"A wager!" she cried. "To think I was used as the stake in one of his games!" She put her hands to her face and wept.

Brandon took her in his arms. "Hush, sweetheart. Had your husband not made his unholy wager, we'd never have found each other. Forget I deceived you. Remember only how much I love you."

His handsome face swam above her in a crystal haze. "Brandon," she breathed, speaking his name in passion for the first time.

"Love me honestly," he said. "There's no need for pretense."

Her restraint slowly ebbed away as the fire in his touch, his mouth, kindled an inferno in her blood. They clung together, mouths and bodies burning as one, then Brandon lifted her off the ground, pinning her against the white-hot throb of his passion. Marie Fleur's blood thundered like the sea.

"Love me," she whispered, "as I thought I'd never be loved again."

MARIE FLEUR
by Patricia Phillips
author of TOUCH ME WITH FIRE

Marie Fleur

Patricia Phillips

A JOVE BOOK

MARIE FLEUR

A Jove Book/published by arrangement with
the author

PRINTING HISTORY
Jove edition/June 1983

ISBN: 0-515-07251-6

Jove books are published by Jove Publications, Inc.,
200 Madison Avenue, New York, N. Y. 10016. The words
"A JOVE BOOK" and the "J" with sunburst are trademarks
belonging to Jove Publications, Inc.

PRINTED IN THE UNITED STATES OF AMERICA

THE CRIES OF homing swallows circling the ornate rotunda on the south lawn shattered the tranquility of the early June evening. When the blue-black birds finally disappeared beyond the cypress hedge, an eerie stillness crept across the twilit garden.

Marie Fleur stood at the open French windows gazing at Langley Chase's landscaped gardens. Great flowerheads of hydrangeas flanking the terrace steps gleamed ghostly in the murky light; vast black shadows of wind-swayed oaks and elms flitted like spirits about the velvet lawns.

As she drank in the beauty of her surroundings, a lump rose in her throat, building until she was forced to blink back tears. Usually she did not dwell on her unhappiness, but this lovely Kentish twilight had left her so vulnerable she could not help herself. Loneliness swept over her in a stifling wave. How far away were the familiar things of home. Those broad Norfolk acres surrounding Toppings where she had ridden—unburdened by responsibility, dreaming of a marriage made in heaven—seemed a lifetime away. Yet how could she confess the unpleasant reality of life with William to her uncle, who still viewed her recent marriage as miraculous? And so envious had Cousin Lavinia been, it had taken her over a month to write Marie Fleur a note of congratulations. Marie Fleur suspected Uncle James wished Sir William had courted the older Lavinia instead, but being infinitely more generous than his daughter, he was quick to show his delight that at least one of the girls had made such an advantageous match.

In April of this year, 1813, Marie Fleur du Lac had been married to Sir William Dowling, baronet, in a lavish ceremony in Norwich Cathedral. Barely recovered from the shock that such an eligible man had chosen the dowerless, somewhat naive daughter of Patience Fox and André, Comte du Lac, Marie Fleur had trembled with anticipation as she dreamed of her fairy-tale existence at Langley Chase, Sir William's Palladian mansion. Luxuries only imagined before would be hers. Lavish parties, sumptuous gowns, the opportunity to rub shoulders with the greatest in the land had been the benefits that turned plain Cousin Lavinia green with envy. Though Marie Fleur had to admit these things would indeed be wonderful, it was the prospect of her handsome husband's passionate love that had filled her heart with joy.

She smiled bitterly at the admission. What a fool she had been! What a naive little simpleton! It hardly seemed possible that it had been only two months since she arrived starry-eyed from Norfolk. In those two months she had learned the reality of life at Langley Chase. All the pomp, the ceremony, the sparkle were nothing but tarnished lies.

For over a decade Europe had groaned beneath the iron fist of Napoleon Bonaparte, the despotic emperor of France. England had sacrificed thousands of men on alien shores as she fought to remain free. The prolonged hostilities had also taken their toll on the home front. Hunger riots and smashed machines made battlegrounds of the teeming industrial cities of the North and Midlands, while numerous small businesses failed and some of the gentry, impoverished by unpaid rents, came close to bankruptcy.

Throughout this period of strife and economic gloom, the Prince of Wales and his dissolute friends amassed huge debts. In 1811, when the prince's ailing father, King George III, lapsed into hopeless insanity, the Regency was established. Far from chastening the spendthrift prince, this official move merely spurred him to greater extravagance. He indulged his taste for art, exquisite furnishings, fanciful architecture, lavish banquets, and plump, middle-aged mistresses, all at the nation's expense. It was no surprise that Prinny had been booed in the London streets. There had even been assassination threats, which sent him quaking to the safety of his beloved Brighton.

William Dowling had been a faithful disciple of his royal master. Though barely thirty-five, he already possessed the constitution of later middle age, the brief fire of youth squandered in the heady pursuit of pleasure. His friends were all rich wastrels like himself. Night and day they drank, gambled, and whored, racing their sporting vehicles from London to Brighton and back at Prinny's whim, eager to ingratiate themselves with their corpulent mentor. The *ton*, the *beau monde*, and the Fancy were names Marie Fleur soon learned to despise. Her dreams about the glamorous life of these exotic creatures soon vanished. She discovered that the shallow existence of a class who lived solely for pleasure sometimes made her long for the stolid Norfolk squirearchy she had so eagerly abandoned for this fairy tale come true.

Marie Fleur had first caught William's eye at the local social events where eligible daughters were trotted out in the hope of finding a rich suitor. Though she had danced with him at the hunt balls, shared his table at the squire's hunt breakfast, and ridden several miles beside him during a frosty winter's hunt, Marie Fleur had never considered William Dowling's attentions anything but a polite flirtation, though she had to confess she found the other girls' frankly envious glances most enjoyable. In the vicinity of Edgerton Heath, Sir William was considered a prime catch. The fact that he was in residence only briefly during the hunting season allowed his image to remain unspoiled. Had they known the truth, many of those ambitious parents would have whisked their daughters far out of reach of William Dowling, nobleman or not.

Not until that dark February day when William galloped through a rainstorm to seek her hand did Marie Fleur realize his attentions were serious. His romantic ardor completely swept her off her feet. That day she had not known he was somewhat the worse for drink or that his impulsiveness was more the act of an erratic personality than an expression of devotion. Nor could she blame Uncle James for so eagerly accepting William's suit. When she had arrived on her uncle's doorstep eight years ago, an impoverished French orphan, he had been kind enough to take her in and raise her as his own, despite the fact that she spoke and acted like a "furriner." Lately her uncle's weaving business had fallen on hard times and his farm barely provided enough to live on. It must have seemed a godsend to him when she received William's splendid proposal. Nor had James Fox's enthusiasm for this marriage been entirely selfish, for William's apparent infatuation for his lovely niece gave him few doubts about her future happiness.

Marie Fleur turned her back on the broad lawns where purple shadows gradually obliterated all form. It would be vastly humiliating to try to explain to her relatives that her marvelous marriage existed in name only. Instead Marie Fleur wrote cheerful, glowing letters about her life in Kent. For her cousin's recent birthday she had sent Lavinia a lovely new gown, and she frequently shipped hampers of delicacies to Uncle James.

Never was there a hint that life at Langley Chase was not every bit as wonderful as they imagined.

During her first week of marriage it became all too apparent that William was incapable of a deep love for his wife. His previous sexual experiences had been limited to women of a lower class who gratefully accepted monetary rewards without expectation of affection on his part. The lascivious stories currently making the rounds detailing her husband's escapades with actresses and chambermaids merely increased Marie Fleur's wretchedness.

These unpleasant bedroom revelations were not the full extent of her disillusionment with William Dowling. Palatial Langley Chase, with its elaborate furnishings, William's flashy canary-yellow phaeton, even his stable of fine bloodstock, was not yet paid for. Marie Fleur wondered if the clothes on their backs or the food they put in their mouths was also bought on credit. Despite his already staggering debts, William continued to gamble, confident that fortune awaited him on the turn of the next card.

From the library, that sacred male enclave, came a burst of coarse laughter. Tonight William was entertaining his gambling cronies. The billiard room adjoined the library, presenting the gamblers with a wide choice of vices. In accompaniment to their dice and cards, the guests usually consumed vast quantities of brandy and port drawn from a seemingly inexhaustible supply in the vaulted, cobwebbed cellars of stately Langley Chase.

Her husband had demanded that she bid his guests goodnight and, though Marie Fleur had come close to mutiny, William's brutality drove her to seek a subtle means of defiance rather than an open confrontation. Had her husband been affectionate, or even considerate, she could have forgiven him much. He considered caresses and tenderness a waste of time. Their intimate moments had taken her through disappointment to indifference and finally disgust. In an effort to maintain his passionate mood William resorted to gutter language, which turned her ice cold to his lovemaking. Her lack of response goaded William into reminding her how much other women enjoyed his attentions. In fact, in a recent fit of rage, he had vowed to bed her only to conceive an heir. Tonight was to have been that night. Yet as she listened to her husband's slurred voice roaring the chorus of a bawdy ballad, she realized he would presently be incapable of making good his threat.

Marie Fleur paused before the pier glass between the velvet curtained windows, checking her appearance in the soft glow of lighted tapers flickering in a silver sconce. She smoothed the organdy frill at the low neckline of her lavender silk gown, adjusting the bodice, which fitted snugly over her full breasts. She had always accepted her own beauty as a matter of fact, pleased yet not unduly impressed by people's favorable reaction to her looks. Her lustrous blond curls, classic features, and creamy complexion turned heads wherever she went. One glance from her soft violet eyes, a flutter of her long dark lashes were sufficient to quicken men's pulses. Her small-waisted, full-bosomed figure readily ignited their passions.

With a shuddering sigh for the dying of her dream, Marie Fleur left the lofty, marble-columned drawing room, with its glittering crystal chandeliers and rose damask upholstery. As she neared the gilded double doors of the library, she could hear the gamblers' voices raised in excitement. Too proud to reveal her unhappiness before their guests, Marie Fleur held her head high, thrusting her stubborn chin forward as she entered the large candlelit room. A challenging gleam lit her violet eyes. No fawning, timid creature, she. William had demanded her presence and she had reluctantly complied, but if he thought to cow her by his blustering demands, he was sadly mistaken.

One by one the male heads lifted. The vision in lavender who glided into their midst was breathtakingly lovely, silky blond curls bound by a lavender ribbon, voluptuous bosom rising and falling within the narrow confines of her high-waisted gown. There was not a man present who was not moved to admiration and lust by the beauteous Lady Dowling.

William rose unsteadily to his feet. He was a tall, well-built man. Though a taut belly and slender waist were things of the past, he still looked impressive in his superbly tailored bottle-green coat and close-fitting fawn breeches. His fair complexion was sun-reddened, adding a deceptively healthy glow to his long, fine-boned face with its aquiline nose and pouched hazel eyes. He was the living image of the noble Dowling ancestors who reposed in gilt-framed splendor within the long gallery.

"Ah, Marie," he said.

His slurred greeting irritated her. He insisted on pronouncing her name "Marr" in that flat English fashion because he knew

how much it annoyed her. Since the discovery of her coldness
in bed, William seemed to have taken a schoolboy's delight in
tormenting her.

"I came to bid good-night to your guests." It took much
effort, but she refrained from adding, "as you demanded."

William stepped toward her. Drunk though he was, he did
not miss the open admiration in the faces of his friends. Marie
was the loveliest woman he had ever set eyes on, the perfect
choice to grace his Palladian showplace. She had it all: breeding, beauty . . . he drew in his breath, barbed once more by his
own personal demon. During their first few nights at Langley
Chase, William had been appalled to discover he could respond
to her sexually only with the utmost difficulty. He was not sure
why. True, in the past he had few intimate dealings with women
of the upper classes, whom he had been taught were always
to be treated with deference. Yet surely a female was a female.
There should be little difference between them in the dark. He
even wondered if it was Marie's startling resemblance to his
beloved Mama that succeeded in all but emasculating him.
Whatever the reason, his own mounting frustration made him
lash out unreasonably at the object of his desire, punishing her
for the constant reminder of his failure. The sheer envy of his
friend's faces partially dulled his bitter disappointment. To have
others covet his possessions was manna to his soul.

"Gentlemen: my wife."

A murmur of approval went around the group.

Marie Fleur forced herself to meet their bold stares. Her gaze
flicked over the well-dressed men who had risen as one. As
usual, the tall, sardonic dandy, the Earl of Cranbrook, was
here, regarding her with his pale, strangely chilling eyes. For
a moment they locked gazes, and a wave of uneasiness swept
over her. The earl often had this peculiarly unsettling effect on
her. Though Geoffrey, Earl Cranbrook, was always polite and
most gentlemanly in his behavior toward her, Marie Fleur dis-
liked the somewhat possessive touch of his perfectly manicured
white hands on which a single priceless diamond dazzled in
the candlelight. Though tonight she avoided his touch, she was
unable to avoid his stare, which raked her as she turned from
him to greet their other guests.

Portly Algy Sweet had food stains on the front of his satin-
embroidered waistcoat. Jack Masham and the red-headed Lord
Westerham, bosom friends of the Prince Regent, were eyeing

her with drunken lechery. Poggy Reid, cashiered out of the Life Guards for misconduct, looked like a fish, his loose-lipped mouth agape. They were the usual ne'er-do-wells without whom William seemed unable to function.

Her mouth quirked bitterly when she recalled that one of the few moves he had made without consulting his constant companions had been their own marriage. For her it had proven an unfortunate act of independence.

Two strangers had also risen to greet her. One man remained in the shadows beyond the flickering candle flames; the other pushed forward eagerly.

"It's my greatest pleasure to make your acquaintance, ma'am," said the fair, florid-faced young man. He was impeccably dressed in gray-striped silk, his monstrous cravat seeming to support his chinless face. Marie Fleur voiced a polite greeting as she dipped a curtsy.

"Teddy Brooks—Poggy's cousin, m'love," William introduced him. Turning to the pear-shaped young Brooks, who gazed with open admiration at his wife, William rumbled, "French, y'know, Brooks. Barely spoke English when she was dumped on her uncle's doorstep. After all this time, she still expects me to pronounce her name in the Froggy fashion. *Marie Fleur*," he mimicked with exaggerated accent. "Too big a mouthful by far for a good Englishman to manage, don't ye say?"

Before anyone was given a chance to voice an opinion, William forsook Teddy Brooks in favor of the other man who had emerged from the shadows, tall and broad-shouldered in a well-cut claret coat. Eagerly William grasped his sleeve.

"And here, m'love, last but not least, the Honorable Brandon Nicholas. Burkhart Nicholas's son, y'know, the M.P. who's always butting heads with Liverpool. Brandy's so notorious, you're bound to have heard some spicy gossip about him."

Brandon Nicholas's searching gray gaze made Marie Fleur uncomfortable. "Why, Mr. Nicholas, I'd no idea your exploits were so famous," she remarked with a smile.

"I'm afraid, ma'am, I'm rather considered the black sheep of my illustrious family," the dark-haired man replied in a warm, resonant voice. His firm, well-shaped mouth curved in a sensuous smile as he thoroughly appraised her beauty.

His statement was met by loud guffaws and someone bleated plaintively.

"Brandy can even speak French." William's tone was tinged with amazement. "Damned if I know how anyone could master that outlandish jabber. Someday you'll have to have a good chinwag with him, but not now," he concluded hastily, lest the assembly be treated to an unintelligible discourse.

Marie Fleur was pleasantly surprised by William's revelation. This man was the first of their circle to display any interests beyond gambling, drinking, or philandering.

Brandon Nicholas's next words dispelled her illusion.

"Well, I must admit it's deuced hard to make love to a woman who doesn't understand you. Naturally, when Papa insisted I take a grand tour—brother Henry being too busy to oblige—I had to learn the language or die of boredom," he drawled.

"The very reason you mastered German."

"Italian, too."

He chuckled, his gray eyes hooded as he lazily surveyed the laughing group. "Gentlemen, you astound me with your brilliance. Who says Prinny's friends are nothing but thick-headed dolts?"

The men's coarse laughter, followed by a round of ribald comments, increased Marie Fleur's discomfort. Already the telltale throb of an approaching headache was making itself felt. Bidding them a hasty good-night, she moved toward the door.

Disappointment clouded her face as she gave handsome Brandon Nicholas a final searching look. His hard, masculine features and firm, determined jaw had suggested far more than another dissolute younger son of a titled sire. When he spoke, his large, dark-lashed gray eyes had sparkled with intelligence. Now his heavy lids were lowered, dimming those penetrating eyes. Marie Fleur sighed. She must have only imagined the glimmer of worth that had attracted her to this man. Even Nicholas's broad-shouldered physique appeared sadly diminished, as if he had shrunk in stature before her eyes. His strong, well-shaped hands drooped from lace-frothed sleeves in the prescribed manner of the dandy. Brandon Nicholas was no more than another indolent wastrel.

Marie Fleur had barely crossed the threshold, their chorused good-nights ringing in her ears, when one voice, louder, bolder than the rest, remarked, "The devil take you, Will Dowling. Where did you find such a deuced fine filly? She's utterly splendid. But then, Frenchwomen have always been odds-on favorites of mine."

Cheeks burning with humiliation at Brandon Nicholas's remark, Marie Fleur slammed the door. Her small act of defiance was drowned in the general hubbub as the gamblers resumed their places for the next hand.

When she reached her bedchamber, Nancy, her maid, was waiting for her.

"Are you ready to retire, my lady?" Nancy carefully phrased the sentence, anxious to succeed in her new role as lady's maid. Sometimes the effort proved almost too much for her.

Marie Fleur smiled at the rosy-cheeked country girl, her spirits lifting. "More than ready. All that noise downstairs gave me a headache." She reached to her temples, pressing her cool fingers over the throbbing ache. Until she married William she had barely known what a headache was. Now they had become an unwelcome feature of her life.

Nancy bounded to the dressing table to fetch her mistress's long-handled hairbrush. When Marie Fleur shook her head, Nancy reddened and put down the silver brush. The gown was to be taken off first. Would she never remember?

"Sorry, Your Ladyship."

"Don't apologize. We're learning to be fine ladies together."

Smiling encouragement at Nancy's diligent efforts, Marie Fleur bent this way and that to make the task easier as Nancy's blunt fingers fumbled clumsily with the delicate fastenings of her gown. Perhaps it would have been wiser to have trained one of the household maids to wait on her. When she chose Nancy as her maid, she had thought to repay some of her deep indebtedness to the girl's family.

"When are we going to Brighton?" Nancy asked, her tongue peeping between her lips as she concentrated on the satin bows fastening her mistress's pink wrapper.

"Soon is all William told me."

Nancy made a face when their eyes met in the mirror. "It don't seem like he makes you very 'appy," she grumbled.

"We've only been married two months."

"Plenty long enough to know if you're 'appy." Nancy wielded the engraved silver hairbrush with fresh determination. "My Ned'll 'ave to make me 'appier than that, or I'll soon be on me way."

"A fisherman has few obligations when he's ashore. I'm

sure you'll be happy with Ned. William has many . . . things . . . to
take his time."

Why was she making excuses for him? Marie Fleur wondered uncomfortably as she glanced away from Nancy's probing gaze. It was all very well to send Lavinia glowing letters
about her happiness, but Nancy was able to observe the truth
firsthand. Many's the time Marie Fleur would have gladly
exchanged Nancy's humble sweetheart for her own noble catch.

"When we does go to Brighton, 'appen I can pop 'ome to
me mum. She's been poorly lately. And what with Betty gone
too, she's by 'erself when me father's at sea. I've not been
'ome for two months," Nancy reminded indignantly.

"Of course. I'll insist on it. You must take her a basket of
nourishing things. And I'll come with you."

"Ooh, would you? She'd be ever so pleased to see you."

Nancy's mother had been Marie Fleur's own mother's maid
before Patience Fox went to live in France. When the Comte
du Lac was executed during the Terror his wife and young
daughter were forced to flee the country and return to Patience's
native England. It was faithful Lucy who had come to her
former mistress's rescue. Marie Fleur's first year in England
was spent at Lucy's cottage in Rye, on the south coast. Later
Patience and her daughter moved to the émigré district of London, and Lucy had come there to nurse Patience when she was
dying. It was Lucy who had later sent Marie Fleur to her
maternal relatives at Edgerton Heath in the county of Norfolk.

She had not visited Rye in years and looked forward to the
proposed visit. Mentally arguing the point, Marie Fleur quickly
anticipated all William's likely objections to her visit. Experience with her husband's dictatorial manner had taught her she
would have to fight for independence. Her proposal to hold a
school for the children of their poor tenants he had greeted
with hoots of derision. Even her modest suggestion that she
take lessons from their cook had been dismissed out of hand.
William had curtly informed her that a woman's place was at
her husband's side. Unhappily Marie Fleur realized she was
expected to live in William's shadow, an obedient doll deco-
ratively attired for all occasions.

"Why not take some of yer tonic? It allus makes them 'eads
better," Nancy suggested kindly, reaching for the despised
medicine when she observed her mistress continuing to knead
her temples to relieve the iron band of pressure.

Marie Fleur agreed and propped herself against the down pillows. The tonic had been prescribed by a local doctor hastily summoned one day by William to treat his wife's hysteria. Hysteria indeed! She had bluntly demanded an accounting of the true state of their indebtedness. Worse than that, she had even demanded an explanation for his shameful philandering while he treated his wife like a stranger. Both were issues guaranteed to drive him into a frenzy, and when she became upset at his towering rage, he deemed her reaction hysteria. Dr. Slope had fended off her inquiries about her supposed ailment with that old catchall "female complaints." She had quite shocked the old gentleman by refusing to be sedated into acceptance of William's excesses. To placate the doctor, who visibly trembled before William's wrath, she finally relented and accepted a small dose of the nauseating concoction. When William demanded to see the bottle to assure himself she was actually taking the medicine, she dutifully produced her dwindling tonic, which she had been pouring into the shrubbery. Not to be outdone, however, he insisted she take a dose in his presence. That was the night she discovered Dr. Slope's prescription relieved her sick headaches.

Nancy held out a spoonful of the black liquid. She had been distressed by her mistress's defiance of doctor's orders. In common with most of the ill-educated, she was greatly impressed by book learning, and Dr. Slope even spoke Latin!

The dark sticky substance crawled over her tongue and down her throat, making Marie Fleur shudder. She gratefully accepted the cup of warm sugar water mixed with brandy, which Nancy proffered as her own never-fail remedy for all ills.

"Thank you, Nancy. I usually sleep soundly after taking this poison."

Smiling affectionately at her mistress, Nancy tucked the flowered bedspread about Marie Fleur's slim body, brushing her mistress's dainty oval-nailed hands with her own broad, reddened ones as she bid her, "Good-night, my lady. Sweet dreams."

"And to you, Nancy."

After the door closed Marie Fleur lay contentedly listening to a bird singing sweetly below her window. The birdsong and an occasional burst of laughter from the library were the only sounds to disturb her rest.

In her drifting, semiconscious state her mind returned to her recent meeting with Brandon Nicholas. When she pictured his handsome face she felt a foolish fluttering in her stomach. On the surface he was highly attractive, yet inside he was as corrupt as all the rest. Like a shiny red apple with a rotten core. The comparison made her smile. No more apt description for William's dissolute friends could have been found.

Presently she heard the clop of hooves and the rumble of carriage wheels as William's guests departed. Marie Fleur was pleased to discover she was no longer sad. She no longer felt anything. Perhaps that was the sole object of Dr. Slope's elixir—total oblivion.

She closed her eyes, her rose-pink mouth set in an expression of absolute contentment. A few minutes later she was sound asleep.

"By God, I'll not let you get away with it," William bellowed as he leaned across the table, his face brick-red. "Give me a chance to recoup my losses. It's the gentlemanly thing to do."

"Have a heart, it's three in the morning! My eyes feel as though they're full of sand. What about tomorrow? I'll play you tomorrow."

"No. This is my house, my brandy, and my cards. I say we play tonight."

Brandon Nicholas raised a dark eyebrow at the belligerence in his host's voice. "Very well, if you insist, but I warn you, it won't be a fair contest. I'm dropping for want of sleep. Too many late nights eventually take their toll. You'd as well play whist with a sleepwalker."

William thrust back his chair and stood up. His jowls were mottled, his hazel eyes bloodshot. The fine aquiline nose with its permanently rosy hue was lifted haughtily. "Then, by God, we'll roll the dice—I'll not be accused of taking advantage of any man."

Lord Westerham and the Earl of Cranbrook also remained in the candlelit library. All four men were the worse for drink, but only William was losing his temper—only William was almost forty thousand pounds in debt.

"Come on, Will, call it a day," suggested Westerham, yawning behind his hand. "Brandy'll give you chance enough to win back your losses at White's."

"To hell with White's! He'll not get my new phaeton without a fight."

The men glanced at each other, unsure how to proceed. William's fists were clenched on the table and his eyes bulged like an aggressive bulldog's.

"Settle it quickly with dice then, gentlemen, so we can all go home to bed," suggested the Earl of Cranbrook.

"The phaeton's mine already. I'm not prepared to wager it again." Nicholas scooped up his winnings. The money clinked and crackled as he placed it in his gold-buttoned pocket. "You're far from sober, Will. We'll settle it some other time."

"You bastard! So you're refusing to give me a second chance?"

"You've had a lifetime's chances already. Have you forgotten how much you already owe me?" Nicholas asked tersely. "In fact, you owe us all so much, I'm deuced if I can see what you can possibly put up to make another game worth my while."

Uneasy glances were exchanged. William's houseguests usually did not remind him so bluntly of his debts.

"By God! All you care about's your own gain. Well, I've something of value left to wager, all right."

"Indeed."

"Aye, indeed," William repeated, his breathing heavy. Drink and the sickness of gambling possessed him. A chance was all he needed—one more chance to win back everything he had lost to that insufferably cocksure Nicholas. The highly irregular wager he was about to propose revealed his own desperation. Tomorrow his recklessness would likely be attributed to the bottle. No one would actually believe the stakes he had offered. But, then, he had no intention of losing. He suddenly felt very lucky.

"I'm for bed," Nicholas announced, nodding to Cranbrook. "See that our friend finds his, won't you?"

"Stay. On one throw . . . everything you've won tonight."

"And what, pray tell, my friend, are you putting up against it?"

William swallowed. The longer he considered, the more difficult it became to speak the stakes aloud. "Tonight . . . with . . . my wife."

An incredulous gasp went round the table.

"I'll put that suggestion down to too much brandy."

"No, damn you, listen!"

William lurched from his chair and grabbed Nicholas's coat sleeve, drawing him back. The others stood by, ready to intervene if the two came to blows.

"No gentleman makes such an offer," Nicholas spat.

"Be damned to gentlemen. In this room we're gamblers. Do you think for one minute I'd make such an offer if I thought I'd lose?"

"What makes you think I'll accept?"

William leaned heavily against the table. "You'll accept. I saw you looking at her. All of you watched her like panting dogs. Don't you think I know how much men envy me that woman? Seeing that Nicholas has turned so damned chivalrous, I'll make the same offer to the rest of you."

There was a moment's hesitation while the exact terms of the extraordinary wager sank into brandy-fuddled brains, then the two other men leaned across the table, eyes lecherous.

William slumped in his chair, his chin sunk on his bottle-green chest. "First you must promise that not a word of this leaves this room."

"Agreed."

Their quickened breathing rasped in the stillness as each man took his turn, the dice clinking before they spilled across the green baize tabletop.

William's confidence returned by leaps and bounds. At Cranbrook's suggestion he took first roll and drew eleven. Westerham had five, Cranbrook eight. His surely must be the highest score.

His face grave, Nicolas asked, "If I win, Dowling, you do intend to keep your bargain?"

"Of course. I'm a man of my word."

The others turned toward Nicholas, intent on his roll. The dice were cast. A whistle of astonishment escaped the earl's thin lips.

"Christ! A pair of sixes!"

"No! No!" William cried, his eyes bulging in shock as he stared at the table. "No. It's a trick. A trick!"

"Are you accusing me of cheating?" asked Nicholas icily.

Bleary-eyed, William looked up, finding it difficult to focus on the angry face above him. "It can't be true," he muttered, "not true."

"It's true. But as I'm a generous man, you can take back half your stake."

"Half? What do you mean, half?" William muttered as he wiped his hand across his sweating brow.

"You either keep the money and the phaeton or the prized night with your lady wife."

Utterly wretched, William held his head in his hands, the decision weighing heavy on his conscience. The sleek canary-yellow phaeton was the fastest vehicle he had ever owned. Prinny himself envied him the bright yellow conveyance. The cash that supercilious Nicholas had in his pocket would pay his tailor's bills for the past two years, and probably his household expenses to boot. Yet the word for what he proposed was ugly. Men of his class did not sell their wives' affections. . . .

"I'm not prepared to wait all night."

"You bastard! I never dreamed you'd hold me to it."

"Had you won you'd have held me to it."

"It's fair enough, Will. The stakes were your idea, not ours," observed the earl with a suitably bored air. His boredom, however, was a ruse. His pulses leaped at the very idea of allowing so esteemed a reward to slip through his own fingers. Not for one moment had he thought Nicholas would turn down so delicious a wager. He had not come by his reputation lightly: Brandon Nicholas was an out-and-out scoundrel.

Already Nicholas was pulling money from his pocket. The paper crackled enticingly before William's mesmerized eyes.

"All this . . . for her."

William's fist closed over the money and a shudder went through his large frame. "She has the suite at the head of the stair," he croaked, his mouth going dry. Mentally he envisioned the thrill of careening along the road in his phaeton, forcing the image until he could almost feel the wind whipping in his face.

Nicholas's mouth tightened. The alcoholic stupor that had beset him evaporated at the electrifying prospect of what lay before him. "What if the lady protests?" he asked belatedly, his hand on the door handle.

"Cuff her into submission. In the dark she'll never know the dif—" William paused, unwilling to allow the others such a telling insight into his marital relations. Caressing the money before him, he said, "Your oath, Nicholas, that it won't go beyond this room."

"You have it."

"And you, gentlemen?"

The others nodded, solemnly pledging their vow, sacred as a religious oath.

"Aren't you going to wish me luck, Will?"

Bellowing in anger, William lurched to his feet. "The devil take you, Brandon Nicholas."

"He undoubtedly will, my friend."

Chuckling, Nicholas opened the library door and stepped into the darkened corridor beyond.

~ Chapter 2 ~

MARIE FLEUR WAS not sure what had awakened her. She fancied she heard a rustling beyond the sprigged silk curtains of her gilded bed. Yet Dr. Slope's elixir held her so firmly in its grasp, she gave only passing attention to the disturbance. The wind must have rustled the curtains, for Nancy had left the broad windows ajar. This being a highly satisfactory explanation, she stretched in the soft featherbed and promptly fell asleep.

When next Marie Fleur awoke, she was aware of a shadow falling across the bed. At first she thought she had dreamed the caress on her brow, but no, a man's hand swept tenderly over her smooth skin, sensitive fingers straying to the short curls framing her oval face.

This unexpected discovery made her stomach pitch. William had not succumbed to drink after all! Yet as she considered his newfound gentleness, her anxiety diminished. He had never bestowed such sweet and tender caresses. In fact, instead of shrinking from his lovemaking, she found to her great surprise she was responding with a delicious rush of heat.

The faint odor of brandy hung in the air, and unfamiliar exotic perfume emanated from the dark bulk beside the bed. William's face was a blur for the night was moonless.

"William," she squeaked, as he turned back the covers and slipped into bed.

Marie Fleur shuddered involuntarily as their limbs touched. It was a reaction no amount of persuasion could erase. Instinctively she pulled away, bracing herself for William's assault.

Almost lazily he began to divest her of her embroidered dimity gown, displaying none of his usual impatience.

"William," Marie Fleur repeated incredulously. His gentle, considerate actions were rendering her husband a virtual stranger.

He chuckled as he slid his arms around her soft body. "Don't be afraid," he said, his voice muffled against her perfumed hair.

17

She found his statement most odd. Surely William was not feeling remorse for the cruel way in which he had treated her. Had a glimmer of reason finally penetrated his besotted brain? Whatever directed this welcome change of heart, Marie Fleur was not going to waste time analyzing it; instead she intended to make the most of it.

Waves of exquisite drowsiness overcame her as she lay contentedly in the warm closeness of his arms. Lulled by his caressing hands, she sighed with sheer pleasure. In the past William's assaults, however futile, were usually soon over. He had never wasted time in preliminary lovemaking.

Marie Fleur's eyes flew open as she became aware of his hands on her breasts. The arousing caress brought a tingling heat surging through her veins. Her resulting gasp of surprise made him chuckle again, the sound rumbling in her ear, for his face was still pressed against hers.

The more intimately William explored her body, the deeper became her own involvement. William had never kindled such a depth of feeling within her. In the beginning her anticipation of lovemaking had been mildly pleasant, for she had so wanted to believe herself in love; of late her feelings had come closer to disgust. Until tonight. Tonight she was being swept into that familiar world of forbidden dreams from which she awakened flushed and panting, yearning for something she did not understand. William seemed to have merged identities with the misty partners of her fantasies, those faceless, nameless lovers who cherished her, who set her afire with sweet kisses and vowed love everlasting.

"Oh, William," Marie Fleur breathed in rapture, her voice breaking, "tonight everything's so wonderfully dif—"

Her words died beneath his hot kiss. The touch of his mouth was so intoxicating, she shook. Even those fantasy kisses had not been so passionate that they bordered on violation.

"Hush, little flower, you talk too much," he admonished when their lips parted.

There was a curiously husky quality in William's voice she never recalled hearing before. In an effort to contain her building excitement, Marie Fleur fought hard against the emotion. When his mouth traced a fiery passage down her neck and across her shoulder, finally coming to rest on her budlike nipple, her restraint was lost forever.

"William, oh, William, I never dreamed I could feel like this."

The sheer amazement in her breathless voice, her ill-concealed passion, fired him further. He trailed passionate kisses the length of her body, sweeping his tongue over her soft, concave belly and across her silken hips.

When his mouth first sought that shadowed secret place between her thighs, Marie Fleur drew back. Never before had she been so intimately approached. His tender mouth, his hot, coaxing tongue made her squirm until she no longer tried to avoid the contact. Burying her hands in his thick hair, she shuddered with delight, moaning deep in her throat for all the pleasure he created.

Now her womanly instincts were fully roused, she was no longer shy and undemanding. Marie Fleur drew up his head, guiding his mouth to her breasts. While his hot tongue darted about her tingling flesh, bestowing exquisite pleasure, she rained grateful kisses on his crisp hair.

"Oh, sweetheart, sweetheart," she moaned, as her arms slid about his smooth shoulders. Marie Fleur marveled at his thick-muscled strength. She had never touched William's body beyond a shy, exploratory caress. Now she longed to know the secrets of his flesh.

"You mustn't be so modest."

In the darkness she blushed, turned uncomfortable by the amusement she heard behind his whispered words. When she had tentatively stretched out her hand, she had gasped in surprise as she encountered the pulsating strength of his manhood burning against her thigh. So furtive had been their coming together on previous occasions, she had not understood the curious working of a man's body.

Gently he took her hand and forced it down, curving her fingers about his flesh. Then he slowly moved her hand, showing her the exact manner in which he wished her to make love to him. His throbbing flesh came alive beneath her fingers, betraying his deep arousal. And the knowledge that she alone inspired such passion sent a quivering burst of heat between Marie Fleur's thighs until she ached.

"I love you dearly," she sobbed, surprising herself with the impassioned declaration. At this moment she could think of nothing beyond the wonderful loving warmth of his body against hers, the searing promise of his mouth, dispelling those shadowy, unpleasant memories of the past. William's kisses and his impassioned love words were the only reality. At last she knew what it meant to make love; this bond, forged by their most primitive emotions, was its ultimate expression.

"Ah, little flower, you're such an easy woman to love," he whispered sincerely.

Her smile was proud as she felt him tremble beneath her caress.

"Why did we wait so long for this?" she said, devouring his hot mouth with her own, drinking in his passion and reveling in the discovery.

"Sheer stupidity, love, and all my fault."

His emotion-charged whisper was music to her ears. From this time forward they would intimately share their lives. Marriage was going to be the way she had always dreamed it would be, after all.

"Love me," he whispered huskily, "now."

It was Marie Fleur who fitted her mouth over his, who drained the hot intensity of his kiss. It was Marie Fleur who eagerly parted her silken thighs beneath him. She did not make him force apart her limbs nor fight to attain union. At this instant there was nothing she wanted more than to join her body with this exciting new William, this skillful lover who had overcome his own twisted emotions to emerge perfectly attuned to her needs, needs she had never before realized she possessed.

He kissed her deeply, his limbs trembling with restrained passion. At first, when his body met hers, fiery hot and demanding, she resisted. Too many times before she had tensed at this point. But with more kisses, more soft, tender caresses accompanied by whispered words of love, the invasion became a highly desired gift. When at last he thrust, when the fire of his powerful flesh moved within her, Marie Fleur cried out in ecstasy.

Gently he fitted her to his body like a silken sheath. She clutched his powerful back, moaning love words, shuddering like one possessed. So inflamed were they, he was forced to lie still while he fought for control. She moaned in frustration as the rhythm they had created ceased.

Aware of her disappointment, he trailed tender kisses about

her ear as he whispered, "Hush, wait but a moment."

Soon he had rebuilt their mood, carrying her to the brink of an unknown abyss from which she drew back in fear.

"No, sweetheart, don't hold back."

His whispered encouragement reassured her. But it was not until he took the matter into his own hands, repeatedly thrusting deep in the core of her belly, that she finally let go. Crying out in surprise, Marie Fleur was swept away in a torrent of passionate heat. He held her while she soared and, when she plunged over the precipice, afraid because she had never journeyed there before, he cherished her, giving comfort until the storm was past.

Tears spilled from Marie Fleur's eyes and trickled into her hair. The moisture splashed on his shoulder, and he kissed her ravaged little face, tasting her salt tears. "You were born to be loved, Marie Fleur," he whispered.

She did not speak, only held him tight and wept softly against his comforting shoulder. All those vague emotions she had never understood had fallen into place tonight. William was right: She was born to be loved. For the first time since she had entered Langley Chase, Marie Fleur was completely happy.

"You were wonderful," she breathed in admiration against his fragrant flesh. Nuzzling her face into the heated hollow of his neck, she gave a deep sigh of contentment. The peace of fulfillment was swiftly combining with the remnants of Dr. Slope's elixir to make her drowsy. "So . . . so wonderful . . . oh, I love you dearly." Her fingers twined in his thick hair, her cheek against his, she finally succumbed to the sweet wave of pleasure washing over her.

Marie Fleur was still sleeping peacefully when he gently uncurled her fingers and laid her golden head against the crushed pillows. Tenderly he drew the silken coverlet over her perfect body, arranging the folds about her slender neck as if she were a child. He even closed the window to keep out the morning chill.

For a few minutes longer he gazed at her. It was hard to leave her thus. He successfully fought the insane desire to kiss her good-bye. This stolen encounter, which he had undertaken in true sporting spirit, had shaken him badly. He had never felt this way about a woman. Of all the damndest luck! He had finally found the one he wanted, and she was married to someone else.

Brandon Nicholas pulled on his wine coat and left the room.

Marie Fleur awoke to sunlight streaming through the open curtains. Nancy stood beside the bed holding a silver tray bearing her customary early morning cup of chocolate and a fresh croissant.

"Good morning, my lady. Did you sleep well?" Nancy inquired brightly as she set down the tray beside the bed.

"Wonderfully well." Marie Fleur's thoughts stole to those secret hours of darkness. She glanced quickly at the crumpled pillow beside her, knowing, even before she looked, that William would have returned to his own room.

"There, you see—the doctor's tonic done you good after all."

Marie Fleur smiled at her own wicked thoughts. It was true, a tonic had done her a world of good, but it was not the one prescribed by bewhiskered Dr. Slope.

On the tray was an unfurling rose of palest salmon-pink. Marie Fleur buried her nose in its perfumed midst, her smile dreamy.

"William sent this, didn't he?"

"The master!" Nancy repeated incredulously. Then, catching her slip, she added hastily. "Well, no, it were Bales who brung it to the kitchen. 'Tis the first flower of that new rose he been growing."

"Oh." Marie Fleur tried to mask her disappointment. "I must congratulate him. The scent's lovely."

Reluctantly she sipped her chocolate. After last night's harmonious blending of hearts, souls, and bodies, the gift of a perfect rosebud had seemed romantically appropriate. Still, William could not be expected to change totally overnight.

While Marie Fleur dressed and assisted Nancy in styling her hair, she hummed a lilting French love song. When she joined William in the breakfast room she would run to his arms and kiss him out of gratitude for last night's heavenly hours. They would laugh and talk. So well attuned had they been in the darkness, she must not allow them to lapse into their former cold relationship. She would shower William with such praise he would be left in no doubt as to her pleasure at his change of heart.

She had chosen a high-waisted, leaf-green muslin gown with puffed sleeves and a lace-trimmed flounce at the hem. Marie Fleur peered at her reflection in the mirror, anxious to appear her loveliest. Nothing must shatter William's loving mood.

Satisfied she was indeed looking her best, she kissed Nancy's cheek and hastened from her chamber.

Her heart thumped erratically as she descended the broad marble stair, as excited as she had been on her wedding day. The ornate molded ceiling overhead, the marble balusters beneath her hand were veritable works of art. The red plush stair carpet had never glowed so brightly, nor had the red patterned draperies shimmered with such brilliance. It was as though her own happiness had changed the world around her.

"Good morning, darling."

Marie Fleur ran to where William was seated at the far end of the ornate rosewood table. His black brocade dressing gown gaped to reveal his sparsely haired chest. Last night William's chest had seemed more hirsute, his body broader, stronger, more overpoweringly virile. It must have been passion that wrought the change in her perceptions.

William blinked in amazement at her effusive greeting.

"Eh . . . er . . . yes, m'love, good morning."

Next she threw her arms about his broad shoulders and eagerly kissed his mouth. Somewhat irritated, William held himself aloof. What was wrong with the woman? This was damned unusual behavior first thing in the morning. And to make matters worse, he had the most vicious hangover.

Trying to hide her mounting disappointment, Marie Fleur became freshly determined not to be put off by his unenthusiastic greeting. She removed her place setting from the opposite end of the table and laid her silver cutlery next to his.

"To begin with, we'll sit closer. I've always thought it ridiculous for two people to sit at opposite ends of this ugly old table."

"Ugly! The confounded thing cost me a fortune! Oh, very well then, suit yourself," he concluded hastily as her full mouth turned down. Another minute and her lip would be quivering. God, he couldn't stand it when she cried! Damnable woman. What was the matter with her? He searched his own recent behavior but could find no change there to precipitate this joyful mood. And then he remembered. Through befogging layers of alcohol the hideous truth dawned. All this lightheartedness,

this bubbling good humor could be attributed to only one cause:
Brandon Nicholas's performance in bed!

"Where's Paulson?" Marie Fleur asked as she glanced about
the sunny morning room. The servants were nowhere in sight
and the polished rosewood sideboard was devoid of its usual
array of steaming dishes.

"Taken my deviled kidneys back," William muttered, running his hand over his face. A shudder went through him as
he looked at Marie Fleur through bloodshot eyes. The woman
had come alive. She glowed like some glittering gem. He
scowled, not liking what he saw. That bastard must have used
every trick in the book. Nicholas had always enjoyed a sizable
reputation with the women.

Marie Fleur smiled tentatively at William before turning her
attention to the view beyond the window. She was hurt and
puzzled by his attitude. Numbly she watched a couple of black-
birds strutting about the velvet green lawn while she dwelled
on the peculiar expression that had crossed her husband's face.
Had she known otherwise, she would have sworn he regarded
her with revulsion. Why? she thought miserably.

It was ridiculous to be sad on this radiant morning, she
finally told herself with fresh determination. Before her ranged
neat borders of snapdragons in myriad shades of red and yellow,
rubbing bright shoulders with fragrant wallflowers glittering
with dew. Lemon, peach, and blue lupins stood straight as
sentries against the rustic fence. In the bright spring sunshine
Langley Chase's gardens reminded her of a painting brought
vividly to life.

"Until today I've never fully appreciated Langley Chase,"
Marie Fleur remarked to her husband. "Our home's really quite
lovely, darling, almost too lovely to be real."

At that point Paulson entered the room, sparing him the
need to reply.

The butler carried a huge silver tray loaded with dishes.
After first bowing to his master and mistress, Paulson whisked
off each domed cover in swift succession to reveal a delectable
assortment of steaming dishes.

"I'm dreadfully sorry for the inconvenience, Sir William.
Cook's had a proper telling off. She sends her apologies and
hopes everything is to your liking."

"Hm . . . well, don't let it happen again," was all William
said. The subject of undercooked deviled kidneys seemed un-

important before this other, more devastating event.

While Paulson served him rashers of crisp pink ham, sizzling sausages with skins bursting to perfection, and golden yolked eggs, William smarted in silence. Try as he might, he could not get out of his mind the odious picture of Marie locked in Nicholas's embrace.

Marie Fleur continued to pick at her food. She had thought once they were alone her husband's humor would improve. It had worsened instead. He slumped over his plate, silently pushing forkfuls of food into his mouth. Though his ill humor had destroyed much of her pleasure, she was too stubborn to admit defeat. While she spread honey over a sliver of fresh brown bread, she prepared a new approach.

Smiling, she casually brushed his hand with her own. William hastily drew away. His action brought a gleam of anger to her violet eyes. He was simply not going to get away with this! There would be no secret life within the darkness of their bedchamber, then a daylight return to the cold indifference of the past. What puzzled her most was how a man who had been so passionately loving toward her could now treat her with such surly ill humor.

"William." He jumped guiltily, as if caught in some secret act. "What's the matter with you this morning?"

"Matter?" he repeated, clearing his throat. "Nothing's the matter with *me*. I was about to ask you the same question."

"You're acting as if I were some loathesome object."

"There you go again with your ridiculous fancies. We'll have to call in Dr. Slope, see what else he can give you—"

"No! Stop treating me like an empty-headed creature with the vapors."

William's face darkened with rage, and he half rose in his seat. "Are you aware to whom you're speaking?"

"My husband," Marie Fleur cried, fighting tears. Of all times to cry—when she wanted to confront him with her faculties intact. "And are you aware that you're speaking to your wife? Your *wife*, William, not some ill-paid slavey hovering at your beck and call. I thought at least after . . . after . . . last night . . . you—"

William winced. "What do you mean, 'last night'?"

"Stop it! You know very well what I mean!" Marie Fleur's voice rose on a hysterical note. Now her tears were flowing in earnest and her lips quivered when she tried to speak. "We mustn't go back to the way we were. Oh, William, sweetheart, last night you were a different person. Please, don't."

Though his gaze remained stony, William felt a flicker of weakening emotion. Marie was so fetchingly lovely. Yet when he softened toward her charms, something inside him revolted.

Tears glistened in Marie Fleur's violet eyes as he stood unyielding before her. "William," she whispered, blinking rapidly, fighting an overwhelming rush of pain. "Please tell me what I've done to anger you."

Steeling himself to overcome the image of her encircled by Nicholas's arms, and worse yet, enjoying every unholy minute of it, William cleared his throat.

"Don't be ridiculous. You've done nothing to anger me. Surely you're not going to treat me to another hysterical scene this morning."

"I don't understand. Last night I know you loved me," she whispered. "You were so wonderfully different toward me."

William sucked in his breath in rage. "You're talking absolute nonsense! Knowing you as well as I do, I can only conclude your coy reference to last night refers to an encounter in bed. I assure you, my dear Marie, any such encounter is pure imagination on your part."

"Imagination!"

"Yes, m'love, imagination. From the time you left the library until breakfast this morning, I never laid eyes on you."

"That's not true! William, you know it isn't."

He noisily pushed back his chair, suddenly feeling in command of the situation. He had intended to ignore Nicholas's visit by pretending it was he who had come to his wife's room in the early morning hours—he and Nicholas were of similar height and build. Now such deception was out of the question. Her calf-eyed gaze, her sickening simper had destroyed forever any hope of deceiving her into thinking he had been her lover. Damn Nicholas for causing him so much trouble! Never once had he thought his friend's drunken performance would be anything but unmemorable.

Still, all was not lost. He had a better grip on things now, and he intended to drive his point home. If he handled matters cleverly, Marie would be as pliant as he required. Frequent hints about hallucinations and urgent calls for Dr. Slope would help substantiate his case. In the future he would sire his heir and he would show off beautiful Marie to his friends, but that would be all. He simply could not have her meddling in his financial affairs. And her constant demands for affection tried his patience to the limit.

"Are you calling me a liar?" he demanded harshly.

"William, why are you saying this? To what purpose?"

"You must have had a vivid dream. You've had them before, you know. Hysterical women often hallucinate. Now come, dry your eyes. We'll send for Dr. Slope, let him give you a once over."

"A dream! You can't be serious. I didn't dream the way you—"

"That's enough! The servants are likely listening at the key-hole. Have you no discretion?"

Stunned, Marie Fleur watched him stride to the door and wrench it open. The corridor was deserted.

"How can you pretend I was dreaming?"

"There's no pretense to it," he snapped, rounding on her. "If you persist in your delusion, I'll seriously question your sanity. Now let's hear no more about it. Tomorrow we leave for Epsom. I hope by then you'll be over your hysteria. I'd hate to be embarrassed in front of our friends."

For a few minutes after William left the room, Marie Fleur did not move. It was as if all the life had been sucked from her body. So insistent was he that she had dreamed last night's wonderful encounter, seeds of doubt had already entered her mind. Surely it was impossible to have dreamed such ecstasy? Yet what reason could William have for wanting to delude her?

"It was not a dream!" she declared defiantly to the empty room, her voice sounding small and tearful. Whatever his purpose in trying to make her think she had imagined their lovemaking, it was simply not so.

Marie Fleur stepped into the quiet garden, no longer noticing the bright summer flowers. Even the birds' song was muffled by the disturbing questions in her mind. Could the medicine have produced delusions? No. That stirring encounter, which awakened every fiber of her being, was reality. Surely she was sane enough to know the difference between dream encounters and those of flesh and blood.

"My lady, are you ready for your ride?"

As Nancy's voice jarred through her consciousness, Marie Fleur was seized with new hope. Anyone coming down the corridor from William's suite had to pass Nancy's door. The floorboards squeaked, and Nancy had always been a light sleeper.

"What time did Sir William come to my room last night?"

"The master were downstairs with his friends till after dawn. Paulson remarked on it 'cause he had to get Becky to clear the library. And a fine mess it were in, too."

"But he must have come to my room," Marie Fleur insisted weakly as her heart began skipping beats.

"'Twere likely a dream if you fancied you heard someone."

"It wasn't a dream."

Nancy slid her arm around her mistress's small waist. "There now, don't fret, 'tis nothin' to be ashamed of. Dreams can often be better than real life, and no mistake. Simplest way to settle it's to ask Sir William."

"How silly of me. Of course I'll do that."

Like an obedient child Marie Fleur allowed herself to be led away while Nancy chatted on, oblivious to her distress. Nancy's gossipy observations, designed to cheer her mood, drifted in and out of her thoughts . . . lovely gowns . . . such a lucky woman . . . all this luxury . . .

"Nancy, do you think my mind's unhinged?"

"Unhinged? What makes you ask a daft thing like that?"

"Just something William said has made me wonder."

"Well, I never! The very idea!" Nancy declared indignantly. "If anyone's unhinged—beggin' your pardon—it's the master. Him and his gambling and drinking something terrible—there I go, talking too much, and it none of my business."

Marie Fleur smiled in relief as she squeezed Nancy's plump arm. "Thank you, Nancy, you've made me feel much better. Now, before we go out, let's decide what to pack for Epsom. We're to leave for the races tomorrow."

Despite Nancy's loyal reassurance, Marie Fleur could not completely dispel the dark cloud hanging over her whilst she selected her traveling wardrobe. All the joy she had anticipated from her marriage was dead. Nor was she sure there had ever been any actual reason for thinking matters had taken a turn for the better.

Lovely face set, lips composed, outwardly as flawless as a marble statue, the sixth Lady Dowling placed a wide-brimmed yellow straw hat on her head and tied the scarlet satin ribbons beneath her stubborn chin. She would outwardly appear as a decorative asset to William's life, but never again would she allow him to come to her bed. Cold-blooded lovemaking was something she could live without. The fleeting pleasure, her revived hopes and dreams merely made facing reality all the more cruel.

"Bring a basket of provisions, Nancy. I've decided to walk into the village."

"Didn't the master say you wasn't to talk to them villagers?" Nancy asked in surprise, somewhat uneasy at being party to such rank disobedience. Servants were whipped for disobeying orders, and she had no desire to feel the sting of William Dowling's wrath.

"Yes, I believe he did say something of the sort. I intend to enlist the minister's help in providing a school for the village children. We may even hold classes in the parish hall. Once the Reverend Millington's involved, William will be too ashamed to forbid it. That would only make him appear callous toward his tenants."

"What a clever trick," Nancy said admiringly as she picked up her mistress's wicker flower basket.

"You'll find the worm's turned, Nancy. I intend to have a life of my own," Marie Fleur announced, her mouth tightening as she spoke. Outwardly she would be Lady Dowling, the gracious, beautiful, adoring wife, but William would pay dearly for each foolish simper.

Chapter 3

BELOW A BLUE sky dotted with fleecy clouds, the racegoers went wild. Thousands cheered as Smolensko, owned by Sir Charles Bunbury, won the Derby by half a length.

As far as the eye could see, Banstead Downs seethed with humanity moving like brightly colored ants in some mammoth colony. The only open space was the broad track stretching between white posts to neatly divide the multitude. The gleaming, muscular horses and their jockeys in brilliant silks mingled with the brightly garbed crowd to form a colorful cavalcade.

"Here, my dear, take some refreshment. I swear, I'm as parched as the desert," drawled Anabelle Reid.

Marie Fleur thanked Poggy's sister for the glass of white wine. She had hoped that William would have delivered her by now from this circle of tittering ladies who picnicked in their carriages on the fringe of the crowd. It was a false hope. Not until the racing was finished for the day could she expect to return to the nearby country house where they were staying with William's friends, Lord and Lady Carew.

In the beginning the color and excitement of the racetrack had stirred her blood, but by now the charms of Derby Week had begun to pale. Had she been close to the rail where she could experience the thrill of the race, perhaps she would not have minded the dust and noise. As it was, she was exiled to the boredom of her fellow female guests, who had taken it upon themselves to entertain her.

A bellowed greeting and a cloud of dust announced the arrival of a horseman. Teddy Brooks's round face beamed from beneath a mole-gray silk hat as he reined in his chestnut. Winking, he said, "'Pon my word, what a bevy of beauties."

The ladies giggled and several of them winked back.

"Are we leaving now the Derby's over?" asked Marie Fleur hopefully.

Teddy grimaced in mock horror. "Leave? I should say not! I'm here to personally escort you ladies to a certain secret spot"—he winked again, inclining his head toward the distant downs—"from where you will view a most splendid entertainment. Follow me, ladies. Tally ho!"

"Absurd, even when sober," remarked Anabelle with a smile. She signaled to the coachman to follow her cousin. Then she lounged back amongst the cushions, waving languidly to the other two carriages of women, indicating they were to follow her to the unknown destination.

"Where are we going?"

Anabelle raised her thin dark brows. "Lud, what ignorance! A mill, my darling. A prizefight. Do you know what that is?"

Marie Fleur agreed she did. And with a sigh she resigned herself to the bumping, dusty ride.

A handsome, dark-skinned gypsy lad ran beside the carriage holding aloft a cage of pink-breasted linnets all chirping sweetly.

"See, lady . . . pretty birds . . . sing like angels."

"Get away, you filthy creature," cried Anabelle shrilly, waving her folded parasol at him. When the lad fell back, disappointment clouding his face, she remarked in an undertone to Marie Fleur, "What do you suppose he'd be like?" Here she winked suggestively. "Such marvelous features! And his skin's smooth as silk."

Marie Fleur shrugged, no longer surprised by anything Anabelle said. "I thought you found him filthy."

"My dear, you've such a lot to learn. One does not come out and say exactly what's on one's mind! You're young, of course . . . yet, maybe you're more the prim little governess sort after all, with no real eye for a likely male. Now, dearest, you simply must tell me again about those darling little ruffians you intend to turn into ladies and gentlemen. Teach them French, is it, and reading? Oh, look there, my dear. What a simply gorgeous specimen!"

A broad-shouldered young man pushed close to their barouche while it was momentarily halted by the crowd. Bare to the waist, he wore ragged canvas breeches and had a red bandana knotted about his unruly blond hair. He winked at them, correctly interpreting the appraising glance Anabelle gave him. Before their disbelieving gaze, he produced a flaming brand and thrust it down his throat, swallowing the fire. Gasps of wonder echoed from the bystanders.

Anabelle clapped in delight. Shouting "Bravo," she threw him a handful of silver from her embroidered silk reticule.

Almost before the coins hit the ground the crowd surged

forward, clamoring about the barouche. Ragged urchins held aloft wooden toys, jugs of ale, feathered marionettes that danced a frenzied tempo at the pulling of a string, bunches of flowers, and all manner of edibles. The bolder of the urchins tried to clamber aboard the barouche while they screeched their wares in high-pitched cockney accents.

Shouting to her driver to go on, Anabelle battered the urchins' filthy clawing hands with the handle of her parasol in an effort to break their grasp. "Quickly, Barnes. For God's sake, man, drive on. These parasites will upend us."

One intrepid crone, shawl-swathed and sporting brass rings in her ears, clung tenaciously to the padded side of the barouche, cackling, "Sixpence, pretty lady. Tell yer fortune fer sixpence."

Barnes did as he was bid, shouting gruffly to the rabble, "Clear orf," while his thin whip snaked over the heads of the matched grays. As they lurched forward, a heap of squealing, cursing humanity tumbled to the ground. The driver stoically ignored the commotion, plunging for an opening in the sparse crowd.

The last Marie Fleur saw of the ancient fortune-teller was a flurry of filthy skirts as she went down. When she looked back a pair of bony legs kicked feebly from a heap of rags.

"Stop! The old woman's hurt!"

Anabelle turned a jaded eye on her naive companion. "Just watch. She'll be on her feet in no time when we don't stop. They're old hands at this game."

Though at first she did not believe Anabelle's cynical prediction, Marie Fleur was surprised to see the ragbag swiftly right herself. The old woman stood shaking her fist after them, her mouth a gaping cavern of obscenities that were drowned by the roar of the crowd.

Though she did not voice her sentiments, Marie Fleur knew by Anabelle's smug smile her companion was inwardly gloating to have been proven right. Deciding not to give her the chance to say, "I told you so," she turned her attention to her surroundings.

Marie Fleur had never seen such a motley crowd as were assembled today on Banstead Downs. Impeccably dressed Corinthians rubbed shoulders with racecourse touts. Jockeys in brilliantly colored silks, looking for all the world like weatherbeaten schoolboys, mingled with the crowds in the paddock.

There were ale sellers, pie sellers, cardsharps, hucksters, and performers of all types and talent. Droves of women of the town, painted and feathered like gaudy birds of paradise, ogled likely customers as they sauntered past. Working men and women by the hundreds had come down from London for the Derby. Ragged children seemed to be everywhere, darting between legs, pushing past skirts, often picking pockets as they went. Dusk would find the roads leading from Epsom choked with returning Londoners, many of them gin-sodden and penniless.

As the barouche rattled over the downs the vast mobs of spectators were left behind, for only a few carriages and horsemen were headed in their direction. The flying wheels flattened scented spikes of fragrant orchids, which spattered the grassland pink. Small blue butterflies fluttered about the clumps of tangled horseshoe vetch.

They finally surmounted a scrubby crest, which overlooked a table-smooth depression. To Marie Fleur's amazement the area teemed with carriages, curricles, barouches and phaetons; even hackneys stood patiently awaiting their customers' pleasure. During Derby Week, illegal but highly popular prizefights drew the cream of the Fancy. Numerous well-dressed gentlemen were placing their bets while their fashionably attired ladies waited in carriages beneath the shade of fringed parasols.

Suddenly the crowd's attention focused on the makeshift ring as cheers and sporadic bursts of applause greeted the two prizefighters and their colorfully dressed entourage.

"Gypsy Dan's the favorite. Albert Price, a Carnaby butcher, is the challenger," said a resonant masculine voice from beside the parked barouche.

Marie Fleur turned in surprise to encounter a pair of searching dark-lashed gray eyes. Before she could speak, Anabelle leaned forward, a practiced smile on her lips.

"Why, Brandy, darling, what a surprise," she gushed, fluttering her sparse lashes coquettishly. "Did you win or lose on the big race?"

"What I lost on that I made up for on the others," Brandon Nicholas acknowledged with a rueful grin. "And you?"

"Oh, a little flutter, nothing serious." Anabelle purposely leaned across the barouche's padded side to force an enticing swell to her blue muslin bodice. "Won't you sit with us?"

"I'm sorry, Anabelle, I can't. I need to be at ring-side to

make sure Gypsy Dan doesn't try any tricks. Price is my man."

Though he spoke to Anabelle, Marie Fleur was conscious of Brandon Nicholas's glance straying to her. Despite the revealing insight into his character she had received at William's card party, she still found him so attractive that her stomach surged with excitement when he smiled at her.

"Lady Dowling, will you accompany me to ringside? Your husband would like you to watch his favorite fighter."

Normally Marie Fleur would have been reluctant to accept such an offer, but her decision was made for her by the approaching carriage full of clucking females, assuring the continuation of today's boredom. "Of course."

"You promised to stay with us," Anabelle cried peevishly. She did not really care whether Marie Fleur went or stayed; it was her handsome escort she coveted.

"When William asks me to join him, it's more than my life's worth to refuse."

Her legs stiff from sitting so long in the barouche, Marie Fleur found it a relief to walk over the springy turf with the fresh breeze blowing in her face.

"Have you ever seen a prizefight?"

"No. And I've no great desire to watch two men batter each other to a pulp, yet even that seemed preferable to more tedious hours of nonsense."

"You do surprise me, Lady Dowling. I thought all women delighted in gossip."

"Not all women, Mr. Nicholas," she replied icily, surprised by her sudden need to keep him at arm's length.

When they entered the crowd he took her arm, carefully guiding her through the milling spectators. Marie Fleur could not prevent herself from shuddering as the pressure of his warm fingers penetrated her frilled muslin sleeve. If her reaction betrayed her, Brandon Nicholas did not acknowledge it.

"Marie, m'love, over here. Meet my lad, Dan," William bawled like a fish porter.

Marie Fleur felt a tinge of disappointment. A few minutes before she had indulged the foolishly romantic notion that perhaps Brandon Nicholas had invented the message in order to be alone with her.

Gypsy Dan was a broad-shouldered man with bulging biceps and fists like ham hocks. When he grinned appreciatively at her, Marie Fleur noticed his front teeth were missing, imparting a roguish air to his smile.

"Pleased to meet yer, m'lady."

"Good God, Brandy, you here too! Get back to your boy. You'll ruin my luck."

Brandon Nicholas gave William a mocking bow and spun about. "I wish you the most damnable luck, Will."

The jest brought blood surging to William's face, and his breathing noticeably quickened. Marie Fleur was amazed by his reaction. She had thought the two men the best of friends. It had certainly appeared so the other evening when William had eagerly introduced them. Now she saw that William's fists were clenched, the knuckles whitening as he watched Nicholas stride away, his muscular legs rippling beneath his skintight cream breeches.

William snarled an oath under his breath as he turned back to Gypsy Dan. "All right, m'boy," he began with forced joviality. "I've got a fortune riding on you. Beat the hell out of that trumped-up butcher."

"Betcha, guv'ner," agreed Gypsy Dan, winking a scarred eyelid.

At William's mention of a large bet, Marie Fleur's heart sank. How long could he keep this up? Week after week he frequented the fashionable West End gambling clubs; she had even discovered he was a regular at Gordon's, a notorious gambling hell in Jermyn Street. If that were not ruinous enough, he both attended and gave parties at which gambling in one form or another was the featured event.

"Penny for your thoughts—or perhaps I should say a few thousand, m'dear, seeing that you're dear Will's beauteous wife."

She had no need to turn about to identify the source of that sarcastic remark. She shuddered slightly with revulsion as she felt the Earl of Cranbrook's hand on her shoulder as he gently turned her toward the ring.

"You'll miss the opening ceremony. They've already thrown their hats into the ring."

William had disappeared in the mob pushing its way to the ropes for an unobstructed view of the fight. Now she could see him, his black hat visible above the crowd as Gypsy Dan's motley assortment of hangers-on stood aside to allow their aristocratic backer an unobstructed view. Several of William's friends were with him.

Gypsy Dan scrambled inside the ring, where he proceeded to peel off his sweat-soaked shirt. His opponent moved more slowly, methodically divesting himself of a crimson coat and lace-trimmed shirt, which sat ill on his bulky, thick-necked frame.

A man wearing a narrow-brimmed top hat, superbly tailored black coat, and cream breeches stepped forward, motioning the two fighters to the center of the ring. Marie Fleur recognized him as Lord Westerham, his red hair blazing like fire in the sunlight.

"Gentlemen . . . and ladies, we're about to see the fight of the century. On my right, the champion, the famous Gypsy Dan, backed by Sir William Dowling and Mr. Algernon Sweet. On my left, the challenger, Albert Price, backed by Mr. Jack Masham, Mr. Brandon Nicholas, and several gentlemen who wish to remain anonymous."

Loud cheering disrupted the rest of his speech as the two prizefighters paraded around the ring, displaying their splendid physiques to their supporters.

To Marie Fleur's untrained eye, William's investment was unusually secure. Gypsy Dan, with his bronzed muscular body and lithe, quick movements, appeared the likely winner. The butcher, while a mountain of muscle, was pale and lethargic, seeming too slow and blundering to go the distance with the gypsy champion.

A frenzy of last-minute betting was taking place as the Corinthians reassessed the fighters' potential. Valuing the humor of the act, the Earl of Cranbrook placed a thirty-pound bet on Marie Fleur's behalf against William's man.

Bare to the waist and clad in tight-fitting white knee-breeches, their muscular bodies flexed, the two pugilists assumed their fighting stance, fists up, elbows level. Each man feinted before bobbing about the ring. Their preliminary sizing up evoked boos of dissatisfaction from the Fancy, who had not come to watch them dance.

Gypsy Dan grinned his gap-toothed smile, taking time out to bow in acknowledgment to his audience, his unguarded action displaying his contempt for his slow-moving opponent.

Somewhat dim-witted though he was, Albert Price knew by the crowd's burst of laughter that he had been insulted. Grunting with rage, his walleyes alight, he lumbered forward. When he swung wildly, the gypsy danced aside. A loud round of applause, followed by catcalls and shouts of encouragement, greeted this flurry. Gypsy Dan continued to dodge Price's blows. Anger mounting, the butcher renewed his efforts. His movements quickened, and he landed several blows on his opponent's body. Gypsy Dan, wanting to teach the challenger a lesson, returned a barrage of punishing blows to Price's body, leaving reddened patches on his lard-white flesh, but failing to stop him. His enormous fists doubled, Price lumbered forward like a great cart horse to land his first damaging blow to Gypsy Dan's face. The champion was caught off guard, playing to the audience. The sheer force of the blow staggered him.

Shouts of dismay came from Gypsy Dan's supporters; there was a burst of cheering from Price's backers. After this crushing delivery, Gypsy Dan no longer viewed his opponent with scorn. The fight began in earnest, igniting the crowd's emotions.

Round after gruelling round was fought. Gypsy Dan continued to land blows then dance away while Albert Price stood his ground like a brick wall, never wavering or buckling under the onslaught.

Marie Fleur turned away in revulsion for both men's faces were little more than a bloody pulp.

Gypsy Dan visibly weaved on his feet while the Carnaby market butcher staggered on, oblivious to the blood trickling down his face. With supreme effort, Price's battered, bleeding fists finally connected with Gypsy Dan's jaw, audibly splintering bone.

Cries of alarm came from the Corinthians at ringside as the champion screamed in agony and went down. Moaning, the gypsy clutched the shattered remains of his jaw while his seconds worked to patch him up to continue the fight.

Despite many angry shouts of protest, Lord Westerham stepped into the blood-spattered ring to declare Albert Price the winner in this, the twentieth round.

Pandemonium broke out as men scrambled over each other to reach the ring. The earl caught Marie Fleur's arm and steered her to safety.

"Thank you. I didn't realize there'd be such an uproar."

"There's a lot of money riding on this fight. Men never like to lose."

"Who did you back?"

"Both. I'm no fool."

She laughed at his answer. "You do surprise me."

The earl smiled, but only with his thin, fine-chiseled mouth. "You yourself have some winnings coming, Lady Dowling. Do allow me the pleasure of collecting them for you. I'd also be obliged if you'd let me collect your derby stake whilst I'm in town on Monday."

"Yes . . . of course, how kind of you," Marie Fleur agreed absently as she glanced about for William. It was unforgivable of him to have abandoned her like this.

The earl led her to a nearby table and chairs where several of William's friends sat squabbling over money.

"My dear Lady Dowling, were it possible I'd stay with you until your husband's return, but I've a pressing engagement at the track. Would you prefer me to escort you back to your carriage?"

"No, thank you, this will be far enough. You've been most thoughtful."

The earl bowed slightly over her extended hand. A few minutes later his tall, beaver-hatted figure disappeared in the crowd.

The air seethed with disgruntled voices dissecting the unexpected outcome of this bout. Some angry gamblers accused their opponents of cheating by drugging the gypsy champion to make him unfit to fight. There were even demands that the challenger be disqualified.

It was not William but Brandon Nicholas who finally came to her rescue. "This is no place for a woman," he observed gruffly.

He had not said lady, and Marie Fleur wondered if he intended to insult her. A quick glance at his serious countenance assured her he had not.

"I'm still waiting for William."

"He's embroiled in a dozen arguments. You'll have a long wait."

"All the same, it would be wise for me to wait."

He shrugged nonchalantly, a smile twitching the corner of his sensual mouth. "Has my evil reputation filled you with dread?"

Marie Fleur smiled also, but her expression was strained. "Not at all."

While she spoke Marie Fleur discovered she was nervously

twisting her hands, and she attempted to mask the agitated movement in the folds of her skirt. Brandon Nicholas had the most infuriating habit of making her feel schoolgirlish and inadequate. Besides, when he stood close to her, his muscular legs brushing her frilled skirt, she felt dangerously attracted to him. A now-familiar emotion surged in her limbs while a curious feeling, almost like a half-forgotten memory, tugged at the back of her mind.

"Very well, madam, I remain your obedient servant," he said with a formal bow. "Like a dutiful wife, you must await your lord."

His mocking words brought a flush to her cheeks. Marie Fleur was about to make a sharp retort when she was seized from behind and swung about.

"William, for heaven's sake! What's the matter with you?" she cried shrilly when she found herself staring up into her husband's flushed, belligerent face.

Thrusting her aside, William stood his ground, squarely facing Brandon Nicholas. His jaw jutted forward; his lips were set as pugnaciously as the prizefighters'.

"Leave her alone."

"I can assure you nothing untoward has taken place. I merely asked Lady Dowling if she would like to be escorted from this . . . place, the language hardly being suitable for a lady's ears."

"She'll go where and when I tell her," William rumbled, lurching slightly. He firmly replanted his feet.

Marie Fleur was appalled by the building menace of this scene. William had been drinking; the scent of liquor wafted about him like a cloud. He had also lost heavily. Yet neither fact excused a public quarrel.

"William, let's go home. Nothing's happened. Mr. Nicholas has been most chivalrous."

Brandon Nicholas inclined his head toward her in sarcastic acknowledgment of the compliment.

"His man cheated!" William finally bellowed in rage, reaching for Nicholas's collar. "Cheated, do you hear! Gypsy Dan should have won that fight."

"Gypsy Dan was beaten fairly," Brandon ground out.

William glared back at him. Thoughts unrelated to the fight and to his tremendous losses floated disembodied through his befuddled brain. Hateful visions of Marie Fleur locked in Nich-

olas's embrace, reacting with passion he had never been able
to release, finally overcame his reason.

"You bastard!" he thundered.

A gasp went round the crowd that had gathered about these
two well-known men, curious to learn the nature of their dispute. It was naturally assumed this was an argument about the
prizefight.

Brandon's hand shot out and he grasped William's lapel.
"Don't call me that again. This time I'll forgive you because
you're stinking drunk. You're a bad sport, Sir William Dowling." With that Brandon turned on his heel.

William stared after him, his eyes bulbous with shock.
"Nicholas," he bellowed suddenly, lurching forward as he came
to his sense. "Nicholas, you'll pay for that. Give me satisfaction. I demand it."

Marie Fleur gasped, knowing full well what that statement
implied. William had challenged Brandon Nicholas to a duel.
In his current drunken state he probably had no idea what a
serious threat he had made. She grabbed his coattail, trying to
pull him away. He shook her free. So determined was William
to be heard, he even pushed aside several concerned friends
who tried to march him to safety.

"Satisfaction? You're drunk. I make it a practice never to
accept challenges from drunks."

"Drunk am I? Well, you damned coward, I won't be drunk
tomorrow. I'll be sober enough to put paid to you. You're a
coward and a cheat. Now, will you give me satisfaction?"

Brandon drew in his breath. There was little he could do.
The insult must be answered, the challenge accepted. A mounting buzz of voices from the nearby spectators reminded him
they were awaiting his decision.

"Very well, Dowling," he said gruffly, "name the place."

"The Cup, outside town. Anyone will show you—"

"I know where it is."

"Choose your seconds," William spluttered, lurching about
to collar Poggy Reid, who stood behind him, frowning over
this unexpected ending to today's glorious prizefight. "Stand
by me, Poggy, old boy."

"You mustn't fight, Will, you don't know what you're—"

"Are you calling me a drunk, too?" William rumbled menacingly.

Poggy sighed. "No, Will, not that. I'll be there in the morning. Dawn's the accustomed time." He wanted to ask William if he had ever even handled dueling pistols, but decided against the question. It would likely be taken as another insult.

Brandon Nicholas's friends surged around him, amazed by this unexpected hostility between former friends. Only two other men knew the actual reason for the challenge, and they had been sworn to secrecy.

The soft summer dawn stole across the downs. Unusual activity for so early in the day had turned the normal tranquility of the countryside into a hubbub. Men and women had ridden over from the surrounding country houses where they congregated for race week, all headed for the Cup.

The local landmark, a former sheep pond gone dry, was outlined by a fringe of juniper scrub. Beechwoods straggled over the spine of the surrounding hillocks, sheltering the spot from the road. Here numerous spectacles, ranging in severity from duels to illegal prizefights, had been held.

As expected, the Fancy placed bets on the outcome of this duel. Brandon Nicholas, having a certain reputation with dueling pistols, was the overwhelming favorite. Besides, those who knew him well surmised correctly that Sir William would likely fortify himself with a few tumblers of brandy, which might greatly hamper his aim.

Long before dawn Marie Fleur resigned herself to the inevitable. She had squandered much of the night in trying to persuade William to apologize to Brandon Nicholas. She had seen signs of forgiveness in the other man's face. If only William would swallow his pride, own up to being the worse for drink, and make an apology. William refused.

Poggy Reid and Lord Cranbrook were to act as William's seconds; Lord Westerham and Jack Masham were to stand for Brandon Nicholas.

The sky was already bright in the east. A salt-tinged wind blew chill through Marie Fleur's thin white morning gown. She turned up the bead-embroidered collar of her yellow spencer in an attempt to block the wind.

William had not yet spoken to her this morning. There had been no loving farewells, not even an attempt to explain his need to avenge an imagined wrong. Nothing but silence. He stood awaiting his opponent in his shirt-sleeves on the scrubby grass, his buff kerseymere waistcoat unbuttoned. She felt she ought to plead with him one final time before it was too late, but when he turned to look at her without a glimmer of affection in his face, her concern faded and died. This morning William's features sagged, his normally healthy complexion reduced to a greenish pallor. She bit back her plea. It would do no good. He was as unyielding as a stone wall.

A rising clamor from the assembled gentry announced the arrival of Brandon Nicholas and his seconds. They walked purposefully up the rolling hillock, heading toward the make-shift arena in the center of the scraggly juniper growth.

"Lady Dowling."

Marie Fleur turned in surprise when Brandon Nicholas spoke to her. Suddenly a disturbing realization struck her: William might kill this man! During all those hours of fruitless pleading, never once had she given a thought to the danger to Nicholas. From the first she had naturally assumed William would be the loser.

"Yes?" she said, finally finding her voice.

"Please, don't distress yourself, Lady Dowling. You've no cause."

His words, delivered in an undertone, were meant for her alone. Wide-eyed, Marie Fleur gazed up at him, searching his hard face for a clearer meaning. He smiled slightly, nodding before he turned about to continue his walk to the dueling ground. Had he been telling her he intended to spare William? Was it possible to make such trickery appear genuine? What if William fired a lucky shot? Fools sometimes had the most amazing fortune.

The sun struggled through the clouds, promising another glorious day as Marie Fleur ran toward the dueling ground, her buff kid slippers darkening in the dew-soaked grass. She could overhear the duelists conferring with their seconds. A doctor, summoned by the owner of Carshalton House, where Brandon Nicholas was a guest, spoke a few words to the combatants before turning aside.

Brandon stood his ground, quickly taking in the state of the grooved land. He wiped his hand across his tan leather breeches before leveling the silver embossed pistol, getting the feel of the weapon and assessing the distance. He did not carry his own pistols; these were on loan from a friend.

Twisting her hands in agitation, Marie Fleur watched as the two men stood back to back. With the exception of William's waistcoat, they were virtually identical in dress, height, and coloring.

The count was begun and the duelists paced off the prescribed distance. When the count of ten was reached, each man spun about and leveled his pistol. Smoke puffed out as two shots were fired.

Marie Fleur felt faint. Forcing herself to look, she found both men still standing. William grasped his upper arm as blood trickled between his fingers; his own bullet lay harmlessly embedded in the earth ten yards from Brandon Nicholas's feet.

Surprised shouts, laughter, and congratulations rang out. No one had wanted a fatality to result from this foolish quarrel, nor was there any wish to see either man badly wounded. Though so tame an outcome was rather an anticlimax, the fashionable guests were satisfied.

"I don't know what happened," Brandon muttered as he examined his smoking pistol. "The sight must be off. My aim was true."

Marie Fleur caught his eye, and her lips moved imperceptibly in thanks, which now, before the others, he refused to acknowledge. It did not matter. She knew his misfire had not been accidental.

Men gathered around, jovial and eager to be off to the racetrack, patting first William on the back, then Brandon. Numerous rounds of drinks were proposed, and Marie Fleur sighed with relief when she saw William smile as he reached for his coat. Quite sober this morning, despite the two swift tots of courage he had taken before leaving, his outlook on events was greatly improved from yesterday.

"No hard feelings, Brandy?"

"None, Will. It was a fair contest."

The doctor bustled up to cut away William's sleeve, exposing a wound that barely broke the flesh. William grimaced as the doctor applied alcohol, but his discomfort was soon relieved. Brandon Nicholas offered him a flask of spirits from which he took a hearty swig. Then, patched up to his satisfaction, William marched away with his seconds.

Everyone hurried noisily past, leaving Marie Fleur standing alone on the windswept downland. How lovely it was here! The air smelled of bruised thyme and marjoram still wet with dew. For an insane moment she contemplated walking away from the noisy throng, losing herself in the herb-sweet solitude

of the open downs. Sense overruled her impulse as she resolutely turned her back on the tempting view and followed the
eager crowd.

Ladies who had been waiting in their carriages were now
passing around refreshments. The Reid family's wine-red barouche stood beside the road. Anabelle waved to her, holding
aloft a plate of food.

Heaving a great sigh of mingled relief and resignation, Marie
Fleur waved back. One more disaster averted, she thought, as
she headed for the barouche. Yet after a day's drinking William's mood might be drastically altered. She had no assurance
tonight would not bring a new calamity.

It was as if Marie Fleur had experiencēd a premonition of doom
on the windswept downs, for by evening the situation was again
near boiling point. William, being very much the worse for
drink, had turned belligerent.

Today all over the racecourse men had laughingly discussed
the duel. Most observers considered Brandon Nicholas too good
a shot to miss by accident; they assumed he had deliberately
spared William's life.

"Don't be ridiculous!" Marie Fleur cried when William angrily presented his case to her. "The man missed. Can't you
be satisfied with that? Had he not missed, you drunken fool,
you'd be lying on an undertaker's slab."

"Drunken fool?" William repeated, poised in mid-step.

"That's what I said because that's what you are. Between
your drinking and your gambling we'll soon be in the poor-
house. When will you come to your senses? Surely today, of
all days, should show you how far you've sunk. A man spares
your life, and instead of being grateful you're boiling with
anger. I think you're insane!"

Marie Fleur stood panting, the gathered white muslin bodice
of her gown heaving. Her words, though true, had been spoken
recklessly. Only now, when it was far too late to retract them,
did the extent of her imprudence register.

"Insane am I?"

"Yes, that too."

William's hazel eyes narrowed almost to slits. His face,
which she had formerly found handsome, showed all the marks
of dissipation; his jowls sagged, his eyes were puffy. Now, to
add to nature's handiwork, he was flushed with rage.

"You French bitch! I dragged you out of the gutter! I made you Lady Dowling, and you dare address me so."

"Out of the gutter? My father was a *comte,*" Marie Fleur cried, her eyes flashing.

"Well, let's see how your fine French ancestry helps you now."

"No, William . . . don't," she screamed as his fists lashed out. He pummeled her viciously about the breasts and shoulders, then delivered a glancing blow to the side of her face that set her ear on fire. Sobbing, Marie Fleur crumpled to her knees, clutching her head.

"If I weren't in such a hurry to face that cheating bastard, I'd beat you senseless," William threatened, kicking out blindly. The hard sole of his riding boot connected with her soft flesh, and Marie Fleur yelped in pain. "I'll deal with you when I come back. By God, if I won't make you eat those words, madam!"

When he picked up his riding crop Marie Fleur raised her arms to defend herself, but her husband's thoughts had already shifted to another target for his venom.

He paused in the doorway, his lip cirled as he threatened, "I'll be back far sooner than you expect. We'll settle matters then."

Shaking with pain, anger, and fear, Marie Fleur fought for breath. When she eventually took her hands from her swelling face, William had gone.

She scrambled to her feet and went to the window. The stable yard was visible from here. There was William now, rattling under the arch in his phaeton, the yellow paintwork gleaming in the fading light. Like a Roman charioteer, he went to avenge his honor. She had supposed he would ride out to Carshalton on horseback to challenge Brandon Nicholas. The comfort of his adored phaeton must be meant to bolster his courage.

At a discreet knock on the door she turned to find Nancy standing wide-eyed on the threshold.

The maid ran inside the room crying, "Ooh, that rotten— oh, look what he done to you—oh, my lady!"

Marie Fleur laid her head on Nancy's shoulder and wept deep, relieving sobs. Crying in sympathy, Nancy guided her mistress to the satin upholstered chaise beside the hearth. There she settled her against the tasseled pillows.

"Lie still. I'll be back in no time."

Marie Fleur's head buzzed, and strange bubbling, fluttering sounds filled her ear. While she lay in the gloom awaiting Nancy's return, she frankly assessed her position. Life with William had become intolerable. She would sooner return to embroidering linen in London's dingy émigré quarter than endure such harsh treatment. She was too ashamed to run home to Norfolk to beg charity from Uncle James. Her reappearance under such circumstances would set the local tongues clacking, and she had no wish to cause an unpleasant scandal for relatives who had treated her so kindly. Besides, it would be far too easy for William to follow her to Edgerton Heath.

But there must be somewhere she could go. In England she assumed a man had the right to forcefully return his wife to their home, but if she were clever enough he would not know where to find her.

"Here, love, drink this. 'Twill soothe the hurt."

Marie Fleur accepted a cup of warm milk laced with spirits. Nancy's genuine concern and the loving touch of her strong hands were infinitely more comforting than her timeworn remedy. Outspoken though she often was, Nancy respected her mistress's right to privacy. She would not ask the nature of their argument, and for that blessing Marie Fleur was exceedingly grateful.

With the candles lit and the rose damask draperies shutting out the dark night, the rather austere room had taken on a welcome coziness.

Nancy bathed Marie Fleur's injury with warm water to which herbs had been added. Though she doubted Nancy's concoction had any actual value, Marie Fleur would not have dreamt of hurting her maid by refusing it.

"I'm sleeping here," declared Nancy at bedtime after she had blown out all but one candle. "Just in case 'is lordship be in a randy mood when he comes 'ome. He don't dare throw me out, not with you looking like something the cat's brung in. Lord and Lady Carew would have plenty to say about that, all right."

"Thank you, Nancy."

Nancy squeezed her mistress's hand.

A small coal fired burned in the green tiled hearth, and Nancy settled down before it on the chaise. Though the room was peaceful, sleep eluded her. She seethed with anger while she awaited Sir William's return. Oh, she would give him a piece of her mind for treating her darling lady so cruelly! This time he had gone too far. A grim expression on her pretty face, Nancy finally pulled a blanket over her head and willed herself to sleep.

Marie Fleur lay awake for hours making and discarding a multitude of plans. Eventually she reached the unpleasant conclusion that William had the upper hand. At present she had not one penny to call her own. But when the Earl of Cranbrook delivered her modest winnings, she would use them to buy a stage ticket to freedom.

At Marie Fleur's request breakfast was brought to her room. She had no desire to go down to the dining room in this condition. The ensuing flurry of gossip would be more than she could face. A glance in the mirror had confirmed her worst fears; bruises circled her eye and her reddened cheek was swollen. Despite Nancy's patient ministrations, there was no way to camouflage her injuries.

"Shall I go down to see what's going on?" Nancy suggested. "Sir William should've been back hours ago. 'Appen he's too ashamed to show his face."

"Never mind. I'm in no hurry to talk to him."

It was likely that William, intoxicated as he had been, had been sidetracked by a willing female. There were numerous inns between here and Carshalton. Perhaps he was sleeping off a debauch in the arms of some barmaid.

In midmorning a rap sounded on the door. When Nancy answered it she found the Earl of Cranbrook and Lord Westerham outside.

"Yes, my lady's able to see you if it's very important," she answered reluctantly.

"Please leave us, Nancy. I'll ring if I need you."

Marie Fleur did not speak until Nancy had left the room, yet she realized the maid might listen at the keyhole. Seating herself in a dim corner in the hope that her visitors would not notice the bruises, she said at last, "I suppose you've brought me word of William's latest fiasco."

"Yes, my dear, I'm afraid we have."

Afraid! Then the news must be truly bad. Marie Fleur glanced from Lord Westerham's serious countenance to the earl, who likewise was frowning. When she met their eyes she saw shock register in both men's faces. The light had not been dim enough to hide the truth.

"A token of my husband's affection," she dismissed bitterly, indicating her injury. "And now that's out of the way, tell me how badly he's hurt."

"I'm afraid William's . . . dead."

Her eyes grew round as she held the earl's pale stare. His almost colorless eyes reflected the light until they glittered like glass. No emotion was visible in his finely chiseled aristocratic features. As her silence continued, he absently flicked dust from the sleeve of his black broadcloth coat. She had to be mistaken! Surely he would not appear so calm if he had said what she thought he had said.

"I think I misunderstood you," Marie Fleur began, reaching to her brow, which felt warm and sticky. "Did you—did you say . . . William's . . . dead?"

"Come, lie down. You've had a shock."

Lord Westerham solicitously led her to the striped satin chaise, supporting her against his body as if he expected her to faint.

"Call the maid, Cranbrook. There's a good chap."

The earl opened the door, and Nancy virtually fell across the threshold. Tears were trickling down her rosy cheeks. She scrambled to her feet and, ignoring the earl's supercilious smile, ran to attend her mistress.

The only tears in the room were Nancy's. Marie Fleur was in shock. Westerham and Cranbrook must find her lack of grief unusual, to say the least, she thought. To her own surprise, she did not even experience a feeling of release although last night, after William's brutality, she had longed to be free of him.

"How?" she asked, finding her voice at last.

"He took his phaeton too fast round a curve. It overturned, and he was pitched out. He struck the Carshalton milestone. It must have been quick. He probably felt nothing."

"For heaven's sake, Cranbrook, have some consideration," admonished Lord Westerham sharply. Kneeling, he took Marie Fleur's small hands in his. "Shall we send one of the women up to you, my dear?"

She shook her head, mute. He searched her violet eyes, squeezing her hand and murmuring sympathetic platitudes.

"Don't know where he was going at such a furious pace, do you?" Cranbrook asked languidly, his gaze fastened on Marie Fleur's pale face.

"I've no idea. William was a law unto himself," she answered quickly, glancing away.

"We'll leave you now. Don't worry your pretty head about a thing. We'll make all the necessary arrangements. Just rest. You have friends aplenty to help you."

"Thank you," Marie Fleur whispered. "You're both very kind."

Taking their leave, William's friends hastened from the room.

Marie Fleur tried to think, to plan, but found herself unable even to arrange events in logical sequence. In the background Nancy wept constantly, her sobs forming a comforting rhythm. She could not imagine why the girl was weeping—last night she had been ready to kill her master. Perhaps Nancy's concern was more for the future than for the past.

Nagging worry about William's vast debts invaded Marie Fleur's thoughts. After his death his estate would be liable for all unpaid accounts. Their tenants' rents, paid quarterly, would not come due for some weeks. She must hope there was cash enough to settle matters.

Marie Fleur's shock gradually disappeared until a single idea was left surging through her brain: she was free. Her brief, ill-starred reign as William's wife was over.

⟵ Chapter 4 ⟶

EVENING SUNLIGHT SPLASHED the cream brocade walls with gold. Marie Fleur stared at the shifting light, desperately trying to accept what had just been revealed to her in this elaborately furnished drawing room. She was virtually penniless! William's debts were even greater than she had imagined. If she were lucky, there would be a paltry thousand or two left after the creditors were paid. Fortunately, out of deference to his widow, some of William's close friends had declined to press for payment of his staggering gambling debts.

"Lady Dowling, are you quite well?" inquired Silas Lawrence, the family solicitor. While he spoke he fussily rearranged papers with his gnarled, age-spotted hands.

"Well is hardly an apt description. If you mean, do I understand what's been said—yes, I understand. By the time I've settled William's accounts I'll be without a roof over my head."

"Perhaps I can have a few minutes alone..." The Earl of Cranbrook, William's executor, glanced toward the lawyer.

"Yes, yes, of course. I'll be in the anteroom if you need me."

When the black-suited solicitor had left the room, Marie Fleur forced herself to meet the earl's pale gaze. Defiantly she asked, "Now are you about to tell me you've changed your mind and intend to press for payment?"

"Would it do any good?"

"Hardly. I'm as good as out on the street."

"You're overdramatizing the situation. There's still the small Norfolk estate. Yew Trees Lodge, isn't it? Then there's the Mayfair property."

"When they're sold will they bring enough to cover my debts?"

"I'll discuss it no further today. You've had a grueling two weeks. Here, my dear, you must be badly in need of this."

Marie Fleur gratefully accepted the glass of pale sherry he proffered.

Since William's funeral the earl had been unusually attentive. As he and Lord Westerham had promised, she had to concern herself very little with the funeral arrangements. During the past days, however, his attentiveness had become disturbing. Though he was still polite and appeared genuinely concerned over her welfare, a dangerous undercurrent passed between them. Today was as good a time as any to bring her feelings into the open.

Marie Fleur smoothed her black silk skirts while she carefully chose her words. "I've noticed a change in your attitude toward me this past week," she began as he turned to face her, his expression unfathomable. As he remained silent, she blundered on, avoiding mention of her actual fears, reluctant to be so blunt. "Is there something you wish to discuss? Don't try to spare me. I'm strong enough to stand one more shock."

"My dear, I think you've already guessed," the earl said softly, almost to himself. He extended his perfectly manicured hand to her. "Before we progress further, I must insist you call me Geoffrey. To address each other as Lady Dowling and the Earl of Cranbrook is excessively formal."

Marie Fleur swallowed uneasily, a premonition of what was to come causing her stomach to churn. "Very well, Geoffrey. Please call me Marie Fleur."

He inclined his head, smiling at her suggestion. "My dear Marie Fleur, though I chose not to press for payment of Will's notes, as long as they are on the books I could still demand it."

"You told me that once the will was settled—"

"Don't misunderstand. I've no intention of pressing. In fact, my dear, I'm prepared to tear up the mountain of IOUs in your presence in return for one small consideration from you."

"And that is?"

"I wouldn't have thought such a lovely woman would need to have matters spelled out."

Marie Fleur gasped. How naive she had been!

The earl's thin mouth twitched to a scornful smile while he poured himself a glass of brandy. "You sound shocked."

"You dare suggest I sell myself to pay William's debts?"

"Not at all. I merely suggest that I ignore your indebtedness in exchange for certain considerations. You're a beautiful woman. It would be my pleasure to escort you to the opera, to dinner, eventually, perhaps, to present you with a suite of rooms in my London mansion."

"Never!"

The smile faded from his thin lips. "You do yourself no service with so vehement an answer."

"It's not my intention to be self-serving. I merely wish to remove all doubt that I find your proposal repellent."

He bowed stiffly. Crossing to the window, he stood staring at the purple-shadowed garden. The sun was setting beyond the oak wood, a dying crimson disk in the violet sky.

"You'd give up all this?" he said.

"I've been given little choice."

"On the contrary, you have a choice. When a respectable time has passed, if you become my—" he hesitated, carefully choosing the word, "fiancée, I'll purchase *all* William's outstanding notes. You'll be free of debt, able to live just as before. This house, these furnishings, everything will stay as it is."

"With one disagreeable exception."

Turning slowly from the window, the earl stared at her, his pale eyes cold. "Would you prefer debtors' prison?"

The menacing words stabbed her with fear. Determined not to flinch before him, Marie Fleur spoke with a confidence she did not feel. "William's friends wouldn't allow you to put me in prison."

Quirking one eyebrow, the earl moved toward her. "How assured you sound. I admire courage in a woman, however misplaced it may be. Are you sure Will's friends would be so loyal? After all, most of them share similar designs on your person. It's just that I'm richer and more powerful than the rest—and I made the first offer."

Marie Fleur's palms were sticky with sweat. "Get out of my house." When he smiled sarcastically, she added, "At the moment it is still *my* house."

"You need not be hasty, my love. I'm prepared to allow you ample time to consider. After all, a public declaration so soon after Will's demise would hardly be in good taste. There'll be time enough for you to contemplate your future sewing grubby linen in a rat-infested garret. It hardly sounds appealing. Good evening, Lady Dowling."

He bowed and left the room.

Marie Fleur glared after his retreating back, her legs trembled with emotion. Fists clenched in anger, she reviewed his audacity in openly propositioning her. Worse than that, he was trying to blackmail her into accepting his terms by dangling the threat of debtors' prison before her.

It was likely he was right to assume some of William's friends had similar ideas. Morality was not the vogue in Regency society. She might even receive a proposal from Prinny himself, if she took his eye. The idea of a romantic involvement with the infantile, grossly overweight regent made her shudder.

Perhaps she could clarify her financial state with Mr. Lawrence. Before she had reached the threshold on her way to find the solicitor, Marie Fleur stopped. Silas Lawrence was an associate of the Earl of Cranbrook. Their discussion would hardly be confidential. Knowing the earl as she now did, he had probably instructed the solicitor to repeat all discourse between them. However difficult it became, she would have to keep her own counsel.

William had no surviving male relatives to assume his title. Only two maiden aunts in Tunbridge Wells had expected to benefit from their nephew's estate. Fortunately, the will had to go to probate, thereby giving her a little time to arrange the sale of whatever assets she owned. She hoped she could raise enough money to satisfy William's many creditors, including the odious Earl of Cranbrook. Once her debts were paid he would have no further hold over her.

During the following months the earl became a frequent visitor to Langley Chase. Each time he called, Marie Fleur refused to see him, but eventually he managed to bribe the servants to admit him. When she rode on the downs or walked in the gardens, even when she retired to her room, she was never sure whether she would find him waiting for her.

Now he insisted he was not bargaining for her body, that she had grossly misunderstood his motives; it was only her incomparable beauty he desired to grace his mansion. So sincerely did he plead his case, Marie Fleur almost believed him. However, young though she was, she knew no man would be satisfied forever with such arrangements. In time he would demand a far more intimate relationship.

She shuddered at the thought of lying naked in his arms. So many rumors circulated about the earl's unholy vices, she did not know which of them to believe. There was even a rumor that he kept a padded room in his fashionable London residence where he indulged his sadistic tastes without complaint from the neighbors. Anabelle Reid swore he had been active in a Satanic cult in his youth. Yet again there were those who cackled uproariously at the salacious stories, insisting the earl's passions were to be spent more in the arms of his young footmen then in those of a pretty woman.

Whatever the truth about the Earl of Cranbrook's intimate preference, Marie Fleur had no desire to make the discovery for herself.

Summer lingered and so did the earl. At her wits' end by now to avoid him, Marie Fleur decided to escape to Rye, traveling with Nancy on a long-postponed visit to her mother, who was now ailing. She had at first considered going to Norfolk, but when Uncle James and Cousin Lavinia attended William's funeral, they had told such tales of woe about their need to pinch pennies that she decided they could not afford another mouth to feed. In the back of Marie Fleur's mind nagged the disturbing thought that Uncle James had been angling for a loan from Will's estate. Though she had revealed to him there were many debts, she had withheld the full truth. It would be a bitter blow to him when James Fox learned his niece was virtually bankrupt.

Because she did not want to be nearer the earl, she had refused numerous invitations to Brighton. Undaunted, her suitor rode back and forth from the seaside resort, traveling with his valet, a sinister Frenchman named Gaston. When he failed to make any progress with his wooing, the earl became so desperate he finally proposed marriage.

Though Marie Fleur was surprised by his proposal, she quickly turned him down, saying she had endured one unhappy marriage and had no intention of repeating the mistake.

She often thought about the night when she had been swept into the heady world of passion. It seemed ridiculous that she could ever have considered William a tender lover. Now she was more inclined to agree with his dismissal of the incident as a dream, perhaps induced by Dr. Slope's powerful medicine.

After William's death, Marie Fleur had supposed Brandon Nicholas would join the many friends of William who came to offer condolences. She had been wrong. Not since the morning of the duel had she laid eyes on him. From Anabelle Reid she later learned handsome Brandon had temporarily dropped out of society. He was rumored to be sharing a romantic hideaway with his latest mistress, the wife of an influential member of Parliament. This unexpected news had been a blow. Angrily she told herself it was ridiculous for her to care what he did, or with whom. Yet she did care. And far more than she chose to admit.

The day of their departure for Rye dawned cold and sunny. Amber and russet already tinged the distant trees, and the nip of frost was in the air.

Marie Fleur discarded her widow's weeds in favor of a high-waisted pink silk traveling dress with a matching pelisse trimmed in white military braid. Beneath the light garments she wore a fine wool chemise. Her fawn kid boots and matching gloves were fastened with pearl buttons. On her head she wore a fashionable tall-crowned French bonnet of pink silk and maroon velvet trimmed with a black feather. This lovely outfit had been ordered during the first month of her marriage in preparation for traveling down to Brighton. By appearing out of mourning so soon, she knew she would probably cause many raised eyebrows, but she was tired of being dowdy as an old crow, hypocritically marking the passage of a man she had grown to despise. Let them gossip. Marie Fleur had little intention of running her life to suit society.

Delay after unexpected delay postponed their departure.

"Oh, my lady, 'twill be dark before we get there," moaned Nancy in anguish as her brown eyes filled with tears. "Jemmy says Mum's taken awful bad. We can't wait. There be no one else. Our Betty's too close to her time. Besides, Dorset be too far away. I've got to get 'ome as soon as possible."

"Don't cry, Nancy. I promise we'll soon be on the road."

Marie Fleur's optimism was misplaced, however. The coachman, after assuring her everything would be repaired within the hour, found numerous faults with the equipage. Broken axles, rusted springs, blown horses—there seemed to be no end to the disasters that befell them. Inwardly seething with anger, Marie Fleur endured the inconvenience with grace. She had never been at ease with William's servants, who had always treated her more like a guest than mistress of the house. Perhaps it was only her imagination, but she got the impression she was being deliberately deceived.

When, soon after noon, the Earl of Cranbrook's distinctive four-in-hand with its bold coat of arms emblazoned on the door rolled into the stable yard, she finally understood the reason for this trail of disasters.

"What, my dear Marie, you've not departed yet! I came to

make sure the servants had secured the house as ordered, and here I find you, surrounded by bags and boxes. Whatever is the matter?"

Her eyes glittered with anger as she approached him. "Perhaps you can tell me."

"How should I know what happens at Langley Chase?"

"You seem to be here nearly as much as I am," she retorted angrily, picking up her rose-flowered valise. "Never mind, Horrocks," she called to the coachman. "We'll set out first thing in the morning. That is, if you think the coach will be roadworthy by then."

Coloring uncomfortably at her sarcasm, Horrocks nodded. He could not meet her eyes. "Yes, my lady, I'll have things taken care of by then." This deception was not to his liking. He had no particular loyalty to the French bit, but neither did he care much for the earl. It was only the man's gold he was partial to.

"Please, my lady, can't we go when 'Orrocks gets the wheel remounted?" Nancy pleaded. She was becoming distraught, her dark hair sprouting untidily from under the brim of her Sunday bonnet. "We could allus spend a night on the road. As bad as me Mum's taken, I don't want to wait." Nancy's accusing glance also said, "Especially after all she's done for you and your mum." Marie Fleur felt a pang of guilt. It was true, they could stay the night on the road, yet she was not partial to highway inns.

"Have no fear, ladies. I'll be happy to escort you."

"Thank you, Your Grace, that won't be necessary."

"I insist. How about you, Miss Cross? Wouldn't you be obliged to leave without delay? My carriage stands at the ready. A faster vehicle would be hard to find."

The sheer joy in Nancy's smile stabbed Marie Fleur afresh. She shook her head, and Nancy's face fell. "Thank you, but Nancy will be happy to abide by my decision. We'll wait until tomorrow."

Marie Fleur had almost reached the side door when Nancy grasped her skirts.

"Please, oh, please, let's travel with the earl. He be a fine gentleman. We'll come to no 'arm. What if Mum . . . if Mum . . . passed on! Oh, I'd never forgive myself." Ending on a wail, Nancy buried her tearstained face in Marie Fleur's pink skirts.

Above her maid's bowed straw bonnet, Marie Fleur met the earl's gaze. Triumph glittered in his face, so blatantly obvious that she ground her teeth in fury. How clever he thought himself, how artful at arranging other people's lives.

"Can you refuse so pitiable a request?"

"I appear to have been outmaneuvered," Marie Fleur announced stiffly. "Very well, Your Grace, we'll accept your kind offer. Come, Nancy, stop crying."

Still sniffling, Nancy eagerly helped to unpack the coach and transfer the baggage to the earl's sleek conveyance.

When everything was aboard, Marie Fleur climbed inside the coach to find Gaston, the earl's French valet, already seated with his back to the horses.

"Would madame prefer me to ride on top?" the Frenchman asked.

"Not at all. I've no wish to inconvenience anyone. I insist on you staying inside." Marie Fleur was rewarded by a glimpse of the earl's angry face before he quickly concealed his emotion. Good, she had at least won one round in their battle. She had no desire for a tête-à-tête with him all the way to Rye. Though Nancy was to accompany them, she knew once they were underway her maid would go to sleep.

The two men sat with their backs to the horses, the women facing them. Though this was a roomy, well-upholstered vehicle, Marie Fleur found the earl's long, booted legs brushing against her skirts. The intimate contact was most unpleasant.

"I'm glad you're not traveling alone—the roads to the coast are far too dangerous. Lately the marsh has been seething with smugglers. There've even been rumors of highwaymen holding up coaches. Smugglers have always plagued the marsh, but highwaymen—they went out with powdered wigs."

The earl flashed a reassuring smile when the two women voiced their alarm. "Have no fear, ladies, both Gaston and I carry pistols. The coachman has a blunderbuss. We're absolutely safe, I assure you."

Soon Nancy began to snore, her head lolling against her mistress's shoulder. Marie Fleur would have liked to watch the passing scenery, but she feigned sleep to avoid conversing with the earl. It was sheer misery to have to keep her eyes closed with his pale gaze probing her consciousness.

At the Hare and Hounds outside Tenterden they paused for refreshment. Here again, Marie Fleur cleverly maneuvered places so she avoided sitting beside her would-be seducer. As she had hoped, Gaston and Nancy acted as perfect buffers. Nancy giggled hilariously, her good humor assisted by two tankards of small ale. The Frenchman, sensing her susceptibility to masculine compliments, was flirting outrageously with her.

All the while the earl's irritation mounted. He shrewdly concealed his ill humor behind his usual languid manner while he complained bitterly about the tasteless mutton and stringy carrots the landlord palmed off on them.

As they headed south the air was freshened by a salt breeze. Stretches of open countryside, broken by stands of beech and oak, sped past the windows as they rolled along. From time to time Marie Fleur risked small glances at the passing scenery. When at last the earl dozed, his face in repose, she felt safe in openly studying the low lying fields, yellow with gorse and dotted with grazing sheep. Suddenly she was aware of his pale eyes gazing at her. She had been caught.

"Ah, so you're no longer sleepy."

She promptly closed her eyes. "I'm just like Nancy; I can't keep awake once the carriage starts moving," she declared.

Resigning herself to more hours of boredom, Marie Fleur seethed inwardly. Yet boredom was preferable to sharing an intimate conversation with the earl. Soon after they left Tenterden, Gaston too had fallen asleep. Now his snores rattled noisily as they sped along country lanes bounded by tangled hedgerows and festooned with honeysuckle and woody nightshade.

After a brief twilight, night descended, blanketing the countryside in black. The plaintive baaing of sheep echoed in the distance, audible until they closed the windows to keep out the sharp wind. A silver moon struggled from behind the clouds as they skirted the marsh, traveling west toward Rye. In a search for better roads, the earl's coachman had taken a roundabout route, adding over an hour to their journey. They were drawing close to their destination and would soon be warming themselves beside Lucy Cross's crackling hearth.

Marie Fleur dozed in earnest, finding it no hardship to exclude unwelcome thoughts. Suddenly the coach lurched, throwing her into the earl's lap. There was a loud confusion of shouts and snorting horses as the coach clattered to a standstill. The coachman bellowed in anger, then another voice penetrated the ensuing quiet.

"Stand and deliver!"

A shot rang out from the box as the coachman produced his blunderbuss and took aim. An answering pistol shot drew a shrill cry of pain, and the heavy blunderbuss rattled to the ground.

"This is outrageous," growled the earl, starting forward.

Gaston snapped up the leather curtain to reveal bright moonlight spreading ghostly fingers across the road. Then the light was blocked as a horseman rode close to the coach. He ducked to look inside the window.

"Oh, lord 'ave mercy—a highwayman!" shrieked Nancy.

Wide-eyed, Marie Fleur stared at the black-masked visage studying them through the window. She shuddered with a mixture of fright and excitement. In popular novels the masked highwayman had evolved into a romantic figure usually depicted as a noble "Gentleman of the road."

"Don't go for your pistols!"

The earl and Gaston simultaneously drew in their breath. Each man had been surreptitiously slipping a hand inside his coat to withdraw his pistol. The highwayman poked two huge pistols inside the coach, their yawning muzzles pointing straight at the earl.

"How dare you! I'll have you know I'm the Earl of Cranbrook. The home secretary will hear about this!" sputtered the earl as the door was wrenched open.

"Yes, Your Grace, I'm well aware of your identity. It's emblazoned across the door of your fine carriage," the masked man remarked gruffly, his rich voice tinged with humor. For the most part the highwayman spoke with the local accent, but his pronunciation of certain words betrayed an educated background.

Four riders loomed out of the darkness. One of the men dismounted and pulled the wounded coachman from the box. The goggle-eyed footman came down without a murmur of resistance to stand meekly beside the robber's horse.

"Out! All of you out," commanded the highwayman.

It was cold standing on the exposed highway, and Marie Fleur shivered in the raw night wind, wrapping her arms tightly about her body. One of the thieves made a bawdy suggestion about what would keep her warm, and the others guffawed.

"What ye say to lettin' me 'ave that pretty piece, Nick?"

"All in good time, Jake. First I want to see what fine rewards the great earl has for us."

The other men fell back, not questioning their leader.

"So you're the scoundrel who calls himself Black Nick!"

"That's right, Your Grace, Black Nick it is."

"I'll see you hang for this."

The highwayman grinned, only the lower half of his face visible beneath the concealing black mask. His tall crowned hat, his many-caped greatcoat, even his sleek mount were black.

The highwayman stretched out his hand demandingly.

Without a word the earl reached inside his pocket and produced a handful of coins, which the highwayman slipped inside a purse. He held out his hand a second time. The earl unlooped his gold watch chain and slipped two rings from his fingers. Nodding approval, the highwayman ordered one of the men to relieve the valet of his possessions.

"What about them pretty pieces? Who's going to search 'em?"

Marie Fleur shuddered at the thought of being pawed by this band of ruffians, who were eagerly crowding around at the exciting prospect of examining the women.

"Perhaps you'll give me your valuables, my lady, or do you intend to resist?"

Marie Fleur glared at the masked man while she eased off her wedding ring. The only other jewelry she wore was a gold locket on a slender chain; this, too, she unfastened and dropped into his gloved hand.

Turning to Nancy, who was standing beside her mistress speechless with shock, the highwayman said, "And what about you, pretty? What have you got of value?"

"Me?... N-nothing. I'm only a maid."

"Aw, she's a maid. Reckon I can take care of that," guffawed one of the others, deliberately misunderstanding Nancy's statement.

Her courage returning with a sudden leap, Nancy turned on the speaker. "You touch me, m'lad, and you'll be doubled over puking in yon ditch."

"She's going to kick you where it 'urts, Jakey lad. Ain't you scared?"

The men's masked leader ignored their banter, too intent on searching the coach. He sharply ordered an accomplice to bring him a light. A hooded lantern was produced from behind the hedge, and when the cover was lifted, yellow light beamed across the road to illuminate the carriage interior.

Marie Fleur exclaimed indignantly as one of the thieves spilled the contents of her cloth valise across the road.

"Bain't nothing worth 'avin' 'ere," he snorted in disgust. "Just women's folderols."

"Bring me a knife."

The earl growled his anger as the masked man held the glittering steel poised above the coach's black leather upholstery. "Perhaps you've got some more valuables you'd like to share with me before I rip your fine upholstery to ribbons. A man of your station travels with more wealth than this. I'm no fool. 'Tis the oldest game around—coughing up a few miserable offerings to pacify me while the real stuff's cleverly hidden."

"There's nothing more. I'm merely escorting these ladies to Rye."

"We'll see about that. Strip 'em."

After loud protestations from the earl, the highwayman allowed the valet to help his master undress. Each garment was carefully searched before it was pitched into the hedge. Finally the two men stood shivering in their drawers and hose, their flesh gleaming ghostly white in the moonlight.

"You see. I told you we had nothing hidden," declared the earl triumphantly, fixing his captor with a glare. "Now kindly allow us to dress before we catch our death of cold."

"Not so fast. Jake, Towzer, watch them."

Ignoring the earl's protests, Black Nick slashed the leather seats. He cried out in triumph as he extricated a pouch bulging with money. Yet still this was not enough. He continued to search the coach, delving amongst the springs and stuffing before finally tipping the seats on the ground in disgust. With the assistance of his henchmen, he proceeded to break apart the paneling. They even uncapped the wheel hubs in their search for valuables. At last, when the fine coach stood in ruins, Black Nick abandoned his search.

"The wimmen. Let's search 'em."

"Let me do it, Nick. I'll do a good job," urged an eager volunteer.

"Ladies, have I your word you've no valuables concealed on your persons?"

"You have. Here's my reticule. It's the only other thing of value I possess."

The highwayman bowed politely as Marie Fleur handed over

her pink silk reticule. He searched it before handing it back. "Keep it. It's an admirable match for your costume."

She smiled, surprised by his courtly remark.

"You may not be aware of it, but Black Nick always exacts a payment from the ladies he robs."

A wave of panic tingled Marie Fleur's blood. Or was it excitement? By his speech and refined manners, the highwayman appeared to be a gentleman. She could not see him clearly in the darkness, yet what little she could see below the black mask and overshadowing hat was highly intriguing. His firm jaw and well-shaped mouth invited her to discover what he looked like without his mask. In fact, the set of his features reminded her of another handsome man who had set her pulses pounding. Suddenly catching her treacherous vein of thought, she drew herself to her full height and prepared to voice an indignant protest.

Black Nick gave a hearty laugh. "Sorry to disappoint you, my love. I merely expected a kiss."

Her face colored as the others roared. Damn him! Surely he could not have sensed that betraying ripple of excitement. "I don't give kisses to common thieves," she declared hotly.

"Ah, but I'm far from common, Duchess, as you can readily see. I'm really quite refined."

The others roared again, and her discomfort mounted.

"What about you, sweetheart?" the highwayman asked, turning his attention to Nancy. "What's your name?"

Instead of retaliating as she had threatened to do earlier when the black-garbed highwayman took her arm, Nancy giggled flirtatiously. Nor did she resist when he drew her closer, his arm sliding about her waist.

"'Tis Nancy, sir."

"Well, Nancy, you'll be able to tell your granchildren you were kissed by the infamous Black Nick." He bent his masked face to hers and kissed her soundly on the lips.

"If you think I'm going to be half as willing, you've another think coming," Marie Fleur declared angrily as she unconsciously voiced one of Nancy's favorite sayings.

The masked man had just turned toward her when the lookout sounded the alarm. A second coach had been sighted rolling around a distant bend.

Black Nick cursed his misfortune. The prisoners were dragged toward the hedge. Young Jake took charge of Nancy, whom he pulled with him into the nearby shrubbery.

"And you, my love, are all mine."

The highwayman's mocking words sent a chill of fear through Marie Fleur's veins. Without more ado she was imprisoned in his strong grasp. Seizing his horse's reins, he blundered through the tangled undergrowth beside the road. Marie Fleur fought her captor, kicking at his booted ankles but succeeding only in bruising her own toes, vulnerable in their soft kid boots.

Black Nick cast a final glance toward the road, where the ruined Cranbrook coach blocked the way, before he drew her against him.

"Little bitch, stop kicking," he admonished with amusement.

A certain familiar quality to his voice intrigued her. When he laughingly chided her, a responsive chord had tugged deep within. Marie Fleur gasped in surprise as he locked his arms about her. His hard legs cut like steel through her thin skirts. There was no further time for thought as his mouth clamped over hers, his kiss making her throb with passion. She gasped, she choked as she fought for breath, all but swooning in his embrace as that well-remembered fire was rekindled. Devastated, she stared into his unfathomable eyes behind the mask slits, but could distinguish nothing. There was something so agonizingly familiar about this highwayman, yet at the same time so alien, that her emotions were in a turmoil.

"Would that I could stay longer, my sweet, but duty calls," he whispered huskily, his mouth against her hair. Her bonnet had fallen off and dangled by its pink ribbons about her neck. He sank his hands in her curls, turning her face up to his for a final kiss. Then, with near brutality, he thrust her from him.

Marie Fleur staggered, managing to right herself in time to see him swing agilely into the saddle. Calling to his companions to follow and without a backward glance, the black-garbed stranger plunged through the undergrowth to the open country beyond. He disappeared from view in a thunder of galloping hooves as the approaching coachman halted his team.

Thoroughly shaken, her emotions raw, Marie Fleur stumbled back onto the road. A few minutes later Nancy joined her. The earl and his valet kept out of sight behind a hedge, calling for help in finding their clothes.

"'Pon my soul! What a state! Oh, my word, a crime's been committed!"

An elderly gentleman emerged from an old-fashioned coach to examine the wreckage. He clucked in amazement when he recognized the coat of arms of the Earl of Cranbrook. His consternation increased when he beheld the disheveled women and heard calls for help coming from behind the hedge.

Slowly he and his servant located the men's scattered clothing, not distinguishing between master and servant, but thrusting the bundle at the thankful pair behind the hedge. Then he leaned over the groaning coachman lying neglected in the ditch. The young footman knelt beside his friend, blubbering incoherently.

The elderly gentleman offered Marie Fleur smelling salts, but she declined his kindness.

Nancy wept softly, somewhat ashamed of her imprudent behavior with the dashing highwayman. Though she had intended to fight back, during his exciting romantic attentions she forgot to resist.

When the earl finally emerged from behind the hedge he was fully dressed and had regained most of his dignity. He profusely thanked their rescuer, reiterating his threat to see Black Nick hang for the audacity of destroying his luxurious coach.

Soon Marie Fleur was safe inside the elderly gentleman's coach, a soft merino lap robe tucked comfortingly about her cold limbs.

The traveler, a country squire bound for Winchelsea to visit his married daughter, was most avid for details of their adventure. While the earl held forth with a highly embroidered account in which he vastly exaggerated his own bravery, Marie Fleur sat silent, locked in a miserable world of her own making.

The touch of the highwayman's mouth still burned on her lips, the weight of his arm still warmed her back. What was wrong with her? She had virtually swooned in a stranger's embrace—a common criminal on whom she would never set eyes again. During that fleeting pleasure she had even compared his arousing kiss—and certainly not found it wanting—to those kisses experienced during that ecstatic, trancelike night.

Resting her head against the upholstery, she closed her eyes, thinking to shut out the highwayman's tormenting image. On the contrary, the action merely revived forgotten details, making her memory of him more vivid. The pressure of his hands on her face, the heat of his skin against her chill flesh, the sweet fragrance of his mouth came vibrantly alive. Disturbing visions of what might have been, had they had more time, only added to her discomfort.

Eventually Marie Fleur slept, her lips upturned in a smile as, in her dream, she galloped into the night clasped before the highwayman astride his sleek ebony horse. The salt wind blew fresh in their faces, sheep bleated from the misty marsh, yet safe in his strong arms, lulled by the even beat of his heart, she lay still, her face buried in the fragrant hollow of his neck.

Nancy shook her arm, saying, "Wake up, my lady. We be home at last."

"What? Home? Where?"

The earl leaned forward and patted her hand. "Poor dear, she's quite overwrought," he commented solicitously, a devilish gleam in his eyes.

"It's an outrage! Something should be done about the crime hereabouts," grumbled the elderly squire. "Smugglers have the run of things, so my Dorcas says. They feast in the open at the inn, and no government man's brave enough to arrest them."

"The times are to blame. There's unrest everywhere."

"I heard tell, on the quiet like, a new lot of agents be coming to clean things up. And not before it's time, if you ask me."

The coach rattled along the narrow cobbled streets of the ancient port, tilting at a precarious angle toward the harbor. They stopped outside the blue door of a fisherman's whitewashed cottage. The door opened, flooding the street with light and revealing a burly, bewhiskered man, who stepped out into the night to greet them.

"It's me father—oh, 'ow's poor Mum?"

Nancy flew weeping into her father's arms and they clung together while Marie Fleur waited uncertainly in the background, feeling out of place during the affectionate family reunion. The earl came to stand behind her whilst the squire's servant neatly stacked her bags beside the doorstep.

"I'll call for you in two weeks," he said, his smooth voice exceedingly pleasant. "I should think, with winter coming on, that will be ample time in this rustic hovel." A disdainful expression crossed his haughty face as he glanced about at the poor dwellings tumbling pell-mell toward the small harbor.

"You needn't put yourself out. I'll return when I'm ready."

"Two weeks, Lady Dowling. Do enjoy your rest."

With that the earl reentered the coach. The corpulent squire waved good-bye to her, extending his sympathy for the hundredth time over her terrible ordeal; then, satisfied all was well, he commanded his coachman to transport the earl to a nearby inn to await the daylight.

"Welcome to our humble cottage, my lady," said Sam Cross, fumbling for words, vastly in awe of this familiar child transformed into a titled stranger.

"Oh, Sam! You've known me since I was a poor waif. I'll not have you treating me different now," Marie Fleur chided, giving him a hug. "How's Lucy?"

"Middlin' . . . better'n last week," he allowed gruffly as he ushered them indoors.

The low-ceilinged whitewashed room glowed brightly with firelight. Shining brass utensils hung on the wall above the rugged stone hearth, where water was bubbling in a blackened cauldron hanging over the flames. The cottage's furnishings were sparser than Marie Fleur had remembered. A three-legged stool, a gnarled oak table, a high-backed settle brightened by a handwoven rug, and a lopsided dresser, which held their treasured dishes, comprised the main room's furnishings.

"Lucy be sleeping upstairs."

Marie Fleur followed Nancy, who was taking the narrow stairs two at a time. They found Lucy in bed, a heap of patchwork quilts pulled up to her chin. A candle stub burned on a saucer beside the bed.

"Mum it's me. And I brung Her Ladyship with me."

"Eh, who?"

Nancy bounded to the bed where she eagerly embraced her mother.

"Her Ladyship—you mean our little Marie?"

"Hello, Lucy. I've brought you a basket of goodies, things to make you strong again." Marie Fleur glanced warningly at Nancy and shook her head. She had decided it would be wiser not to frighten Lucy with the story of their adventure.

Nancy pouted. She was eager to reveal the greatest excitement that had befallen her since she was asked to go to Langley Chase to wait upon Mistress Fox's daughter. Like her mother, Nancy had never been able to accept Patience Fox as the Comtesse du Lac. And though Marie Fleur bore a decidedly French name and spoke with a peculiar accent, Nancy had never considered her anything but English. The Frenchies were their enemies; she could never be friends with one of them!

"How you feeling, Mum?"

"Lots better now you're here. Just a chill, girl, nothing to get in a flap over, nothing much at all." Lucy chuckled, propping herself on her elbow the better to see her guest. "Get that man of mine up here. I've a mind to go down to the fireside."

Marie Fleur smiled in relief, content that Lucy was not nearly so ill as they had believed.

Within the next few days Lucy was back on her feet with only a nagging cough to betray her recent illness. She bustled about the dark cottage scolding Nancy for her slovenliness. Lucy tried hard to be deferential to their guest, but despite all her good intentions, she usually treated Lady Dowling exactly like her own daughter.

Marie Fleur shared Nancy's attic room nestled beneath the gray slate eave, sleeping in the narrow bed vacated by Nancy's older sister Betty, who had gone to Dorset to marry a farmer. At night, through the latticed window overlooking the narrow harbor, they gazed at the masts of boats anchored below where pools of moonlight glittered silver on the rippling water. And they dreamed of romance. Nancy's dreams were of Ned, her fisherman sweetheart, while Marie Fleur dreamed of a nameless lover, a combination of her most stirring dreams rolled into one.

Nancy told her mother about Marie Fleur's unhappy marriage and how, now that she was in Rye, she seemed to be miraculously cured of her terrible headaches. Nancy also extolled the kindness of the Earl of Cranbrook in bringing them here. Because Marie Fleur had never confided to her the earl's outrageous proposition, the maid remained oblivious of the nastier side of his character, seeing him only as an impeccably dressed gentleman who flatteringly referred to her as Miss Cross.

One blustery October evening Nancy hurried into the parlor and signaled to Marie Fleur to join her outside. Wrapping herself warmly in an embroidered wool shawl, Marie Fleur followed, wondering at Nancy's ill-concealed excitement.

"Ned's 'ome!" Nancy squeaked once they were safely outside.

"There, I told you he'd be back soon. And you thought he was shipwrecked—what's the matter. Is he hurt?" Marie Fleur asked, seeing the happiness fade from Nancy's round face.

"Not that . . . it's just . . . well, Mum'll never let us marry now."

"Why?"

"Ned's joined the smugglers on the marsh."

"Talk him into unjoining."

"You don't know them smugglers—nasty pieces of work they be. Ned says he's in it for good now. In for a penny, in for a pound, as they say. But that's not really why I wanted to talk to you."

"What then?"

"Will you come to a party with me?"

"Me? What kind of party?"

Nancy smiled as she eagerly gripped Marie Fleur's arm. "It's in the Mermaid's back room. It be Yorkshire George's birthday—he's the smugglers' cap'n. They be holding a party, and Ned invited me."

"Go if you want."

"Not by meself! I'm scared to death of them ruffians. Now if you was to come with me..."

"I wouldn't fit in."

"Yes, you would. We'll say you're me cousin visiting from—where?" Nancy put her head on one side, puzzling. "With your funny way of speaking, how about Bristol? That be far enough they wouldn't know how you's supposed to talk. You can wear one of me best frocks. Oh, come on, it'll be fun."

"No, Nancy, you go. You'll have Ned. I don't know anybody," Marie Fleur declined, vastly tempted but allowing her good sense to stifle the reckless idea.

"Please, I've never asked you a favor, my lady..."

"You'll have to remember not to call me that."

"Ooh, you'll come! Oh, I'd never dared go by meself. Come on, let's hurry."

Generously Nancy insisted on Marie Fleur wearing her best dress and new red wool shawl with a deep knotted fringe. Her rough leather shoes were too wide for her mistress's narrow feet, so she reluctantly agreed to let Marie Fleur wear her own black kid slippers.

Nancy's red-striped Sunday dress fitted snugly over the breasts before falling straight to the ankles where it ended in a double flounce. A black embroidered peasant bodice laced in red completed the outfit. When she saw her mistress wearing her best gown, Nancy was delighted, exclaiming that the dress suited Marie Fleur better than herself. Because Nancy was a head shorter than her mistress, the dress barely came to Marie Fleur's ankles. A tempting display of slender white-stockinged ankle was revealed.

When Marie Fleur reached for her bonnet, Nancy squealed in protest. "Not that! Local girls only wear bonnets to church. Put the shawl round your head. And no reticule."

Marie Fleur returned her possessions to the cupboard. She knew this escapade was insane, yet tonight a sense of adventure possessed her, turning her deaf to the remonstrances of her sensible inner self.

Somewhat reluctantly, Marie Fleur admitted the earl had been right. After living at beautiful Langley Chase, and even before that, having grown accustomed to James Fox's spacious farmland, she found Lucy's cramped cottage terribly confining. This newfound boredom had sharpened her taste for adventure, and though she was perhaps ill-advised to agree to Nancy's deception, Marie Fleur found the prospect exciting.

As they hastened along the narrow streets, puffing as they toiled uphill over rough cobblestones, the sky began to spit rain. Marie Fleur drew the red wool shawl closer about her head. At last they turned into Mermaid Street. In her excitement Nancy had quickened her pace, virtually racing her companion along the steep streets. As they passed, welcoming lights shone through latticed panes, shedding golden haloes over the damp cobblestones. The street was deserted. Before they reached the Mermaid the raucous voices of its patrons could be heard.

Shunning the brightly lit front entrance with its swinging lantern, Nancy led Marie Fleur through the archway into the innyard. Here, through a side door, they gained entrance to the white and black-timbered coaching inn. Marie Fleur glanced about with interest at the Elizabethan paneling, but Nancy was far too eager to join her sweetheart to dally.

The party was being held in a back room bright with firelight. Here the hefty blackened beams were so low they brushed men's heads, while the uneven floorboards tilted like the deck of a ship at sea.

"Ned! Ned!" Nancy dragged Marie Fleur with her as she ran to greet her sweetheart. "This 'ere's me cousin Mary from Bristol. 'Tis all right for her to come too, b'ain't it?"

Ned shrugged, glancing sharply at the mysterious female swathed in the red shawl.

"Reckon," he allowed, pulling Nancy close.

Marie Fleur was temporarily forgotten as the lovers embraced. Someone gave her a foaming tankard of ale and a fresh honey cake.

The men around the blazing hearth were singing loudly to the accompaniment of a reedy pipe, banging their tankards on the scarred trestle in time to the music. A second table was filled with pewter plates heaped with food. There was a wide array of contraband bottles of gin, brandy, and rum. Half a dozen local girls giggled shrilly at the smugglers' humor as they boldly sat on their laps and helped themselves to the food and drink.

Nancy guided Marie Fleur to a quiet corner farthest from the hearth where they took off their damp shawls. Several men had already cast approving glances in their direction, but Ned curtly informed them it was hands-off his Nancy and her cousin, so they did no more than ogle them.

Pungent pickled herrings and brown bread, moist apple cider cake, hot smoked eels, all were piled on a plate and thrust at Marie Fleur. She had not tasted these simple foods since childhood.

Presently Yorkshire George climbed onto the table and danced a hornpipe amid the laughing catcalls of his companions. The smugglers' merriment grew even louder until it echoed along the darkened street. Rain still pattered gently against the windowpanes, but the sound was drowned by the merrymakers.

Clattering boots thundered up the stair, and the door crashed open to admit a group of latecomers who squeezed inside the crowded room. They were greeted warmly, slapping backs and shaking hands all round. Drinks were pressed upon them. From where she sat Marie Fleur could not see the men, but she assumed they were fellow smugglers. Nancy was far too occupied flirting with Ned to pay attention to Marie Fleur's questions.

Still feeling hungry, Marie Fleur took her plate to the table for a second helping of cider cake. As she reached for the cake her wrist was trapped in a viselike grip. Gasping in pain and surprise, she looked down at a man's black-gloved hand. Her gaze traveled slowly upward until she encountered the lower half of a grimly set face beneath an ominous black mask.

"Black Nick!"

"Who's this wench?" he shouted, swinging her about. The merriment lessened as the smugglers stared at the woman struggling in Black Nick's grasp.

"'Tis Nancy's cousin from Bristol," Ned explained, puzzled by the highwayman's anger. "She be all right, Nick."

"Oh no, she's not. The wench is an imposter. I know *who*

she is because I relieved her and her finely dressed companion of their valuables on the Tenterden road." An angry rumble went about the room as smiling faces turned sullen.

"How do we know she hasn't led the customs men here?" someone asked suspiciously.

"Nancy, you told me—"

"I meant no 'arm, Ned. She's all right. 'Tis only me mistress. She won't give you away," Nancy explained tearfully, afraid of the smugglers' hostility.

"I didn't know you'd be here," Marie Fleur hissed, trying to free her wrist. Black Nick let her go. She made a great play of rubbing her bruises.

"No doubt. You never expected your deception to be exposed."

"There was no harm intended. I did it to please Nancy."

"What else would I expect you to say?"

Angry men moved closer, their expressions menacing. Two ruffians grasped Marie Fleur's arms, pinning her against the trestle table. No one laughed or sang now as a distinctly threatening mood possessed the guests. Treachery was something smugglers did not regard lightly.

"What shall we do with her, Nick?"

The ensuing silence was suddenly broken by banging on the inn's front door. Accompanying shouts could be heard as the thundering racket increased. A bellowed command to "open in the name of the king," produced startled cries of "Revenue men!"

"'Tis true then, she brung 'em to us."

"You were making so much noise, they didn't need anyone to lead them here," Marie Fleur shouted in defense, trying to make herself heard above the commotion.

No one listened. Chairs scraped and heavy boots clattered over the bare floorboards as men raced for the door, anxious to be away before it was too late.

Nancy stood wide-eyed, alternately clutching Ned to her and urging him to go. After a parting kiss, he bolted for the door, joining the general scramble. The table of food had been upended in the rush, and ale puddled a tawny river over the floorboards.

"You little traitor! I'd best keep you with me," growled Black Nick, seizing Marie Fleur before she had a chance to escape.

"No! You let her alone."

Nancy's protests were in vain as the highwayman dragged Marie Fleur with him, fighting his way through the scuffling crowd.

He covered her with his flowing cloak as they raced outside into the spattering rain. In the dark he swiftly located his tethered horse. Lifting Marie Fleur, he dumped her in the saddle, ignoring her squeals of protest. Then he sprang up after her and urged the animal forward, hooves beating a noisy tattoo across the innyard.

Most of the smugglers were on foot and steathily disappeared into the narrow warren of streets surrounding the Mermaid.

As they galloped through the black night, a sharp wind blew. Marie Fleur tried to call for help, but Black Nick kept his gloved hand over her mouth. Eventually tiring of her resistance, he cuffed her gently across the face. Only then was she quiet.

The lovely dream she had cherished of riding into the night with him on his great black horse was destroyed. No sweet whispering, no passionate stirring, only force and anger radiated from this masked man.

She endured the remainder of the wild ride in silence, trying not to lean against his hard body. Eventually she had to relax her taut spine, and as the terrain grew bumpier, she clung to him to keep her balance, finding that his body imparted welcome warmth. Tonight the highwayman was not wearing his many-caped greatcoat. Beneath a voluminous traveling cloak he wore a dark, double-breasted coat fitted close to the body. His heavy cloak kept out much of the fine rain, but trickles from his tall-crowned black hat splashed against her cheek. When Marie Fleur stole a glance at his shadowed face she found his mouth grim beneath the sinister mask.

Chapter 5

THEY HAD NOT gone far before Marie Fleur heard pursuing hoofbeats. Black Nick heard them too, for he increased his horse's pace, running him flat out.

The sharp tang of salt in the freshening breeze told her they galloped near the shore, yet she could distinguish nothing in the surrounding black void. Marie Fleur's heart was in her mouth as the large-boned animal thundered along at breakneck speed. The marsh was treacherous; one stumble, one ill-chosen path, and they could flounder up to their necks in sucking mud. Yet the masked highwayman appeared to be familiar with the terrain, for he wove unerringly along narrow trails, always heading east.

When the sound of the distant hooves faded into the night, Black Nick slackened his desperate pace, patting the horse's neck and whispering words of praise. They were crossing firm sand, she realized, for the hoofbeats had changed to a dull thump.

"Where are you taking me?"

"You'll not be harmed. I've a place on the marsh."

"The government men will catch you," she pronounced with conviction, straining for the sound of horses in pursuit.

"That's why we're taking a detour."

Out of the darkness loomed a tall round tower where signal lights flickered yellow in the night. The structure appeared close, yet the flat landscape was deceptive, for they rode another five minutes before they came within hailing distance. Marie Fleur wondered where they were headed until she realized this was one of the new martello towers ringing England's southern shores, erected as defense against a surprise French invasion.

"Hey, O'Grady. 'Tis me, Nick."

"Why are we stopping here?" she demanded as the highwayman pulled the reins up short, jarring her against his body.

"We'll be safe here. I know the officer in charge."

An answering shout came out of the darkness, and a man

holding a lighted lantern guided them closer.

The circular stone tower was over thirty feet high. A twenty-four-pound cannon was mounted on its flat roof to provide the main armament. This strategic tower and its sister defense three hundred yards to the east, protected the sluice controlling the water level of Romney Marsh.

Black Nick dismounted and reached up to help her down. Disdaining his assistance, Marie Fleur slid clumsily to the sand. Now she could hear hoofbeats echoing in the damp air. Anxious to waste no time, the highwayman thrust her before him toward a ladder leading to a door high above them in the tower wall.

"Go on, wench, get up the ladder," he commanded, shoving her at the first rung.

"I can't climb up there!"

"Move! I'll not be hanged because you've turned coward."

To her shock Marie Fleur felt the cold muzzle of a pistol poking her back. Gasping, she lifted her skirts and clambered onto the first rung of the rain-slick ladder. The experience proved to be not as frightening as she had expected; in fact, she would have managed the precarious climb quite well had not Black Nick kept pushing her upward, almost toppling her from the ladder as the approaching hoofbeats grew louder.

A door opened below, and someone led the highwayman's whickering horse inside.

A slight, uniformed man was awaiting them at the top of the ladder. He held a lantern, shielding the light with his hand.

"By all that's holy! And who's this?" he asked with a pronounced Irish accent. He raised the lantern to peer closely at Marie Fleur and whistled his approval of her pretty face. Then he quickly drew them over the threshold and secured the door behind them.

"She's my hostage. Pretty as a picture, ain't she, O'Grady? But I'm afraid it's hands off."

The Irishman groaned his disappointment. "Now I thought you'd finally brought me something worthwhile. And what've you got in your saddlebags tonight, you scoundrel?"

"Rum, good Holland, and lacy folderols for pretty Eileen."

"Hm, s'pose it'll have to do. If they come inside, she's to keep quiet, now."

"Got that, wench?"

Marie Fleur glared at the masked man. He was treating her like some village ninny. Yet she supposed he was doing her a favor by not calling attention to her identity. After his initial scrutiny the Irish officer did not question her presence.

Lit only by weak lantern light, the round tower was gloomy. Much commotion came from the adjoining room where the common soldiers were playing cards. Captain O'Grady shouted to them to be quiet, then warned them to prepare for an official visit. Following his announcement a general scuffle ensued while the men hastily restored order. Several curious soldiers peered around the door, their faces lighting up when they saw the highwayman, whom they greeted like an old friend.

Captain O'Grady ushered Marie Fleur inside his own small quarters to the left of the main entrance. The bed was hard and the furnishings meager.

While Marie Fleur waited, the Irish captain and the highwayman talked in an undertone. Then, saluting jovially, the captain reached to the musket stand surrounding the central pillar and withdrew two muskets. He handed one to the highwayman, who disappeared into the gloom.

"Don't be afeared o' me," O'Grady said to Marie Fleur when he came back inside the room. "Your friend's gone upstairs awhile. Now, my lass, into the cupboard with ye, for if I'm not mistaken His Majesty's officers are due any time now. And keep quiet. I'd hate to have to disfigure your pretty face."

When Marie Fleur resisted, the wiry Irishman rammed the muzzle of the musket into her ribs, helping her inside the cupboard. There was barely room to squat in the base below the shelf. He pitched her a pillow and blanket from his bunk in an attempt to make the makeshift quarters more comfortable.

Shouts sounded outside, and he slammed the rickety door closed and secured the wooden latch.

Inside the dark cupboard the events that followed were muffled. Snatches of conversation and several alien voices could be heard, followed by laughter and much talking.

It had been quiet for a long time when Captain O'Grady finally opened the cupboard door.

"Out you come, me beauty. The coast's clear."

Feeling as if she would never walk again, Marie Fleur crawled out of the cupboard on her hands and knees. Gingerly she stood on cramped legs.

"Sorry to be so ungallant. It couldn't be helped," Black Nick said from the doorway. He was still wearing his black hat and cloak.

"I wouldn't be surprised by anything you did!"

The Irishman chuckled at her angry retort. He whispered something to Black Nick, who laughed at his suggestion.

"Come on, Your Ladyship, we've got a long road ahead," the highwayman announced sarcastically, grabbing Marie Fleur's arm and yanking her across the room.

The rain had stopped, leaving the night misty and dank. She followed him down the treacherous wooden ladder. When she was within a few feet of the ground, Black Nick grabbed her around the waist and yanked her from the ladder.

"Sorry to rush you, love, but time's awasting."

He ignored her shrill protests as he plopped her unceremoniously into the saddle. He leaped up behind her.

"Did you get your pay, O'Grady?"

"That I did, and it's the best ye've brought yet," said the Irishman, waving good-bye.

Clapping his heels to the horse's flanks, Black Nick careened in a circle before the martello tower, seeking a guiding light that flickered occasionally in the black vastness.

Except for the hoofbeats there was no sound save the distant waves and the moisture dripping from the sodden foliage of alder and willow thickets. The sheer desolation of this vast marsh made Marie Fleur shiver. Much of the lonely region was barely above sea level, an endless expanse carved across by dikes and crisscrossed by narrow tracks. It was said that only a man born and bred in these parts had any hope of staying alive in the dark.

Sleep gradually overcame her. Her head drooped against Black Nick's shoulder and she jerked awake, resisting such intimacy. Sensing her fatigue, however, the highwayman pressed her head down against his chest, imprisoning her there until she ceased to struggle. Later Marie Fleur was not sure whether she imagined the pressure of his mouth against her hair. At his touch, a treacherous ripple of pleasure invaded her blood. She was surprised to discover she was not afraid of him. Despite his angry betrayal of her at the Mermaid, his subsequent gruff kindness had erased her fear.

Marie Fleur stirred to find herself being lifted from the saddle. They stood before a cottage, firelight spilling from its open door. She was only vaguely aware of voices, light, and warmth. It was not until Black Nick deposited her on a bed that she came fully awake.

"Where am I?"

"You ask a lot of questions, Lady Dowling."

"None of which you ever answer."

"In that case it surprises me that you continue to ask them."

When his back was turned she lifted the edge of the homespun curtain to look outside. The blackness was pierced by bobbing lights flickering like fireflies in the night. After her eyes adjusted to the dark, Marie Fleur saw a line of men carrying casks and boxes. When she looked closely at the building, she was surprised to find it was a church.

"St. Martin's in the Marsh."

"You hide your stolen goods in a church?"

"Men hide contraband wherever they can. A church is as good a place as any."

"How long do you propose to keep me here?"

"Why? Do you find your surroundings objectionable?"

"Most definitely."

His mouth, visible beneath the mask, was set in a straight line. "Be careful, Lady Dowling," he warned.

"Why?"

"Because you may soon regret your viper's tongue."

"Ha! Your threats don't frighten me."

Black Nick kicked the door closed and took a menacing step toward her. A flicker of fear touched Marie Fleur when she realized that, aside from Black Nick's fellows, they were alone on the marsh. Desperation making her agile, she leaped at him, grasping a copper kettle from the window ledge behind her as a weapon. Snarling an oath, the highwayman easily deflected her blow. Then he hurled her aside, sending her careening into a basket of peat and upending it on the stone floor.

"Damn you, you ruffian!" she yelled, nursing her bruised side.

Her temper flared anew as Black Nick came to stand masterfully over her, his face grim. Marie Fleur shouted an especially satisfying French curse remembered from childhood, then she found herself roughly swung to her feet. She lashed out at him, trying to bite the gloved hand he struggled to clamp over her mouth.

The highwayman swiftly retaliated in the same language. She gaped at him, eyes round with surprise at hearing her native tongue.

A smile tugged the corners of his mouth. "That took you aback, didn't it? I've no wish to keep a wildcat prisoner. You're free to leave whenever you choose."

"You don't mean that?"

"I mean it."

Hope brightened her face as Marie Fleur scrambled backward, wary lest he try to grab her again. When he did not move, she seized her shawl, which he had tossed across a chair, and threw it about her shoulders. She wrestled desperately with the iron door latch, surprised to see that the highwayman still had not moved. Hardly able to believe her good fortune, Marie Fleur finally wrenched open the door and stumbled out into the night.

Black Nick did not pursue her. Her confidence rising, Marie Fleur ran from the cottage. When, after a few minutes, he had not come after her, she thankfully slowed her steps. The chill mist eddied around her like smoke, wafting a white halo about her head. It was becoming so dense St. Martin's steeple had already disappeared from view. As she headed for the narrow path leading across the churchyard, the enveloping blanket swallowed the gabled roof.

Her heart began to thud in fear as she stood in the swirling mist, wondering which path to follow. She had slept during the final stretch of their journey and had no idea from which direction they had come. She sniffed the air for the betraying scent of the sea, but from every direction came the smell of water and decaying vegetation. The wetness was already oozing through her kid shoes and between her toes.

Finally deciding on a path, Marie Fleur circled the scattered tombstones in the small churchyard, summoning courage as ghostly shapes emerged like lost souls from the mist. There was no sign of the men who had been storing goods inside the church. She supposed they had retreated to their hideouts on the marsh. There was a remote chance that not all the inhabitants of this godforsaken land were smugglers. The realization gave her fresh hope, and she decided to ask for help at the first cottage she came to.

Vastly naive about the nature of this marshland, Marie Fleur soon floundered ankle-deep in icy water. She retraced her steps, striking out in a different direction. Matted vegetation was slick underfoot, and she slid dangerously close to a squelching, bubbling quagmire before regaining her balance. As she picked herself up, tall, poker-straight reeds raked her face while marsh creatures, startled by the intruder, stirred in the undergrowth.

She stood still, waiting for her heart to quieten its frenzied beat, vainly trying to pinpoint a guiding light in her search for habitation. Tears of despair welled in her eyes and trickled warmly down her frozen cheeks. Her feet were already numb; her wet skirts wrapped slickly about her legs, whilst her sodden wool shawl slapped her back at every step. If she did not soon find help she would either drown or freeze before dawn. Then she heard hoofbeats slipping, splashing in the marsh. Head to one side, she listened intently, praying she was not mistaken.

"Hello," she called, trying to still her chattering teeth long enough to hail the passing traveler. The wind cut icily through her soaking clothing. In every direction streamers of mist wreathed sinuously over the waterways like disembodied spirits emerging from the marsh.

No answering shout came, yet she could still hear hoofbeats. Perhaps it was only a riderless horse, lost like her in this bone-chilling mist.

Halfheartedly Marie Fleur called again. "Is anyone there? Over here! Oh, please, please, don't leave me." Clutching her trembling hands, she huddled under her waterlogged shawl. "Please, don't leave me," she repeated hoarsely.

"I'd not do that, you little fool. Did you really think you could find your way out of the marsh?"

The scornful words echoed out of the mist. Marie Fleur's spine tingled as she recognized Black Nick's voice.

"Oh, God! You, of all people!"

"No one else knows you're here. Come, you'll catch your death—"

"Don't touch me!"

"Do you fancy a watery grave then?"

"I fancy it a sight more than I fancy you."

To her annoyance he laughed heartily at her angry retort. Suddenly he loomed out of the mist, a tall black shadow astride a great black horse. Marie Fleur turned and ran back along the path. For a few minutes she was on solid ground and her confidence increased, then, as before, the path ended in an oozing sea of mud. With a shrill cry of alarm she floundered to her knees in icy wetness, desperately trying to regain her balance.

The horse snorted directly behind her, its hot breath penetrating her clothing. Strong arms reached down, and Black Nick jerked her off her feet. Kicking at her captor and shouting in outrage, Marie Fleur soon found herself pinned before him on the saddle.

In growing exasperation he growled, "Be still, you wayward little bitch, or you'll drown us both."

His anger released her waiting tears, and Marie Fleur sobbed with frustration, cold, and fear.

Grimly the highwayman switched course, seeking safer ground. He urged his horse through the mist, traveling more by instinct than by sight. At last the cottage loomed ahead. The door was open, fire and lantern light making puddles of spilled gold in the shifting haze.

"Get indoors," Black Nick commanded gruffly as he swept her from the saddle. "The poor horse deserves a rubdown. If you value your life, you'll still be here when I come back."

She was waiting for him when he pushed open the door and walked inside. Tearstained and wet, Marie Fleur huddled before the fire. She glanced up in mingled relief and apprehension.

"Thank you for rescuing me," she mumbled, the words hard to voice.

"You surely didn't think I'd let you wander the night out there?"

"I don't know. Perhaps you ought to have."

He grinned at her. "You're right, I should. Here, drink this; it'll get your blood circulating."

She accepted the cup of brandy. The burning liquid made her cough, then seared her throat and gullet on its way to her stomach.

"Get those wet things off. Before you start protesting— here, wrap yourself in this blanket."

Marie Fleur grudgingly accepted the dark blue blanket. It was difficult to manage, but she undressed inside the shielding tent of blue wool.

Black Nick pulled off his cloak and coat and removed his hat. He ignored Marie Fleur while he tended the food cooking in a blackened cauldron swinging over the flames. Soon the delicious aroma of stewing meat and vegetables filled the room. He took her wet clothing and draped it over two chairbacks before the hearth. The drying fabric emitted clouds of steam.

Clutching the blanket around her, Marie Fleur tried to main-tain her dignity as she crossed the stone tiled floor to the hearth where he was ladling stew into pewter bowls.

"Thank you."

Black Nick nodded before retreating to a dim corner where he proceeded to eat his own meal.

Rankled by his silence, Marie Fleur finally snapped, "Why are you still hiding behind that ridiculous mask? You can take it off. I've no interest in identifying you."

"I was under the impression ladies found masked men intriguing. You disappoint me."

Marie Fleur decided not to attempt to talk to him. As she ate her stew, the combined warmth of food, fire, and brandy slowly relaxed her; it even soothed her annoyance. In the flickering firelight she found her captor every bit as captivating as when she had first seen him. Now that he was hatless she saw that his hair was black and curly. And when he had spoken to her a few minutes ago, she had noted his speech was devoid of the local accent. In fact, his diction was so fine he might have been a guest at one of William's gaming parties, although his speech was straightforward with none of the popular affectations of the *ton*.

"Who are you?" she asked at last, setting her empty bowl on the hearthstone.

"Black Nick."

"And who is Black Nick?"

"Someone who'd rather remain anonymous," he grunted, moving even deeper into the shadows. Her blanket had slipped to reveal an expanse of milk-white throat, and he found the glimpse highly enticing. "Here, you can wear these. They aren't fashionable, but they're dry."

Silently Marie Fleur caught the bundle of garments he tossed to her. She retreated to the bed to dress, knowing the change in his attitude was directly related to her probing questions. While she fumbled with the clothes, dressing beneath the blanket, she puzzled anew over the highwayman's reluctance to reveal his identity.

The brandy was creating strange, unexplainable feelings. Her limbs felt heavy, and the blood tingled palpably through her veins. When she looked at Black Nick standing in his shirtsleeves warming himself before the hearth, she felt a shiver of renewed excitement. He was tall and muscular, his legs and buttocks well-shaped in the clinging black breeches and mud-spattered boots. And as he leaned forward to stir the coals, his broad shoulders strained against the white shirt fabric. A delicious memory tugged in the back of her mind, something half-forgotten, or was it half-remembered? Marie Fleur giggled, surprising herself with the unexpected sound.

Black Nick glanced up. "You're tipsy, my lady. It's bed for you."

"Yes, I think I am, just a little."

As they faced each other across the small room, a tingle of heightened awareness rippled along Marie Fleur's spine. Why did this stranger kindle such strange emotions? His eyes were hidden behind those shadowy slits, yet she could feel their burning gaze. He did not speak, nor did she. Suddenly the fire flared brightly behind him, flooding his masked face with gold.

He held out his arms. Feeling as if another being moved within her body, Marie Fleur took a step toward him and stopped. What was she doing? If she went to his arms she knew instinctively what would happen. Yet an inexplicable force drew her on, giving her no time to reason or to evaluate the probable consequences.

"I thought you'd never come," he whispered huskily as his arms closed about her.

Marie Fleur blinked in amazement as he enfolded her in his strong embrace. She could not remember taking those final steps, yet here she was in his arms, listening to the thud of his heart, his quickened breathing.

"I . . . I . . . shouldn't . . ."

"Yes, sweetheart, you should. There's nothing more right than this," he whispered as he uptilted her chin in his lean hand.

She gazed up at his sensual mouth, finding such familiarity in those lips. The lean, strong hand that cupped her face was not that of a rough criminal. Her eyes closed, and she imagined his hands on her body, arousing the dormant fire slumbering in her soul; his caressing fingers would reawaken the delight of her forbidden dreams. Fire leaped afresh in her veins as he drew her even closer. Now she was aware of the tantalizing throb of his body against hers, his stirring passion, which produced an answering rhythm in her. When his mouth came down on hers, she was rocked with emotion.

She shuddered as she grasped his strong shoulders, as she slid her arms around his back, no longer aware of her surroundings, knowing only the compelling thrill of his nearness.

"Marie Fleur, you're the most beautiful woman in the world."

From a vast distance his impassioned words finally registered, penetrating the brandy-induced warmth, the passionate rush to oblivion. She was chillingly returned to the present. Gasping, Marie Fleur pulled her face from his, her violet eyes dark circles in her pale face.

"How do you know my name?"

He did not speak. Instead he reached behind his head to unfasten his mask. Mesmerized, she waited for the black cloth to fall and reveal his identity. A primitive inner knowledge already told her the answer.

"Brandon Nicholas!"

He smiled. "At your service, ma'am."

"To think it was you all along! You deceived me!"

He laughed at her outrage. "Does it really matter who I am? It's Black Nick who fascinates you so."

"Why are you pretending to be a highwayman?"

"Hardly a pretense," he pointed out with amusement.

"All right, why are you a highwayman?"

"For reasons I'm not at liberty to divulge, at the moment."

"Surely it was not so important to you to take me unawares that you had to go to these lengths."

"You flatter yourself, Lady Dowling. No man takes such grave risks solely to deceive a woman."

"Why did you put me in danger by denouncing me to the smugglers?"

"Why did you put yourself in danger by idiotically pretending to be a village wench? They're desperate men. You're lucky you weren't dumped on the marsh with your throat slit."

"Which I might well be, now that you've aroused their suspicions."

"You little fool, do you think I'd expose you to such peril? You can return home safely. They'll go about their business, no questions asked. They'll assume I disposed of you as I saw fit."

"I can't believe—is it thrills you're seeking? Is danger that appealing? Oh, you're such a fool!"

"Hardly a fool. I'd hoped to be called a patriot," he said with a grin, his statement further confusing her. "I assure you this desperate flight was unplanned. I'd never intentionally involve you in danger—you mean far too much to me."

Her head came up as she recognized the sincerity of his

words. His face unsmiling, his gray eyes dark in the glow of
the fire, he wordlessly held out his arms.

"Come, now you know my identity, it will only make our
kisses sweeter."

Marie Fleur bridled in indignation at his boldness. How dare
this imposter, this rake, this dissolute dandy assume she would
welcome his arms, his kisses, his lovemaking?

"Please *cherie,* I've waited so long," he pleaded, his voice
husky with emotion.

Moving as a sleepwalker, she finally reached him. Her arms
went around his muscular back, and she rejoiced in the hot,
hard feel of his body pressed against hers.

"Waited for me? I don't understand."

"Kiss me."

Their lips seared together, remembered ecstasies surging
afresh at the touch. Marie Fleur gasped at the strength of her
passion. His groin swelled, burning through her clothing until
she yearned to join her body with his. The primitive urge
shocked her, and she drew back.

"Don't you remember, sweetheart, a night so long ago it
seems an eternity? How often I've relived those hours. You
were like no other woman I'd ever known."

"You're mad! What night?"

"It was early summer, and a bird sang sweetly below your
window. You didn't think me mad then, *cherie.* You loved me
with total abandon."

A chill swept over her as Marie Fleur finally understood.
"That night! Oh, no!"

"Don't sound so shocked. Didn't I acquit myself well in
your bed?" he asked, the warm intimacy receding from his
voice. His grip on her arms tightened, and he thrust her slightly
away from him. "Christ in heaven, you surely didn't still think
it was William."

Tears filled Marie Fleur's eyes, her mouth trembling as she
whispered with difficulty, "Oh, now things are much clearer.
I'm so ashamed, so embarrassed—"

"Because you made love to me? The sin, if any was incurred,
was all on my behalf. God, that's rich! You thought it was
William! How unfortunate I can't share the amusing situation
with our friends."

Hurt by his changed mood, she stared furiously at him, tears
welling to her eyes and spilling over to her cheeks. "Always

you deceive me. How could you let me think . . . that—that—
you were William?"

"What else could I do?" Angrily he released her and swung
away. "Seeing that you feel so terribly deceived, my lady, I
apologize. My idea of rekindling what I assumed to be mutual
passion was a mistake. If you wish, I'll escort you back to
Rye. Get your things. If we hurry we can be there before
daybreak."

Numb, she stood there, all her emotions raw. Those wonderful dreams she had cherished, the blissful awakening of her
heart, her body, her blood had been based on a lie. William
had not acted differently toward her the next morning because
he had never made any concessions in the first place. Her tender
lover had been more of a stranger than she realized. Swallowing
her pain, feeling so terribly bleak and alone, she finally asked,
"Did William know?"

"He made the wager."

"A wager! Oh, God, my shame's even greater than I supposed. To think I was used as the stake in one of his games!
That's why he hated you, why he challenged you to a duel. It
didn't make sense until now." She put her hands to her face
and wept.

For a few moments Brandon listened to her sobbing. When
he finally took her in his arms she did not resist. "Hush, sweetheart, it doesn't matter now," he whispered, brushing her brow
with his lips. "Don't cry. Had he not made his unholy wager
we'd never have found each other. Forget I deceived you. No
ill was intended. Remember only how much I love you."

Through tear-glazed eyes she gazed up at his handsome face
swimming in a crystal haze. "Brandon, oh, Brandon," she
breathed, speaking his name in passion for the first time.

"Love me honestly. There's no need for pretense."

Her restraint slowly ebbed away as the fire in his touch, his
mouth kindled an inferno in her blood. They clung together,
mouths and bodies burning as one.

In his eagerness to claim her Brandon lifted her off the
ground, pinning her against the white-hot throb of his passion.
Marie Fleur's eyes were dark with desire, and her blood thundered like the sea.

"Love me, sweetheart, as I thought I'd never be loved again,"
she urged.

Brandon carried her to the bed where he laid her down

gently. She could hardly endure the wait until he lay beside her. Eagerly she pulled him against her, molding herself inch for inch against his body. Growing desperate for his mouth, she pressed her lips against his, shuddering as the fire of his passion was transmitted in their kiss.

Swiftly Brandon unlaced her homespun bodice. Impatiently thrusting aside the constraining material, he spilled her full breasts from her gown, shuddering at the sight. He had dreamed of this moment, of feeling that throbbing, milk-white softness come alive beneath his touch. With his hot tongue he teased her nipples to attention, tormenting her until she cried out in anguish.

Marie Fleur grasped his head, dragging his mouth up to her own. She sank her hands into his thick dark hair, imprisoning him there. Their lips parted, and his tongue stabbed furnace-hot inside her sweet mouth. The kiss brought excitement tingling through her veins, arousing her to even deeper passion. Now her breasts were crushed against his chest, demanding the pressure that imparted pleasure with pain.

Soon her gown lay crumpled beneath them. Impatiently Brandon kicked it aside. He gazed in wonder at her perfect body: full white breasts, marble-smooth, narrowing to a tiny waist, flaring again over pearl-white hips and ripe thighs. He buried his mouth in her perfumed flesh, imparting hot kisses until Marie Fleur thought she could not endure the pleasure. His kisses grew fiercer, more savage as his desire mounted.

Her hands slipped inside his white cambric shirt and she marveled at the hot strength of his body. Crisp dark hair sprang beneath her fingers as she explored the smooth perfection of his chest and broad shoulders. She unfastened the garment, her inquisitive fingers moving lower until she felt the restricting waistband of his breeches. That other time, when she had grown so bold, he had chuckled in amusement at her naiveté. Tonight he did not laugh. Instead he helped her unfasten his clothing, to discover what she so eagerly sought. Silk smooth, velvet tipped, his surging organ throbbed hot beneath her caress. Had she not known the ecstasy he was capable of delivering, she would have shrunk in fear from his towering manhood. Smiling with pleasure over her secret knowledge, Marie Fleur bent to bestow a butterfly-gentle kiss on the tip of his quivering flesh.

Brandon shuddered, groaning aloud at the unexpected delight. And though her kiss filled him with pleasure, he knew he must halt the dangerous pastime. He kissed her, he caressed her, exerting the utmost control to fill her body with heat whilst holding himself back from his own satisfaction.

"Love me tonight for myself," he urged, his voice husky with desire.

The tension in his face made her shudder; desire tautened his features and darkened his eyes.

"I want you so much . . ." she whispered.

He caught her to him, yearning to join their bodies in mutual passion. Gently he spread her legs, and Marie Fleur eagerly opened them wider to receive him, hardly able to endure the anticipation until his thick manhood consumed her belly with fire. His hungering mouth devoured hers as he slowly entered her. Deeper, deeper he drove, until she sobbed with pleasure, reaching for him, straining to absorb every inch of that rigid, pulsing brand. He moved rhythmically, pacing himself as he gauged her response.

Time hung suspended in that lonely mist-wrapped cottage on Romney Marsh. Marie Fleur strove to keep this moment for eternity, longing to stay enfolded against his virile body, impaled upon the sweet embodiment of his desire.

"Come, my lovely, torture me no longer," he urged at last, making a supreme effort at control.

"No, 'tis you who are tormenting me," she replied huskily, taking his tongue inside her mouth, shivering in delight as he simulated the very ecstasy that turned her limbs to molten heat.

Wild abandon possessed them as he surged anew inside her, plumbing her depths with throbbing passion. Her pleasure mounted to such intensity, Marie Fleur wondered if she could bear it as he moved slowly, surely, allowing her to experience each rapturous quiver. Quickly she soared to that ecstatic height so well remembered and now so readily achieved. A sob escaped from her trembling mouth. Brandon held her against him as she plunged into the dark, star-shot world of fulfillment. Deafened by her roaring blood, consumed by the heat of his body, never before had she experienced such pure pleasure.

Afterwards she lay sobbing quietly in his strong arms, devastated by the storm of desire. She needed the assurance of his presence and his love. They lay closely wrapped in each other's arms.

"Marie Fleur," Brandon whispered, breaking the spell. "Promise to trust me whatever happens."

Bemused, she readily agreed. "Trust you? What a foolish thing to ask. Of course I'll trust you."

His mouth turned upward in a grim smile. How easily such promises were made. "You mean so much to me. Don't make those vows lightly."

She snorted softly in the firelight. "Haven't I forgiven you two deceptions already? Is that not trust?"

Sighing in relief, he planted a kiss on her soft hair. "You're right, you've already stood the test." But when she dozed in his arms, Brandon frowned, his mind straying to dangerous tasks ahead.

"I must leave before dawn," he said at last, the words heavy on his conscience. "Not because I want to, because I must."

"Dawn," she repeated, nestling against the safety of his strong body. "Oh, 'tis such a long time till dawn, *mon cher*. Let's not discuss it now."

"We must discuss it. I've a dangerous mission ahead—"

"Smuggling contraband. I know what you're up to. And you so rich you've no need to do so. For shame!" Smiling, she traced his chin with her tongue. "And yet, wicked though you are, an outlaw though you are, I'll forgive you because you make love to me so splendidly."

"Listen, *ma chere*, things are not what they seem. My life will always be in danger. For that reason alone I can make no lasting vows to you. Would that I could—"

"Be quiet. We've plenty of time for promises. If you're to be away at dawn, we've only time enough to make love."

Sighing in exasperation, Brandon ground his teeth, fighting anger. But her soft hands were already working magic on his body. And her tongue, hot, sweet, was probing his lips. Groaning, he welded her to his body, aching to possess her. He wanted never to stop possessing her. He wanted never to leave this bed or the sweetness of her arms.

"All right, I'll make love to you, though it's not what I'd intended—" He ducked as she aimed a glancing blow at him.

"How dare you," Marie Fleur said indignantly.

He smothered her mouth with kisses, fighting her resistance until he had possessed her. All those dark thoughts about the waiting danger must wait for daylight. At this moment the passionate woman trembling in his arms was all that mattered.

∽ Chapter 6 ∾

BEYOND THE COTTAGE window pale rays of sunlight gilded the heavy mist. Excitement surged through Marie Fleur's veins as she realized where she was. This poorly furnished room could not have delighted her more if it had been a palace. The nicked furniture, the rag hearthrug were part of the magical night she had shared here with Brandon.

A tall figure suddenly emerged from the fog that shrouded the churchyard. Her heart began to thud—Brandon had not gone after all. But the stooping man who thrust open the unlatched door was a stranger.

"Awake at last, are ye, girl? I thought you'd sleep till doomsday."

Hastily Marie Fleur pulled the covers up to her chin, and she slid down in the bed, hiding her bare shoulders from the stranger's gaze. The man was dressed in a fisherman's boots, knit watch cap, and rugged sweater.

"Where's Nick?" Marie Fleur had enough presence of mind not to refer to Brandon by his real name. If at times the secrecy he demanded seemed overly melodramatic, she still intended to maintain it.

"He's been gone since first light."

The fisherman smothered the rosy fire, then hefted a cloth bundle of supplies over his shoulder. Marie Fleur watched him while she fought a wave of disappointment that brought her absurdly close to tears. Brandon had gone. Last night, even when he warned her that he must leave at dawn, she had not actually expected him to go without saying good-bye.

"Come on, shift yourself, girl. We'd best be on our way. I'm taking you back to Rye."

After issuing this curt command, the fisherman turned and walked outside. Marie Fleur heard the jingle of harness as he saddled their horses.

Reluctantly she slid from the warm covers. Without the fire the room was chill, and she shivered as she struggled into her clothes. Though dry, her borrowed garments felt chafingly stiff.

When Marie Fleur stepped outdoors she shuddered at the desolate sight of the mist-locked marsh. As far as she could see the table-flat land was layered with fog. Around the cottage steps, vegetation lay sodden and dripping. Those tentative rays of morning sun had long since disappeared in the murk.

"It be a raw day for the journey, and no mistake. Had it pegged right, he did, when he said you'd never make it without me," observed the fisherman with relish. "Get on the nag, girl. The master said we was to be in Rye before noon."

"Did Nick hire you to guide me to Rye?"

"He be the master, b'ain't he?"

Marie Fleur nodded, disliking the man's attitude. He offered her no assistance in mounting, so involved was he in struggling to fit two battered wool overcoats over his knitted sweater. She clung to the saddle and pulled herself up, scrambling clumsily astride the horse. The animal seemed sturdy enough and even-tempered, for he waited patiently. The fisherman's horse was little more than a pack animal, scabbed, swaybacked, and possessing a baleful stare.

For the first half hour they traveled in silence, weaving back and forth between narrow stretches of water, the gray ceiling of mist less than six feet overhead. The wind began to rise, gusting icily off the water. Marie Fleur pulled the wool shawl closer about her body, but the icy blast soon penetrated the thick fabric. In a few minutes her teeth were chattering.

Becoming aware of her need, the fisherman threw her a rough wool blanket out of his saddlebag.

"It be clean, girl, no need to curl your lip," he admonished sharply as she eyed the blanket. "Master never said what a hoity-toity bit of muslin you was. Expect he reckoned I'd find out for meself soon enough."

This chuckled comment made Marie Fleur seethe, yet she bit back a scathing retort, aware that she needed this stranger too much to risk alienating him. They ploughed ahead into the teeth of the wind, which was sweeping vast streamers of fog aloft to reveal tall stands of dead saw thistle and mournful tangles of thatching reeds stripped bare of leaves. The blurred white shapes that had edged the perimeter of their vision were revealed as a flock of sheep.

"Are you a smuggler?" Marie Fleur asked the man presently when they rode abreast along a wider track.

The fisherman squinted at her dubiously before nodding. "Most folks hereabouts are smugglers."

"Has Nick been with you long?"

"Since he was a little shaver—well, not 'with us' like, knowed to us. Stayed summers here with the curate at the church. A distant relative of his. Got to know the marsh like a native. You could've blowed me down when up he pops, full growed, wearin' 'is mask. Still, as I says, even fine gentlemens can fall on 'ard luck these bad times."

"You know he's a gentleman then?"

"Oh, yes, natural-born. You can't 'ide that, though he tries, bless 'im. S'pose it's family troubles what drives 'im down 'ere. Then again, maybe he just wants a bit of excitement."

That was the extent of the information the man was willing to divulge. The rest of their journey was conducted in silence. It was a relief to Marie Fleur when she finally saw the outline of Rye perched high on its sandstone hill above the steel-gray River Rother. Now situated two miles inland, she found it hard to believe that in the Middle Ages Rye had been a great port.

"Don't s'pose you'll want me coming too far. I'll watch till you're safe inside the gate," suggested the fisherman with unusual consideration. "Reckon you've got explaining aplenty to do without adding me to it."

She thanked him, smiling in genuine surprise at his thoughtfulness. The man nodded his acknowledgment whilst gumming a battered briar pipe in his toothless jaw.

Marie Fleur rode ahead feeling terribly conspicuous. It was as if the events of the past twenty-four hours were written on her face. It took her some minutes of stern reprimand to quiet her misgivings. No one could possibly know what had taken place. She intended to reveal only that she had been held hostage by the highwayman. She hoped Nancy had not panicked and alerted the authorities to her disappearance.

At the massive stone Landgate, Marie Fleur paused to wave good-bye to the fisherman, no more than a blur now in the distance. It seemed as if he raised his hand in farewell before turning back to the marsh, but he was too far away to tell. Urging her mount forward, she rode under the twin-towered arch and along the narrow cobbled street, turning to her right at the bottom of the steep cliff, from which vantage point she had a magnificent view of Romney Marsh.

If the townsfolk had been alerted to the abduction of a lady of quality, she must produce a satisfying explanation of her absence. Brandon had to be protected at all costs. By the time she reached the old monastery, Marie Fleur had already settled

on her story. She would say she had been treated well while
held captive, without revealing her knowledge of the highwayman's true identity or her own involvement with him. A
pang of guilt stabbed her over the planned deception, for this
was the story she must repeat even to Nancy.

When Marié Fleur arrived at Lucy's cottage, the street was
virtually deserted. To her surprise no one responded to her
knock. Unsure of what to do with the horse, Marie Fleur got
an urchin to lead the nag to the Mermaid's landlord to hold for
Black Nick.

Just as she was creeping stealthily toward the back entrance,
skirting the ramshackle outhouse and coal shed without detection, Nancy's startled shriek of surprise nearly made her jump.

"Milady! Oh, thank heaven. When did you get back?"

"Ten minutes ago."

"Shh!" Belatedly remembering they stood beneath her mother's window, Nancy put her fingers to her lips. "Mum's been
taken poorly again. I told her you was feeling under the weather
too this morning and was sleeping late. I was at me wits' end
to know what to do. Another few hours and I'd have gone for
the law. Are ye safe? Nothing bad happened to you?" Nancy
inquired suspiciously, noting her mistress's disheveled appearance.

Eyes downcast, Marie Fleur shook her head. "No, I'm quite
unharmed. The highwayman kept me prisoner overnight. One
of his men just brought me back."

Nancy's piercing gaze made Marie Fleur uncomfortable.
Though she had revealed nothing about the rest of her adventure, Nancy's expression suggested she was not convinced this
was the whole truth.

"Funny. Somehow that don't sound like what I've heard
tell about Black Nick. All the girls hereabouts says—but never
mind, you're safe now." Nancy hugged Marie Fleur, then pushed
her impatiently across the threshold. Clucking in dismay, she
marched her mistress to the blazing fire. "You be chilled to
the bone! Oh, Lord, if you takes a fever I'll never forgive
meself."

"I'll be all right, Nancy. None of this was your fault. I
agreed to go to the party. You couldn't know what would
happen."

"You'll never convince me I'm not to blame, so you'd best
stop trying."

Nancy chewed her lip in agitation as she measured milk into a pan, adding a dollop of butter and a generous serving of brandy. She heated the mixture over the fire and when the posset had reached the desired temperature, she urged Marie Fleur to drink it.

"Them smugglers believe you brought the government men, milady. What with them all over the place, it's not safe for you to be on the streets. You'd best stay indoors till we decides what to do. Reckon they thought Black Nick would do for you. Happen when they sees he let you go, they won't be too 'appy. I tell you, though he's a gentleman, I had me doubts how you'd fare."

"I 'fared' as well as can be expected." Marie Fleur buried her face in the large earthenware mug, eyes downcast, her guilty expression shielded by her tumbled hair. It would be a great relief to be able to confide in Nancy. The need to hide such joyous knowledge was almost more than she could bear. But Nancy's reminder about the smugglers' anger gradually turned her thoughts from a need to protect Brandon to anxiety over her own safety. In a matter of hours the news could leak that she was back. She shuddered to think what action Yorkshire George would order as punishment for informing on his men. It was far too dangerous to remain in Rye. She must return to Langley Chase without delay.

The next morning Marie Fleur departed for Kent in a hired coach. She shared a tearful farewell with Nancy, who, afraid for her mother's declining health, begged to be allowed to stay in Rye until Lucy had recovered.

The morning was half over before a reluctant sun struggled through the clouds to shine like a feeble lantern across the drab landscape. The glories of autumn were quickly fading as high winds stripped burnished leaves from the trees. Scarlet rose hips strung jeweled necklaces about the browning hedgerows. As they clattered along the country lanes, the horses startled a dun hen pheasant from the grass verge, and an army of red squirrels fled up the gnarled trunks of sweet chestnuts ablaze with ochre foliage.

Had it not been for the treasured secret nestled in her heart, Marie Fleur would have found this journey depressing. Whenever she thought of the empty winter days stretching ahead, of the loneliness of cold, palatial Langley Chase, she only needed to recall the treasured warmth of Brandon's embrace, the sweetness of his kiss, the wonder of his love for her heart to soar. Marie Fleur did not know when she would see him again, but she was confident Brandon would come to her as soon as he was able. It was for that reason alone that she decided not to spend the winter at the Norfolk hunting lodge. If Brandon came ashore briefly, there would not be time for him to travel to Norfolk, even assuming he knew where to find her. So intense were her feelings for him, she would be devastated if she missed his visit. A day, even an hour in his arms, was worth enduring much.

Beyond the coach window the landscape faded into a misty blur as light rain spattered the glass. They entered the village of Langley where children, ill-clad to face the approaching winter, stood at their cottage doors to watch the passing coach. They appeared half-starved.

Marie Fleur's attention was riveted on their wan, big-eyed faces staring dully at her through the drizzle. In all her gloom about losing the estate to her creditors, she had given scant thought to what would become of her impoverished tenants. William had never been a generous landlord; now the extent of his indebtedness was disclosed, she understood why. The money for repairs to rental property had been desperately needed to support his flamboyant way of life. Never a prosperous village, Langley had lost four men in the Peninsula War, and two more had been crippled. Compared to England's vast losses during the preceding decade of strife, Langley's casualties were small. Yet the loss of a blacksmith, two yeoman farmers, and a thatcher was a stunning blow. Under William's faltering leadership, the shabby hamlet had never recovered.

Rousing herself, Marie Fleur waved to two barefoot children she knew by sight. Not recognizing the coach, the children merely stared at the rain-spattered window without responding. Those were the poor creatures she had anticipated teaching to read and write! Gloom settled over her as they turned into the oak-lined avenue leading to the white-columned mansion. Unless their bellies were full, she realized she had little hope of teaching the village children anything. The future promised them an existence on the edge of humanity, toiling, begetting, living out their lives in hopeless ignorance and poverty like their parents before them. Though in Regency England rural poverty was less visible than that of the cities, it was nevertheless as real.

Unable to push the memory of those dejected waifs from her mind, Marie Fleur decided her most pressing task was to try to improve the village children's future by educating them. The Reverend Millington had pledged his support in founding a school, so at least she had one ally in her seemingly insurmountable task.

Marie Fleur's charitable intentions were to be delayed for a few days. She had forgotten that this weekend began the local hunting season. By tradition, the owner of Langley Chase always received the master and the pack in the frosty dawn to offer a stirrup cup. The hunt breakfast, partaken of after the hunt, was also traditionally served by the owner of Langley Chase. Though Marie Fleur's recent bereavement would have been an acceptable excuse for breaking with tradition, the thought of going on a hunt through the autumn countryside filled her with pleasure. This would be her first time out with the Langley pack, although Marie Fleur and her cousin Lavinia had ridden regularly with the Edgerton Hunt, enjoying every minute of the exhilarating ride. Her enthusiasm for the sport overcame her nervousness in presiding alone over so important a local function.

The November morning was forbidding, the bare landscape steeped in mist as Marie Fleur went down the steps of the stately mansion to greet the master of the hunt. Belatedly she discovered the Earl of Cranbrook was master of the Langley pack. Clad in a bright red wool coat, skintight white breeches and black boots, he waited astride his enormous chestnut hunter, surveying his surroundings with the utmost arrogance. The earl's gaze flickered toward Marie Fleur as she descended the steps. Three servants followed her carrying silver trays filled with glasses of mulled wine.

The nip of frost was in the damp air, its sharpness taking her breath. Today Marie Fleur wore a figure-hugging redingote of navy broadcloth with a white silk stock at her throat. On her head was a tall crowned black silk hat with a floating gray veil. Severe, as befitted a woman in mourning, the dark costume was also admirably suited to her fair skin and blond curls.

"Welcome to Langley Chase."

The master of the hunt removed his black hat in acknowledgment of her greeting, being the first to partake of the mulled wine.

"May the hunting be good," Marie Fleur added, stepping

back as the earl leaned from the saddle, his face unpleasantly close to hers.

"Welcome home, my dear. I see you grew impatient for Langley Chase. No doubt the glories of the hunt drew you from your rustic retreat," he mocked, his pale eyes holding hers.

"It was quite by accident that I returned in time for the hunt, yet an appropriate accident at that. Considering the local custom, I'd hate to cause the pack a disastrous year by breaking with tradition."

The earl nodded his approval, flicking imaginary dust from the lapel of his formfitting scarlet coat.

"Will you do me the honor of riding at the head of the pack, at least till we reach the crossroads?"

"Is that traditional as well?"

He smiled sarcastically. "So you still consider my company odious? A pity, my dear. I'd hoped by now you'd have learned sense." His smile faded as he urged his horse forward, leaving her standing on the bottom step.

The groom brought around a saddled bay mare, which Marie Fleur had not seen before.

"Where did she come from? Oh, she's so fine!" she exclaimed in delight as she patted the animal's velvety nose. The bay was tall and well proportioned, amply suited for hunting. William had a number of good bloodstock, yet to her knowledge this young mare with her sleek lustrous coat and perfect lines was not one of their stable.

"Purchased some time ago, milady," mumbled Sefton, his eyes downcast. "Arrived while you was gone."

"You know I'll have to return her, don't you? I can't afford the mounts I've got, let alone take on a new animal. Yet..." Marie Fleur looked wistfully at the lovely bay. Perhaps she could ride the mare once before returning her.

The groom knelt and offered his locked hands for her to mount. Marie Fleur felt like a queen as she settled in the saddle. Taking a deep breath of the damp air redolent with woodsmoke and decaying foliage, she surveyed the misty countryside stretching from horizon to horizon. For a brief time at least, Langley Chase was still hers. Today might be the last time she would ride the boundaries of this land.

Urging the mare forward, Marie Fleur called over her shoulder. "What's her name, Sefton? I forgot to ask."

"Madonna, milady."

· It was an unusual name for a horse. Marie Fleur leaned close to the animal's velvet ears, whispering endearments to her and patting her neck. She would call her Donna, she decided. The mare seemed in favor of the nickname, for she whickered in pleasure as Marie Fleur whispered it, gentling her as she grew restless when the hounds milled about her legs.

The hunt cantered down Langley Chase's spacious drive in the lifting haze, moving between tall oaks where dwindling bronze leaves clung sodden to the stark branches. The distant hedgerows and fields were obscured from view, cottages and barns looming sinister through the murk. Autumn filled the air with its own peculiar fragrance. The deathlike hush of the damp country lanes was broken only by the steady clop of horses' hooves. At the roadside, red-and-white spotted toadstools nestled beneath dripping foliage. Peppery yarrow stood dingy white on the grass verges and scarlet pimpernel peeped shyly from the browning grass.

Poignant memories of Brandon and their shared love made Marie Fleur smile wistfully, her secret thoughts excluding the earl, who kept glancing toward her, awaiting an invitation to join her. She was glad Cranbrook was master of the hunt. Having far too many important duties to perform, he was prevented from monopolizing her time.

Over barren farmland the Langley Hunt rode. Heads down, sterns high, the pack of hounds picked up a scent. Eagerly they barked the announcement of their discovery. Immediately a current of excitement rippled through the field, generated by those distinctive cries echoing through the mist-shrouded countryside. The chase was on.

Faster they went, then faster, fanning out over the fields where the wheat stubble had been ploughed under, the fresh-turned furrows white with frost. Skirting the copse where rusty bracken dripped with moisture beneath the beeches, the riders pursued the pack of hounds who were excitedly giving chase.

The cold air whistled past Marie Fleur's ears, stinging her cheeks and bringing tears to her eyes as she quickened her pace. The mare kept up with the leaders of the hunt, amazing her mistress by her unexpected speed. At a brush obstacle, Donna soared, needing little guidance. Airborne for what seemed minutes, she landed gracefully on the other side without breaking stride. With every mile Marie Fleur found herself falling deeper in love with the dainty mare.

The huntsman's horn shrilled as the fox was sighted on open ground. The pursuing field thundered over fences and pasture, eager to be in at the kill. After a worthy chase, the large fox was eventually cornered and quickly slain by the excited pack.

The master of the hunt awarded the mask, pads, and brush to outstanding riders. With great ceremony the novice riders in the field were bloodied on both cheeks, initiating them as members in good standing of the Langley Hunt.

The chase over, the riders retraced their paths, having come virtually full circle, for Langley Chase's white chimneys were visible through the trees.

Riding alongside Marie Fleur, the earl shouted, "You should have taken an award, Lady Dowling. Your performance was superb."

"Thank you, Geoffrey. That's high praise coming from the master of the hunt."

"How do you like your mare?"

"She's marvelous. I've never known an animal so responsive. I've already fallen in love with her."

He smiled, his expression hard to interpret. Then he rode ahead to assume his rightful place as leader of the pack. The scarlet-coated huntsmen, the whippers-in, the hounds all streamed in a colorful cavalcade across the winter-black Kentish landscape. Villagers stood on their doorsteps, gaping at the gaudily dressed riders while farmers cursed the gentry who galloped indiscriminately over their land with little regard for livestock or crop.

A roaring fire blazed in the vast grate of the red-curtained dining room of Langley Chase. At the far end of the room a sumptuous banquet was laid. Two large tables were filled with an elegant array of silver topped dishes to revive the hungry hunters. Paulson nodded politely to his mistress, awaiting her signal for the breakfast to begin. Platters of crisp fried ham; deviled kidneys and mushrooms; scrambled eggs; tureens of steaming oxtail soup; rich, dark ale fruitcake; rosy, spiced baked apples; and heaped boards of cold beef, pork, and lamb awaited the guests. Copious mugs of mulled ale and fortifying glasses of port, claret, and champagne were eagerly consumed whilst the hunters discussed the merits of the season's first outing.

Marie Fleur moved among the guests, receiving their sympathy as well as their congratulations for having the fortitude to continue this sacred tradition despite her recent loss.

After a couple of hours the company had dwindled to a mere handful of William's close friends, who tipsily bewailed the loss of their host. The Earl of Cranbrook also lingered, awaiting an opportunity to speak to Marie Fleur alone.

"My dear Marie Fleur, I'm immensely pleased to have you home," he began pleasantly, offering her a cup of spiced claret.

"It's most pleasant to be home. I've missed the countryside." Almost as soon as she said it, Marie Fleur knew her honest statement had been ill-advised.

With a speculative smile, the earl moved closer, slipping his hand gently beneath her elbow. "All the more reason for you to consider my most generous offer," he said in an undertone, assured they could not be overheard.

"I've already considered your offer. The answer's still no."

"You're a stubborn female. Still, your spirit intrigues me. Will you keep the bay?"

Marie Fleur turned, surprised by his question. "Surely that's no concern of yours."

"Ah, but it's of the utmost concern. She comes from my stable."

The news was an unpleasant shock. So well attuned had she become with the spirited animal, Marie Fleur had been wracking her brains for a means to keep this particular horse when the others went to satisfy her creditors.

"Your stable," she repeated stiffly. "William bought her from you?"

"Not exactly. She's a gift from me to you."

"Then you must take her home with you. I çan't accept your gift."

"Oh, come, what's a gift between friends?"

"A gift obligates me to something I've no wish to be part of. You can't buy me, Geoffrey. When will you realize that?"

"But so small a gift. You said yourself you were enchanted with her. . . ."

"I'll never accept gifts from you. Never."

With this she turned from him and walked from the dining room, stoically ignoring his sharp command to return.

Marie Fleur seethed with anger to think she had so easily fallen prey to temptation. For a minute back there in the dining room, she had caught herself debating whether to keep the gift, just this once. But if she accepted the seductive lure of a bay mare, the earl would only renew his efforts to sway her to his will. His was a generosity she could not afford.

On Monday morning, warmly clad in a plain wine wool dress and matching pelisse, a dark paisley patterned shawl about her shoulders, Marie Fleur set out for the rectory beside Langley's Norman parish church. She was eager to discuss the establishment of the parish school with the Reverend Millington, and she hoped that in her absence he had not lost his enthusiasm for the project.

Mrs. Millington opened the door to her. The minister's wife was a faded little woman, perpetually tired from childbearing and the burden of maintaining her family in this drafty, cavernous rectory. After she led Marie Fleur into the austere drawing room, Mrs. Millington disappeared.

"Welcome home, my dear Lady Dowling. I trust you recuperated during your brief holiday."

Marie Fleur smiled and agreed politely as the Reverend Millington strode briskly into the room.

"Yes, I'm quite rested, thank you."

"Good. Good. Emily, bring some tea for her ladyship—no, I insist," he added sternly when Marie Fleur opened her mouth to protest. Then, the matter settled, he ushered her closer to the struggling coal fire, which had been lit in her honor.

Langley's vicar was the younger son of lesser nobility, a fact he had regretted all his days. But for an accident of birth he might have become a comfortable gentleman farmer in the Weald instead of trying to save the souls of illiterate peasants who found the perpetuation of lifestock infinitely more important than the state of their souls. He often wondered if the bishop had sought to punish him with this appointment. The Reverend Millington sighed, turning his attention back to the charming noblewoman who had deigned to grace his hearth.

"My dear Lady Dowling, what can I do for you this cheerless morning?"

"I came to discuss our village school."

"Ah, yes, well, I must admit, I'm most disappointed in the response from the villagers. A couple of mothers wanted their children to learn to letter, as they call it. Beyond that, nothing. Really, my dear Lady Dowling, I'm not one to squash so admirable a project before it has been given a chance. . . ."

"Are you saying I have no students?"

The Reverend Millington smiled wanly and nodded agreement.

Marie Fleur pursed her full lips, deep in thought. "The local children look so ill-fed and poorly clothed. I wonder . . . if we offered them bread and cheese as an incentive, do you think they'd come?"

"Your observations certainly have merit—" The Reverend Millington broke off as Emily crept into the room, two young children clutching at her skirts. She set the tray on a mahogany drum table beside the hearth and just as quietly retreated. The two small children cast wide-eyed backward glances at their finely dressed visitor before they, too, disappeared into the drafty corridor. "My wife's not a very sociable woman, and I apologize for that. She means well—"

"Give it no thought. We're not responsible for the dispositions of our spouses." Marie Fleur exchanged sympathetic smiles with the minister, who well understood her meaning. William had never been a favorite of his.

"Well put, my dear lady, well put. Now, tea?"

As they talked, it was decided that Marie Fleur would use the small room adjoining the parish hall. The minister had collected for her some paper, a half-dozen cracked slates, a tattered first reader discarded by one of his own children—but no pupils.

"I shall go to their cottages myself." she declared finally, determined not to be thwarted in her plans.

These past days her desire to start a village school had become increasingly strong. Somewhat guiltily she admitted she might be using the project to fill her mind instead of pining for Brandon. Yet the idea of holding school had been born long before her involvement with him. At that time, however, she suspected her motive had been to relieve boredom. Inherent honesty brought her to these conclusions, yet neither could she deny she wanted to save the youngsters from the unending grind of poverty. Marie Fleur continued to smile blandly at the Reverend Millington, deeming it imprudent to confide thoughts that might tarnish his ideal.

"I must warn you, my dear Lady Dowling, these people may not be what you're accustomed to," the Reverend Millington went on uncomfortably. Mentally he visualized the packed dirt floors in the meanest hovels, the overflowing chamber pots, the odor of unwashed bodies, and the all-pervading stench of festering cesspools which, though set at a distance from the habitations, were always pungently apparent. For a genteel lady such unpleasant revelations would come as a decided shock. "Will you allow me to accompany you?"

"By all means. I'd welcome your company."

"When do you wish to make your visit?"

"This morning if possible."

The Reverend Millington blinked behind his steel-rimmed spectacles, his thin aristocratic face disclosing his surprise. He had hoped the visit might be postponed until a more clement season, spring perhaps.

"Yes, very well. I have a couple of free hours. Allow me to fetch my coat."

Marie Fleur hid a smile as he strode from the room. Poor man, he hardly seemed suited to this shabby, backward post. She rather imagined he would be more at home chatting to chokered dowagers and their plain daughters or soothing the ruffled tempers of the ladies' sewing guild.

The dirt road through the village squelched unpleasantly underfoot as Marie Fleur accompanied the minister on their first call. His appearance was much altered by a black overcoat, black top hat, and tattersall check muffler. The first hovel they stopped at was deserted as were the second and third. The families were out in the muddy fields grubbing for late potatoes. At the fourth cottage they were more fortunate.

"Come in, reverend . . . milady," whispered the flustered tenant, her eyes round with surprise. She ushered the two honored guests into her smoky home.

The beaten earth floor was strewn with straw. The chimney piece of lichen-spotted fieldstone covered an entire wall. Above the flames swung a blackened cauldron containing watery gruel, which the housewife stirred slowly with a dented spoon.

"Now, Mrs. Neave, we've come to see if you're still interested in Juby and Sid learning how to read. Lady Dowling is most enthusiastic about our school."

Mrs. Neave ducked her head, suddenly flustered. "Well, reverend, Lord knows I'd like the lads to get some book learning, but our Bert says it's a lot of rot, farmers don't need to read. And he's going to be 'is own boss next year. He's already got that acre beside the birchwood."

When they encountered a similar story at the next four cottages, Marie Fleur's enthusiasm was definitely dampened.

"Why?" she asked, as they trudged back through the slimy mud redolent of cow manure and another, human effluent. "Why don't they want something better for their children? The world's changing, yet here time's passed them by. They're living an almost feudal existence."

"Ah, yes, my dear, but what can we do? It's the way things are. Many of them leave to work in the towns, and there they endure even worse squalor. Ignorance is the cornerstone of poverty, yet you'll never convince them of it. Here, in this last house, they might be a little more receptive. The mother reads a little herself. Her daughter Maudie's a bright little thing, eager to learn how to read and write. The husband's an insensitive brute, but thankfully he's usually at the Seven Stars at this hour."

A vine twisted about the brown painted door. Though devoid of flowers or leaves on this chill November day, the plant showed that someone cared about the outward appearance of the house.

A thin woman wearing a voluminous white apron answered their knock. "Oh, Reverend Millington, what a surprise! My Dan's not 'ome at the moment."

"It's you and Maudie we've come to see, Mrs. Leach. May we come in? I've brought Lady Dowling to meet you."

"Oh, my lady, 'tis an honor," mumbled Mrs. Leach, creaking to a flustered curtsy as Marie Fleur stepped inside the cramped room.

A movement in the corner directed their attention to a ragged bed where three young children slept. A fair-haired girl of about thirteen leaned over them, tenderly adjusting the patched covers. The girl turned to the visitors with a bright, alert smile, and she, too, bobbed a deferential curtsy.

"This 'ere's 'er Ladyship from the 'all," announced Mrs. Leach, nudging the girl. "Tell 'er 'ow welcome she is, Maudie," she urged in an undertone.

"You're most welcome to our humble home, my lady," parroted Maudie, obviously well rehearsed in the speech.

"Thank you, Maudie. I'm very pleased to be here."

"Maudie is your most enthusiastic pupil. Isn't that right, Maudie?"

The girl nodded her pale curls, gazing adoringly at her exalted visitor. "Is you really going to learn me to read and write?"

"Teach, Maudie, teach," corrected the minister with a shudder. "Yes, Lady Dowling is prepared to take her time to instruct you. But you must promise to work diligently."

"Oh, yes, sir, Maudie promises," said her mother, answering for her daughter. "Don't you, Maudie?"

"Yes, Ma, I promise," Maudie mumbled, made uncomfortable by her mother's interference. "I can already letter and read a bit," she said, darting to a scarred Lancashire dresser from which she produced a slate and chalk. Laboriously she spelled out, "Maudie Ann Leach, Langley, Kent." Triumphantly she held out the slate, awaiting approval.

"Oh, that's very good," exclaimed Marie Fleur, genuinely surprised by the exhibition. The letters were formed well, a skill obviously taught to Maudie by her mother, who beamed with pride. "You'll soon be able to write whole sentences."

"Things like, 'I saw the moon shine silver on the pond'?" asked Maudie breathlessly, her blue eyes turned dreamy. "I think up ever so many things I want to write about the trees and the animals. Sometimes I—"

"Maudie," admonished her mother, "that'll do."

Later, when the Reverend Millington was politely inquiring about the health of the younger children and of the older son who worked as a farm laborer, Marie Fleur turned to Maudie. The girl had not taken her eyes off her. "We'll write down all those things. You just tell me what to write, then I'll teach you how to read and write it also."

"Oh, would you? I do poems, too—leastways, Ma says they's poems."

When they left the Leach's cottage, Marie Fleur saw young Maudie staring wistfully after them before her mother yanked her back indoors to return to her spinning.

"A remarkable child, don't you think?"

"She's wonderful! So eager! In fact, I'd run the school just for her if necessary."

The Reverend Millington smiled ruefully. "After our lack of success this morning, I'd say you might be doing just that, Lady Dowling."

Chapter 7

TO MARIE FLEUR'S great disappointment, Maudie did not come
to the parish hall the following morning. The Reverend Millington assured her he had delivered the message via his own
daughter. It seemed the brutish father had something to do with
Maudie's absence, considering it time taken away from her
spinning, on which he depended for ale money.

Seething with resentment, Marie Fleur had just made up her
mind to confront him and insist he allow his daughter to attend
school when two grubby-faced boys peered around the doorjamb. She did not recognize them from yesterday's visit.

"Come in. You're my first pupils."

The boys shuffled over the dusty floorboards, their filthy
toes projecting from worn boots. Twisting their threadbare cloth
caps in wizened hands, they stood diffidently, not knowing
what to do next.

"What are your names?"

"Joe and Dick," mumbled the taller boy.

"And your last name?"

The two looked blankly at each other, not comprehending.

"Who is your father?"

"Ooh, 'im be Tyler, Earl Cranbrook's cowman."

"Earl Cranbrook!"

"At your service, my dear Lady Dowling," said a smooth
voice from the dusty shadows of the parish hall.

Marie Fleur's face tightened as she beheld the superbly
outfitted figure of her would-be suitor emerging from his hiding
place beside a stack of dusty hymnals.

"So I owe the arrival of these pupils to you."

"Naturally. And I'll round up as many eager scholars as you
care to teach. This is a most admirable pursuit—most admirable."

Their eyes met, and Marie Fleur felt an icy chill travel down
her spine. Nothing had changed. There was still that barely
masked predatory gleam in his pale eyes, the assured manner,
as if he owned her already.

"My school was for the children of Langley."

"Where are they? I don't see any children from Langley here."

"Their parents wouldn't allow them to come." It was mortifying to have to admit her idea had not borne fruit. To any but he, she would not have minded. Yet far from gloating, the earl's haughty face was touched by a flicker of sympathy.

"The peasants are generally reluctant to be elevated, my dear. Did you not know that? Still, all's not lost. These two are ready lads, and I guarantee there'll be a dozen more join them before noon."

"How did you know about the school?"

"Well, it's hardly been a secret. But I do confess to a certain stealth. I learned of your current difficulties from the esteemed Reverend Millington. He does not hold me in quite the same low regard as you do, my dear," he added a trifle bitterly.

Becoming aware of the urchins' rapt attention, Marie Fleur decided it would be wiser not to pursue the subject. "Thank you for your kindness in bringing my first pupils," she concluded with a dazzling smile. "Come, boys, this is where you are to sit."

The boys glanced toward the earl, awaiting further instruction. He nodded reassuringly. Obediently they went to the small chairs and flopped down, their gazes roaming about the room whilst they awaited the unknown. Trying hard to ignore the earl's offending presence, Marie Fleur began her first class.

True to Cranbrook's word, by noon another half dozen children arrived at the parish hall. The earl was also aware of her proposal to provide them with refreshment. A groom from nearby Cranbrook Place, resplendent in buff livery faced in maroon and wearing a black top hat cockaded in gold, carried forth a wicker picnic hamper filled with assorted breads and cheeses.

Though the earl had been helpful, Marie Fleur had no desire to be beholden to him. Unfortunately, before she could inform him of her feelings, the Reverend Millington had thanked their noble benefactor most effusively. After the minister's unbridled enthusiasm on behalf of the local unfortunates, it seemed uncharitable of her to inform Cranbrook that his efforts were unwelcome.

Later in the week, following the minister's suggestion, Marie Fleur conducted school during the afternoon only to enable working children to complete a morning's toil. Bread, cheese, and milk were provided as added spurs to learning. She also outfitted the neediest scholars from a parish relief basket donated by the Reverend Millington's father-in-law, the vicar of the neighboring parish.

After the enthusiasm of the first week, however, only a handful of children continued to come to the drafty schoolroom, and Marie Fleur wondered if these few came more for the meal than for the lessons. Those who did attend had to wear their ragged outer clothing indoors because the room was so cold. Marie Fleur was not overly disappointed by the decline of students for as the inclement season progressed she had expected a drop in attendance, especially amongst those who had to travel from the earl's estates. One afternoon the last runny-nosed, grubby-handed waif was seated and the alphabet begun when she noticed a pale face peering hesitantly around the door.

"Maudie! Oh, come in. How glad I am to see you."

Maudie was uncomfortable sitting with the younger children so Marie Fleur led her to the teacher's table, hoping to put her advanced pupil at ease.

This was to be the first of many rewarding days. During the following weeks Marie Fleur lent Maudie books from the library at Langley Chase. Some of the volumes had illustrations, and Maudie pored over the pictures by the hour. Together they read simple poetry. Marie Fleur even began elementary French, hardly able to keep from joining Maudie's embarrassed laughter over her novel pronunciation of the French verbs. Each day when Marie Fleur arrived, Maudie was waiting on the doorstep, eager to begin her lessons. Friendship blossomed between them. So delighted was Marie Fleur with her pupil's progress, she could have hugged Maudie out of sheer joy. The few times she actually attempted to embrace her, however, Maudie drew away, uncomfortably reminding her of the difference in their stations.

By December, Maudie had learned to write a simple story, which, with much assistance, she read aloud to the others. The village children listened with varying degrees of interest, failing to appreciate the natural poetry of Maudie's prose.

When class was over and most of the younger children were trailing outside into the dusky afternoon, Marie Fleur caught Maudie's arm, urging her to stay.

"Not for long, milady. Really I can't," Maudie protested, glancing nervously toward the disappearing scholars.

"I won't keep you long. You see, we might be able to have a Christmas pageant in the church. The rector says he will assist us. I've plenty of things at home we can use for costumes. Can you help me with the little ones? I know everyone would enjoy it."

"Ooh, yes—but I—I mightn't be able to come tomorrer."

"Why not?"

"Me dad doesn't like me being gone so long."

Maudie's downcast eyes and uneasy manner alerted Marie Fleur to some problem as yet uncovered. "Doesn't your father want you to learn to read?"

"He says learnin' be wasted on a girl."

"Ignorance has little to do with sex. In fact, it would be good for your father to learn to write his name. Do you think he'd be interested?"

"No." Maudie shook her head, and she sidled around the doorjamb, anxious to be gone. Her crude cloak fashioned from a worn blanket snagged on a nail. "Bugger it," Maudie muttered, dragging at the coarse fabric.

"Here, let me help you," offered Marie Fleur, choosing to ignore Maudie's language. The girl's changed attitude puzzled her. During these past weeks they had become the greatest of friends, yet lately she had sensed a change in Maudie. Gone was the laughter, the exchanged confidences: Maudie had become unusually withdrawn.

As she was wrapping the rough homespun cloak about Maudie's thin frame, smiling as she tucked in the tie ends to form a scarf, Marie Fleur was shocked to feel a protrusion in the girl's abdomen. Surely Maudie could not be pregnant! Mrs. Leach did not allow her daughter the freedom of field and hayrick like most of the other youngsters. Maudie's morals were beyond question, or so she had been assured by the Reverend Millington.

Not waiting to be questioned, for her discovery was apparent on Lady Dowling's shocked face, Maudie bolted for the door. Marie Fleur was left standing on the threshold, watching the ragged little figure trudging home in the cold winter wind.

On Monday morning the Earl of Cranbrook's carter arrived at the parish hall with a dozen scarred desks, a table and chairs, and a huge box of teaching supplies. Swallowing her pride,

Marie Fleur did not refuse to accept this further attempt to woo her. These gifts were for the children, not herself. By such rationalization she salved her wavering conscience as the carters hefted the secondhand desks into place.

Marie Fleur could barely contain her excitement. To be honest she had already accepted that for the most part the village children would probably learn little beyond writing their own names, but Maudie Leach was different. In the wooden crate was a copy of Shakespeare, several volumes of poetry, and reams of beautiful pristine paper as well as ink, inkwells, pens, and a box of nibs. She could have danced for joy. Almost guiltily she realized Maudie was the one she wanted all this for because Maudie would appreciate it the most. Now she could replace Maudie's splintered slate with paper, pen, and ink. The girl would be able to take pride in her work. They could rewrite her story and make it into a book in time for Christmas.

After noon the handful of faithful scholars shuffled indoors, streaming noses and hands painful and reddened by chilblains ignored while they stood gaping at the transformation. To Marie Fleur's great disappointment, Maudie was not amongst them. When the girl did not show up for the rest of the week, she decided to visit the Leaches' cottage to find out what had happened. Her recent discovery might well be the reason behind Maudie's prolonged absence.

After Marie Fleur closed the school for the day, she walked up the deeply rutted lane in the gathering dusk. The winter sunset spread silver wisps in the sky, and a pale sulphurous yellow penetrated the mist over the distant hills. Trudging uphill to the cottage, she smiled ruefully as she considered her appearance. Her cloak was trimmed with faded red braid; the hem of her plain wool gown was worn. In her practical, unfashionable attire, she looked every inch the governess.

Mrs. Leach opened the door, her face paling when she beheld Lady Dowling on the doorstep.

"Is Maudie ill?" Marie Fleur asked, coming straight to the point.

"Not 'zactly, milady, not proper-like," mumbled Mrs. Leach.

"What's the matter with her then?"

"I can't say—"

"Oh, Ma, stop it!"

Maudie's shrill, tearful voice echoed from the smoky depths

of the room. Without waiting to be invited, Marie Fleur stepped inside and closed the door behind her. To her horror she saw Maudie dressed in a ragged shift, her hair matted, her face blotchy. There was no longer any doubt about her impending maternity. Maudie looked like a stick figure, her thin white arms and legs jutting in an ungainly fashion from her swollen body.

"Maudie!"

Defiantly the girl raised her head. "It ain't wot you thinks, milady," she declared fiercely.

"Hush, girl," admonished her mother.

Maudie broke away from her mother's restraining hand. "No, Ma, I won't hush. We can't hide it forever."

"It's all right, Maudie. There's nothing to be ashamed of." Marie Fleur reached for Maudie's thin, rough hand. "Tell me about it so that I can help you."

"'Elp me? 'ow's you going to do that?"

Marie Fleur was shocked by the sudden gleam of age-old knowledge in Maudie's thin face. This girl was a stranger. What had happened to the eager scholar, the poet, her friend? "I can try to help you, Maudie."

"'Ow?"

"The father of your child must be made to marry you."

The girl's bitter laughter chilled her. Mrs. Leach turned away, shuffling to the fireplace where she turned over potatoes baking in the ash.

"Won't do no good. Go on, you'd best leave me alone. Beggin' your pardon, milady, but I don't belong with you no more. Out here it's a different world from what you knows, ain't it, Ma?"

The bitter question went unanswered. Maudie trudged disconsolately to the rag-covered bed in the corner beside the hearth.

"Mrs. Leach, surely you know the father of Maudie's child. He must be made to support her—"

"No, milady. No—you'd best go like she says."

"Why won't you let me help you? I care what happens to Maudie. I don't know how I can mend matters, but I intend to try."

"You've been me friend, and I'm happy for that," Maudie said, her eyes dark pools in her pale face. "I know'd the school wouldn't be for me. But I wanted to learn so bad...." She broke off, her eyes filling with tears. "It's no use now," she whispered, swallowing and staring into the fire. "It's too late. Don't make no trouble for me."

"You mustn't protect him. He has a responsibility to you."

Maudie shook her head.

"Don't you even know who he is?" Marie Fleur asked at last, loath to brand the girl immoral yet knowing no other reason for her reluctance to name her child's father.

Maudie's blue eyes gleamed fiercely in the fire's glow. "Though I'm poor and dirty, I'm not a slut, Your Ladyship. Yes, I knows who he is!"

"Who then?"

The imperious demand went unanswered for a moment as the two Leach women exchanged glances. In that moment Marie Fleur was sickened by the similarity between them. During these past weeks Maudie had aged until she was a younger version of her mother. The hope, the intelligence, the vitality were gone.

"My Dan'l be the one. Our Maudie's a good girl," Mrs. Leach explained, raising her head defiantly as she salvaged a little pride.

For a moment Marie Fleur did not comprehend. "Daniel?" she repeated. Then suddenly she understood. Daniel was the name Mrs. Leach used when speaking about her husband. "You surely don't mean—"

"Me father—that's right. 'Appens all the time 'round 'ere."

"But you . . . why didn't you stop him?" Marie Fleur demanded angrily of Mrs. Leach. "How could you stand by and allow it?"

"It's clear you ain't never been in my shoes, Your Ladyship. And no disrespect to you, but you'd best be leaving. Dan'l comes 'ome about now. 'Tis best you be gone when he comes in."

"No. I want to speak to him. Someone needs to give him a—"

"Give him a what?"

All three women raised wide eyes to the doorway where a huge bear of a man filled the space. As he lurched indoors the odor of stale ale filled the room.

"Oh, Dan'l, Her Ladyship be just leaving."

Maudie merely turned away, burrowing defensively in the bedcovers.

"I've just discovered your daughter's condition is due to you, Mr. Leach," Marie Fleur began, facing him with flashing eyes. "What do you have to say in your defense?"

The red-faced laborer blinked owlishly, then lurched forward, tipping over a wooden stool. "Condition? That's a fancy word and no mistake. Whelping you means, don't ye? Let's call a spade a spade. Don't you go gettin' the wrong idea. Our Maudie's no slut. We keeps 'er 'ome of a night." He brushed aside his wife's ineffectual efforts to quiet him. "Aye, 'appen I know about it, Your Ladyship, seeing as 'ow I done it."

"You don't even deny it! You sound almost pleased with yourself."

The shaggy head, large as an animal's, came up, his red, piggy eyes glaring with hostility at the noblewoman who dared cross-examine him in the sanctity of his own home.

"Do you think any man'd want to mount *'er?*" he spat, jerking his thumb toward his wife. The woman's grayish face under its mop of stringy hair tightened in pain at his insult. "Why, boar'd be hard put to service 'er. Now, me fine lady, before you comes in here laying' down the law, let me remind you Maudie's mine to do what I wants with. And that's the way it is. Now I'll thank ye to get out and take yer fancy book larnin' with you. Puttin' ideas into the little cow's 'ead—it's not right. Her life's 'ere in this muck 'eap, not prancing about at tea parties. . . ."

Daniel Leach stopped in mid-speech as he was grasped from behind and swung about. Everything happened so quickly, the women stood like figures in a tableau. Framed in the open doorway, surrounded by whirling mist, stood the Earl of Cranbrook and his groom. The earl's face was hard as granite, his pale eyes gleaming like slivers of ice in the weak light.

"How dare you address a lady thus, you swine?" he demanded, his voice clarion clear in the muffled night. "By God, I'll have your neck for it!"

Large though he was, Daniel Leach stumbled against the wall, thrust aside by the earl as he strode inside the room. Ineffectually Leach raised his huge fists, threatening the nobleman in a false show of bravado. "Get out, you bloody toff. This be my 'ouse. If ye don't—"

He never finished the sentence, for the Earl of Cranbrook lashed him across the face with his riding crop. "Silence, you animal!"

The farm laborer clutched his bleeding face, moaning in shock and pain. His wife, darting a frightened glance at the angry earl, went to his side to comfort him. "You've 'urt my Dan'l bad," she wailed, as he thrust her aside, swearing at her.

Marie Fleur watched the unfolding scene in horror. Desperately she looked at Maudie, mutely pleading for support. The girl refused to meet her gaze.

"Maudie?"

"I told you to go. You should've listened," muttered the girl.

"Yes, you should've listened. We both told you to go. Now my Dan'l's 'urt bad," shrilled Mrs. Leach, glaring at them defiantly.

The odorous room whirled slightly in a nauseating blur before righting itself. A leaden weight settled in her heart as Marie Fleur resolutely turned her back on the proud cottagers. She felt betrayed. Her hope, her trust, her ambition for Maudie had been turned back upon her in open hostility. These people were no longer the obsequious, cap-twisting peasants of her acquaintance. A rebellious, dangerous mood had been generated, leaving her uneasy, almost fearful as she beheld their undivided loyalty despite the crime Maudie's father had committed against his daughter.

"Come." Cranbrook's voice sounded gentle, distant. "As for you, you swine, you'd better lie low for a while, or I'll have you horsewhipped," he threatened, spinning about to face Daniel Leach.

The sweating, bleeding laborer swayed as he tried to maintain his balance. When he faced the nobleman in whom centuries of power and breeding had created contempt toward him, Daniel Leach's bluff facade crumbled.

"No 'arm was meant. 'Er was interferin' in family matters," he mumbled, his eyes moving shiftily from one to the other. "No 'arm was meant, Your Lordship, no 'arm," he repeated as a wave of sobriety flooded his muddled brain to remind him of the danger in crossing the ruling class.

"Thank you, Geoffrey. I'm more than ready to leave," Marie Fleur whispered, fighting weak, betraying tears. She took the earl's proffered arm and, holding her head high, without another word she walked into the misty night.

The earl took Marie Fleur onto his own horse, where he wrapped his caped cloak about her to keep out the cold. Tears of humiliation stung her eyes. When she had set out for the Leaches' cottage she had never expected such a horrible ending to her visit. Even Maudie had turned on her. All her hope, her enthusiasm for teaching a bright disadvantaged child lay trampled on the beaten earth floor of the Leaches' rank hovel. Though she would have liked to rest her head against the welcome masculine shoulder so conveniently accessible and give vent to her bottled emotions, Marie Fleur steeled herself against the temptation, too aware of the identity of her rescuer.

"Thank you for your timely intervention," she said stiffly. "I'm very grateful to you."

"You should've known it was unwise to confront the boar in his own sty."

"I went to see what was wrong with Maudie."

"Maudie? Oh, the dirty little filly in the corner. One of your students?"

"Yes."

"Well, my dear, I take it you found out."

"Yes."

"And the terrible truth is?" he prompted, urging his mount along the oak-lined drive of Langley Chase.

A dozen lights gleamed from the windows of the house, promising welcome warmth. Marie Fleur shivered at the sight. Never before had she been so glad to see her own home. The hateful incident in the Leaches' primitive dwelling had left a foul taste in her mouth. "She's pregnant by her own father," she said finally.

"I see." The earl glanced sideways at his lovely passenger, able to understand her deep concern while feeling none himself. "Surely you knew those things went on."

"Oh, yes. I've not spent my life in a convent."

"Then why are you so angry?"

"Because Maudie was an excellent pupil. She wasn't like the others—dull as ditchwater. She had vitality, curiosity, and she was coming along so well," she ground out, anger radiating from her being.

They discussed the matter no further, riding the few hundred yards to the entrance in silence. The groom took the horses, and the earl escorted Marie Fleur indoors.

Over a glass of mulled wine before the blazing hearth, Cranbrook resumed his inquiry.

"You know, I should be horsewhipped myself for allowing

you to get so heavily involved with the peasants."

"You have little to do with it."

"There you are wrong. I know what insensitive animals they can be. There's no excuse for my allowing you to visit their filthy hovels, none at all."

Marie Fleur's eyes flashed. "You don't own me."

He smiled slightly at her angry retort. "Do I not? What of your vast debts, both monetary and intangible?"

"Debts?"

"Surely you've not forgotten. This house, the furnishings—"

"Stop it! I'm in no mood to reopen that discussion tonight."

"When will you be in the mood?"

"Never!"

The smile faded from his haughty features. "I see. Never's a long time, Marie Fleur. Rather longer than you have, I'm afraid."

"What do you mean?"

"Only that my patience has run its limit. I've tried to behave in a gentlemanly manner toward you. I've even proposed marriage to placate your missish scruples. And what do I have to show for it?"

"From the beginning I told you I wasn't interested in your suit."

"I've even supported your foolish little schoolteacher charade by purchasing desks and writing materials for creatures who don't know one end of a pen from the other—"

"I never asked you for a thing," she blazed, matching his mounting anger.

"You're right. You did not. I provided the gifts merely out of a desire to see you happy. You owe me nothing for them."

"Thank you."

They glared at each other. Marie Fleur's hand hovered around the bellpull as she prepared to call the servants to forcibly eject the earl if necessary. "You're always trying to be a part of my life. It's an attention I do not wish, nor can I endure it a moment longer. If I'm indebted to you, it's only my husband's debts that are owed—nothing else. I've thanked you for the school supplies. And I thanked you for rescuing me from a situation that was of my own foolish making. Now, will you please go? I'm tired, and I wish to retire."

"And if I decline?"

"I'll have you thrown out."

Cranbrook stood before the hearth, the firelight leaping over his dark blue high-collared coat, dancing flashes from his embroidered white marcella waistcoat. Impeccable, menacing, he stared at her as if unable to comprehend her final statement.

"You'd dare to do that?" he asked at last, his tone incredulous.

"I hope such drastic action won't be necessary. A gentleman usually does not remain where he is not welcome."

The earl studied the mirror finish on his black Hessian boots. "You're a very foolish woman," he said at last, his voice smooth. "You have everything to gain and nothing to lose from an alliance with me."

Marie Fleur raised her hand and pulled the gold tasseled cord. The bell jangled discordantly through the empty marble-floored corridors. Soon the steps of a servant hastening to his mistress's summons could be heard drawing closer.

"I will not be thwarted," the earl declared as he turned to pick up his cloak and top hat. "Perhaps you're unaware of my power. I'm a bosom companion of the heir to the throne. My best friends number the great of this nation—"

"You're no longer welcome in my house."

"But soon it shall be my house. And then, my dear Marie Fleur, I shall do as I damned well please."

With that final snarled threat, the earl picked up his riding crop and, slinging his cloak about his shoulders, he strode toward the double doors as a servant entered the room.

"Please show the Earl of Cranbrook out."

"*Au revoir* . . . till next time, my dear Lady Dowling."

Long after he had departed, Marie Fleur stood trembling before the hearth. Tears dammed until now, trickled down her cheeks. She felt betrayed, battered, assaulted. It was possible she was reacting too strongly to tonight's disturbing events. There was no denying she had hoped for much for poor Maudie Leach, a hope that was now dashed. Yet might she not find a place for Maudie in her own household? The earl's threat that he'd soon possess Langley Chase hovered menacingly about the room. It meant she would have nothing to offer Maudie Leach. Besides, Langley Hall was too close to home to offer much improvement in the girl's situation. Here she would be ostracized by the other servants, who were mostly locals, at the same time as she would be readily available for her father's lust. Marie Fleur was no longer sure Maudie even wanted to be saved from her sordid circumstances. The unfathomable expression on the girl's blotchy, pale face seemed far from one of friendship. Uncle James's favorite maxim, "Blood is thicker than water," had certainly been proved true at the Leaches' cottage. After being degraded by her husband, that poor drab woman had rushed to comfort the brute. Maudie, too, appeared to side with her parents.

Not usually one to crumble at the first salvo, Marie Fleur nevertheless felt defeated by the unexpected outcome of her generosity. She knew the Reverend Millington's eldest daughter had expressed an interest in serving as a teacher in the parish school, and feeling as she did, Marie Fleur wondered if it would be wiser to withdraw from a situation in which she had become too personally involved.

As if the brush with Maudie's father had not been unpleasant enough, she now had the added injustice of Cranbrook's anger to bear. The earl had left, but there would be tomorrow and the next day, next week, next month . . . and soon the settlement of Will's debts would be demanded. So far no serious buyers for the house had come forward. Though the solicitor assured her these things took time, she suspected the earl of having a hand in the situation. Perhaps no one dared make a serious offer for what he so obviously considered his own.

Marie Fleur paced before the hearth, her fists clenched. Treacherously her mind strayed to Brandon, and a rush of delicious weakness invaded her body. How she longed for his arms! Why had he not sent a message to her? Surely his latest smuggling venture was over by now. Had she placed too much trust in a man's heated avowal of love?

The marble mantel felt ice-cold as she placed her blazing cheek against its welcome smoothness. Out of the corner of her eye Marie Fleur glimpsed a folded white card edged in gold propped against the cherub-adorned timepiece. It was an invitation from Anabelle Reid to spend Christmas in London. She could virtually recite the bubbly missive from memory. A heady round of parties, dinners, visits to the theater and the opera, glimpses of titled personages and even an audience with the prince regent himself were all mentioned as tantalizing incentives to accept. When she had first received the invitation, she had mentally declined with a shudder, for she had expected to spend Christmas in Norfolk. Then a letter arrived from Ed-

gerton Heath urging her not to come because Lavinia's latest
ailment was thought to be contagious. She wondered if she
could stay at Yew Trees Lodge and avoid whatever infection
was brewing, but the realization that Cranbrook would never
allow her any peace dissuaded her from the journey. She was
not anxious to find an unwelcome guest on her doorstep.

She had not yet declined Anabelle's invitation. While she
was not overjoyed by the idea of spending Christmas in London,
the prospect of the increasing gloom of winter alone in the
country, bombarded by the Earl of Cranbrook's unwelcome
attentions, was far worse. It almost seemed worth catching
Lavinia's rash to be free of him.

She could accept Anabelle's invitation, safe in the knowledge that she would be in the company of others. Perhaps an
overdose of frivolity and mindless twittering would be the perfect antidote for her current melancholia. Regency society in
festive mood might even mend the heartache caused by Brandon's neglect. He did love her—he had vowed as much, she
repeated stubbornly—yet why had he not visited her, or even
written?

Resolutely Marie Fleur marched to the inlaid writing table
and took out pen, ink, and paper.

"My dear Anabelle," she wrote.

Chapter 8

MARIE FLEUR STOOD at the window overlooking the square, its bare trees shrouded by mist behind tall iron railings. The December dusk, thick with coal smoke and London grime, swirled around the chimney pots before finally settling on the plane trees in the deserted gardens below.

The Reids' elegant town house stood near St. James's Park in the area made fashionable since the Prince Regent had lavishly remodeled Carlton House. In recent years the Reid family's stately Georgian dwelling had been renovated, its plain brick facade camouflaged by the now-fashionable stucco. Bowed iron railings had been installed to form balconies on the upper floors. Flanking the steep front steps were twisted wrought-iron railings, while an elaborately designed staircase with iron balusters adorned with vines and ivy leaves climbed the four stories to the attics. Even the mansion's furnishings had been given an up-to-the-minute look with the addition of lavish silk draperies and lacquered Oriental pieces. The drawing room, of which Anabelle was most proud, was hung with yellow silk *á la mode chinoise* in slavish imitation of the Prince Regent's own drawing room in Carlton House.

Marie Fleur had been in London for two weeks. At first the gaiety of the dinner parties and visits to the theater had diverted her. But gradually the entertainment began to pall. Anabelle, amusing at first, had become boring at best; at worst, she was positively nerve-jarring. As Marie Fleur gazed into the darkening street, virtually deserted except for two ragged, barefoot crossing sweepers, she fought a mood of increasing melancholy. Christmas lay around the corner. Thank goodness they were to spend the festive season at a mutual friend's country house; it would make a welcome change from grimy London's glittering pleasures.

"There you are—my dear, you aren't even dressed!" shrilled Anabelle from the doorway.

"I'm almost dressed. Perhaps you should go without me. The prospect of another of Lettice Beardsley's soirees doesn't seem inspiring. Why don't I meet you later at the theater?"

"I won't hear of it! You'll have no escort."

"Surely Poggy will have returned by then."

"Given Poggy's excesses, that's hardly predictable."

"Once I arrive there'll be escorts aplenty. You forget, Anabelle, I'm still officially in mourning."

"Ha! Mourning! No widow ever looked lovelier. Tongues are wagging all over town. Very well then, you aggravating chit, I'll go without you. I don't know what Lettice will say. Besides, what will you do with yourself? It's a good two hours before the opera."

"I'm going to write a letter."

"A letter! Lud, what a bore you are! No one stays home from a party to write letters."

"Except me. Now, go on, enjoy yourself. Find out all Lettice's secrets. I'll meet you at the theater. What's tonight's performance, by the way?"

"Heaven knows—some boring dirge most likely. Very well, love, I must fly." Anabelle placed a cool kiss on Marie Fleur's cheek before she rustled from the room. The skirt of her gown, blue silk overlaid with gauze, formed a feather-trimmed train that swept majestically over the polished parquet floor. Anabelle casually slung over her arm her blue velvet spencer edged with fur and sparkling with diamond-adorned frog closings, allowing it to trail the floor as she left.

A few minutes later Marie Fleur watched Anabelle depart for Lettice's early supper. It was quite dark now. The twin carriage lamps cast great glowing haloes in the hazy atmosphere. After the opera a second meal would be taken at Viscount Lindsay's Portland Place mansion. All those elaborate rich dishes washed down by copious quantities of champagne sometimes made Marie Fleur long for a simple piece of bread and honey accompanied by a cool glass of fresh milk.

As the horses clopped away, their steel-shod hooves echoing over the cobbles, she drew the heavy orange velvet curtains, shutting out the cold December night. Marie Fleur went to the deep rosewood wardrobe and withdrew her opera gown. While not formal mourning, the garment was subdued, almost plain. The deep wine velvet of the high-waisted, puff-sleeved gown glowed richly in the firelight. The front of the gown was covered in Brussels lace dyed to match the velvet. A heavy velvet and lace cape, deeply edged with Russian sable, completed the costume. A discreet feathered fan, low-heeled black silk shoes, and pristine white kid gloves reaching to the elbow were the accessories she had chosen for this evening. A velvet headdress capped by two wine ostrich plumes completed her outfit. Anabelle herself had approved the accessories, favoring the plumes over a floral cluster because plumes were somehow funereal: "One must bow slightly to convention. After all, my dear, it's barely six months since poor Will's passing."

Marie Fleur spread the dress across the bed. More than a few raised eyebrows had greeted her emergence into society. And though she often wore black, it was more because black contrasted superbly with her blond curls than out of deference to a custom she deemed hypocritical and outmoded. She was aware she had set a multitude of tongues awag with her cavalier attitude. Let them wag.

Marie Fleur pulled a face as she settled down at the carved rosewood desk. A pearl-domed lamp shed a pool of soft light over her writing materials as she sat thinking about what she would write. On arrival in London she had written to Maudie Leach offering her a position in Norfolk at the local vicarage; the girl's sordid home life and impending maternity had been explained and charitably accepted there. An added nudge from the Reverend Millington might encourage her to accept this chance for a new life. With that in mind she penned a brief, informal note to the reverend urging him to action on her behalf. Though she could never feel quite the same about Maudie after that dreadful scene, Marie Fleur had begun to understand why the girl had sided with her own kind. Subsequently her feelings of betrayal had slowly evaporated, leaving concern for the girl's future in their place. The wife of the vicar to whom she was sending Maudie was a kindly soul and would give the girl the utmost encouragement.

The letter to the Reverend Millington sealed, Marie Fleur stared at the flickering oil lamp, wondering what news she should tell Nancy, whom Marie Fleur had taught to read some years earlier. Any information about London would be of interest to her maid, who had always longed to visit the capital. She began the letter in a chatty vein, telling Nancy about last night's supper party. Soon her mind strayed from Nancy, from London itself, to that mist-locked night on Romney Marsh. Her heart lurched at the vivid memory. Why, Brandon, why? Her lips mouthed the question while her hand, poised above the paper and seemingly possessed of a will of its own, wrote his name. She was desperate to know his whereabouts, yet she dared not ask Anabelle for news. Empty-headed and vain though Poggy's sister was, she was as sharp as a ferret; a few chance questions followed by a betraying blush, and Anabelle would guess the truth. At this time Marie Fleur could not risk exposure. If exposure there was to be, it had to come from Brandon himself.

The Reid family carriage clopped along Pall Mall toward Covent Garden. The gas lamps lining the Mall shed soft haloes over the damp pavement, gleaming and shimmering in ever-shifting pools. Seated within the dark, swaying conveyance, Marie Fleur felt cut off and alone. It was strange to be riding through one of the greatest cities in the world, teeming with multitudes of people, and to consider oneself alone. She straightened in her seat and fussily adjusted her bobbing plumes. It wasn't just strange; it was ridiculous! Mooning about like a lovestruck girl because some conceited dandy had withdrawn his attentions. If, and when, Brandon chose to contact her, she would listen to his explanations of his absence. If his story was plausible, she might even accept it. If not—well, that remained to be seen. Marie Fleur sat even straighter against the quilted leather upholstery. How she ached to see him. She wanted to fly into his arms, eager to forgive him all transgressions in exchange for the comforting passion he so readily ignited. Her mouth tightened. And if she did just that, she condemned herself to a lifetime of indifferent treatment. Their love had bloomed untainted on Romney Marsh, yet here, in Mayfair's luxurious perfumed salons, affairs of the heart were conducted to a different set of rules. Boredom, indifference, and languor were the mode, pursuit of a love object generally veiled behind a set of movements as carefully structured as a dance. Brandon was used to women of his own upbringing. Perhaps her eagerness marked her as provincial.

Before the brightly lit theater, Marie Fleur alighted from the carriage, feeling conspicuous as top-hatted heads swiveled eagerly in her direction. As Anabelle predicted, Poggy had not returned from his engagement in time to accompany her, so she had traveled unescorted to Covent Garden. She held her head high as she entered the theater, conscious of the finely dressed gentlemen who ogled her appreciatively. Because she had arrived without an escort, they probably assumed her to be a Cyprian, one of the professional ladies of the *ton* whose showcase was a box at the opera. The front line boxes were often rented for the season by these beautiful courtesans to be used as shop windows for their charms.

Marie Fleur kept a fixed smile on her perfect features, hurrying so as not to allow them an opportunity to approach her. In a way, she supposed such avid appreciation was flattering; on further consideration, she decided it was definitely preferable to being ignored.

Anabelle's party had gathered in the chandelier-lit Round Room. The women wore a veritable hothouse of artificial blooms adorning bright gowns or intricately entwined into chignons and sleek coiffures of cascading ringlets. The men in the group were the epitome of fashion in their perfectly tailored black coats and black silk breeches popularized by the dandy, Beau Brummell. Flat-heeled patent leather pumps replaced the men's usual tall Hessians. Many a pearl or diamond stickpin gleamed amid ruffled cravats or was centered elegantly on the excessively tall, plain white cravats favored by some gentlemen in imitation of the prince regent, who, it was rumored, began the fashion to conceal a bout of swollen glands.

Marie Fleur was greeted eagerly, swept into the welcoming arms of Anabelle. Her bevy of female cousins, after their first effusive greeting, began to eye her with jealousy. Marie Fleur saw the spite, the envy reflected in their pinched faces, and this newfound hostility made her uncomfortable. She turned her attention to admiring the opera house. Everywhere she looked she was met by a blaze of light, glinting flashes from crystal chandeliers, gilded moldings, and jeweled patrons alike, its golden brilliance dazzling to the eye. Swagged velvet draperies, Venetian mirrors, and richly patterned carpeting set the elegant tone.

"My dear Marie Fleur, I hope you won't be too disappointed. Tonight's a positive mishmash of pieces. An act of this, an act of that, with some Neapolitan songs sandwiched in between. It's as if opera were an array of pies from which slivers are casually selected," remarked Teddy Brooks glumly. He had taken it upon himself to act as her escort.

"I'm not as familiar as you with the operas, so perhaps I'll not be critical," Marie Fleur remarked with a charming smile, glad to take young Brooks's arm. His company would be a

shield against the unwelcome attentions of a group of unat-
tached young bucks who were even now moving in for the kill.

Swishing back his black satin-lined cloak, Teddy Brooks
straightened his rounded shoulders in an effort to appear more
manly and, bursting with pride over his good fortune in being
allowed to escort so lovely a creature, he sallied forth with her
to his box. They were accompanied by three pale-faced females
attended by a formidable dowager whose husband was well
into his fifth port. "Distant cousins from Hampshire," whispered Teddy half-apologetically.

Even after she was comfortably seated in her gilded chair,
her feathered fan spread before her, Marie Fleur was still conscious of the lascivious glances cast in her direction. She was
a beautiful newcomer to society, and she appeared unat-
tached—what more encouragement did the young blades need?
And though she was a houseguest of the Reids, Anabelle's own
amorous adventures, rather than dissuading would-be admirers,
served merely to encourage them. She need not fear being
embarrassed by a proposition now that she was in Teddy Brooks's
protective custody. His presence would temporarily halt the
avalanche of unwanted interest. For this evening at least, slav-
ishly abiding by their own code, the predatory males considered
her Brooks's territory.

Anabelle had contrived to sit in an adjoining box with a
handsome houseguest of her cousin Olivia. The young man
had recently returned from a grouse shoot in Yorkshire, and
though usually bored to tears by sporting tales, tonight Anabelle
hung on her companion's every word, pumping him for details
of his adventure. Marie Fleur smiled knowingly. Though unable to hear what was being said, she knew Anabelle was
flirting shamelessly with her unsuspecting quarry. Oh, he might
think it was his charm that had wooed her, but Anabelle had
singled him out weeks ago as likely prey.

The orchestra was tuning up, discordant notes floating up
to the tiers of boxes, which were gradually filling as titled
patrons noisily gravitated toward their seats. Finally the red
velvet gilt-edged curtains slid open to reveal an exotic, if slightly
confusing, scene of Oriental splendor. All around her Marie
Fleur heard muttered questions over this staging for the first
act of the Pacitta opera.

A stiff gold-lettered program was thrust into her hand. Marie
Fleur turned to thank her benefactor, discovering to her surprise

that Teddy Brooks's mousy cousins and their chaperone were gone. Instead a lone male figure stood in the shadows against the closed red velvet curtains at the rear of the box. He stepped forward, swishing a voluminous cloak across an empty chair before sitting beside her.

"Where's everyone?" Marie Fleur whispered hoarsely, her attention fixed onstage.

"Sent conveniently to another box, thank God." The unexpectedly supercilious tone of the Earl of Cranbrook froze her to the marrow.

"You! How dare you?"

"I dare, my dear Marie Fleur, because I pay the rent on this box."

As he slid into the gilt chair beside her, she began to rise, but he placed a firm hand on her arm to restrain her.

"Don't be a little fool. You'll cause too much comment if you leave now," he hissed menacingly.

She swallowed and sat down again. He was right, of course. The first duet was coming to an end, and the diminutive tenor and his fat soprano were preparing to take their bows. Polite applause rippled through the house interspersed with an occasional boo in protest against the inappropriate stage set, which the patrons surmised had been orchestrated in deference to the prince regent's obession with things Oriental. Tonight, however, the royal box was conspicuously empty.

Between acts Anabelle bobbed her head around the partition of the adjoining box, her conspiratorial smile telling Marie Flcur she had been a willing party to the earl's deception. Before she was able to leave, or even tell her noble suitor what she thought of his foisting himself unbidden upon her, a crowd of mutual acquaintances filled the exit to the box. Amid much chat and laughter, much pumping of hands and proffered glasses of champagne, Cranbrook received their congratulations on his winning stable, his mounts having earned a respectable purse during the year's race meets. Marie Fleur sat in uncomfortable silence, stewing over the heated dialogue she would inevitably exchange with the earl. From a box in the upper tier Teddy Brooks, looking decidedly uncomfortable, waved sheepishly to her. It seemed he had not been as willing as Anabelle to play along with the earl's demand. Marie Fleur smiled and nodded to him, anxious to show she did not blame him for giving up his place in her box. The earl could hardly cause her

unpleasantness before an audience of thousands. Besides, if he
reopened a discussion of his demands, she would silence him
in order to listen to the music.

Between operatic acts a young, strikingly lovely Italian soprano, Gabriella Vasco, was scheduled to sing. The young
blades set up a thunderous cheer, pounding uproariously when
she appeared, their enthusiasm increased no doubt by the intermission champagne.

Marie Fleur studied the dark-haired young woman through
the earl's opera glasses. At such close inspection her beauty
was undiminished. Dressed in a voluminous full-skirted tulle
gown strewn with garlands of pink roses, the petite Italian
woman had the appearance of a beautiful china doll. Her perfect
face, though clearly accented with cosmetics, was serene.
Heavily lashed dark eyes and a pouting underlip added the
suggestion of passion to an otherwise madonna-perfect face.
Her full breasts, tiny waist, and daintily exposed ankles were
further objects of wonder. Gabriella Vasco took a deep breath,
the movement eliciting gasps of masculine approval as her
swelling bodice threatened to expose even more of her charms.
Countless opera glasses focused unmovingly on her considerable assets as she began the first of a medley of hauntingly
lovely Neapolitan songs.

"She's beautiful," Marie Fleur commented to Cranbrook,
who was leaning forward on the edge of the box in rapt attention.

"Yes, isn't she. Yet I far prefer blonds," he remarked chiv-
alrously. "Rumor has it she was mistress to Murat, Boney's
puppet king of Naples. Her affections are currently captured
by a gentleman of our acquaintance. . . . Oh, *brava, signorina,
brava.*"

The ensuing wave of applause ended their conversation. A
pang of unease churned Marie Fleur's stomach. She was not
to know its cause until the following intermission. Through the
next boring act of yet another opera sandwiched in this mixed
bill, she fought to stay awake. Boredom made her sleepy, yet
to openly fall asleep in so conspicuous a box would be social
suicide. Anabelle would never forgive her for the lapse, and
she supposed she did owe the Reids some consideration.

The intermission parade began almost before the second act
was over. The final presentation was to be the second act of
the opening Pacitta opera, and it promised to be lengthy. The

ton was in dire need of fortifying beverages to weather the storm. The earl leaned over the front of the box to wave to someone in the pit before suggesting, "Why don't we go downstairs to meet the little Neapolitan nightingale."

The Round Room was packed with glittering patrons, an avid group surrounding the sensational new soprano. Gabriella Vasco seemed even more diminutive beside the tall, broad-shouldered males who pressed bouquets upon her and plied her with crystal glasses of sparkling champagne. The vivacious Italian woman bubbled with gaiety as she basked in the compliments of her many admirers.

"*Signorina,* your beauty is as exquisite as your voice," complimented the earl as he bowed over her tiny hand glittering with diamonds. "When you sang I was transported. . . ."

"Flatterer. But you charm me so beautifully, you're forgiven," laughed Gabriella. Her musical, prettily accented speech vastly enhanced her appearance.

"And here's another lovely creature to sparkle in our midst."

"Together they form the perfect representation of light and dark."

The flattering chorus of male voices grew louder as Marie Fleur smiled and inclined her head in acknowledgment of their praise. It was not enough. Eager hands propelled her through the throng until she stood beside Gabriella Vasco. Assorted gasps of approval sounded as several gentlemen studied the charming couple through their pince-nez, fully appreciating this delightful contrast in feminine beauty.

"Allow me to introduce Lady Dowling. She's a houseguest of the Reids. Signorina Vasco," said the earl.

The two women smiled politely at each other, but there was little genuine warmth in their exchange. Gabriella Vasco resented Marie Fleur's intrusion in her province. To be contrasted, however favorably, with this blond amazon, was not to her liking. In truth Marie Fleur's height was little more than average, but beside the diminutive Italian she appeared unusually tall.

"Your recital was most charming, Signorina Vasco."

"*Grazie.* Very kind of you to say so."

The brief exchange at an end, Marie Fleur stepped back. At that moment there came a flurry of movement from the far end of the room, and the admirers fell back to allow someone to come forward.

"Caro!" shrieked Gabriella, her dark face animated with pleasure. Casually Marie Fleur turned toward the newcomer who was shouldering his way through the throng.

"Didn't know you were back in town till this afternoon when I saw you large as life in Almack's window. Welcome back, old fellow."

The greetings echoed and reechoed amidst hearty slaps on the back. Gabriella raced forward, virtually leaping in the gentleman's arms as she crooned endearments in her native tongue.

When Cranbrook stepped forward to offer his own greeting, Marie Fleur glanced up in curiosity, wondering which gentleman of her acquaintance was Gabriella's lover. The smile froze on her mouth as she encountered large, dark-lashed gray eyes studying her over Gabriella's flower-festooned curls. The handsome face that haunted her dreams swam before her in sickening clarity. To make matters worse, Brandon did not say a word to acknowledge her presence. Marie Fleur opened her mouth and closed it soundlessly like a fish. The earth-shattering encounter lasted only a few moments, yet it seemed an eternity that she stood frozen with shock, their gazes locked, a multitude of unvoiced questions passing between them.

"Brandy, you devil! Trust you to beat us to the punch. Didn't even know such an exquisite creature existed," thundered Poggy Reid, who had belatedly joined the opera party.

Aware of Cranbrook's searching gaze, Marie Fleur desperately fought to regain her composure. A hollow feeling spread through her stomach and circled upward, threatening to become nausea.

"Of course, my dear, you already know Brandon Nicholas." The earl's precise voice finally penetrated her numbed brain.

"Yes, Mr. Nicholas is known to me."

Brandon stood before her, politely inclining his head. He was dressed more appropriately for riding than an evening at the theater. When she noticed a folded cape and riding crop on a gilded chair beside the refreshment table, she decided he must have just arrived. Brandon's black serge coat was impeccably tailored; his cream skintight breeches were molded like a second skin. Black, highly polished boots turned down with scarlet and an elaborately tied snowy cravat completed his dress. Between his closely curled black cap of hair and his broad, sculpted black shoulders, his face appeared unusually pale as he spoke and politely touched her hand.

"My dear Lady Dowling, how pleasant to see you again."

His fingers glanced off hers, and Marie Fleur shuddered, afraid she would swoon. Gabriella Vasco was watching them closely, a predatory gleam in her brown eyes. The Italian woman clearly considered Brandon her property.

After greeting Marie Fleur, Brandon stepped aside, turning his attention back to Gabriella and his laughing friends. He continued to ignore Marie Fleur, and the pain of his betrayal felt raw as a fresh wound.

"Come, my love, the next act will soon be starting."

As if in a dream, Marie Fleur moved to Cranbrook's side. Brandon watched her, his expression questioning. While she had hardly expected him to reveal their recent intimacy before the others, she had not been prepared to be treated as a virtual stranger. How could he ignore her after the passionate love they had shared. the vows they had exchanged? Was it because Gabriella watched for signs of betrayal? The Italian woman appeared perfectly capable of clawing out her eyes if she as much as suspected Marie Fleur had more than a casual interest in her handsome lover. Had Brandon allowed everyone to think they shared merely a passing acquaintance to spare Gabriella? She must also be the reason behind his puzzling absence from Langley.

Resentment and anguish welled up inside her, threatening to choke her in its intensity. So devastating was her discovery of Brandon's infidelity, Marie Fleur stumbled blindly on the hem of her gown. The earl, ever considerate, bore her up, remarking solicitously upon the dangerous wrinkles in the Oriental carpet. She glanced over her shoulder to find Brandon's gaze riveted on her. A band of heightened color suffused his high cheekbones where the skin appeared taut. His sensual mouth was thinner, sterner than she remembered. He watched her, his features impassive, no trace of tenderness or love softening the sculpted perfection. His remote expression was a further blow until she realized its probable cause. Brandon assumed she was attending the opera with Cranbrook! He might even think the earl was her lover. Hysterical laughter surged within her and tears glittered in her violet eyes, adding an unnatural sparkle as she gripped the earl's arm.

"Geoffrey, what would I do without you," she said gaily, praying Brandon would hear, wanting to wound him as painfully as he had wounded her. Damn him for making her want him, for taking her heart and crushing it under the finely turned heel of his mirror-bright Hessians. He deserved pain in return, far more than any chance remark she made to the Earl of Cranbrook could produce.

Somehow Marie Fleur found her way back to her box. She shivered with cold. Her hands were like ice, her legs trembling. She drew her cape around her, barely conscious of the earl's mumbled inquiries about the chill within the box.

Onstage the red velvet curtains swished open and once more the audience was plunged into brilliant pagoda land. Brightly garbed dancers tripped about the stage, their patterned satin kimonos catching the footlights. The girls scattered clouds of flower petals while they sang, and bursts of applause broke out in appreciation of the enchanting scene.

Marie Fleur gazed glassy-eyed at the stage, lights and color running together into a shimmering blur until a flurry of movement below their box attracted her attention. Nausea churned her stomach anew as she recognized the broad-shouldered man possessively chaperoning a dimunitive doll-like creature in pink. She knew Cranbrook watched her. It was too dim in the box to clearly see his face, but she could feel his penetrating stare. Surely he had not guessed. She did not think her manner had been that revealing.

"You'd think they'd have some consideration for others," she hissed angrily as the cloud of tulle subsided into place.

"Brandy's never been very circumspect," murmured the earl. During the next thirty minutes his attention frequently strayed from the stage to the lovely woman beside him.

Marie Fleur wanted to scream beneath his scrutiny. There was no way he could guess what had taken place between her and Brandon Nicholas. It had to be her own guilty conscience that attributed such knowledge to him.

The interminable performance finally came to an end. In the glare of flickering yellow light Marie Fleur's eyes were riveted on that beautiful couple who were surrounded by a crowd of well-wishers. It appeared their alliance was being congratulated on all sides. A well-known society rake and a beautiful foreign artist—the perfect coupling.

Swallowing a fresh surge of nausea as she stared at Brandon in profile, Marie Fleur stumbled to her feet. The earl draped her cloak about her shoulders and he handed her feathered fan to her. Below them the dispersing crowd swept Brandon and his ladylove away.

"Are you going on to Lindsays'?"

"No. Please, go without me. I've a terrible headache. It must be too much champagne."

"More likely it's too much opera."

Marie Fleur managed a tight smile. "Yes, you're probably right."

"You've lightened my heart this evening. I expected anger and heated words when I changed places with young Brooks," the earl added warmly as he led her to the stair.

Again that tight smile. Marie Fleur did not want to encourage his attentions, yet tonight she could muster no will to do battle. She wanted to creep away in the darkness, slinking like a wounded animal to its lair to lick her wounds.

Marie Fleur was revived by the blast of cold air sweeping indoors as they neared the theater entrance. Sidestepping opera patrons who thronged the vestibule eager to dissect the performance, or those crushing through the gilded doors to the street anxious to proceed to one or another of the parties that would soon be in full swing, she successfully fought the desire to succumb to nausea.

Outside the theater hansoms vied for space with curricles and phaetons lined up to receive their titled passengers. The horses snorted and stamped their feet in the crisp damp air. The earl quickly secured her a carriage.

Marie Fleur was vaguely surprised to find neither his own elaborate equipage nor the Reids' more sedate vehicle drawing up before the theater. She was about to question his choice when she noticed a familiar broad-shouldered figure detaching himself from the glittering crowd. He stood a moment, searching for someone, then he started forward. Her heart lurched. It was Brandon.

Hastily bidding Cranbrook good-bye, Marie Fleur gathered her cloak around her and darted inside the waiting carriage. The earl gave the Reids' address to the coachman, who tipped his hat and picked up the reins. As the coachman snapped his whip, urging the horse forward, Brandon called her name. People milled about the pavement, faces blurring through the grimy window as the carriage swayed into motion. Brandon even ran a few yards along the pavement in pursuit, trying to attract her attention until, realizing his behavior was becoming conspicuous, he fell back with a muttered oath.

What had he wanted to tell her? Marie Fleur's mouth tightened. She could guess well enough. "Forgive me, sweetheart. Gabriella's only a friend. She means nothing to me. You're the one I love." Like a well-rehearsed dialogue the words fell in place, each guaranteed to twist a little deeper. She wanted to cry, but grief lay buried beneath her pain. It was true she did not know what he had wanted to say, she could not know. Perhaps he had a plausible explanation for his seemingly damning conduct with the Italian woman, yet she doubted any explanation he could give would ease her hurt. All those wonderful dreams of abiding love were dead. She had given her heart away only to have it returned mangled and trampled. Of course, Brandon would never have dreamed she had come to London. He supposed her to be safe in Kent at isolated Langley Chase faithfully awaiting his next visit. He must have felt secure in believing she would never know what he did in London's sparkling theater world and with whom. Their confrontation tonight must have been as much a shock to him as it had been to her.

Her head throbbed like a bass drum, and she rested it against the cool leather upholstery. The odor inside this hired conveyance was objectionable; the leather smelt musty and the floor was unclean. After a few minutes she opened her eyes and sat up, forcing composure she did not feel. In a few minutes she would be at the Reids' house. There would probably only be servants to take note of her devastation, but even they must not know. Anabelle cleverly wheedled scraps of information from the maids, blackmailing them with her knowledge of their own indiscretions.

At whatever cost to her own nerves, Marie Fleur was determined to present a perfect facade until she reached the safety of her bedchamber. Then and only then would it be possible to allow herself the comfort of grief.

The street slipping past the grimy window seemed unusually dim. Marie Fleur leaned forward and peered through the murky glass. There were few lights here, and the buildings were small and dilapidated. The thin mist had changed to rain, and the narrow cobbled streets gleamed with moisture, reflecting small lamps above corner shops and taverns from which echoed raucous singing. This wasn't the broad, well-lighted Mall! The driver had gone the wrong way!

Angrily she tapped on the window to alert the man on the

box. He must have misunderstood the earl's directions. She rapped again with the ivory handle of her fan, thinking perhaps the man was deaf. The horses clattering over the cobbles made a steady background noise, yet surely he must be aware she wanted his attention.

Her impatience mounting, Marie Fleur let down the window on its leather strap and poked out her head in the drizzle. "Driver, didn't you hear me? I want you to stop. Turn back. We're headed in the wrong direction." To her amazement, the man merely quickened the horses' pace. Faster they went until they lurched around a corner at breakneck speed.

Growing afraid for her safety as they entered an even narrower street, Marie Fleur swiftly drew in her head. Her heart was pounding, and she was aware of a strange fluttering in her throat. She was being abducted! Why else would the man have quickened the pace? Why else would he bring her down these murky side streets, moving ever farther from lighted Mayfair? Perhaps he thought she had jewels or money to steal.

Jerking to her senses, Marie Fleur struggled to open the door. The foolishness of jumping from a moving carriage did not enter her mind. To her dismay the catch would not budge. Next she yelled for help from the open window. The few shabby passersby walking close to the buildings to keep dry glanced at her, then looked away. No one cared enough to come to her aid.

The horses galloped around a corner into a livery yard, the body of the carriage scraping the stone wall as they turned. Cursing angrily, the driver yanked on the ribbons, bringing the horses up short. Marie Fleur was flung jarringly against the upholstery from which she slid to the filthy floor. The impact, however, removed whatever had obstructed the door for when she grasped the handle in a wild effort to save herself, it came open.

Fresh hope surged in her veins as she grabbed her cloak and leaped from the carriage. At first, preoccupied with inspecting the damage to the side of his vehicle, the driver did not see her. Then as he noticed her shadow passing behind the carriage, he shouted a warning to stop. Marie Fleur ignored him as she scrambled over a refuse pile and bolted for the street.

"Oy, you! Git back 'ere!"

Heedlessly Marie Fleur ran on, her chest pounding, her mouth dry. She had no idea where she was going, yet surely escape to the unknown was preferable to whatever fate awaited her at the hands of the unscrupulous coachman.

Twisting, turning, she stumbled through a warren of narrow streets. She finally reached a squalid courtyard where rats squeaked in agitation about a grate through which fetid water trickled. Though the night was cold, this quarter's stench took her breath. She gagged and coughed, fighting for air. A furry body darted over her feet, and she recoiled in horror. The thump of approaching steps brought her quickly to her senses. Braving the rats was nothing to what she would endure if she was caught.

Marie Fleur ran on down a narrow alley leading out of the courtyard. At the end of the alley the uncertain light of an oil lamp flickered against the wet pavement. When she drew closer she could see four women standing in the shadows beyond the light, each holding an infant. She ran up to them, gasping in an effort to catch her breath. To her dismay she found no welcome on the young-old faces.

"Garn, you bloody fancy tart, we've got this spot."

"There's no toffs round 'ere, princess. You're off yer beat."

Marie Fleur stopped in the murky halo of light. These painted young girls defensively holding their shawl-swathed babies were prostitutes who definitely did not encourage encroachment on their territory.

"I'm being chased. Can't you help me? My life's in danger."

"Garn, get on wiv yer."

She did not need to feel the blow the taller of the girls aimed at her to understand there was no salvation here. Marie Fleur skidded on the slimed cobbles as she chose a different route, the women's catcalls echoing in her ears. The heavy pursuing steps were drawing closer. Desperately she fled into another refuse-heaped courtyard from which there was no exit. Close at hand a door creaked as a man emerged from a fetid privy.

"Hey, girlie—want to make thruppence?"

Recoiling in horror from his lewd pantomine of his needs, Marie Fleur ran back the way she had come. The man uttered an angry bellow and ran after her. Repeatedly turning her ankle as she slipped on the cobbles slimy with sewage, she was almost too weary to go on. As she reached the lamplit corner she ran into a burly, cloth-capped man who grabbed her.

"Got 'er, Mick. Yer can breav' easy."

Now the man who had propositioned her in the court caught

up with them. "Get your 'ands orf 'er. The tart's mine. We agreed on a price."

"Fuck off, yer bleeder! She ain't for sale!"

A brief tug-of-war ensued before the latecomer was neatly laid out on the cobbles. Two other men joined her captor, and together they raced Marie Fleur back to the livery stable. Struggling, fighting, screaming for help availed her nothing. When they passed the four prostitutes a rousing cheer greeted her capture.

"Let me go. I'll pay you well," she finally pleaded as they entered the livery stable. The men ignored her plea as they grimly hauled her against the wall beneath a stark lantern. Marie Fleur could no longer contain her tears.

"Pretty piece, ain't she," muttered one of them. "Fancy done up. Reckon she's worth a bit."

"Garn, you got yer pay."

Licking his slack mouth, the man in the cap moved closer. He fingered Marie Fleur's hair, and she jerked her head away from him. "Why not 'ave a sample first? Who's ter know?"

Her heart lurched and began a flurried, frightened beat. The others were clearly contemplating his suggestion when the driver appeared carrying a blanket.

"Come on, yer bleeders, get on wiv it."

"'Ow's about a taste of the merchandise first?"

The driver paused, his florid, thick-lipped face a study of temptation.

"We could all 'ave a go, free-like."

"Naw. Flash cove give'd me fifty quid to deliver 'er un'armed."

"'Ow's 'e ter know, Ned? 'Ow's 'e ter know?"

"Yer right there. Still, I's got me reputation to fink of."

Marie Fleur shook off their pawing hands and jerked free of inquisitive fingers sliding inside her bodice. "Don't you dare touch me!"

Unsure how to proceed, the grubby foursome stared at her.

"Naw, we'd best get 'er over there. If we's late we might lose the lot."

"We'll still 'ave 'er, Ned. Reckon she'd be worth a bit at the Craven. We can't lose either way."

The man grabbed Marie Fleur. Ignoring her shouts and kicks, they struggled to get the odorous blanket over her head until, tiring of her resistance, the driver cuffed her on the side of the head with his hamlike fist, silencing her protests in a shower of sparks.

She heard the clatter of hooves as she jolted inside the smothering blanket on the journey to her final destination. Streets sounds filtered through the wool so she knew they were still in the city. Next she heard men's voices. The horses stopped, and she knew the door was opened because she felt a sweep of icy air. She was pulled ungently from the coach and tossed over a shoulder like a sack of potatoes. With many muttered oaths and furtive whisperings she was conveyed down a flight of area steps. A door opened, and there was a brief exchange with a manservant, followed by the clink of coins. A swift "Right you are, guv'ner," and she was being handed over to someone else.

The place where Marie Fleur had been brought was lighted, for the dirty yellow blur penetrated even this thick blanket. Up more steps. This time her abductor, not being as strong as his accomplices, huffed and puffed. Seizing her opportunity, Marie Fleur jerked and bumped about in his arms, twisting as much as she was able inside her blanket prison. With hands and feet bound there was little she could do to escape.

The filthy gag in her mouth threatened to choke her as she fought for air. At last she was dumped on a spring bed, bouncing a couple of times when she landed. Still bumping around in a desperate bid to free herself, she heard a muttered oath followed by a snarled command to be still, which she ignored. The man followed up his threat with a painful thump on her head. She sank down, down, into the feather mattress and was still.

Chapter 9

"HERE, MISS, DRINK this."

Coming out of a daze, Marie Fleur tried to focus her burning eyes. A small pinched face emerged whitely from the mist; red-rimmed brown eyes peered into her own, curiously at odds with the young face.

"Where am I?"

"Never mind that. Drink this tea. It'll warm you."

Thankfully Marie Fleur accepted the mug, warming her hands around the thick crockery. The tea was strong and sweet. She managed a smile for her benefactor. "Who are you?" she asked, hoping perhaps that question might be answered.

"Rose, mum, that's me name. Rose Wilcox."

"Are you a maid here?"

Rose nodded, her pinched mouth curving slightly. "Upstairs chambermaid. What's your name?"

"Marie Fleur."

"Ooh, you're one of them foreigners."

Rose waited until Marie Fleur was finished with the cup. While she waited she smoothed her starched apron and nervously pleated the skirts of her gray striped gown. "Got to go now. I'll be back later," she whispered as heavy footsteps sounded in the corridor outside. "I've got to lock you in," she said apologetically. "Them's me orders."

Marie Fleur nodded, watching as the maid scuttled outside. She heard a key turn in the lock, then Rose's footsteps hastening away.

Inching to a sitting position, she discovered she ached in every limb. Last night's events slowly returned like some hideous nightmare. At first she had hoped it really was a nightmare and that Rose was a servant in the country estate where she had intended to spend the holidays with Anabelle. Reality provided no such comfort.

Though bare, her prison was clean. When Marie Fleur slid from the bed she saw the skin around her slender ankles was chafed. To her relief she found she was still able to walk. She had no idea how long she had been here, but she hoped it had been merely overnight. Through the grimy window she could see leafless trees and a gabled roof line; beyond that stretched gray winter sky streaked with rain. This room was identical to the attics in the Reids' town house, so she concluded this was an establishment of stature. She was not being held captive in a dingy Whitechapel tenement after all.

It was even possible that the owner of the house had no knowledge of her presence. Young Rose could be a link in a chain, surreptitiously hiding kidnapped women for Ned the coachman. What was to happen to her after she left these temporary quarters, she dreaded to think. Lurid rumors about white slavery rings flourished throughout London. Yet women of quality were not usually captured for that purpose. Impoverished girls, often orphans without friend or family to miss them, were the perfect choice. Once her abductors learned her identity, she was sure to be released unharmed.

It was not until dusk blotted out the stark branches tossing beyond her window that Marie Fleur saw Rose again. This time the girl scuttled inside the room carrying a tray of food. After setting it down, she scuttled away with no more than a mumbled greeting.

The food was unusually good. Roast beef in a succulent gravy, pureed brussels sprouts, roasted potatoes, greengage pie, and a foaming glass of milk. The quality of this meal merely reinforced Marie Fleur's conviction that the owners of the house were well-to-do. This was obviously food from belowstairs, not the splended delicacies served to guests in the mansion's stately dining room, yet a kitchen that provided its servants with such wholesome fare had to be a household of good standing.

Revitalized, Marie Fleur crossed to the window. She still wore her wine velvet opera gown, though by now it was much the worse for wear. Her cape was gone. In its place she had been given a rough black-and-white woolen shawl with a deep black fringe. This must be one of milady's castoffs, for the cashmere, though worn, was of fine quality.

The tree branches beyond the window looked close enough to be reached. She could loop the bedsheet over a branch and fashion an escape route. Excitement surged through Marie Fleur's veins at the prospect. She pushed the window, finding the pane reluctant to open. Eventually the warped frame yielded and a rush of damp smoky air entered the room. To her disappointment, the branch was too far away to reach. After a few tentative throws of the shawl, she realized her chances of snagging a branch were slim. Still, it was not impossible.

Marie Fleur felt the bricks below the window for a handhold. A thickened wisteria vine grew about a foot below, winding over the wall where it was secured by iron loops. The wisteria grew from ground floor level, twining around the windows of the three lower stories. Its gnarled branch seemed supportive enough. Could she climb to freedom?

"I don't advise jumping, my love. Four stories is a long way down."

Marie Fleur gripped the window ledge until her knuckles whitened. That supercilious voice! Surely it could not be!

"Don't you recognize me?" the Earl of Cranbrook asked as he stepped behind her and slipped his hands over her shoulders. "Marie Fleur, my darling, welcome home."

"Don't touch me!"

"You're mine now."

"No! I'll never be yours. I should've known you were at the back of this. I demand you set me free at once! How dare you keep me prisoner? And those hideous creatures you paid to kidnap me—oh, I hate you! All the time I thought they—"

"Sorry if I spoiled your visions of adventure. Unfortunately, you declined to come to me any other way. I told you I'd run out of patience. Still, all's not lost. You're here now, my love. Merely cooperate, and all will be well."

"Cooperate? What do you mean, cooperate?"

In the dwindling light she could not see his face, yet his voice chillingly betrayed his intentions.

"You're in my home now, and here you will stay. The choice of lodging remains entirely with you. This uncomfortable little room or my spacious bedchamber. Surely there can be little choice."

"How dare you? You can't keep me prisoner!"

"Can I not."

"My friends..."

"Who, bless them, realizing how Will's demise has affected you, will assume you've departed for the country alone, no longer able to face the festive season without him."

"They'll know it's a pack of lies."

"Not wholly lies. You will be in the country as soon as I make the necessary arrangements. But not at Langley Chase. Though I don't usually fancy the somewhat primitive accommodations of Braithwaite Hall at this uncharitable time of year, I'm sure it will suit our purpose admirably. It will be a change to spend some time in the wilderness, and decidedly less expensive. I can keep a carriage there for half the cost of keeping one in the city. The Yorkshire yokels ask few questions. In fact, we could tell them we're husband and wife."

"What makes you think I'd go along with your deception? How could you even dream I'd be agreeable to such a preposterous scheme."

His hands slipped around her slender waist, and he pulled her against him, pressing her buttocks tightly against his body. "I never gave your refusal a thought, my love. After all, you've nothing to lose and absolutely everything to gain."

Marie Fleur struggled in his grasp as he put his mouth on her neck. The touch of his lips on her flesh chilled her, and she shuddered. The earl chuckled in the darkness, mistaking her reaction for passion.

"Not such a stone-cold creature after all, are you, my dear Marie Fleur?"

"I hate you! Don't touch me! I'm asking you one final time to let me go. Perhaps, if you're considerate, I'll keep your crime a secret."

"My, you're uncommon generous tonight," he mocked, stepping backwards.

She stood her ground beside the window, warily awaiting his next move. "Mockery's exactly what I should've expected from you."

"You do disappoint me. I assure you, my dear lady, I've far more spirited entertainment in mind. I trust you'll come to your senses before long. This climb is devilish hard on the constitution."

Long after the earl had descended the stair, his footsteps echoing in the dark, Marie Fleur stood unmoving beside the window. Anger surged within her. How dare he assume she would welcome his attentions? How dare he subject her to such horrid indignities as her flight through that hideous quarter? It made her shudder to recall those girls soliciting customers, their babies in their arms. True, Cranbrook could not have anticipated she would try to escape, but he was to blame for the unpleasant experience nonetheless. Marie Fleur thumped her fist in the palm of her hand, longing to physically attack him. However, his superior strength, coupled with the ready assistance of his servants, would render such efforts pointless.

She crouched against the wall in the dark, contemplating her next move. Plans half formed and were discarded as the hours slid by. A pale moon haloed by mist finally rose above the treetops. The weak light barely lit the room sufficiently for her to make out the furnishings and this only after she became accustomed to its meager glow. Tonight the earl would probably leave her alone, wanting to give her time to consider the tempting choice of his bedchamber over this dark, unheated room. Why wait? She could try to escape tonight.

She opened the window, and cold dampness filled the room. Finding the wool shawl not warm enough, Marie Fleur pulled the blanket from the bed and wrapped it around her shoulders. She was feeling for the first handhold where the vine was bowed to form a support when an unexpected voice startled her.

"'Ere's your supper, miss."

Marie Fleur spun about. So intent had she been on escape, she had not heard the door open. Rose stood in the doorway, a candle in one hand, a plate of food in the other.

"Take it away. I'm not hungry," Marie Fleur called, her voice tight.

"I can't do that. You've got to eat." Rose came inside the room and placed the candle on the wooden chest beside the bed. "Please, Miss, I'll be in lots of trouble if you don't."

Marie Fleur reluctantly moved from the window, knowing the girl must guess what she had intended when she saw the pane ajar. "All right. Put it there."

Rose was immediately aware of the cold air blowing inside the room. Though Marie Fleur had pushed the window to behind her back, the draft had sucked it open again. Without comment, Rose banged the window shut.

"You'd best not try that, miss. 'E keeps guard dogs. They'll 'ave your leg orf in no time."

Marie Fleur swallowed. She had heard nothing to betray a dog's presence.

"Why am I being imprisoned?"

"Dunno. S'pose you knows that better'n me."

Because the maid perched on the foot of the bed to wait, Marie Fleur decided it would be expedient to eat the meal. The steaming stew had large pieces of beef and vegetables floating appetizingly on the surface, unlike the soggy mush that often passed for stew. Gambling recklessly that the maid might side with her, Marie Fleur asked impetuously, "Will you help me escape?"

"Me! It'd be more'n me life's worth!"

Marie Fleur continued to eat in silence, wondering how she could enlist the maid's sympathy. "I'm Lady Dowling of Langley Chase," she said finally. She felt a flicker of satisfaction when Rose's eyes widened in surprise. "Your master has been pursuing me for some time. Seeing that I refused his suit, he decided to take matters into his own hands."

Rose nodded, craning forward. "'E do like to get 'is own way."

"I have friends who'd not hesitate to rescue me. Only they have no way of knowing where I am. Will you take a message to the Reids' house, number 25—"

"Here, Rose, it's time you was out," snarled a voice from the door.

Rose leaped from the bed in a fluster. Without asking if Marie Fleur was finished, she snatched the plate and spoon from her and dashed to the door.

A wizened-faced housekeeper dressed in a musty, unfashionable black gown eyed the prisoner in distaste. "S'pose you's another of 'is fancy pieces. 'Struth, don't know what gets into 'im, really I don't. Bringing 'em 'ere by the bushel he be, and no mistake. I don't 'old with it. Not in the least."

The door was slammed, and the key grated in the lock. The shuffling footsteps receded into silence. Clouds obscured the moon, plunging the room into blackness. Marie Fleur closed her eyes as overwhelming heat moved through her body. Sweat beaded on her upper lip, and a wave of nausea washed over her. She hastened to the chamber pot in the corner, thinking the stew had not agreed with her.

She did not vomit. In a few minutes the sensation had passed, leaving in its stead a feeling of well-being. Marie Fleur lay down on the bed. The blanket was still on the floor, but she no longer felt the cold. As she drifted peacefully in and out of consciousness she realized something must have been added to that stew. Cranbrook intended to drug her into submission.

Marie Fleur did not know how long she had slept when a

rattle at the door jerked her awake. A liveried footman stood in the doorway, then strode boldly inside the room.

"All right, you, time to go downstairs."

Marie Fleur contemplated refusing to go, but decided against it. Meekly she obeyed, allowing the servant to lead her. Once she had the freedom of the house she would find more opportunities for escape.

The man gripped her arm and propelled her along narrow corridors and down the servants' backstairs. Here it was dimly lit and in a poor state of decoration. Eventually they reached the more splendid family rooms, which were plushly carpeted and expensively furnished. Stopping before a closed door, the man knocked.

"Come in."

Marie Fleur shivered at the unpleasant sound of the earl's voice. The room they entered was a small book-lined study, pleasantly warm with the glow from a coal fire in the iron grate, delft tiles forming a colorful surround to the orange flames. A green silk-shaded lamp burned brightly on a vast mahogany desk, casting a pool of gold over Cranbrook's aristocratic features.

"Thank you, Martin. You may leave us now."

The manservant bowed and backed out, closing the door behind him.

"Why did you send for me?"

"I didn't go to such elaborate lengths to secure your company merely to keep you upstairs in that dingy room."

When he came around the desk to stand beside her, Marie Fleur saw that the earl was wearing a rose-colored brocade dressing gown and matching tasseled slippers on his narrow feet. She managed not to flinch when he fondled her cheek. Though it was hard to stay calm in the face of what she assumed would be an attempted seduction, she knew she must fight this sarcastic nobleman with his own weapons. A cool, calm head was required to outwit him.

Her reaction pleased him, and he smiled as he lounged against the broad mahogany desk.

"You must feel in need of a bath. And a change of clothes after your adventure."

"They would be much appreciated."

"Very well. Next door in my bedchamber you'll find a bath drawn. I assure you I'll stay safely beyond the door. One of the women will assist you. When you're refreshed, you may join me in here."

Very wary of his intentions, Marie Fleur did as she was bid, thinking perhaps the other room would furnish an opportunity for escape.

The adjoining bedroom was like an Oriental palace. A shimmering circle of pleated gold satin was suspended from the ceiling above the bed, its long draperies brushing the red-carpeted floor. The mantel ornamented in gold was of white marble. The furniture was a mixture of elegantly gilded pieces and preposterous chinoiserie of black lacquer inlaid with mother-of-pearl. Slowly Marie Fleur took in the vast bed, gilded dragons forming the foot, their talons sinking into the plushly carpeted dais. At the head of the bed was poised an even larger fire-breathing dragon. She blinked, amazed at the sight of smoking incense issuing periodically from its brazen mouth.

"Miss, is you ready for your bath?"

The unexpected voice startled Marie Fleur. A young maid was standing beside the window, her dark dress blending with the black velvet curtains. She indicated a large copper bath beside the hearth.

"I didn't see you. Everything's so magnificent."

"Yes, miss."

The girl stood beside the bath, awaiting Marie Fleur. Clearly she was not going to be talkative. Perhaps she was under orders from her master not to engage in conversation. Like an automaton the maid helped her disrobe. The bath water was scented with oil, which the girl replenished from an elegant glass bottle. While she luxuriated in the heavenly scented water, Marie Fleur examined the bottle on the nearby table, finding the name Bourgeois Amick & Son printed on a flower-edged label. Milk of roses and a green bottle labeled oil of jessamine both came from the exclusive *parfumiers* patronized by the prince regent.

Methodically the girl soaped her, then rinsed, then soaped and rinsed again. It was wonderful to be enfolded in a soft plush towel warm from the hearth. Marie Fleur glowed all over, the hot water merely intensifying that warm feeling of relaxation she had felt in her prison. The sudden reminder, however, put her immediately on guard. Like a fool she was playing into his hands.

The maid handed her a diaphanous red garment shaped like full pantaloons gathered at the ankles. A jeweled waistband curved over the hips to reveal her navel. The matching red silk top was little more than a minute waistcoat trimmed with dangling gold coins; it barely covered her breasts. When Marie Fleur protested the scantiness of the garment the maid handed her a gold silk dressing gown that provided ample coverage. She knotted the silk fringed sash about her tiny waist with determination. This luxurious bath in these exotic surroundings, the theatrical costume all made her wonder what strange fantasies the earl expected to enact.

When Marie Fleur reentered the study a strange odor like burnt grass hung in the air. Cranbrook lounged before the fire, drawing reflectively on a long-stemmed pipe, his eyes half-closed while he awaited her return. The click of the door latch alerted him, and he smiled his approval of her appearance.

"Exquisite. A golden vision. Now, do you not feel much revived?"

"Yes. The bath was divine. But why are you going to such trouble?"

He shook his head, a bemused smile on his thin mouth. "Aren't we the suspicious little matron. Indulge yourself, sweet girl. There are so many pleasures you've not even dreamed of."

"And likely they're pleasures I can well live without."

He smiled as he uncoiled his long elegant frame from the armchair. "Trust me."

"Why? You've hardly proved trustworthy in the past."

"Will you take some brandy?"

Marie Fleur shook her head. His movements languid, the earl unstoppered a crystal decanter and poured an inch of amber liquid in his glass. Raising the glass, he toasted her silently.

Marie Fleur was gradually becoming aware of muffled sounds from an adjoining room rising above the hissing moisture on the coals and the soft pattering of rain against the window. The earl appeared unconcerned by the noise. Eventually he put his empty glass on the mantel.

"Come," he said, motioning for her to follow him.

Warily Marie Fleur obeyed, her bare feet sinking into the dark plush carpet. Though she had expected to find an escape route, this suite of rooms proved to be interconnecting. A small sitting room, its walls decorated in scarlet and white brocade outlined in gilt, opened off the study. Now the mysterious sounds were explained. Two girls of about ten and twelve stood arms about each other beside the hearth. They no longer cried, but sniffled constantly while they cast fearful glances about the luxuriously appointed room. Tears had made white rivers down their grimy cheeks. Their dirty feet were bare, their garments ragged, yet despite their obvious poverty, their huge blue eyes and flaxen hair gave tham an angelic beauty.

"Perfect," breathed Cranbrook in rapture, his eyes glittering as he studied the two. The footman who had brought Marie Fleur downstairs stood beside the urchins, gripping the older girl's arm in an unrelenting grasp.

"They're fine specimens even if I does say so meself. Found 'em selling oranges in St. Giles, milord."

"Irish?"

"As Paddy's pig."

"How would you like a chance to earn a few shillings?"

The older girl looked squarely at the tall nobleman, the mention of such unimagined wealth snagging her interest. "Shillings?" she repeated incredulously.

"That's right, shillings. Likely you're used to being paid pennies for your labors; I pay in shillings."

"We would, Your Honor," the older girl spoke quickly for her younger sister, who merely nodded.

"Name's Maeve, and Kathleen," the footman revealed in an aside before he took the girl's arms and marched them away.

Unease radiated through Marie Fleur's body as the door closed on the two urchins. "What are you paying them to do?" she asked suspiciously.

"Don't concern yourself over their welfare, my dear. The London streets are full of waifs eager to earn a few coppers. Those little Micks will be able to support their family for a month on what I give them, and the working conditions are luxurious, to say the least." The earl waved her to a red-and-white striped satin sofa near the hearth. "Before I take you to see my valuable collections, there's something I want to say."

Marie Fleur perched uncomfortably on the edge of the sofa with its elegantly turned mahogany legs. The earl leaned against the mantel, drumming his long fingers on the marble as he spoke.

"You're wise to have acted civilized this evening. I'm being honest in saying it's more than I expected. Your acceptance pleases me."

Her tight smile was wary. At the moment she would not tip

her hand. Wily as her opponent was, she must use her utmost skill in letting him think she *might* acquiesce. How else would she be given a chance to escape? On the other hand, too sudden a submission would plunge her into deeper trouble. Her mind strayed to the footman. His attitude was much too familiar for an ordinary servant. She wondered what his exact duties were inside this household.

"We'll enjoy ourselves immensely this evening if you continue to show such good sense," Cranbrook was saying.

"If that means what I suspect it does, you're going to be disappointed."

He smiled unpleasantly. "Oh, no, I don't think so. You see, I'm privy to certain secrets, which, if revealed, could prove most embarrassing to you."

"Secrets?" Marie Fleur swallowed uncomfortably. Had she been right when she suspected Cranbrook knew about Brandon? It was impossible for him to know. No one but the lovers themselves could know what had taken place on Romney Marsh.

"Think back to a certain summer night. Your husband hosted a card party at which I and several other gentlemen were guests. A wager was made, a most astonishing wager."

Marie Fleur's hands flew to her cheeks, which burned with humiliation. The earl smiled triumphantly as he stepped toward her.

"Ah, so you do remember after all. Think what a scandal it would be, my dear. Think of the ridicule, the unkind cuts if the terms of that wager were made public. You would be labeled a whore. As for the gentleman involved, being largely without honor in affairs of this kind, he would no doubt consider the notoriety an advantage."

"You wouldn't dare!"

"Wouldn't I? Think again. When I want something very badly I go to any lengths to get it. If you haven't learned that by now, you're more foolish than I thought."

"And your payment for silence?"

His tone was soft, almost seductive as he reached for her soft curls, damp after her bath. "You."

"Never!"

"You've little choice. You're my prisoner—a prisoner of love, if you will. Besides, do think of the Reids. After housing you, after introducing you to their titled friends—they'd be the laughingstock of London."

Eyes glittering fiercely in anger, Marie Fleur leaped up. "I can hardly be held responsible for a drunken fool's wager. You're no gentleman if you reveal—"

"What? I'd be telling no more than the truth. But enough of this pointless discussion. Come, I've something I want to show you that I think you'll find interesting."

Cranbrook ushered Marie Fleur into yet another adjoining room with a curtained dais at the far end. The walls were lined with alcoves set behind silk screens. In the center of the room stood a low horseshoe-shaped table around which were grouped silken tasseled cushions in rainbow hues.

"This is my petit banquet hall. I have a passion for things theatrical, as have many of my friends. Here we sup in Roman splendor like the emperors of old. And while we eat, certain . . . entertainment . . . is provided."

"Those little girls are to provide it?"

"A portion . . . yes. I've yet to find two young boys." His eyes became remote as, half to himself, he said dreamily, "Preferably dark-skinned and black-haired—but that's none of your concern."

Nausea roiled Marie Fleur's stomach. She needed not ask what entertainment the children were to provide; that it would be some sexual spectacle was obvious.

"In all that's whispered about you, never once did I hear tell of this. Perhaps it's not yet known how you corrupt children."

"'Corrupt' is hardly the word," he snapped, the pleasure fading from his face. "Don't threaten me, my dear. For your information, these *children* you're so eager to protect often sleep six to a bed with the pig thrown in for good measure. You can rarely get girls untouched at that age anymore. Filthy creatures their own age take them if their own fathers and brothers don't get to them first."

Stunned by his gritted speech, Marie Fleur leaned against a mahogany chair for support as she fought the sickening memory of young Maudie Leach defending her father in his crime.

Cranbrook smiled unpleasantly as he interpreted her thoughts. "Ah, yes, the little filly at Langley. I assure you, my words were not designed to stir unpleasant memories. If you wish, when you're permanently established here, you may attend one of our little entertainments. We dress as Roman senators or Eastern potentates. At times we have medieval banquets. Some of the more decent of the Drury Lane company are among my acquaintances. We have had farces direct from the boards performed for us. Prinny himself has attended our theatricals, but vastly indulgent and ofttimes labeled degenerate, our Prince Regent has little predilection for the more refined entertainments."

They proceeded to a smaller room leading off the banqueting room. Was this the secret place people whispered about, the room where the earl and his degenerate friends took their sadistic pleasure? When Marie Fleur held back, desperate to escape, he pulled her inside the room and slammed the door.

"Don't be a little fool. These are things I want you to enjoy as much as I. There's no reason to be afraid. Thousands of pounds worth of treasures are in this room. Look"—he took down from the wall an iron device roughly two feet long, with places for the head, hands, and ankles. "This is quite a rare piece called the Scavenger's Daughter. Once locked, it compresses bodies in a crushing stranglehold—"

"I don't want to know how it works."

His smile was faint as he replaced the instrument of torture on the wall. "Here then, perhaps this will interest you—an iron bridle for scolds. Sharp-tongued women were locked into this bridle, the iron insertion depresses the tongue. This particular piece came from the Tower. There were originally two. Prinny admired the other, so I presented it to him to be placed on exhibit."

"Most generous of you."

"We have a collection of manacles and fetters out of old London prisons. This, however, is my *pièce de résistance*. It's unique."

An iron flambeau jutted from the wall over a metal frame about six feet long with three wooden rollers. It reminded Marie Fleur of a weaving frame, but in this lurid museum she knew its function was far more sinister.

"The rack. It still works most effectively."

Her horrified gasp was drowned by the creak of the machine as he cranked the lever operating the pulleys to demonstrate its crippling potential.

"Please, don't show me any more. I've seen enough," she choked, turning away. All that was needed was a flaming torch in the flambeau and rats scampering underfoot to reproduce the terror of a medieval torture chamber.

"As you will. I find your reaction most disappointing; my friends are generally fascinated by it."

"Then you must reserve the pleasure for them."

A narrow door in the wall gave access to yet another small chamber, the sight of which made Marie Fleur recoil in horror. This was the infamous padded room! A row of manacles were suspended overhead and fetters were attached to the floor. Several tall padded devices with cutout openings were propped against the wall. A movement from a bench under a display of whips attracted her attention. There a youth lay sleeping, his head pillowed on his hand. Marie Fleur's stomach churned in distress when she noticed he wore an outfit identical to hers.

"Vicente!"

The dark head snapped up, revealing large soulful brown eyes dazed with sleep. "My lord," the youth mumbled.

"We're nearly ready for you. Come here, let me look at you." Cranbrook beckoned with his finger.

Vicente moved with a dancer's grace, his swarthy skin gleaming like the finest silk. His oiled body was devoid of hair, smooth as a woman's. The earl ran his hands appreciatively over the youth's flat, branching shoulders and rippling midriff. "Is he not a fine specimen?"

Observing Vicente's blank stare, Marie Fleur realized he did not understand English. "Is he another waif you kidnapped off the streets?"

"The son of an Italian hurdy-gurdy man. He dances beautifully and sings like an angel. He'll join us presently."

Eagerly Cranbrook grasped Marie Fleur's hand and led her through a narrow door padded in blue fabric that opened into his bedchamber. The door on the other side was concealed behind the black velvet draperies shrouding two walls of the large room.

"This room is the most exquisite of all," he said, his face animated as a child displaying its favorite toy. "My dragons even breathe fire. Prinny clapped his hands in delight when he saw them. And he pouted for a month when I wouldn't give him the bed."

The earl strode to a black lacquered cabinet and took out two glasses and a crystal decanter. He poured colorless liquor into them and handed a glass to Marie Fleur. Tentatively she sipped the strangely bitter yet sweet fluid flavored with a hint of anise. Growing bolder, the earl slid his hand over her neck and inside her shawl-collared dressing gown. She backed away.

"I've told you many times I'm not interested in forming an alliance with you. I'm interested only in my freedom."

"Which you shall regain after you've proved obliging. I demand to be repaid for my past generosity."

Marie Fleur sidestepped him. The apparently innocent liquor had wrought an unpleasant change in his behavior: Gone was that calm exterior, that supercilious, almost bored air; his eyes were dilated, his nostrils flared.

As in a sinister dance they waved and bobbed about the room. Marie Fleur dashed for the door and miraculously she reached it. Yanking on the handle, she raced into the adjoining study where she collided with the footman, Martin. To her horror she saw he had changed from his gold-braided livery to a costume similar to the Italian boy's.

"Back we go, dearie. Don't want you leavin' just yet."

Marie Fleur screamed as he grabbed her. Making it appear an accident, he grasped her breast beneath the robe, thoroughly exploring the delight of her flesh. Taking malicious pleasure in her helplessness, Martin squeezed her breasts until she gasped. Only Cranbrook's harsh command from the lighted room brought him to order.

"Don't be impatient, Martin. Our little French gazelle's feeling skittish. We'll soon tame her. Vicente!"

The smooth-skinned Italian boy emerged from behind the black curtains, moving like a automaton to obey his master's bidding. Perhaps he had been drugged, or maybe he was drunk. Or had the earl an even more sinister hold over these men, which forced them to carry out his commands like animated dolls?

Struggling desperately in their grasp, Marie Fleur was hauled back into the padded room, which was now lit brightly by candles and oil lamps. She had always privately discounted the sinister stories about the earl's strange lusts enacted in a private suite of pleasure rooms. Now, on the second floor of Cranbrook House, she was to learn the truth about those forbidden delights.

To her horror, Marie Fleur was manacled to the wall. In vain she tried to sink against the padded satin wall to relieve the drag on her arms. Her gold silk robe lay at her feet, and she felt horribly exposed, ashamed of her near-nakedness before this strange trio. In the bright light her filmy silk pantaloons afforded little cover, while the minute red silk waistcoat gaped wide to reveal her breasts.

"They're magnificent," breathed the earl. He could not resist fondling her full breasts, tantalizing as ripe fruit beneath the coin-edged scarlet bodice. He felt her heavy flesh, squeezing until she cried out in pain. Marie Fleur's cries brought a strange expression to his face, and his breathing quickened as he crushed even harder, imprinting her white flesh with bruises.

"Pain is often the companion of pleasure. Oh, you're going to discover untold delights. You'll never want to leave." His moist lips were slack with anticipation as he gazed at her, a captive slave to do with as he wished. Silently Cranbrook motioned to Vicente to take down a narrow thonged whip. "A delicious love instrument, my sweet Marie Fleur, to sting and caress until you beg for mercy."

Her screams of terror rang shrill, but the three remained unmoved. As if performing an age-old ritual the two servants stepped to their master's side and slowly removed his brocade dressing gown. His pale slender body was revealed, hard and muscular, clad only in scarlet pantaloons of gleaming satin, which fitted over his hips like a second skin, flaring out again beneath the knees in graceful bells. As the earl stared in rapture at his captive, a telling bulge appeared in the satin. Across his genitals the scarlet pantaloons went taut, revealing each muscle, each fresh surge of blood. Legs planted wide, the earl raised his arm, and the cruel whip snaked out.

Marie Fleur gasped in pain as the thong snapped lightly across her exposed breasts, flicking aside the scant protection of her red satin waistcoat. Again he struck, and she screamed as twin red tracery crisscrossed her white flesh in stinging tracks. Next he allowed the thong to caress her narrow waist, to curl lovingly about her buttocks, directing the narrow leather as if it were a biddable creature, never higher or lower than he intended, the blow neither softer nor harsher, demonstrating his skill in the art of sadistic lovemaking.

"Tears?" he cried incredulously, seeing the silver shimmering over her pale cheeks. "Surely this is joy!"

Blinded, Marie Fleur tried to focus through the daze, unable to speak because her teeth were gritted against the burning torment.

"Come, do the same favor for me, my love. If I release you, will you oblige?"

She blinked free the blurring tears. "Whip you?" she whispered through bitten lips, salt tears burning her flesh.

Without waiting to be told, Martin stepped forward to un-couple her wrists from the manacles. Marie Fleur sank to the floor with a sob, chafing her wrists, trying to cover her nakedness.

"'Ere, best do as 'e says."

Martin thrust the whip in her hands. Cranbrook stood manacled in her stead, awaiting his punishment, a smile of expectation on his thin mouth.

"No, I won't whip you."

"You'd better do 'as 'e says, ducks. 'E don't like to be crossed," Martin urged in a whispered aside. "Do it for all our sakes."

Marie Fleur gripped the leather handle, suffused with rage for her ill treatment. Now was her chance to avenge herself, to inflict upon her tormentor the pain he had inflicted upon her. Drawing back her arm, she swung the whip with all her strength, sending the narrow leather thong snaking about his white body, wrapping about his chest, his flat belly, his waist, even licking across his swollen genitals. Far from pain, the punishment elicited cries of joy. Marie Fleur recoiled in disgust from the ecstasy reflected on his pale face glistening with sweat. And she threw the whip into the corner.

"Now you and Vicente," gasped the earl as he was freed from his manacles. He mopped rivers of sweat from his body.

Marie Fleur huddled defensively in the corner. Martin dragged her up, thrusting her toward the bench where he quickly lashed her down with two broad leather straps. Desperately she tried to free herself before Vicente's smooth young body overlaid her own. Above the boy's curly black head she saw that the earl had donned a silver turban centered with a glittering jewel in which he appeared like some Eastern potentate.

Thinking she was about to be raped, Marie Fleur tried to draw up her legs and push the boy off her. Her efforts failed. She later realized her fears were unfounded; her violation was only to be simulated. Vicente moved rythmically, blending their limbs, grunting convincingly at appropriate moments. Marie Fleur stared into his eyes, finding them dark and unfathomable. She tried desperately to understand why he was a willing participant in this spectacle. Then she realized there was no heat, no demanding pressure against her thighs, only the rythmic grind of his pelvic bones against hers. Vicente was unaroused. Simulating the pinnacle of ecstasy, he partially rose up, gasping aloud as the whip lovingly caressed his shoulders. Then, when his whip-wielding master nodded approval of his performance, Vicente dropped upon her to rest, his face beaded with sweat.

Impatiently Cranbrook pushed Vicente from the bench. He uncoupled Marie Fleur's restraints and swung her to her feet.

She fought him, but he was far too strong, stronger than she had ever imagined he could be. Locking his arms about her, sweat gleaming on his hairless chest, the earl crushed his mouth to hers. He took her lip between his teeth, biting until she whimpered with pain. Then, with a triumphant cry, he swept her from her feet and carried her to that hideously grand bed guarded by fire-breathing dragons.

Marie Fleur was dropped on the scarlet satin bedcover where she lay panting for a moment trying to catch her breath. Her head was spinning with nausea and revulsion; her flesh stung from the whip. Too late, she tried to roll away from him, but the earl entangled her in his long legs, keeping her prisoner on that down-filled island. This time the sexual assault would not be a charade. She was becoming unpleasantly aware of the steel hard pain of his manhood driving relentlessly against her bruised body. Cranbrook fumbled with the jeweled waistband of her flimsy pantaloons, ripping until the fabric gave. Then he sank his hot face against her soft abdomen, his tongue probing her navel. Desperate to escape, Marie Fleur beat his back and shoulders with clenched fists. In anger she had torn off his swathed turban, revealing his light hair sweat-damp and tousled. Without the protective covering her blows easily found their mark, yet so intent was he upon his own gratification, her resistance proved ineffective.

"A rape's more to my liking anyway, dear heart," he murmured, his face buried against her flesh.

The hours spent within this pleasure palace were becoming a never-ending nightmare. This was a madman, a monster, resistance seemed more to delight than to deter him. Perhaps cool, calm logic would prevail where all else failed.

"Geoffrey," Marie Fleur began in a futile effort to appeal to his sensibilities as she tried to hold him at bay. "Don't do this. We've mutual friends who—"

He drowned her protests with a smothering kiss. Quickly he stripped off his satin pantaloons. Now he knelt above her naked, the scented dragon's breath swirling about his head. She stared in morbid fascination at his towering erection pointing sword-stiff toward her. He raised himself on his knees, pausing a moment to allow her a better view, proud of the length of his organ. Marie Fleur twisted in an effort to roll free of him, but she found herself imprisoned by his knees. Angered by her sudden resistance the earl slapped her face, the stinging blow bringing tears to her eyes. Ignoring her futile defense as she dug her nails in his back, raking his flesh like an angry cat, he forced himself between her thighs, thrusting, battering until, with a sob of passion, the barrier was finally breeched.

Time stood still in that garishly ornate room. Watching and participating in the ritual whipping had readily aroused him, the simulated assault by the smooth-skinned Italian boy bringing him even closer to the pinnacle of desire. The fire-breathing dragons with their gargoyle's faces puffed smoke above their heads while Marie Fleur steeled herself to endure his almost insatiable lust. When at last the earl rolled from her, she saw a network of red on his ravaged back where her nails had drawn blood. She lay panting on the sweat-drenched bed feeling horribly defiled.

He looked down at her, lids half closed. "I've waited a long time for you, it was well worth the wait. Tomorrow we'll invite some good friends to help us enjoy our pleasure. I'm not selfish with my toys."

Almost as if a command had been given, the maid who had bathed her and Martin, the footman, came inside the room. Marie Fleur shuddered as she realized there must be peepholes in the wall. There was no other way the servants could have known the precise moment to enter.

Cranbrook staggered to his feet, arms outstretched for the enveloping robe Martin held out to him. "Where's Gaston?" he asked, his voice weak as he slumped against his servant.

"Waiting for you in the dressing room, milord."

"Good, good. See to her, Liza, there's a good girl." And the earl, leaning heavily on young Martin, went into the dressing room next door.

Liza obediently did as she was bid. She looked down at Marie Fleur, her dark eyes bright. "You can go to bed now and sleep," she said. "S'pose that'll be a relief."

This evening of horror was over.

Chapter 10

"BY ALL MEANS, Brandy, I'd love to have you," said the Earl of Cranbrook, guiding his white stallion safely through the melee of riders in this late afternoon parade through Hyde Park. Tomorrow would see a mass exodus for the country as the titled Corinthians joined splendid house parties for the Christmas season.

Impeccably dressed in a teal-blue tailed coat, cream doeskin breeches, and highly polished Hessians, Brandon made a perfect picture of the fashionable gentleman. His mount gleamed like satin, its body rippling beneath his well-muscled legs.

"I'll be leaving for the country myself tomorrow."

"Really? Going up to Norfolk, old chap?"

"Yes, get in a bit of hunting before the weather turns."

"Devilish cold. Suspect it's going to be a bad winter."

"By all reports."

This pleasant exchange brought them to the end of the Row.

"At eight then, old chap?"

"I'll be prompt."

"The little Neapolitan nightingale keeping you busy?"

"Not that busy. I'll be there." Brandon grinned, and patted his black's neck. "I hear you've been up to some theatricals of your own. Very hush-hush, or so I heard."

The earl's smile was tight. "I didn't know your tastes ran to such extravaganzas. I'll drop you a line when next we have something arranged."

Brandon smiled, hiding his own revulsion for the entertainment in which the earl and his tight-knit group of cronies reveled. You could say what you wanted about Prinny. It was true the future King George IV was grossly fat and an infantile voluptuary, yet he did not indulge in the depravity whispered about Cranbrook's "by invitation only" evenings. In fact, Prinny didn't believe a damned word about it and he said so. "A splendid fellow, Cranbrook, red-blooded as any other Englishman," he had spluttered in rage when questioned about the matter.

"Shame that deuced fine little Dowling filly slipped out of the traces. Dowling never knew when he was well off," Brandon remarked casually, slowing his horse's pace in order to hear the earl's comment.

"You should know, Brandy, you old dog. Yes, it is a pity. Still, with those French pieces you never know. You could've blown me down with a feather when I heard the story. The man's in the Home Office, they say. Not naming any names, but—"

At that moment a phaeton came bowling along and the two men parted, tipping their top hats to the fur-swathed lady in the carriage.

"Georgina Stanhope has her eye on you, Brandy," remarked the earl, glancing after the disappearing phaeton. "You should arrange a meeting when her tabby's not in attendance. You could sing some sweet songs together." Cranbrook winked meaningfully and, tipping his hat in farewell, he turned in the opposite direction, heading home.

Brandon dismounted and leaned against the white-painted railing at the Row's boundary, his mouth grim as he watched the earl's tall, elegant figure disappear in the gathering mist. The current rumor about Marie Fleur running off to the country with a nameless minister in Liverpool's cabinet was ridiculous. He was sure Cranbrook was responsible for its manufacture. Brandon of all men was in a position to know just how ridiculous it was. After that disastrous meeting at the opera he might have expected her to flee to Langley, her nose out of joint, yet judicious inquiries in that direction had unearthed nothing. Even Poggy Reid was at a loss to explain her whereabouts. What had become of her?

Brandon remounted, swinging himself with ease into the saddle, oblivious to the admiring glances he was receiving from a carriageful of elegant ladies wrapped to their delicate chins in furs. Cranbrook knew more than he was letting on. He must! He had been the last person to see Marie Fleur. And Brandon was convinced she would never confide a secret love affair to Cranbrook.

He tipped his hat to several people of his acquaintance, declining to stop. Feeling unusually reticent, he wrestled with disturbing thoughts about Marie Fleur. Not a night went by that he didn't wake thinking of her. Surely she had not plunged into a whirlwind romance to punish him for Gabriella. Could it be possible that she was cozily ensconced in some cabinet minister's country hideaway? No! He knew her too well for that. Once he explained the difficult circumstances of his relationship with the opera singer, she would not hold Gabriella against him. He grinned sheepishly—at least he hoped she would not hold the fiery little Italian against him. With Marie Fleur it was hard to tell.

Brandon arrived at Cranbrook House promptly at eight and was shown inside the opulent drawing room where several guests were already assembled. The plum-colored walls picked out in white glowed richly in the candlelight. Brandon tried to appear his usual languid self, yet he felt as tense as a coiled spring. Not only had he accepted this dinner invitation in an effort to discover more about Marie Fleur's whereabouts, he was also here on official business. Cranbrook's French valet had been recently uncovered as a Napoleonic spy. This time Gaston was preparing to pass vital documents containing English troop movements to the Froggies. Protected as he was within Cranbrook's household, the Foreign office had been unable to get at him. Brandon's Uncle Ben, who, like Brandon's father, held a high post in the government, had personally asked him if he would take the risk and intercept the stolen documents. Burglary was not his usual operation, but recklessly Brandon had succumbed to the line about doing his duty for his country and agreed to tackle the job. A replacement document crackled uncomfortably inside his royal blue coat, a constant reminder of duty.

Dinner was drawing to a close. Brandon sat back feeling pleasantly full. The combination of roast goose with glacéed chestnuts, asparagus with *hollandaise* sauce, brussels sprouts, apricot soufflé, and copious glasses of dry white wine had married surprisingly well. Soon he could excuse himself on the pretext of a call of nature. Already armed with knowledge of the location of the French valet's room, he needed only slip away for a few minutes to accomplish his job. If he hadn't missed his guess Gaston would be belowstairs gorging himself on the dinner leftovers. That would give him a few minutes leeway.

Cranbrook looked over at him, smiled, and raised his glass. Brandon replied with his own freshly filled glass. Damn him! Nothing about Marie Fleur had been allowed to slip despite the attempts of several curious gentlemen to pump the earl to reveal how he knew where the delicious Lady Dowling was hiding. He had even attempted to grill the servants, but they either knew nothing or had been instructed to hold their tongues. Brandon could not demand outright to know Marie Fleur's whereabouts; he would be considered a madman. Short of doing just that, he did not see how he would discover anything Cranbrook did not want him to discover. Cranbrook was far more wily than Brandon had given him credit for. There was even the remote possibility that the earl knew no more than he about her disappearance, but Brandon doubted that. He had grown accustomed to working by instinct. And instinct told him Cranbrook was guilty as sin.

Occasional sounds filtered upstairs from the large farewell dinner party. Marie Fleur lay on her bed, feigning sleep beneath a mountain of blankets. For two days she had not seen the earl. Rose had told her they were preparing to leave for the country tomorrow. She could not allow him to take her to Yorkshire, where all hope of escape would be dashed. Her food was usually drugged to keep her docile. Today, in order to keep her mind clear, Marie Fleur had merely pretended to eat. Rose was not nearly as conscientious as she used to be. Lately, while Marie Fleur ate the maid stood at the window peering beyond the leafless trees to the street below where she could glimpse the passing parade of horses and carriages turning into the Mall. Marie Fleur had been able to dump her food in a towel. For almost twenty-four hours she had eaten nothing. Her stomach growled continually in protest.

In a few minutes Mrs. Medley, the housekeeper, would come by on her rounds to see if she was asleep. It would be much later, if at all, when she would be required to amuse the earl. Because she had not yet chosen to come willingly to his arms, Cranbrook had to keep her hidden from mutual acquaintances. This fact made him violently angry for it had destroyed his dream of revealing to an envious society that he was the secret lover the beauteous Lady Dowling had chosen from the cream of the *ton*.

Last week the Regent himself had been a guest at Cranbrook House. Marie Fleur grimaced as she reflected on that Roman banquet. She had only glimpsed the future king from behind the silken draperies. Grotesquely overweight, Prince George had been a decided disappointment. Dressed in a voluminous toga the size of a tent, he lay on silken cushions gorging himself as if he hadn't eaten in a week. That was the night when, unguarded for a moment, she had made a bid for freedom, intending to burst in on the guests and beg for their help. Westerham was there; she knew he would help her. Unfortunately, Martin, who seemed to know her thoughts almost before she thought them, grabbed her, his large hands nearly suffocating her as he stifled her protests.

There, the key was grating in the lock! Making her breathing soft and even, Marie Fleur lay still, trying not to tremble with the anticipation of what lay ahead. A faint pool of candlelight splashed across her face and was gone. Not until she heard the door lock again and the footsteps die away did she stir.

Following her new ritual she picked up the towel of food and took it to the window, then she flung the contents into the garden. Snuffling and a chance yap from the earl's usually silent watchdogs told her how much they had enjoyed her meal. She hoped the drug the earl used to sedate her would work equally well on the animals, enabling her to escape unharmed. For over a week she had plotted this daring escape, knowing she must remain alert if she was to follow through with her plan. Not until today had she been able to put the plan in action.

Marie Fleur wore the blue wool gown and thick red-and-white shawl she had been given for everyday wear. She wished she had a dark cloak because she was afraid the white shawl would be noticeable in the dark. The idea of leaving it behind occurred to her, but she decided it was far too cold for that. She had also been provided with a pair of leather shoes so she wouldn't have to tramp the London streets barefoot.

The small window opened easily, and she thrust her head through the aperture. Wriggling, straining, she pushed her shoulders through. With supreme effort she struggled to a sitting position on the sill. The sounds from the lower floors were much louder now, and she realized someone had opened a window below. Singing drifted upward. It was a decidedly bawdy ballad she recognized from William's parties. The gnarled vine was rough on her hands, and she scraped her knuckles on the brick wall. The voices sounded even closer, and she crushed herself close to the wall as a man said, "Egad, stars big as diamonds! Beautiful sight!"

Not as entranced as he by the heavens, she waited, not daring to descend because the vine twined about the window of the ground floor dining room. On second thought she wondered if it would not be wiser to climb inside the open window below and try to move unseen through the house. The room below hers belonged to the earl's valet, Gaston. She had heard him singing a French round one evening when she lay in her usual after-dinner stupor. At this hour he would be belowstairs eating his supper. If she climbed to the garden one of the earl's guests might see her. There were occasions when discovery would have been ideal, yet tonight she did not know who had been invited. If the men did not know her, they would believe any lie the earl told them. This past week she had realized just how inventive he could be when Rose had recounted the current gossip about town suggesting that she was sharing a romantic tryst with a member of the prime minister's cabinet. That cleverly spread rumor was the reason no one had been concerned over her disappearance. When Parliament reconvened after the holidays the ruse would be discovered, but by then she would be buried in the wilds of Yorkshire.

The earl's guests finally moved away from the dining room window, allowing her to put her plan into action. It was not nearly so easy as she had imagined to cling to the vine with her skirts impeding her movement. The shawl kept slipping down, and the bricks grazed her hands. Afraid she would lose her shoes, Marie Fleur gingerly put one foot over the sill of the valet's room. The room was dark, yet she fancied she could smell a freshly lit candle. With a sigh of relief, she dropped from the windowsill to the uncarpeted floor beneath. For a few minutes she crouched there trembling, sick with weakness and excitement.

"What the devil are you doing?"

Her hands went numb and her heart thundered like a drum. It was not the Frenchman, yet the man's voice was terribly familiar. In her current state of nerves Marie Fleur could not place it. She struggled to her feet and was immediately imprisoned in a man's strong grasp. It was too dark to identify him. Instinct told her to fight for freedom. Kicking, punching, she tried desperately to repel him, terrified he would summon the earl.

"Look, you fool woman, stop struggling."

She cried out in pain as the man exerted even more pressure on her wrists, swearing in exasperation over her struggles. Subdued and weeping, Marie Fleur finally hung her head, her courage, her will, crumpling in the face of defeat. The man lit a candle. That was why she had smelled candle grease. She must have startled him when he saw her descending from the floor above, and he had blown out his candle. She fought the throb of pain in her temples as he turned toward her, his bulk throwing grotesque shadows on the plaster ceiling.

"Brandon!"

"Sweetheart! God—I don't believe it!"

They stared dumbfounded at each other, the wavering candle flame a halo of gold between them. Marie Fleur was aware of a choking sensation in her throat. For a wild moment she supposed his presence to be a product of her imagination. When he put down the candle and pulled her into his embrace, she knew he was real.

"Oh, God, Brandon! How glad I am to see you."

"What are you doing climbing through windows?"

"It's a long, terrible story," she gasped, burying her face in his warm neck. "Just hold me. Comfort me. Oh, I thought I'd never see you again."

Tremoring as he pressed her against the safety of his body, Brandon held her tight, trying not to hurt her. In his joyous discovery he wanted to crush her, to blend muscle and sinew and blood. The sudden reminder of his actual task in this room brought him quickly to earth.

"We've got to get out of here. You can tell me everything later," he said tersely, turning to the opened desk where he had been searching for the papers. This was where his informant told him they would be found, yet so far his search had been unsuccessful.

"I can't go downstairs and let everyone see me. You don't understand—"

"First I've got to find something, then we'll go out the back way as quickly as possible."

Her delight at being rescued by Brandon slowly receding, Marie Fleur began to consider how odd it was to find him going through Gaston's desk. He refused to answer her questions. He continued searching inside the desk before turning his attention to its back, at which he looked for a catch to a secret compartment. Exclaiming in triumph, he finally found what he was looking for. A narrow drawer shot open to reveal a bundle of folded papers, which Brandon quickly exchanged for the packet inside his coat.

"I'll explain everything later. We've got to get out of here," he muttered, blowing out the candle flame. Then, grasping Marie Fleur's arm, Brandon propelled her into the drafty hallway.

They hastened down the back stairs, expecting to be confronted at every turn as laughter and clattering steps frequently made them hug the wall until the danger was past. They finally reached the house's rear entrance where the maids hung their outerwear on pegs outside the scullery door. Brandon grabbed an enveloping cloak and threw it to Marie Fleur.

"Put that on."

"But, Brandon, listen, there's so much I've got to—"

"Not now. When we're safely outside you can tell me everything. Keep quiet and follow me."

Hardly able to believe their good fortune, Marie Fleur hastened after him. The cold damp air took her breath as they walked outside. Brandon slowed his pace, adopting a more leisurely stride as they headed for the stables. Before they reached the lantern hanging over a doorway, he pulled the dark hood down to cover Marie Fleur's face; then, his finger to his lips, he cautioned her to keep quiet.

A sleepy groom emerged from the straw, rubbing his eyes and yawning. "Yes, sir."

"Saddle the black for me, there's a good fellow. By the way, have you any ponies for hire? I'll have it back in the morning." The man shook his head. Not accepting that for an answer, Brandon leaned closer and grasped the man's arm. "I'm prepared to make it well worth your while. I'm in a bit of a spot, actually. I arrived alone, but decided to leave with company." Here he indicated the cloaked figure standing beyond the lantern glow. The groom's face brightened and he nodded understandingly, a grin spreading across his flat face.

"Ah, nice bit o'skirt, milord. Which one?"

"The new girl. Damn it all, fellow, who bothers to ask their name?" Brandon chuckled, hoping his answer would suffice. It did.

"Now, don't reckon it makes much difference what they's called. I'll see what I can do."

The groom promptly reappeared leading a slender chestnut saddled for the road; Brandon's black stallion walked docilely behind him.

"Capital! I'll send a lad over with the hoss. Can't thank you enough." Brandon winked at the groom and money changed hands. "Come on, girl, let's not waste time. I'm eager to sample my ill-gotten gains. Not a word to the old harridan. Wouldn't want the little gel to be punished," he added in an undertone.

"Right, milord. Me lips is sealed." The man winked and touched his forelock as the two mounted and turned the horses around before the stable.

Brandon raised his hand in farewell. Catching Marie Fleur's reins, he guided her beside him as they clopped through the side entrance into the street. A commotion erupted at one of the doors, making her gasp in alarm. Brandon ignored the voices and kept on going. Not until they were within sight of St. James's Park did he slow the pace. There he drew her under the shielding branches of a lime tree, positioning the horses so they faced the direction of Cranbrook House.

"Now you can explain why you were climbing through a window. In fact, you can tell me what the devil you were doing in Cranbrook's place to start with."

Though eager to be avenged for the humiliating treatment she had suffered at the earl's hands, Marie Fleur heeded an inner warning of danger. Whatever Brandon had been doing in the valet's room was decidedly outside the law. Yet if she revealed the extent of her mistreatment while captive in Cranbrook House he would be at the earl's throat. For his own safety she prudently decided to tell Brandon only part of the truth.

"I was trying to escape."

"I gathered that."

"The earl appears to be somewhat touched in the head."

"I gathered that also."

"He invited me to come to his house and he kept me captive there in hope I'd agree to become his—"

"By God! I'll have his neck!"

"No," she cried in alarm, grasping his arm as he swung about. "I'm safe now. To go back would only cause a scandal."

"He shan't get away with it! You're as touched as he to even suggest such a ridiculous—"

"Listen. Tonight you can't afford to return or to tell them how you found me. The earl's friends don't usually engage in thievery beneath their host's own roof."

"The door was unlocked." He grinned, his anger coming under control. For a moment he had completely forgotten his purpose for being in the French valet's room. Marie Fleur was a decided deterrent to duty.

"You're right, at the moment I daren't risk it. But, by God, Cranbrook shan't get away with this. To dare keep you prisoner, then to spread lies insinuating you were tête-à-tête with a politician—the blackguard! I'll demand satisfaction just as soon as I'm able."

Marie Fleur swallowed uncomfortably, thankful for the cover of darkness. Were Brandon to examine her closely and see fading bruises from the loving ministration of the earl's whip, there would be no stopping him. The memory of those hideous evenings made her shudder.

"Tomorrow he's leaving for Yorkshire. While he's gone you can decide what to do."

"I don't need time; I merely lack opportunity," Brandon growled, glancing toward the wrought iron portals of Cranbrook House. He could distinguish little in the misty night. The distant rumble of a carriage, the clop of hooves alerted him to possible danger. He motioned to her to continue their journey.

Out of the city they rode, heading south. Brandon said little after he had revealed their destination. Marie Fleur's heart sank when she learned they faced yet another parting. Brandon was bound for France. Had they met last week they would have had time to spend together. As it was, he had barely enough time to find her lodgings before he must be away.

They galloped along the highway, the searing, salt-laden wind sweeping over the exposed countryside, chilling them to the bone. Marie Fleur's joy at the sight of Brandon gradually evaporated. He had not taken her in his arms, nor had he kissed her since their initial meeting. In fact, he had barely spoken to her, staying deep in thought as they rapidly swallowed the miles to the south coast. Was it because he puzzled over how to explain his Italian woman that he was robbed of speech? The more she dwelled on the picture of beautiful Gabriella in his arms, the stronger grew the jealousy curdling in her veins. At last, unable to stand the suspense any longer, she reined in.

"Brandon, let's rest here. There's something I must ask you."

"Why was I stealing from Cranbrook's valet?" He stopped his horse somewhat reluctantly. They had little enough time as it was. Still, a few minutes lost here could be made up closer to their destination.

"Yes, so long as you mention it, why were you stealing

from him? Surely a valet hasn't valuables of interest to Black Nick."

"No, not to Black Nick, but they're of the greatest interest to the British government. Once I asked you to trust me. It still holds true. I've a job to do, a dangerous job as far removed from my supposed public self as can be. Suffice it to say that every day I'm away I'm in constant danger. For your own safety you must know no more."

His intense speech surprised Marie Fleur. His revelation of heightened danger temporarily took her aback, yet still that jealousy gnawed, prompting questions that would not be silenced.

"Is Gabriella Vasco part of your dangerous second life?" she asked, venturing to make her question sound lightly humorous. The venture was a failure; tension and anger overlaid her words.

"Yes."

"And you're not going to offer the slightest explanation," she gasped incredulously. "They say she's your mistress. Am I to blindly accept that gossip without question?"

"Your acceptance would certainly make matters easier." He smiled as he reached for her, but Marie Fleur pulled away. "Yet I suppose blind faith would be too much to expect from a woman like you. You must accept the fact Gabriella means nothing to me. I'm not in love with her. She's merely valuable to my work. She has a direct link with one of Napoleon's commanders. Listen, sweetheart, I daren't tell you more. My life depends on secrecy. I'm not what I seem—"

"Let's not go into that again. Those words carry a sense of déjà vu."

Anger spread a dusky banner across his cheekbones, and his mouth tightened. "I don't owe you any explanation of my actions. If I choose ten women as mistress I have no need to explain myself."

"Indeed! I thought we were lovers."

"We are lovers. Love makes the difference between our relationship and that which I share with Gabriella."

His blunt words made her gasp. "So, you aren't even going to deny you sleep with her, that you keep her as your mistress. Am I supposed to accept that, to quietly acquiesce?" Her words dissolved in tears.

Brandon's anger mounted when again she repelled his attempt at comfort. "You can do what you damned well please, you contrary chit. Now, come, we've wasted enough time. I've pressing business at the coast."

"No. I thank you for rescuing me, but I thank you also to ride ahead without me. I'll not share you with that Italian woman. How dare you even expect me to? Especially when I've more than enough knowledge of your criminal activities to condemn you to the hangman."

"Don't ever threaten me!"

"I'll do as I please!"

"You'll do as you are told!"

Marie Fleur cried out shrilly as he seized her reins and yanked the horse to action. With a shriek she gripped the mount as it lurched forward in a drunken rush. "Let me go! I'll not travel with you. What do you propose to do with me while you adventure on the high seas?"

"I'll rent you a room, and there you're to stay. Or do you fancy going back to Cranbrook? He has some very unsavory tastes, my love, in case you're not aware of it. Now shut up and ride."

Tears poured down Marie Fleur's cheeks, stinging painfully in the cold wind. Why was she following him? Why did she meekly obey? Brandon had virtually confessed Gabriella was his mistress as he had also shown in no uncertain terms just how little he cared for her feelings in the matter. Damn him! She should pull free and ride in the opposite direction. Yet her anger was already cooling, allowing common sense to come to the fore. Without money, proper clothing, or any knowledge of the region, she would not get far. A woman alone on a cold winter's night would be fair game for the lawless fringe of society patrolling England's heaths and moorlands.

Several hours later, with the plaintive bleat of sheep echoing in the fog-shrouded distance, Brandon turned onto a side road. Here a thatched cottage nestled behind shielding hawthorn hedge. A single uncurtained window winked brightly in the dark, spilling a flood of lantern light over the tangled grass.

"Wait here a minute. This is where I change clothes."

A woman opened the door, peering out as the horses' hooves thudded outside the cottage.

"Is she another of your useful business contacts?" Marie Fleur demanded sarcastically as she indentified the mobcapped female as young and comely.

Brandon's mouth was grim as he swung from the saddle. "Yes, for your information, my dear, she is."

Like a fool Marie Fleur waited for him, huddling inside her borrowed cloak to shelter from the wind. The high hawthorn hedge formed a windbreak, and she moved closer to it. What manner of man was he that he did not even attempt a lie to cover his amorous connections? Most men would have lied if only to salve her pride. Yet would she have loved a cheat? Had Brandon lied to her she would have known it. Perhaps it was this inherent, if brutal, honesty that was one of his attractions.

When he finally emerged at the now-dark doorway, Brandon was masked and clad in a voluminous black cloak covering that same long military-style coat he had worn during his last mysterious assignment across the Channel.

"Black Nick?"

"At your service, madam. Come, we must press ourselves now. The Ship and Anchor's almost ten miles away."

Marie Fleur refrained from questioning him about the woman whom she fancied she saw watching their departure from the upstairs window. How had he explained his female companion to the cottage wife? Given Brandon's general reticence on that subject, she decided he had probably made no attempt to explain her at all.

The stinging salt wind made her lips sore. Eventually a lighted lantern swinging above the painted sign of the Ship and Anchor appeared through the misty darkness. The whitewashed inn stood alone on the windswept headland overlooking the Channel. This was where Brandon intended to lodge her. Quietly Marie Fleur dismounted and allowed the groom to take her horse. He appeared to know Black Nick for he tipped his forelock and discreetly kept his eyes downcast.

They entered the old inn, virtually deserted at this late hour.

"Bench, good man, are you here?"

The corpulent landlord straightened up from behind the counter, an ale-stained apron tied around his ample girth.

"Nick, lad! 'Tis a while since you been this way. Got another job?"

"And fast. However, I've a slight encumbrance. Can you lodge this lady for a few nights till I return?"

The landlord eyed Marie Fleur's serving girl's cloak.

"Reckon, if it be that important to 'e."

"It's extremely important. I'll pay you well for her board when I come to get her."

"Ye are coming back?"

Brandon turned to look at Marie Fleur, whose damp blond curls had escaped her hood and trailed in wisps over her smooth brow. The brisk wind had whipped color to her cheeks and reddened her softly delectable mouth. His heart lurched—and it was not just his heart. "Wouldn't you?" he asked gruffly, gripping the landlord's beefy arm. "A man would be a fool to let that one get away."

The landlord showed blackened stubs of teeth in a wide grin. "Agreed, my lad. And I'm nigh on fifty years old."

Brandon drew Marie Fleur aside, indicating they needed privacy, and the landlord obligingly busied himself in clearing the littered taproom.

"You'll be safe here, sweetheart. Bench is crude, but honest. This is a quick job. I'll be back in a couple of days. You will wait—won't you?"

She gazed up at his handsome face, mysteriously shadowed in the candlelit room. Beyond the creaking latticed pane the wind howled, sounding so lonely her heart ached anew for their need to part. "Yes, I'll wait. Any woman in her right senses would—"

"—do exactly the same thing if she loved me like you claim to do." A tinge of humor crept into his voice as he tried to lift their parting from heartrending sorrow to a casual farewell. "I'll come back for you, I swear. Trust me, darling, whatever happens. That's all I ask . . . and that you love me."

"I love you," she whispered, her mouth against his cold cheek. She kissed him. His skin tasted of sea and wind and salt marsh. Tumultuous emotions stirred within her, and tears pricked her eyes.

They kissed deeply, arms locked tight, trying to make the moment last forever. Then, resolutely, Brandon set her aside. Nodding to the landlord, he walked out into the windy night.

Marie Fleur lay awake a long time in the small chamber beneath the eave at the Ship and Anchor. Late though the hour had been, the landlord had provided her with a generous meal of mutton pasties, bread, and cheese. It had seemed like a banquet. What luxury to be able to eat and know the food needed for sustenance would not disable her. Whenever she thought about those frightening weeks at Cranbrook House she could not suppress a shudder. Now that she was free of her prison and the sadistic earl, everything blended together like a horrendous nightmare. Perhaps she could eventually block the memories from her mind. If only Brandon had not been in such haste to leave. She had intended to tell him about those poor little street girls, about captive Vicente, about the half-dozen other waifs who had trailed through that magnificent mansion during her stay. She knew if she made her knowledge public few would believe her, and even if they did, fewer still would care what befell the countless poor. In London's squalid streets rich sadists like the Earl of Cranbrook could find an inexhaustible supply of actors for their charades. If by accident the pleasure became too intense and a life was snuffed out, obliging Martin had contact with a gang that provided bodies to medical students for anatomical experiments. It was common knowledge such gangs often sped likely victims on their way. And few citizens cared enough about the crime to bother to remedy it. What hope had she of being believed when she tried to expose the perversions of one of England's richest peers?

Resolutely Marie Fleur thrust the disturbing memories to the back of her mind. Perhaps someday she would be able to tell Brandon the whole story. At present his swift temper would create far too dangerous a situation; it was just as well she hadn't had the opportunity. Drowsily she sank deeper in the feather mattress. All she had to do now was rest and eat and wait. In the space of two sunsets her beloved would be at her side. The nightmare was over.

Sometime in the night Marie Fleur was awakened by knocking on the door. The landlord's agitated voice could be heard conversing with someone who sobbed rather than spoke. Fear alerted her to possible danger, and she sat up.

"What is it?"

"Someone to see yer, missus. Says it's a matter of life and death."

Her heart thumped uneasily. "Who wants to see me?"

"Jake—maybe you don't remember. Open the door."

Jake? Marie Fleur grabbed her cloak from the bed and pulled it around her as she padded to the door. The only Jake she knew had been the lad who rode with Black Nick! Her heart skipped a beat as she drew back the bolt.

"Did you come from your master?" she whispered, wide-eyed in the dark.

"Be all right to leave 'im, missus?" questioned the landlord dubiously. He stood shivering in a voluminous nightshirt, his candle dribbling wax on the floorboards.

"Yes, I know him."

Marie Fleur half pulled young Jake inside her room. He was swathed in a thick overcoat. With trembling hands she lit her candle and held it aloft to see her visitor. His face was white as a sheet, and he swayed where he stood.

"What is it? Are you hurt?"

"Bad, Missus. Can I?" He indicated the bed and she nodded. "Ran into constables on the sea road. They's working with the customs men to get smugglers." Jake winced and eased himself to a more comfortable position. "Was on me way 'ere to tell ye . . ."

Marie Fleur leaned over him and pulled aside the enveloping garment, gasping in horror at what she saw. The damp patch on the breast of his thick coat was not rain, as she had first thought, but blood. Jake's shirt and jacket had become a mangled part of his chest. "Oh, God, you need a doctor."

"Naw. Too late for that. 'Sides, they'd only haul me away. What I needs is you to listen and listen good."

Chastised, she perched beside him, chilling at the sight of his terrible wound. Soon the blood would run down over the sheets to the floorboards; the landlord would come to investigate.

"Nick's in terrible danger."

Sickness assailed her at his words. "But surely he's safe aboard ship for France."

"That's where the danger is. Don't know if he'd agree with me telling you this—he's a government agent, missus, a spy, if you will."

"A spy!" So that was what he had been hinting, delicately skirting the actual admission of his profession. "I thought he was a highwayman, a smuggler."

"That too. It's a good cover. Now I can't get word to 'im, you've got to. Go after 'im, stop 'im. They won't've sailed yet. If only I'd not run into them blasted constables on the road. Turned tail then, I did, coming 'ere to you, and got both barrels from the revenue men." Jake lay back exhausted, his voice barely audible as he said, "A paper . . . mayhap you know— 'e took it to London."

She nodded, remembering the desk in the valet's cramped room. "Yes, I remember. Yet surely that paper couldn't be important enough to make it a matter of life and death. How could a valet have access to state secrets?"

"Because Gaston's a ruddy Frog spy! Someone high up's been leaking information about troop movements. Only Nick doesn't know the Frogs set 'im up with a false dispatch. Of course, they don't know *who* 'e is, just that 'e'd be at Cranbrook House. They all uses code names. You see, missus, Nick's not just a spy . . . 'e's a double agent."

"A double agent! You mean he works for both sides?"

Jake nodded, shifting positions on the lumpy mattress. "You've got it. And them Froggies twigged it. They plan to catch Nick red'anded with them special papers. That'll condemn 'im as this English spy they've been after. Whether 'e's a smuggler, a gentleman, or Bob's yer uncle, it don't matter to them."

"So you want me to stop him going aboard ship, to tell him the papers are a trap?"

"Aye, they'll be waiting for 'im in Paris to make contact. We can't let 'im sail or 'e's signing 'is own death warrant. Spy's is not well thought of during a war."

Marie Fleur smiled at his small attempt at humor, and she adjusted the pillow behind his head.

"Take the coast road to the quay. Ask around for Nick. Likely 'e'll be at a tavern—Jellied Eel's the name. It's allus been 'is favorite. Now, in case they's reluctant to talk, there's money in me pocket to grease a few palms."

Marie Fleur found the money wrapped in a seaman's pouch in Jake's coat pocket. It was still hard to accept his story. Lately, events had happened too quickly for her mind to absorb. One thing was certain, a truth that set her heart pounding with fear: Brandon's life was at stake. And it was up to her to save him before it was too late.

Assuring her he would be all right, Jake smiled weakly, thankful she was loyal enough to his master to help.

Marie Fleur scrabbled beneath the bed for her shoes, slipping them on as she hurried from the room. She knocked on the landlord's door on her way downstairs and breathlessly recounted her mission. He promised he would do what he could for the wounded man.

The sleepy groom seemed to take hours saddling her horse. There was no mounting block, and the lad seemed unaware she needed assistance in mounting. Seething over his incompetence, Marie Fleur finally wheeled onto the highway, heading for the small harbor that lay to her right. She had gone only a hundred yards before it began to spit rain. She pulled her hood over her hair. As she rode she discovered she was trembling with a mixture of fright and cold, hardly able to believe she was thundering through the night on the strength of a wounded lad's garbled story.

The distinctive rumble of carriage wheels and the thunder of hooves on the macadam surface caught her attention. Rounding a curve she glimpsed through the low hedge a lighted coach traveling at breakneck speed. Someone else was in a fearful hurry. Not until she rounded a second bend, which afforded a better view of the conveyance flying along the road, did she recognize that distinctive equipage. Cranbrook! No one else had such a sleek carriage agleam with silver. And the muscular blacks, straining blood-flecked nostrils for the coast, were as distinctive as the carriage. He must have followed them from London! He might even have learned her current destination from the helpful innkeeper.

Fear gripped Marie Fleur as she urged her horse faster along the narrow road. The salt smell in the air intensified as she drew nearer to the sea. Ahead through the gloom she could distinguish the harbor's bobbing lights, while farther out yellow blurs shimmered as anchored vessels dipped on the water. To her horror she found she was not outdistancing the coach. It drew ever closer. When she pulled onto the open stretch of highway she would be spotted. Desperate to outwit her pursuer, Marie Fleur plunged her reluctant mount through a break in the hedge, galloping him flat out across the open country. The carriage and four made such a racket no one would hear her animal's hooves. The coast road curved around cottages whilst her route was direct. Flushed with triumph, Marie Fleur prodded the horse onward, praying she could coax these last few miles out of him.

Plunging between two ramshackle barns, she finally emerged on the cobbled apron before the quay. Even now she could hear the coach clattering through the deserted streets. Marie Fleur approached the first seaman she saw loading boxes aboard a small vessel. When she asked him about Nick, the man sensed her desperation and did not feign ignorance. He pointed through the dark to a cove several hundred yards downshore from whence the highwayman had sailed less than an hour ago.

Marie Fleur wrung her hands in anguish. Brandon lay out there, bobbing close to the horizon and awaiting the swelling tide. Perhaps she could get a message to him using the seamen's lantern code for signaling ships at sea. Yet before she could inquire if anyone could deliver such a message, thundering hooves and deafening wheels announced the reckless descent of Cranbrook's coach as it hurtled around the corner and skidded onto the quay. With a cry of horror, Marie Fleur leaped from her horse. She could never outpace them astride the blown animal; her only hope lay on foot.

Casting about for a hiding place as her ears rang with the sharp tones of Cranbrook's valet inquiring about a lady from a nearby fisherman, Marie Fleur chose the loading vessel. The gangplank was still down, and she raced aboard. She hoped the earl would not think of searching a ship for her. Once he had given up his hunt she could safely emerge.

Scrambling over crates and barrels in the fetid darkness, she lost her footing. Everything seemed to shift underfoot as she grabbed frantically for a handhold. She landed with a bump on the far side of the stack. Picking herself up, she nursed her bruised shins and elbows. There was a lantern bobbing up on deck, and she headed for the light, hoping no one had seen her come aboard. She had no wish to meet these sailors, who might well be strangers to whom the name Black Nick meant nothing.

A great meshed bundle blocked her way, and Marie Fleur climbed onto it, scraping her shins against projecting metal bands on boxes and casks. She was almost at the top of the heap, the lantern light darting in macabre dance over the narrow stairway overhead, when everything began to move. With a shriek of fright she toppled sideways. Marie Fleur fell to the deck with a bone-jarring thud, striking her head against the bulwark. She groaned in pain, clutching her bursting head before everything slipped away beyond that bobbing light.

Chapter 11

SOFT HANDS BRUSHED her brow as Marie Fleur tried to focus through a confusing blur. "Brandon," she whispered, "is that you?"

French voices. Laughter. Fear shot through her limbs. She thrust off the caressing hand with a resurgence of strength and struggled to a sitting position. The room rocked giddily before finally righting itself.

"Eh, you're still alive then."

"You've got a lump like a pigeon egg."

A man in rough seaman's garb leaned against the wall while a young woman in a scarlet wool skirt and black shawl sat beside the bunk.

"Who are you, *cherie?*" the woman asked kindly. "Are you a stowaway?"

The word did not assume meaning until Marie Fleur became aware of the ship's creaking timbers and the curious lurching of the cabin, which told her they were under way.

"Oh, God, we're sailing!" In alarm she tried to rise from the narrow bunk. She fell back helplessly as a fresh wave of giddiness assailed her. "Please, you must help me get ashore," she whispered, finding the French unfamiliar on her tongue.

"There, there, *cherie,* don't fret. You're safe with us. What's your name? I'm Corinne, and that ugly lout is my brother, Yves."

"Marie Fleur."

"See, she is French," Corinne announced triumphantly to her brother. "Are you running away from home?"

Marie Fleur nodded. How much could she safely tell them?

Assuming she was reluctant to divulge her story before Yves, Corinne shrilly flapped him away. The big seaman cursed beneath his breath as he thumped up the narrow stair, leaving the women alone. "Men!" Corinne exclaimed, rolling her eyes heavenward.

The captain's sister was in her early twenties, pretty in a coarse, bold way, with curly red hair, green eyes, and that

175

brick-dust complexion that sometimes afflicts redheads. She helped Marie Fleur to a sitting position and thrust a pillow behind her.

"There . . . now he's gone and you can tell me your secrets."

"First tell me where we're bound?"

"Some craggy point in Brittany, though officially we're headed for Cornwall. Why?"

"I must find someone. You must put me ashore. I can't sail to Brittany."

Corinne pulled a face. "You can tell Yves that yourself. Anyway, what's so important ashore?"

Marie Fleur swallowed, trying to formulate a believable story without revealing anything to endanger Brandon. "My lover was to sail on the morning tide. I ran away to follow him."

Corinne grinned, her interest immediately aroused. "He'll be on his way by now. Where was he bound?"

Panic-stricken, Marie Fleur realized she did not know. On the quay she had learned only the name of his ship, while from Jake she discovered Paris was his eventual destination. "Somewhere in France. He was on the *Wasp*."

"Yves will know. Your man's a smuggler then?"

Not knowing how she should answer, Marie Fleur mumbled, "He's really a highwayman who works with the smugglers out of Romney Marsh."

Corinne returned a few minutes later, a smile of achievement on her full mouth. "You're in luck. Yves knows the *Wasp's* captain. They were bound for Normandy."

"Normandy! Oh, we'll never catch him!"

"The *Wasp's* not as fast as we are. Besides, in our business we never linger. You know, you're a fool to chase after him. Men aren't worth it. Will your papa come looking for you?"

"He won't know for a while. They're in Yorkshire for Christmas."

Marie Fleur was growing more inventive by the minute. After Corinne readily accepted her story, she felt somewhat guilty about the deception.

"Lie still. You need rest. We'll be putting out to sea in a few minutes. Hungry?" Marie Fleur nodded, only just realizing that fact. "I'll get you something. While we eat you can tell me more about your handsome highwayman. He is handsome, isn't he?" Again a nod. Corinne smiled in anticipation of the forthcoming gossip, and she sped upstairs to the deck.

By the time Corinne returned with the meal, however, Marie Fleur did not feel like eating. The rolling vessel made her stomach heave, and she felt sick. Corinne laughed sympathetically when she saw her clutch her mouth at the smell of food.

"Not a sailor, eh? Too bad. Well, I'll eat for both of us."

Though she tried, Marie Fleur was unable even to keep down last night's meal. Chuckling good-naturedly, Corinne held Marie Fleur's head while she vomited until she thought she would heave out her insides. Instead of adjusting to the swell of the waves as the hours passed, Marie Fleur grew worse. Soon she was groaning in misery, her face green, as the boat rocked unmercifully.

"Sea's a bit rough—usually is at this point. That's what you get for sailing in winter."

Corinne sponged her brow with cool water; she brushed back her hair and fussed with the bedcovers. Marie Fleur was grateful for the woman's ministrations, but she felt too ill to offer more than whispered thanks before the heaving began again.

"Oh, I feel like I'm going to die."

"No such luck, *cherie*," Corinne replied cheerfully, grabbing a basin. "Come on. You can't have much more left in you."

For two days Marie Fleur lay on the narrow bunk wishing for death. She had never felt so ill in her life.

The driving wind had brought them to their destination earlier than expected. Last night, in rough seas that had threatened to capsize them, they had taken aboard their contraband goods, which were stored in a secret compartment behind the bulkhead. The *Amelia* had a false stern specially designed to conceal the true purpose of their voyage. The crew, a mixture of Bretons and Cornishmen, hauled goods for trade along the western coast. Their actual wealth came from the hidden half ankers of French brandy, laces, and Holland gin, luxury goods eagerly sought by those with cash enough to pay the extortionate prices demanded. Now, on this sunny becalmed morning, they had left behind the craggy shore of Brittany.

"We'll dock today," Corinne told Marie Fleur when she brought her a dish of gruel and a slice of honey-dipped bread. "Eat this. Your man won't want a skeleton in bed."

The food tasted delicious and it stayed down. Corinne helped her brush her hair and wash away all trace of her illness. While she worked, the French captain's sister repeatedly exclaimed over Marie Fleur's beauty. Corinne even lent Marie Fleur a fine lace-trimmed lawn petticoat, which she supposed to be from the contraband goods.

"Are we ahead of the *Wasp?*"

Corinne gave a Gallic shrug. "Maybe."

"What will I do if he's already gone?"

"Follow him. You've come this far. Don't grow fainthearted now."

Corinne's reassuring words rang in her ears as they came into port. The unprepossessing town comprised a ramshackle collection of cottages grouped about the quay and a gray rock fort perched on high ground, two huge guns trained on the harbor. Marie Fleur shuddered at her first actual reminder that this was a nation at war. Belatedly she realized she had no papers to prove her identity. What if they arrested her as a spy?

"Yves's brother commands the fort," announced Corinne. "That's why we're tying up, bold as brass. I'll tell him you're my maid."

During their exchanged confidences these past days Marie Fleur learned that Corinne was a silk-flowermaker. She had accompanied her English lover home after he was wounded in the war. When the nobleman finally died from his wounds, Corinne had walked to the coast to await her brother's vessel. Marie Fleur no longer need wonder why Corinne had so readily accepted her own wild story—adventure was part of Corinne's life. Experiencing a wave of affection for her kind-hearted friend, Marie Fleur squeezed Corinne's arm as they stood together at the rail.

"Thank you for all you've done for me. I'd never have managed without you."

"Silly goose, following your lover across the Channel. What girl in her right mind would do something like that?" And Corinne grinned impishly as she stepped on the gangplank.

Who, indeed? thought Marie Fleur as she obediently followed the other girl's swishing skirts. The fort's captain awaited them on the narrow quay. Marie Fleur purposely lowered her head in an attempt to rid herself of the proud carriage that was the mark of her birth. It would never do for a servant wench to walk like a duchess.

After a jocular exchange between the brothers, the soldier shook his head when he was asked the whereabouts of the *Wasp*.

"Did it not put in to harbor?" a dismayed Marie Fleur asked.

The soldier shrugged and winked. "Not exactly."

After much arm-waving and raised voices, Corinne finally unearthed the truth. The *Wasp* had put ashore a passenger who was detained until his papers were scrutinized, then he had been released to continue his journey to Paris.

The news sickened Marie Fleur. Now there was no hope of her intercepting those fateful papers. The soldier pointed out to sea where a vessel bobbed at anchor just beyond the gun's range. The *Wasp*, awaiting the return of its cargo, lay at rest.

"Well, now, that's a fine state of affairs. Are you sure this lover welcomes you?" Corinne asked suspiciously as they sat together on the low rock wall edging the harbor.

"He doesn't know I'm coming."

"*Sacrebleu* . . . now you tell me!" Seeing her new friend's tear-filled eyes, Corinne patted Marie Fleur's hand sympathetically.

"I've come for nothing unless I can stop him before he reaches Paris."

"Why not join him there? Though Paris is not so lovely in winter, it's not called the pearl of France for nothing. I think I'll come with you. I've been wondering what to do with myself."

"You? Oh, would you?"

"My journey's not entirely selfless, I've a lover there."

"But I thought your lover died in England."

"Where does it say a girl must have only one lover? Wait. I'll tell Yves."

Within the hour the two women were heading for Paris in a cart transporting apple brandy to the capital. Corinne joked and chatted with the young driver, flattering him outrageously so that he would pay for their meals on the journey. Naturally the man expected far more for his outlay, becoming angry when he pressed his suit and Corinne shrilly rebuffed him. Soon, however, he had recovered his good humor, and they traveled the rest of the way to Paris on amiable terms.

Marie Fleur envied Corinne's expertise in handling men. Having little experience in the art herself, she carefully observed how Corinne manipulated the opposite sex to her own advantage. Marie Fleur suspected such skill was not easily acquired.

From an innkeeper at Mantes, Marie Fleur learned Brandon had asked directions to a tavern in St.-Germain. It was to this sector she asked the carter to take them. As Corinne's lover was the son of a guard who manned a customs post in that quarter, the French girl was familiar with the area.

After much fruitless inquiry conducted first by Corinne and then by Marie Fleur herself, they could learn nothing about the whereabouts of the Englishman they described. Belatedly Marie Fleur remembered Brandon spoke French like a native. Perhaps he had not been recognized as English. So many people came and went in the narrow cobbled streets of this impoverished district it was like looking for a needle in a haystack. Brandon's contact must have been waiting for him at the tavern. By now it was likely all papers had been exchanged. He could be safely on his homeward journey or he could have been arrested. No one seemed able to divulge any helpful information.

Wearily Marie Fleur perched on a stone buttress shoring up a row of ramshackle tenements. She had reached a dead end. A tear trickled down her nose. It was growing much colder and snowflakes blew in the wind. Anger over her current predicament mingled with the love she felt for Brandon; in fact, she almost resented the bond that had brought her all these miles in a desperate attempt to save him.

"Eh, what's this? Tears?"

Marie Fleur tried to smile as Corinne plopped down beside her. "Everything seems so hopeless. I'll never find him now."

"This man of yours—is he tall, black-haired? Not well dressed. A good body."

"Yes, that could be him. He's very handsome."

"The guards aren't as smitten with his looks as you, little goose. I might have news for you."

"Oh, they remember him!" gasped Marie Fleur, her eyes gleaming with hope.

Corinne took her hand, squeezing her fingers in comfort as she spoke. "Hector says such a man was arrested this morning."

The unexpected news pierced like a spear. Marie Fleur stared in alarm at Corinne. "Where did they take him?"

"Never mind that. Wherever it is, you can be sure he won't

be going anywhere for a while. First we must find lodgings.
Come on, we'll catch our deaths out here. I know a place,
cheap but respectable. And that's something to be said in this
quarter."

Marie Fleur wanted to reject Corinne's sensible suggestion
and pursue the lead. She glanced about in the bleak, snowy
dusk to find the street deserted. Snow was falling steadily now,
and the wind cut through her garments with icy intensity. She
knew she would learn no more tonight.

"All right. I've some money left. I should have listened to
your brother when he tried to decline payment. I might be here
a long time."

It was weeks before Marie Fleur had further news of Brandon.
At her wits end by now, she alternately paced the floor of the
drafty garret Corinne had rented and trailed up and down the
steep flight of stairs on her relentless quest for information.

The new year passed unmarked by celebration. What little
money Marie Fleur brought with her was almost gone. Not
wanting to live on Corinne's charity, Marie Fleur was hopeful
of earning a few sous by taking in needlework. Unfortunately,
she found there was little demand in this poor district for the
delicate stitchery that was her only marketable talent. The other
marketable commodity she possessed was one she would use
only if impending starvation gave her no further choice.

While she stitched feverishly in their drab rooms she thought
about Langley Chase. During her absence she wondered what
underhanded scheme the earl would concoct. Yet even he must
be puzzled by her sudden disappearance. It pleased her to
imagine his angry frustration when he discovered what drastic
lengths she had gone to in order to avoid his company. But
her brief pleasure over his pique did not nearly compensate for
his having a free hand with her estate.

Little by little seeds of information came in, mostly collected
by Corinne, who was able to put two and two together in a
most efficient way. Initial rumors that Brandon had been in-
terned at either the Carmes or Abbaye prison proved false, but
little could be discovered about what was true.

One murky day in mid-January Corinne came up the dingy
stairs singing. Marie Fleur was stitching flowers on a shawl
for a local shopkeeper's wife, for which she was to be paid in

bread. Corinne rushed inside the room and struck an attitude before her.

Marie Fleur stared in surprise at Corinne's new blue bonnet heaped with ribbons, at her red fringed shawl, but most of all at the wicker basket overflowing with food resting on her ample hip.

"Where did you get that?"

"I have a suitor—old, fat, and moderately rich. Our worries are over."

"What about Hector?" Marie Fleur asked in surprise, referring to the dark-haired son of the guard who hung about their doorway eager for a glimpse of his beloved.

"Ah, him—he's too slow to catch a cold. We'd starve waiting for Hector to be a man. He was a gross misjudgment on my part, I can tell you. And, *cherie,* better than that, Pilou's the local magistrate and he's arranged for you to visit your lover. Believe me, getting such a paper wasn't easy. Have you any idea what they charged your man with?" Corinne demanded indignantly, her eyes flashing as she waited.

Her humor was not greatly improved when Marie Fleur guiltily offered, "Spying?"

"How did you know?"

"He's English, and France is at war with England. It was a natural conclusion. Sometimes I worry even about myself."

Corinne's pursed mouth relaxed a notch. "You worry! Anyway, he's not in an important prison. Apparently they don't know what to do with him. Still awaiting word from the bigwigs, I suppose. You're to be allowed to see him next week. Well, aren't you pleased?"

Fighting tears of relief, Marie Fleur nodded. *Pleased* was hardly the word. Yet stronger than her delight was an overwhelming sense of impending doom. How did one go about defending oneself from a charge of spying? There was no one here to help Brandon. At the moment he was known only as Nick, an English highwayman—no more, no less. To have such a man accused of carrying state secrets must be quite puzzling to Corinne's fat magistrate.

"Thank your friend for me. Can I take him some food? From what I've heard they don't eat well in prison."

"Yes, take some of this. There's plenty more where this came from." Corinne unpacked the basket on the rickety table, grumbling as she worked. "That ungrateful dog, landing in jail when you've come this far to be with him. Men are worthless—except for certain things." Here Corinne winked meaningfully before waltzing about the room in her new finery.

Snow frosted the refuse-laden streets on the afternoon Marie Fleur set out for the jail. Magistrate Pilou had written a brief authorization for her visit because such prisoners usually were not allowed visitors. She had learned Brandon had been moved twice already. It was only a matter of time before action would be taken in his case. She must get help from his family. He would have to tell her whom to contact. She had already uneasily reviewed the possibility that his own government would disclaim all knowledge of his identity in an effort to maintain secrecy.

Her feet were like ice as she trudged through the dirty snow. A bedraggled stalk of holly lay crushed in a doorway, a mute reminder of Christmas and the lavish houseparty to which she had been invited by Anabelle. Everyone would have accepted the earl's lie about her secret lover. The surprising escapade had probably been discussed avidly around the loaded feast tables. If only Anabelle knew where she was, and why. Today Marie Fleur felt so alone in this alien land of her birth. The thought that she was soon to see Brandon was the shining dawn at the end of the dark night.

When Marie Fleur walked inside the crumbling stone building, the horrid stench of the prison threatened to choke her. Nervously she stood in an anteroom that served as guardroom. She tried to ignore the stares of the guards. It sickened her to think Brandon was in this hole. There were probably worse prisons than this dilapidated pile on the edge of a slum, but none could have more effectively conveyed despair. Châtelet, Temple, La Force, Conciergerie—those hideous names brought back chills of horror from her childhood. It was in those notorious prisons that her parents' aristocratic friends had been held for execution. Obviously Brandon was not considered important enough for imprisonment anywhere but this insignificant dungheap. The risks he had taken for his country were reduced to nothing, seeming hardly worth sacrificing his freedom for.

"Follow me." Marie Fleur's thoughts were interrupted by

the brusque command. Blinking back unexpected tears, she stepped toward the jailor. The slovènly man stank of garlic, tobacco, and an unwashed body. He leered at her while the others inspected her basket of food, extracting a bottle of wine and a wedge of Camembert in payment for their trouble. Brandon still had enough to eat, but it would not be the feast she had intended. A loaf, a small piece of cheese, a bottle of white wine—perhaps to him that would still be a feast.

The terrible chill of the place seeped into her bones as she followed the jailor with his jangling keys. She had expected noise, but the narrow, dimly lit corridors were silent as a tomb. The jailor made numerous suggestive comments, which she tried to ignore. She realized she was at his mercy, yet he did not touch her, undoubtedly because he was wary of her connection to the magistrate. They crossed a littered courtyard in which prisoners paced. Some huddled in threadbare coats or old blankets while others were reasonably well dressed. On the other side of the yard she followed her guide down a flight of steps. A rush of air laden with the stale smell of ages of neglect met them as they entered a narrow passage. The jailor's lantern cast monstrous shadows over the walls as they passed.

"Hey, Englishman, your fancy girl's here to see you," shouted the jailor as he unlocked the door.

Trying to stifle the frantic beat of her heart, Marie Fleur swallowed and quickly composed her features. In the gloom a man's broad-shouldered figure became visible as he moved under the barred window from which spilled a murky beam of daylight. The unmistakable clank of chains chilled her; she had not known he would be in irons.

"I've no money for fancy girls, you fat toad."

Marie Fleur clenched her hands till they ached at the longed-for sound of Brandon's voice. The jailor spat as he lifted his lantern, its yellow light overflowing across her face.

"Now, there's two good handsfull there, my friend," he chuckled, allowing a pool of light to linger on the swelling of her breasts beneath her dark cloak.

Brandon's horrified gasp of recognition was drowned by the jailor's burst of coarse laughter. He appeared dumbstruck as she stepped into the pool of lantern glow.

"It's me, Nick." Marie Fleur dared not call him Brandon. She must help him maintain his pose as a common criminal;

it was his only hope. Her lips trembled so much she found it hard to speak.

"Marie Fleur! What in God's name are you doing here?" he demanded, emotion turning his voice gruff.

"I've brought you food." She glanced toward the jailor, wishing he would leave them alone, but as he lounged more comfortably against the wall, she could see he was preparing for a long stay. "I've been looking for you," she said, gazing at Brandon, searching for signs of deep affection in his set face.

Brandon glanced at the despicable creature who was picking his teeth with a filthy fingernail. The man he'd dubbed Toad might appear cretinous, yet he suspected it was a clever act. He wished to God Marie Fleur had not followed him. How she got to France, or where she was living or with whom, he could not imagine. He knew only she was in terrible danger. His jailors' suspicions must not be aroused or they would take her in for questioning. These days being English was reason enough to be arrested. A wave of relief washed over him as he suddenly realized there was nothing to connect her to England. They were conversing in French, and her accent was so authentic Toad would not suspect she was anything but French. He intended to keep it that way. Brandon racked his brain for a way to convince Toad he had met her whilst in Paris. Short of insulting her, he could think of no credible ploy. Still, if he insulted her sufficiently, she might go away and keep out of danger. His own desperate situation turning him reckless, he decided to impart a message along with the false identity he was now to give her.

"Well, Marie, you certainly surprised me. Did you come to take me home?" He grinned at her, steeling himself against the surprise reflected in her lovely face. Someday, when she recovered from her anger, she would thank him for this. Already Toad was looking at her questioningly. All those devils needed was an excuse to hold her for questioning. Imprisoned women were fair game for the jailors' lust. "There'll be a lot of empty arms while you're wasting your time visiting me." Ignoring her stunned expression, Brandon motioned to the jailor to step closer to the door. "You're a man of the world, Toad. You've laid plenty of women you hardly remember next morning. The food's welcome, but go on, there's a good fellow, take her out. You, of all people, know I've no money for whores. She's pretty, but too expensive. And seeing her is more torture than I can bear."

A sly grin suffused the jailor's beet-red face. At Brandon's nonchalant explanation of her identity, Marie Fleur died a little inside. He seemed so alien, so unlike the man she knew. He must be afraid if he showed emotion she would give him away. It was painful to discover he had so little faith in her. She longed to assure him he would never be condemned from her lips, but the sweating jailor's presence prevented such private communication.

"Right, English. But I tell you, if I'd done that one, I wouldn't want to forget her in a hurry. So you want the food, eh?"

"Of course. I'm penniless, not witless."

Swiftly Brandon grasped the basket the jailor took from Marie Fleur, hungrily picking through the contents. Turning, he bowed mockingly. "Many thanks, sweetheart, it's generous of you. They always say whores have hearts of gold, but until today I never believed it. You can send food every day, if you like. It's welcome as springtime. The slop they feed us here wouldn't keep a flea alive."

"Maybe her belly's swelled," suggested the jailor, turning back to Marie Fleur, who stood white-faced beyond the open door. As English said, a generous whore was most unusual.

"That's quite likely, and as I'm somewhat of a captive audience . . ." The two men laughed, and the jailor nudged her to accept the empty basket. Pushing her out of the way, he clanged the door shut and locked it.

"Be sure to give my love to the girls at the Belle-fleur . . . God, how I miss them. Tell them I think of them night and day."

Brandon's hateful parting words pounded through her brain as Marie Fleur stumbled up the worn steps in the semidarkness, following the panting jailor. He had treated her like a casual acquaintance to protect himself. She could not blame him for his caution, but she was deeply hurt that he should have chosen to label her a prostitute.

As she stumbled along the slime-covered corridors, she remembered the name Brandon had uttered: Bellefleur. It was probably a notorious brothel. Anger slowly began to supplant her pain. Why was Brandon treating her like this? She had been anticipating his joy, his passion, after all those sweet vows, never once expecting such an indifferent reception.

The unanswered question beat a tattoo in her brain as she recrossed the courtyard where all the pale, sun-starved faces blurred into gray. When they reached the warm guardroom, the fat, popeyed man Brandon called Toad snarled a curse at her as he shoved her inside.

"Stupid bitch, trailing me over to the other side—and what did I get out of it? You're wasting your time. He's got no money. Besides, I'm the one who makes the deals here. If you hadn't had that paper from Pilou I'd never've let you through. Next time, if you're stupid enough to come back, I want cash for the privilege of seeing your man. Understand?"

He pushed her roughly against the wall, and she righted herself indignantly, glaring at him, words of defiance hovering on her lips. The guards lounging in the room eyed her speculatively, licking their slack lips as they contemplated the treasure hidden beneath her cloak. She took a few wary steps toward the door. When one of the men got to his feet, Marie Fleur bolted outside, their catcalls echoing in her ears.

Into the snowy cold she plunged, nearly swept off her feet by homeward-bound foundry workers. Some of the men called out hopefully to her; today was payday. Heedless of their demands to stop, she forged ahead, racing back to the safety of the cold garret she shared with Corinne. This longed-for reunion had brought her nothing but confusion. Why had Brandon treated her so casually? Was he afraid they would ask for her papers, for he must guess she had none. Perhaps he had been trying to protect her. Her hopes soared slightly as she skillfully wove between the sweating workers, filthy after their day's toil. This satisfactory explanation of his strange behavior cheered her. The unsettling pangs she felt when she wondered if he had tired of her were thrust to the back of her mind.

"Blessed Mother! What's the matter?" cried Corinne as Marie Fleur virtually fell across the threshold and collapsed on the lumpy bed. "Who's chasing you?"

"No one. I couldn't wait to get home. The jail was horrible. And those awful guards... Oh, Corinne, he acted as if he barely knew me. Do you think he was trying to protect me?"

Corinne's mouth tightened and she cradled Marie Fleur's blond head against her ample bosom. "The bastard," she muttered, ignoring her friend's hopeful question. "Well, I can't

say I'm surprised. Did he take the food?" She glanced at the
empty basket and swore under her breath. "Of course, why
should I ask? Come, don't cry. There are plenty of other men."

Dreary February passed, and Corinne obtained several sewing
orders for her. Corinne still fashioned silk flowers, but her
labors were halfhearted for the aging magistrate was unusually
generous with his money. They had a new bed, a table, and
chairs, even bright red curtains for their dingy window. Corinne
had arranged for Marie Fleur several meetings with local men
of influence, convinced that if she were willing her beauty
would earn her a far more valuable alliance than fat Pilou. But
the assignations were unfruitful. Although she had insisted she
would not, Corinne finally relented and asked Pilou to authorize
a second jail visit for Marie Fleur.

It had been over three weeks since her last visit and this
time Marie Fleur felt uneasy as she set out for the jail with a
large basket of food. Her expectations of Brandon's pleasure
at seeing her again were dashed. Though he was grateful for
her gift, there was little change in his cool manner beyond that
brief animation. This time the jailor pressed them both for a
fee for the privilege of allowing the visit. Brandon handed over
his neckcloth in lieu of cash.

Baffled by his seeming indifference, Marie Fleur left the
guardroom, the laughing taunts of the guards ringing in her
ears. They joked about the Englishman's reluctance to pay for
her, chiding her for her foolish persistence. Now they, too,
shouted, "Give our love to the girls at the Bellefleur," as she
slammed the door and stepped into the street.

Today, again, Brandon had mentioned that hateful place.
He had been noticeably insistent when he asked if she had
remembered him to the others. She snorted in indignation,
freshly annoyed by his reference to her supposed profession.
It was only when he shook his head in warning that she bit
back her angry retort. The more she dwelled on the incident,
the more she wondered if Brandon was giving her a message.
Did he have contacts at a place called the Bellefleur? As she
hastened home through the cold streets, she decided to ask
Corinne if such a place existed. Before now she had been too
ashamed to breathe a word about the humiliating incident.

Corinne's head snapped about, her carroty locks wagging

in consternation at Marie Fleur's question.

"You keep away from that place!" she declared emphatically. "Where did you hear about it, anyway?"

"In the jail."

"No wonder," Corinne snorted derisively. "Half the whores behind bars probably worked at the Bellefleur at some time or other. Seamen and thieves hang out there. If you don't want trouble, stay away."

Surprised but undaunted by Corinne's revelation, Marie Fleur said, "Don't worry. I've had trouble enough since I crossed the Channel. Where is the Bellefleur, anyway, so I'll know to avoid it?"

"I doubt it's on your beat," laughed Corinne, giving her a playful push. "It clings to the walls of Flaubert's tannery like a festering sore. And that's what you're likely to get there too, for a more poxy bunch of sluts you couldn't find."

It was raining the next day when Marie Fleur hastened through the dismal streets toward Flaubert's tannery. She stopped several times to ask directions, guided as she drew closer by the unmistakable stench of this quarter south of the city. Figures huddled in refuse-littered doorways, sheltering from the rain. It was from one of these men she asked to be directed to the Bellefleur. The old man cackled and reached for her arm, but she twitched herself free of his rheumatic grasp. Thanking him and taking care that he not step on her skirts to detain her, she pulled her cloak around her face to shield her identity as she headed in the direction he indicated. This sleazy section of third-rate wineshops, taverns, and greasy cookshops seemed to have blown in the wind and settled in all its squalor against the high brick walls surrounding the stinking tannery, whose effluent spilled down the narrow cobbled street and imparted its own special stench to the surroundings.

The Bellefleur tavern was a timber structure of peeling paint and rotting boards. Even at this early hour the drunken patrons were boisterous. Choruses of ballads, both bawdy and nautical, echoed from the door, which constantly swung back and forth as a steady stream of patrons passed over the threshold. The Bellefleur was the liveliest spot for miles.

Marie Fleur entered the crowded tavern, keeping well back in the shadows, her cloak still pulled about her face. As soon as she stepped through the door a couple of sailors swiveled about on their bench to stare at her. The fact that she kept her face partially hidden gave rise to their supposition that she was disfigured by the pox.

It was not difficult to strike up a conversation in this place, poxed or not. Several men sidled up to her, hands reaching drunkenly for the ripe prize beneath the swathing cloak.

"I'm looking for a man named Nick. Do any of you know him? He's tall, dark-haired, usually dressed in black." She did not tell them he was English because she was afraid that would not help her cause.

The men shook their heads and turned away. Several of those close enough tried to grab her, to grope beneath her cloak, their drunken senses making them oblivious to the threat of disease. Shuddering in horror, she thrust aside their dirty hands as she pushed the men away. Finally she approached the blowsy woman behind the counter who was serving greasy pies and cheap wine to the tavern's patrons.

"So you want Nick, eh?" The woman looked her up and down, although muffled as she was the scrutiny proved unrewarding. "What you want him for?"

"I'm a friend of his. Do you know where he is?" Marie Fleur asked in an undertone, not knowing if it was safe to discuss him openly in this place.

After glancing about to make sure she was not overheard, the fat woman rasped. "Yes. Do you?" Marie Fleur nodded, vastly relieved to have met with success. "What do you want with me then? Are you looking for work?"

"I want to help Nick. I came to see if his friends could help him."

The woman gave her a peculiar look and motioned for her to go through a tattered curtain behind her.

Without question, Marie Fleur ducked past the flowered curtain. Fears for her safety came only while she waited in the stifling kitchen where the air was laden with the smell of rancid grease. A few minutes later the woman joined her.

"Now look, you, Nick's had all the help we can give him. A message was sent weeks ago when he was first taken. The rest's up to them over there." She jerked her thumb expressively to indicate across the Channel. "You can tell him that much. We can't afford to be seen there. He'll understand."

With this crumb of satisfaction, Marie Fleur was rapidly ushered out of the tavern by a side door and left unceremoniously in a fetid alley, where the refuse seeped over her shoe tops. Feeling elated that she had at last done something positive to assist him, even though she had learned little of value from her visit to the Bellefleur, Marie Fleur wended her way homeward to the garret.

It took some time for Pilou to issue another authorization for her visit to the prison. While she waited for the paper Marie Fleur was on tenterhooks. Once Brandon knew he had not been forgotten and was not being left to rot in this French jail like countless thousands, he would be vastly relieved. His joy in her achievement, in her bravery for journeying to that foul quarter, would overcome his pretense for the jailor's sake. She was convinced of it.

Corinne tried to dissuade Marie Fleur from leaving their lodging. In recent months the Grande Armée of France had been defeated, its battalions crushed by the allied troops as they marched across Europe. The citizens of Paris greeted the news with mixed feelings. No one wanted Frenchmen to be defeated, yet the insane thirst for power exhibited by their little emperor had lately lost him many allies amongst his own countrymen. Everyone longed for peace, tired of the privations of war, of the sacrifice they were continually called upon to make. The latest word was that Napoleon had fled Fontainebleau. And the Russian Army was rumored to be outside the city, joining forces with the Austrians and the Prussians to claim Paris for the allies. Word of the soldiers' approach spread like wildfire through the taverns and bistros. Far from exhibiting fear, the Parisians awaited the arrival of these foreign troops with joy, considering this more a liberation than a defeat.

There was no sign of foreign soldiers, nor of resistance by the few troops quartered within the capital. The streets buzzed with a curious air of expectancy as Marie Fleur hurried toward the prison. No one knew how close the allied armies actually were, for these washerwomen and ragpickers rarely left their grubby environs. The army could have been marching down the Champs Élysées and they would not have known it.

Impatiently waiting for the jailor to approve her official authorization, Marie Fleur was told today she would have to pay steeply for the privilege of this visit. She had to give him half of what she had earned yesterday before he condescended to escort her to Brandon's cell.

Her stomach pitched when Brandon did not even bother to

move from the wall where he lounged, surveying his visitor unsmilingly through the open grille. As usual, the jailor was at her side. Lately the man had begun to slyly fondle her body as he stood beside her in the gloom. Though his actions were partially concealed, Brandon, who always suspected the worst from Toad, was not deceived. Anger surged within him, and he longed to beat the jailor to a pulp. They had begun to ask a lot of questions about his visitor, alerting him to their increasing suspicions. It was clear they did not wholly believe his story that they had met in the Bellefleur. Nor did they accept his insistence that he was a smuggler who had stolen those incriminating papers from a traveler with whom he had fought in a tavern brawl.

"Well, and how much is this visit going to cost me? You'll have me naked if you bring her here much more often." He reached to his shirt and the jailor guffawed, thrusting Marie Fleur before him until her face was against the bars.

Anger and pain coursed through her body as she stared at Brandon's unsmiling, bearded face. Beside her the jailor's hands, given a life of their own, slid beneath her cloak; his garlic tainted breath enveloped her in a noxious cloud. "It won't cost you a thing," she snapped, her nerves taut as she recalled her revulsion over the visit to the Bellefleur, the terrible indignity of those pawing hands. In view of her sacrifice his increasing indifference cut her to the quick. "I've paid more than enough for both of us."

Brandon nodded, a slight smile fixed on his face. Toad looked from one to the other while his beefy fists were busy drawing back Marie Fleur's cloak, adeptly dodging her blows as she sought to keep away his pawing exploration.

"I bring you greetings from your friends at the Bellefleur. They are concerned over your welfare."

Brandon did not speak, but he did move from the cold stone. God be praised, she had deciphered his meaning after all. "Is that so," he drawled lazily, an eye on Toad who blinked, alerted to some undercurrent he did not understand. "And how are the poxy little bitches? Well, I hope."

"All well. They've known you were locked up from the first."

"News travels fast."

"Across land and water," she said in an undertone.

"What was that?" demanded Toad, alerted to the possibility

the woman was trying to make secret communication with his prisoner. "None of that. Speak up where I can hear you. Private meetings cost four times what the bitch paid me, as well you know."

"Oh, Christ, Toad, what possible pleasure can you get from eavesdropping on us?" Brandon groaned in exasperation. "Can't we have a minute's privacy. Consider, this may be the last female I'll ever see."

"You could do far more than 'see' her, English," Toad suggested slyly. Now he openly slid his hand over Marie Fleur's hips, waiting for Brandon's reaction. Though it cost him a supreme effort, Brandon did not react; he merely watched casually as Marie Fleur pushed aside the offending hand. He turned away and moved to the far corner of his cell, unable to bear the anguish in her eyes.

"Pay up, English, and you can have her inside with you," Toad suggested, his thick lips flecked with spittle as he contemplated the sight.

"Go to hell!"

Brandon stayed in the far corner of the cell where they could no longer see him. Marie Fleur's heart raced in shock. She had expected that now she had brought him news he would at least . . .

"All right, you, come on. I've got better things to do than stay here."

Marie Fleur was yanked in a viselike grip as the jailor slammed the door. "English bastard," he muttered as he pushed her before him.

Brandon gritted his teeth as he watched them move out of sight. The need to treat Marie Fleur so coldly, when he ached to hold her, tore him apart. At least she had brought him the news that he was not completely cast adrift in the enemy camp, a likelihood he had been all too aware of each time he crossed to the Continent. Yet if his friends across the Channel did not act soon, whatever the French decided to do with him would be his fate. Brandon smiled bitterly as he recalled the day his father had suggested the first of these "voyages," as the old man liked to term it. "A damned sight more use to England than roistering about with Prince George, you dissolute young puppy," he had thundered. Brandon wondered what Papa thought of the matter now, enshrined at High Hill with his hunters and his hounds—that's if he ever thought at all. Uncle Ben would

harumph and offer his deepest sympathy, but clearly they both
probably considered dying for one's country to be a far better
end than dying from drink and lechery.

And what did *she* think? That he no longer loved her?—
yes, that would be her most likely assumption. She would never
know he had sacrificed a final stab at happiness to save her
life. It would have been easy to have welcomed her with open
arms—it was what she had expected, the lovely, naive little
fool—and she would have been imprisoned along with him to
share whatever was to be his fate. She could no longer justify
her presence by any affection in his part. Would to God she
would get out of France whilst she was still able.

The jailor scowled as he huffed toward the guardroom. If
it wasn't for the woman's connection to Pilou, whatever that
might be, he'd take her here and now. It was a fool's game
bringing her to the Englishman, who hadn't a penny to spare
for firewood, let alone whores. He knew plenty of others who
had money, though, and they would pay dearly for five minutes
with this armful.

"Next time you don't need to pay, *cherie*."

Wary of the jailor, Marie Fleur sidestepped his wandering
hand. "Why so generous all of a sudden?"

He grinned, displaying rotten stubs of teeth in wet red gums.
"Out of the sheer kindness of my heart. It's not in me to turn
away a nice little piece like you. I've a dozen men on this side
alone who'd give their last sou for a few minutes with—"

"Thank you, but you can turn your generosity elsewhere."

"You'll do what you're told," he snarled, gripping her arm,
pulling her close so that the foul stench of his breath hit her
full in the face. "Next time we'll make a profitable deal, you
and me. You can forget English. He's not long for here, anyway."

Marie Fleur pulled free of him and moved as far away as
the narrow corridor allowed. Vastly aware of her dangerous
predicament, she chose not to openly display her anger. "I'll
think about it."

"Mind that you do. We could have a nice profitable little
operation going. You're worth a lot. You know, it's strange,
Marie Fleur, and I'm getting curious, but no one at the Bellefleur seems to have heard of you. Now, what do you think of
that?"

She swallowed, her stomach pitching uneasily. There was

no way she could escape him here, deep inside the warren of corridors as they were. Trying to brazen it out, she said, "You don't think I use the same name all the time, do you? That's bad for business. If they say they've never heard of Marie, then they're all liars."

Impressed, Toad thrust her before him along the stench-filled caverns of the jail. At the guardroom door he said softly, "You're far too nice for the Bellefleur, anyway. There are prisoners here with money; they're not all paupers. We can arrange something good, you and me. What about a sixty-forty split on all you take in? That's the most generous offer I've ever made. For that consideration, of course, I'll expect a little something for myself—"

Leaving the sentence unfinished, the jailor slid his hand across her breast. Marie Fleur had to steel herself not to flinch as she backed though the doorway, her thoughts on escape.

"There's no point visiting him anymore. He's no money; he spent it all in the first month."

Marie Fleur nodded, moving warily toward the outside door as the guards got up from their bench and moved closer.

"And I'll tell you this," the jailor bellowed as her hand closed over the cold doornob. *"That* doxy didn't get any sixty-forty, *cherie*. Ten percent is all I gave her. Now don't look so surprised. The man may be English, but he's not gelded."

The door handle turned beneath her grasp, and she stumbled into the alley beside the prison, their coarse laughter echoing after her.

Chapter 12

MARIE FLEUR STOOD gasping for breath in the pale March sunshine. A wave of nausea stirred in her stomach, a mingling of many emotions: humiliation over the jailor's proposition, revulsion for the disgusting memory of his prying hands, anger because she felt she had been duped, and strongest of all, pain over Brandon's indifference. She had been a romantic, starry-eyed fool to have ever trusted a man like Brandon Nicholas. Rising indignation swept away the last illusion that perhaps he was trying to protect her. She had risked her own safety by visiting the Bellefleur, by staying in France in the hope she could help him. And for what? His lukewarm reception was not that of a man who loved her deeply. Once his message had been relayed he had no further need of her. She was a simpleton to have expected more. Brandon habitually used people—by his own admission he had used Gabriella. And he had used her, too, when it suited him.

It was painful to acknowledge that her grand love was no more than a passing fancy. How she longed to reenter the jail and tell Brandon exactly how she felt about his deceiving her, but her pride forbade such a scene. Besides, after her conversation with the jailor, it would be unwise to go back. Inside the jail she was at their mercy, and her probable treatment made her shudder. It was common knowledge the jailors acted as pimps for their prisoners, yet she had never expected to be included in such an arrangement. Brandon's insinuations about her trade were to blame for that insult. Suddenly the picture of Brandon locked in intimate embrace with a nameless woman purchased from the leering Toad flashed through her mind.

She shook her head to clear the sickening vision, blinking back tears. She had been carried away by what she assumed to be undying love; not until today had she finally faced the truth. Her reason for staying in Paris no longer existed, and longing for home flooded through her like a physical ache. By now Langley Chase's landscaped acres might be lost to her, but there was still Yew Trees Lodge. A wave of homesickness moved her to tears as she pictured the Norfolk countryside in the first flush of spring, gold sprinkled with primroses, filled with the cries of marsh birds. . . .

She had become aware of passersby staring at her as she leaned white-faced against the sooty stonework. Self-consciously brushing her hair from her sweating brow, Marie Fleur rearranged her shawl and tucked her package of needlework more securely beneath her arm. The wrapper was soiled after the guard's inspection. After Corinne had warned her of the danger if the city fell to the allies, she had decided to combine her visit to the prison with delivery of her completed sewing to the wife of Citizen Martelot, a watchmaker who resided near the Île de la Cité. The journey would take her across the Seine into the heart of Paris, but she needed every sou she could get to buy a return passage to England.

Preoccupied as she was, fighting to overcome the pain of spurned love, Marie Fleur had not noticed the unusual buzz of excitement in the streets. Not until she drew closer to the city center, trudging along foul streets, threading through alleys, up steps, through gateways dividing quarters, did she become conscious of the building air of expectancy among the crowds heading toward the river.

"The Russians are coming," someone shouted to a passing vendor.

Even now, above the clatter of wooden pattens on the cobbles, came a building roar. Marie Fleur quickly identified the sound as a cheering crowd. There was also the incessant rumble of wheeled vehicles, clopping hooves, and the tramp of many feet.

"What is it? Are we attacked?" she demanded in agitation as the multitude swept past her.

"The city surrendered. Hurry, you can see the soldiers. They say the Russian Czar's leading them," shouted one of the passing girls.

So dense was the crowd, Marie Fleur despaired of ever reaching the watchmaker's house. She finally joined the swiftly moving body, allowing herself to be swept into the heart of Paris. The crowd moved so fast, she virtually ran over the bridge across the Seine.

Now she could actually see columns of soldiers making a broad sweep down the boulevard, a tall blond man on horseback at their head. He wore a green uniform like his guard, with epaulettes and a collar of gold to match his gleaming hair. On his head was an enormous hat set at a jaunty angle and surmounted by a sheaf of cock feathers. Whispers that this was the Russian Czar spread through the crowd, which gave him a resounding cheer of welcome. Hearty cries of *"Vive l'Empereur Alexandre"* greeted the Czar of all Russias, who graciously acknowledged the cheers with raised hand.

There was little fear evident in the jubilant faces lining the wide boulevard. As a body, Parisians were fickle. It was all very well for the patriots of Toulon to resist the advancing armies, but after long years of conflict the capital's inhabitants were weary of war. The terrible losses of sons, husbands, brothers, the harsh demands for still greater sacrifice from their fanatical emperor, who sought to raise more Grande Armées, brought mounting disillusion. Instead of a savior, Parisians now saw Napoleon Bonaparte as he really was: a despot obsessed by his dream of ruling the world. And they had had enough. Peace was long overdue. So today they would cheer the Russians, welcoming them with open arms, instinctively understanding that these allied troops would deal fairly with a city that had capitulated with little or no resistance.

Repeated cries urging the restoration of the monarchy came from all sides. After all, wouldn't the fat Bourbon be eternally grateful for his puppet throne, gratitude making him far more malleable than the fiery little Corsican who envisioned himself as savior of all Europe? And with this satisfying conclusion in the backs of their minds, the cheering Parisians breathed a collective sigh of relief. Napoleon was gone; long live *l'Empereur Alexandre!*

The soldiers kept coming, rank upon rank, their strangely colorful uniforms causing admiring comments from the crowd, which was greatly enjoying the spectacle.

Marie Fleur's stomach sank like lead. The realization that she may have waited too long to leave Paris made her weak. Even after she had been paid for her latest work she might not be able to get a passage to England. The foreign troops might shut the city gates and demand passes from all travelers. Perhaps Magistrate Pilou would give her a pass to leave Paris, though of late he had been most reluctant to exercise his official capacity. She was not optimistic.

Seizing her opportunity whilst the multitude were still absorbed in the parade, Marie Fleur elbowed her way to the nearest alley and set off for the Île de la Cité shop of Citizen Martelot.

After winding miles out of her way to avoid the surging crowd, she finally arrived at her destination only to find the watchmaker's shop shuttered. The neighboring establishments were also shuttered. Word of the imminent fall of Paris must have reached this quarter early. Yet she suspected that once the troops were established in the city the taverns and wineshops would reopen, for Russians, like Frenchmen, could grow very thirsty.

After pounding on the back door for several minutes, she finally raised the watchmaker's wife, who peeped nervously between the shutters.

"You stupid girl! What are you doing on the streets? You'll be raped by the savages," she shrilled, banging the shutter closed.

"I've finished your gown, citizeness."

The nervous woman opened the door a crack, thrusting out her arm for the goods. Marie Fleur hesitated, suspicious that once the citizeness had her gown she might decline payment. But Citizeness Martelot gave her no more time to consider as she snatched the package. A chorus of satisfied mumbles and comments followed, then the fat hand reemerged holding the money.

"Bien fait. I'll have more work for you next week, Marie."

"I won't be . . . yes, I'll come back then," Marie Fleur rephrased as her fingers closed over the money. It would not be prudent to reveal her intentions. The shrewd citizeness might demand part of the payment back if she thought she would not see her again. Marie Fleur placed the money safely in a hanging pocket beneath her skirt before she bid good-bye to the watchmaker's wife.

Crowds milled aimlessly about the Paris streets. People said the Russians were bivouacked on the Champs Élysées, their camp stretching all the way from the unfinished Arc de Triomphe to Notre-Dame. The soldiers were setting up tripods over lighted campfires and making themselves at home. Droves of Parisian women, painted and dressed in their finery, came out to hail the liberators, laughing and linking arms with the allied troops.

As Marie Fleur had expected, the wineshops, the bakeshops, the taverns, and the bistros reopened, eager to serve the combined Russian, Austrian, and Prussian armies.

Dusk was rapidly falling over the huddled city as she tried to fight her way through the crowd heading for the bridge across the Seine. She had not intended to be out this late, and whenever she found a clear stretch she ran, anxious to reach home. Drunken shouts and laughter filled the air as men and women made merry. Unease gripped her as she considered how many triumphant troops had been turned loose in the city. A woman alone would be fair game. Marie Fleur glanced behind her at the hundred firefly lights from the Russians' cookfires. Many of the soldiers were wild Cossacks, part of the advance troops who had entered the city this morning.

The vast bulk of Notre-Dame loomed ahead on the skyline. Not long now before she would be safely across the river. Her journey through the unsavory southern districts would seem calm after this melee of laughing, shouting thousands.

The crowd blocked her way, and Marie Fleur was forced to take a detour down a narrow winding alley. She raced through the horrid entry, anxious to reach the light. As she emerged into the narrow street she was startled by the appearance of a troop of horsemen, whooping and cheering while one of their number galloped over the cobbles, hanging by his feet from the saddle, his light hair brushing the ground as he retrieved a colored handkerchief with his teeth. Giggling woman, already half-drunk, cheered the exhibition, lolling in the arms of foreign soldiers.

"Hey, *mademoiselle . . .* wine?" a young soldier shouted to her, holding aloft a brimming cup.

Marie Fleur tried to sidestep him, but the garishly dressed soldier lunged for her and swung her against his knee-length fur-lined tunic. The man's loose red breeches were stuffed into the tops of high boots. On his head he wore a tall Astrakhan cap with a spindly white plume.

"Drink . . . you . . . me?"

"No." She shook her head as she pulled out of his demanding grasp. Several other soldiers moved closer, all commenting favorably on her appearance.

So diverse were their uniforms and in such a galaxy of colors—scarlet, blue, green—Marie Fleur could not begin to guess which nations they represented. Some soldiers wore Turkish-style baggy pants gathered at the ankle above pointed-toed shoes while others wore splendid European-style uniforms frogged in gold braid. There were several officers in fur-edged capes and plumed shakos. The Cossacks wore a strange assortment of headgear: Astrakhan calpacs, fur-trimmed caps, hats with strange pointed tops.

To her dismay, Marie Fleur saw that she was surrounded. The trick rider still clattered up and down the street performing even more daring feats, the roar of the crowd indicating each successful pass, but these Cossacks were no longer interested in daredevil horsemanship. They were far too intent on other pleasures. Eager women moved amongst them, regarding her with surprise when she continued to protest the soldier's familiarity.

"Get your hands off me!" Marie Fleur screamed, trying to dodge the Cossack's reaching hands. "I don't want wine. Let me go!"

The men grinned and shrugged, not understanding her words. Her obvious reluctance, though universally understood, they chose to ignore. Laughing men addressed her in myriad tongues as they formed an impenetrable barrier around her. Marie Fleur's shrill cries for help were unanswered.

The riding exhibition was over. Men and women linked arms and danced folk dances, singing in drunken revelry as they careened about the square, calling to everyone to join them.

A huge pigtailed man in baggy red trousers wrestled Marie Fleur away from the others and, pinioning her arms, he allowed his companions the freedom of her bodice. She writhed desperately in his crushing grip, helpless to prevent the eager exploring hands, which kneaded and pounded. The stitches of her bodice broke, and the torn fabric gaped to reveal bruised flesh. Soon tiring of this tame sport and eager to be about more serious business, the soldiers dragged her around the corner of the tavern away from the light.

Against the background of gay singing voices, the lustful animal hunger in these foreign faces seemed all the more hideous. Tears poured down Marie Fleur's cheeks. No one heeded her screams for help; no one even cared that she was about to be raped.

Fixing her with opaque black eyes the Tartar in the scarlet trousers loosened the sash that held his clothing in place. A surge of nausea gripped Marie Fleur, and she shut her eyes as the red fabric fell to his ankles, exposing the girth of his turgid organ. Her eyes flew open again as the man slammed her

against the building, preferring not to lie with her on the be-
fouled cobbles. His black eyes burned in his sallow face as he
tore hungrily at her skirts. Behind him the others moved closer
to await their turn, feral eyes gleaming in the smoky darkness
broken only by garish flickers from the nearby campfires and
pools of lantern glow from the tavern.

"Get back, damn you! Get back!"

The thunder of hooves was followed by cries and groans
rippling through the group of soldiers. A uniformed man astride
a white horse was forcing his way through the crowd, dealing
blows with the flat of his sword when men refused to get out
of his way. The lecherous Tartar turned around with a snarl,
cursing the intruder in his own language. The mounted stranger
drew a whip from his saddle bow and curled it stingingly about
the Tartar's naked buttocks.

"Get back to duty, pigs," he snarled, riding into them.

The soldiers fell back, allowing him passage. Glaring mu-
tinously while he rubbed his injured backside, the Tartar grasped
his brilliant trousers and dragged them up to cover his shriveled
manhood.

"You dogs! How dare you disobey your emperor? No woman
was to be harmed. Have you gone mad? Get back to your
camp. Your officers shall hear of this. Nikolai, Sergei," shouted
the man on the white horse.

Two lieutenants in similar uniform rode from behind the
crowd and seized several fleeing Cossacks. A trio of men from
their own regiment had taken to their heels and, laughing uproariously, the avenging angels allowed them to go.

Muttering and sullen, the Cossacks drifted back to their
assorted bivouacs, the name Bezak a curse on their lips. Those
who were drinking in orderly fashion within the tavern the
Cossack officer allowed to stay. By now the two adjutants had
taken Marie Fleur to a bench outside the wineshop. One of
them spoke a smattering of French, and in his stilted tongue
he inquired about her condition.

With trembling hands Marie Fleur tried to refasten her torn
bodice, which the rapacious Cossacks had destroyed. Though
the young officers must have been aware of the revealing
glimpses of flesh protruding from the ripped gray fabric, they
refrained from either comment or stares, not anxious to earn a
reprimand from their superior.

When all was to his satisfaction, their commanding officer

rode back to the wineshop and slid from the saddle.

"My humble apologies, *mademoiselle*. The men are savages. We're under express orders from our Czar to treat the native populace with courtesy. Allow me to escort you to your home," said the Russian in strangely accented French.

While he spoke the young officer proffered a linen handkerchief for Marie Fleur to dry her tears. She was grateful for his consideration, and she quickly scrubbed the stinging salt traces from her cheeks and blew her nose, continuing to clutch her torn dress with her free hand.

"Thank you, sir. You've saved me from a . . . a terrible fate."

Now the man stepped closer beneath the swinging lantern above the wineshop door. A flurry of movement from inside the shop revealed the local patrons were giving him the once over. The Russian officer, resplendent in his dark red uniform and gray cloak faced with light fur, stood arrogantly in the glare of light, lord of all he surveyed. He had seen the gallery of curious faces but chose to ignore them.

"Please, *mademoiselle*, allow me to escort you home."

Again the offer. Though he had saved her from rape and appeared to be genuinely concerned for her welfare, Marie Fleur was uneasy about accepting his offer. Sensing her reluctance, the Russian bowed formally, his face very close to hers in the circle of lantern light.

"I guarantee your safety. Come, it grows late. First allow me to introduce myself. I am Andreas, Count Bezak, of the Sumsky Hussars."

"You are most kind, Count Bezak."

Marie Fleur accepted his extended hand, and he drew her to her feet. Marking her difficulty in keeping her bodice together, he unlooped his red fur-lined pelisse from his shoulder and draped it around her. He even began to close the frog fastenings before thinking better of his actions. She thanked him and fitted the gold braid loops over the gold buttons. One of the count's adjutants had picked up her cloak from the cobbles and returned it to her.

The Russian, appearing preposterously tall in his fur hat with its waving plume, impatiently rapped, "Come." And he pointed his furled whip toward his white charger.

The adjutants lifted Marie Fleur astride the horse, who was so well-trained he barely shifted when her weight was put on his back. After hastily conferring with his adjutants, who seemed most reluctant to allow the count to travel alone, the Russian placed his booted foot in the stirrup and swung agilely into the saddle behind her.

By now the occupants of the wineshop had lost interest in the scene outside. Few of the tipplers even bothered to glance after Marie Fleur and the count, being far too intent on their own enjoyment. The count directed his adjutants to investigate a brawl that had erupted at the opposite end of the alley before he turned the horse in the direction Marie Fleur had indicated.

Over the Seine they went, leaving behind much of the roistering army. "You should not have been on the streets alone," he reprimanded as they cantered along the cobbled street. "What else can you expect?"

Bristling with indignation, Marie Fleur straightened in the saddle. "I expected to be allowed to travel the streets unharmed. Your men acted like wild animals!"

"Only a very few of them were *my* men. They were mostly Cossacks from the remotest regions of Russia."

"That's immaterial. They're part of your army."

"You can't blame soldiers for your own carelessness. A woman alone in the vicinity of taverns and wineshops is usually for sale, or at least amenable to certain proposals."

"Oh, really. I can see you have much experience in the matter."

She heard him chuckle, but he did not reply. If she were closer to home she would demand he let her travel on foot, yet she did not relish more of the same treatment for even here small groups of foreign soldiers idled. Her rescuer had proved to be less a gentleman than she had expected. He was virtually accusing her of leading his men on.

"Where to now?" the Russian asked when they reached a crossroad and she sat smarting in angry silence.

Marie Fleur pointed to the right. The streets were unusually crowded for the hour, and though she hated to appear to give in, she knew it was wise not to proceed on foot.

"I didn't intend to insult you, *mademoiselle*. I was merely giving you advice. In future don't be out after dark when soldiers are on the streets."

"Russian soldiers."

"Russian, Austrian, Prussian, all soldiers are alike. You're a prickly one. Perhaps, had I known, I'd have left you to your fate."

"Then I'm fortunate you have only lately discovered my failing."

"Most fortunate. With your pretty face and divine figure I'd have thought you to be an angel. In actual fact, you're more of a shrew."

Marie Fleur snorted in indignation. "Apparently it's not occurred to you that I was about a legitimate errand."

"And that was?"

"Collecting wages so I could eat."

He clucked sympathetically. "In such dire straights—I'd no idea. But why so late? Surely the day Paris falls to the allies would seem a poor choice."

"I'd been visiting someone in prison, if you must know. The crowd was so heavy I couldn't get back any faster."

This latter information sobered him. For a few minutes the count remained silent, sensing the intensity behind her words. Finally, as they passed into St.-Germain, he asked, "Your husband?"

"No, my . . . my—"

"Lover?"

"Yes, once he was that."

"And no longer?"

She swallowed, fighting back weak tears that came unbidden to her eyes. "No longer," she repeated softly.

"Do you live with your family?"

"No, they're dead. I lodge with a friend. She's helped me since I've been in France."

"Ah, so you are a foreigner too. Where is your home?"

"England, though I'm French-born. My mother fled to England after my father was killed in the Terror."

By now they had reached the corner of the dilapidated tenement owned by Magistrate Pilou's cousin. "This is where you live?" he asked in surprise, glancing about at the crumbling paintwork, the rotten boards, at the faceless human shadows propping up the filthy walls.

"Yes. It's the best I can afford."

"*Mademoiselle*, in all this time you've not told me your name."

"Marie Fleur."

The Russian count repeated the name, making it sound alien in his accented speech. "How very pretty. A pretty name for a pretty woman. Are you sure you'll be safe? I would come upstairs with you, but my horse is valuable. When I return there may be nothing of him but the shoes."

She smiled understandingly. "I'll be all right now. Thank you, Count Bezak, for your trouble."

"May I call on you again, Marie Fleur?"

She shook her head. He slid from the saddle and, placing his hands on her waist, he lifted her down.

"Why? Can we not be friends? Surely no one will object, least of all the man behind bars who was once your lover."

"No. You're most kind, but . . . no."

At the doorway she paused when he called her name, glancing at him where he stood in the shadows, the horse's milk-white coat gleaming silver in the night. A crowd was forming about the foreign soldier, staring at him with frank curiosity.

"I will come. Maybe not tomorrow, but soon. Yes?"

"No." She smiled and shook her head, then resolutely she went inside the tenement and ascended the stair.

When Marie Fleur reached their room Corinne threw open the door. "Who is *he?*" she demanded with a squeak of delight. Not waiting for an answer, Corinne ran back to the window and pulled aside the red curtain to admire the man who had just swung into the saddle.

"A Russian."

"A Russian! Is that all you've got to say? Where did you meet him? When?"

Marie Fleur smiled at Corinne's unbridled eagerness. "Tonight. He saved me from an attack by a horde of savages."

Corinne shrugged and allowed the curtain to fall back in place as the white horse disappeared from view. "Is he rich?"

It was Marie Fleur's turn to shrug. "I don't know. He's an officer. And he says he's a count."

"Hm . . . a count. You're well in there. When's he coming back?"

"Probably never. I told him not to."

"Well, he'll be back if only to get his pelisse," Corinne observed. "It's very fine! Are the buttons real gold?"

In surprise Marie Fleur glanced down at the fur-lined pelisse. She had forgotten to give it back to him. Familiar with the ways of men, Corinne was probably right in thinking the count would return, using the pelisse as an excuse.

Marie Fleur reached under her dress to the secret hanging pocket looped about her waist to see if her money was still there. "See. Citizeness Martelot paid me. I've got money enough to go home."

"If you can. I heard they're closing the gates to the city and demanding travel passes."

"Are you sure?"

"Who can be sure? It's what I heard, that's all."

"I was afraid of that. If only I'd left last week."

"What happened? Last week you were still mad in love with the handsome English bastard. I see you've finally learned sense."

All evening Marie Fleur had managed to thrust her heartbreak to the back of her mind. Stricken by the reminder, she looked up at Corinne, a sinking leaden feeling in her stomach. "He doesn't really care for me. Only before I was too stupid to realize it."

"So now you're free for your Russian. Good." Corinne took the money and placed it in a crack in the wall, their own secret vault. "I wanted to go and watch the troops. I wanted to enjoy myself, but instead I sat here waiting for you to come home. And what were you doing? Riding like a princess in the arms of a handsome prince...."

"Count."

"All right... count. He is handsome, isn't he?"

"I suppose. The light was bad. He's young, tall, broad-shouldered—yes, I suppose you'd say he was handsome."

"Aha, so you did notice, after all. Well, when you tire of him, let me know. He's a better bet than Pilou. The Russians are the conquerors. A girl's a fool not to take advantage of that. They'll be the ones with the good food and the money, who can show you a good time. They say the czar's a handsome devil. Did you see him?"

"I think so, but he was too far away to really see."

"Merde! What a one to send for news. How many soldiers were there? I heard they barely fired a shot. Tell me, tell me, imbecile! I want to know all about it."

"First bring me food and drink, then I'll give you a firsthand report of the fall of Paris."

Corinne laughingly obliged, and Marie Fleur wished she felt as lighthearted as she pretended. Before her eyes danced a loathsome image of Brandon indifferently turning his back on her. Quickly wiping a hot tear from the corner of her eye, Marie Fleur fashioned a bright smile, for Corinne had turned expectantly towards her, eager for her story to begin.

When the Russian count returned the next morning Marie Fleur was not at home. Corinne offered him his pelisse, but he said he would accept it only from Marie Fleur. When her friend returned from the market an hour later, Corinne was all agog.

"You missed him!"

"Who?" asked Marie Fleur as she carefully unpacked her basket, catching potatoes and turnips as they rolled to the edge of the table.

"Your Russian, you dimwit!"

Marie Fleur stopped, clutching a pepper in her hand. "He came back? Did you give him his pelisse?"

"He says he'll take it only from you," Corinne declared triumphantly. "Oh, he's a god! You should see him in the daylight. Thick golden hair, face perfect as a statue, but far, far warmer. Oh, you're in for much pleasure there." Corinne winked and nudged Marie Fleur's arm. "His body's like steel and of the most interesting proportions."

"And to think you didn't capture him and keep him prisoner."

"Fat chance. He didn't even notice I'm a woman. It's you he wants, you goose." Corinne snorted in exasperation over her friend's stupidity. When a man like that showed interest, any woman in her right mind would be only too pleased to oblige.

"Mother of God! Eggs! Where did you get those, *cherie?*"

"Your poor forlorn Hector gave them to me as a love offering for you," Marie Fleur explained as she carefully extracted three brown-speckled eggs from their hiding place amidst the lettuce leaves. Somehow the treasure seemed less wonderful to Corinne now.

"Oh, him. Well, at least he's good for something at last," Corinne dismissed as she pitched the empty wicker basket in the corner. Then, getting out a cast iron pan, she whistled softly as she began to prepare breakfast.

Marie Fleur had met Hector lingering below in the street, anxious to personally deliver his treasure to Corinne. After delightedly accepting the luxury on behalf of her friend, Marie Fleur had asked Hector if she would be able to leave the city. To her dismay, he said only those with authorizations from the allied command would be allowed to travel. While she ate her delicious omelet flecked with green and red peppers, Marie Fleur considered her predicament. Surely the Russian could arrange a traveling permit. It would take only a word from him to prepare a whole sheaf of papers, for he seemed to be in a position of great authority.

"Corinne, I'm going to delight you by seeing the Russian if he comes back."

Corinne spun about, her face alight. "Oh, he'll bring us such good things. No more coarse bread and cheap wine. We'll dine off caviar and champagne. We'll have—"

"You misunderstand. I'm only going to ask him to get me traveling papers. That's all."

"All! You must be insane!" Corinne's face fell. Then, new hope arising, she shrugged. *"Eh bien,* it's a start. You have to begin somewhere."

Marie Fleur was stitching silk roses around the edge of a fine white cashmere shawl, sitting by the window in the fresh spring sunshine, which at this hour crept shyly inside their room, when there was a rap on the door. Corinne was out.

When she opened the rickety door, she found to her surprise a tall uniformed man on the threshold. She swallowed nervously as she looked closely at him in the dim light; his thick hair was blond, his uniform had a multitude of gold braid across the chest. It must be he, for she saw that he clutched a distinctive black bearskin in his lean hands.

"Count Bezak?"

The uncertainty left his face and he flashed her a broad smile, his teeth appearing unusually white and even.

"Ah, you do remember me. At your service, *mademoiselle.*"

"Come in, please." Marie Fleur was somewhat hesitant to invite him in, yet every door of the landing stood open as the old women shuffled out to inspect her visitor. When she admitted the Russian the gossip would be that she was prostituting herself to the foreign troops. But that could not be helped. There was no privacy out here, and she must have privacy to ask her favor of him.

Though the count did not comment on her shabby lodgings, Marie Fleur was aware that he took in everything, from the dingy cracked window to the meager fire struggling in the grate.

"You've come back for your pelisse. I thank you for lending it to me."

"Yes," he agreed with a smile.

Marie Fleur took the fur-lined garment from the end of her bed where it had warmed her during the chilly night. The count walked about the room examining things before pausing to look through the window into the narrow street below where dilapidated buildings crowded out the sun.

"Ah, your work."

He was holding up the cashmere shawl with its pink silk roses.

"Yes, that's how I earn my living. My friend Corinne makes the flowers."

"Corinne introduced herself to me this morning."

Marie Fleur smiled uncomfortably because his expression revealed that the other girl's welcome had been most effusive. "Let me apologize for Corinne. She's a simple girl who's had to support herself for many years. She means well."

He nodded understandingly. "Of course. And I am one of the conquerors. To be greeted with joy is most pleasant. I expected more hostility from the people of Paris than we've received. Perhaps they have fallen out of love with their little emperor. In fact, most people treat us more as friends than enemies."

The count's presence in this small room made Marie Fleur uneasy. Though he stayed at the window, the murky sunbeams dancing off his gold-braided tunic, he appeared overpoweringly close. In the dingy light she studied the Russian, finding unexpected lines on his face though he was still young, his skin clear and sun-golden. His firm jaw jutted aggressively from the high collar of his gold-braided uniform. When he turned toward her his eyes were blue beneath heavy brown brows.

"I brought a picnic hamper. We will picnic, yes? The sun is most pleasant."

"No, I can't. . . . Thank you all the same."

"I have the food, so we'll eat it here if need be."

Before she could protest he had gone out on the landing to shout to someone below. A soldier appeared lugging a wicker hamper up the stair. The count ordered the man to put the hamper in her room, their exchange beyond her comprehension for it was conducted in Russian. The man bowed to her and backed out of the room.

"He'll wait below for me."

Ignoring her feeble protests, the count unpacked white china

plates from the hamper. There was a dish of chicken pâté and
a crusty loaf of brown bread, assorted cheeses, pungently fresh,
early tomatoes, and crisp young lettuce. He placed a glazed
pastry on a linen napkin for their dessert. Then, turning to her
with a grin of accomplishment, he uncorked a tall, slender
bottle of white wine.

"It's not nearly as nice picnicking indoors, but I'm adapt-
able. If you will not go to the picnic, I shall bring the picnic
to you."

Marie Fleur laughed, her protests swept away by his audacity. She was eager to join him in the feast for she had not
eaten since breakfast.

"We can sit here in this patch of sunshine," she suggested,
pulling the checkered counterpane from Corinne's bed. It had
been a recent gift from the magistrate, and she hoped her friend
would not object.

The Russian clapped his hands, delighted by her growing
enthusiasm. "At last you are thawing. I was afraid you were
like some Russian girls, frozen immobile by our treacherous
winters."

"Such delicious food's an eloquent temptation."

For a moment he puzzled over her words, then finally comprehending, he smiled in pleasure. Two pillows made a seat
for her; he sat on the floor, his booted legs stretched toward
the window. Filling two glasses with bubbling wine, he handed
one to her.

"To Paris. Long may she live."

"To Paris."

Marie Fleur smiled at him over the rim of her wineglass.
This impromptu picnic seemed rather like a dream. She knew
she should have sent him away, yet she knew also that he could
provide her with the means to leave France. Last night the
Russian had behaved like a gentleman, and she hoped the wine
and the intimacy of their surroundings would not alter matters.
Belatedly she reviewed the possible danger of her situation,
realizing she might be getting far more than she bargained for
from her blond liberator.

"You will call me Andreas, yes?"

"Andreas," she repeated dutifully.

His stilted French became easier as he briefly recounted his
adventures these past few weeks on the way to Paris, telling
her how they had skirmished with the remnants of Napoleon's

Grande Armée. The wine and the good food relaxed them both, and finally Marie Fleur told him in return the long involved story behind her current circumstance, carefully leaving out any reference to Brandon's actual purpose for being in France. Though the Russians were France's enemy and, it would seem, sympathetic to a foreign spy, she was not sure whether Brandon's exchanged information with the French, however unimportant, would make him suspect.

"So your man's a criminal? I'm surprised. You don't seem the type."

"Since the war many Englishmen have run afoul of the law trying to keep body and soul together. Nick was arrested on charges trumped up by the French because he's English. Do you suppose, now your army is in control, he will be released?"

Andreas shrugged. "I doubt it. The French prisons are teeming with criminals. We don't intend to stay here long enough to worry about them. Besides, most French officials have been allowed to retain their posts; that way we are assured more cooperation." He smiled sympathetically as her face fell. Though she told him one thing, he suspected her heart told a different tale. "So you say he does not care for you now. This man's a handsome adventurer who's tired of you, yes?"

Marie Fleur nodded, finding his simple assessment of the truth harsh. This conclusion seemed to have been apparent to everyone but herself. "You're right, only I was too foolish to realize it until it was too late."

"What of your late husband's property? Is it sold?" he asked next, changing the subject as he noticed a betraying quiver in her lower lip.

"Not yet. The settlement of debts is to be made within a year of his death. The year will be up this summer."

"So, even if you return to England, you have no home."

"There's a country place I hope to keep. And I have friends, relatives there."

He smiled faintly as her head came up defiantly. "How unfortunate men have not treated you kindly in the past. Such a lovely creature. There's no justice, my dear Marie Fleur."

He leaned closer, and she drew back. They had already drunk two glasses of wine. The count drained the last of the bottle into his glass as he lounged against the wall, watching her as he sipped the sharp wine.

"I wonder, Count Bezak—Andreas," she corrected hastily as his heavy brows drew together. "Could you get me an authorization to leave the city?"

"Anything's possible. Yes, I suppose I could, if that's your wish."

"Oh, thank you! When?"

He shrugged noncommittally. Marie Fleur discovered he had inched closer without her knowledge. His somewhat prominent light blue eyes were heavy-lidded and fringed with dark gold lashes. His long, slightly hooked nose ended in flaring nostrils. As she studied his face more closely, Marie Fleur was alarmed to discover Count Bezak had the look of a libertine: that fixed appraising stare, the slight curve of his generous mouth as he studied her appreciatively. Why had she not noticed before? Had it taken the wine to bring that sensual, almost predatory expression to his features? Now his gaze strayed boldly to the swell of her bodice, moving down to her narrow waist and curving hips.

"You're the loveliest woman I've ever seen." The count's compliment was accompanied by a fleeting touch on her shoulder. "Quite exquisite . . . If I give you a traveling pass you'll be gone from my life forever."

Marie Fleur swallowed, not liking the turn of their conversation. "At the moment I'm not part of your life."

"Ah, but I intend to change that," he said lazily, stretching his booted legs. When he crooked his knee, she was given a perfect view of his well-muscled thigh in the skintight breeches. "Would you like me to release your former lover?"

She gasped. The count's brow clouded and his mouth tightened.

"You lied," he snapped.

"No, I've not lied to you."

"You told me he meant nothing to you."

"He no longer wishes to mean anything to me. Our grand love was a lie."

"And you?"

"I must learn not to love him," she admitted honestly. "It will be easier to achieve as time goes by. Since I came here I've thought about little else but helping him. Surely you can understand such concern can't be wiped out overnight."

He drained his glass, brooding as he stared at the leaping

dust motes in the sunbeam. Finally he said, "I understand. I don't like it, but I understand. This man is very important to you still."

Marie Fleur hung her head, wanting to deny his statement. In all honesty she could not. At last, not meeting his eyes, she nodded in agreement.

"If you wish I could have him set free."

She betrayed herself with a gasp of surprise. "Would you do that for me?"

The count studied her with that uncompromising gaze, then he got to his feet and stared out the window. "I'm not here because I find you unattractive; you're surely aware of that." She nodded and he continued. "Obtaining passes and releases is certainly within my power if I care to exercise it, but these are not concessions I make for nothing."

Their eyes met, and in the limpid blue Marie Fleur read the terms of his agreement. Swallowing, she glanced away. The discovery was not a surprise, somehow she had known it would come to this.

The moment of tension between them passed and, laughing, he strode to the table to get the glazed pastry. "Here, this tart is full of pears and chocolate. Most delicious."

They were munching on their shared delicacy, trying to stop the chocolaty fruit juice running down their chins, when the door opened and a startled Corinne appeared on the threshold.

"Oh . . . I'll come back—"

"No, Corinne. We have plenty for you."

The count did not object, realizing, today at least, that further amorous overtures would have been rebuffed.

Corinne joined them on the checkered counterpane, exclaiming in delight over the delicious food. They apologized for having drunk all the wine, but she said the food was so good she had no need of wine. While she ate Corinne scrutinized their guest, delighting in his dazzling smile and gallant conversation.

At last, when all the food was gone, Count Bezak stood. Bowing to the two women, he said, "I must return to my duties. I hope I shall be welcome here again." The veiled question behind his innocent words made Marie Fleur's heart beat uncomfortably. When she did not answer, Corinne, afraid her friend's silence would turn away their golden goose, jumped up laughing.

"You can visit every day if you bring such delicious food. I could kiss you for your generosity."

The count reached for her, his hand demanding on Corinne's plump shoulder. "A kiss will be ample payment, *mademoiselle*," he said.

Corinne slipped her arms eagerly about his broad shoulders, clinging to his splendid uniform jacket. She pressed against his hard muscular body as she planted an eager kiss on his mouth. Above Corinne's fiery tresses the count looked at Marie Fleur, their eyes locking. Highly uncomfortable beneath his gaze, she found she somehow could not break the contact. He did not smile nor wink at her, as she half expected, merely regarded her solemnly.

"Good day, *mesdemoiselles*."

Corinne clattered onto the landing after him, chatting in an excited, high-pitched voice as she waved and bid him good day. Defiantly she glared at the old busybodies who had emerged from their dingy caverns to witness the soldier's leave-taking.

"If you let that one get away I'm going to give up on you," Corinne shrilled as she waltzed back inside the room and slammed the door. "You could have knocked me down with a feather when I turned the corner and saw that Russian holding the horses."

"Horses?"

"He had three horses. I thought you were going for a ride. I nearly broke my neck racing up here to see your count before you left. Why didn't you go out with him?"

"He wanted to picnic. I thought it was too cold."

"Oh, tell me another," Corinne dismissed scathingly. "You're afraid of the twinges between your legs, that's your problem, Marie Fleur. Let yourself be a woman—because he's certainly a splendid man. I get wet just looking at him, I can tell you. Did he write you a pass?"

"No."

"*Sacrebleu!* Why not? What did you do all afternoon? Don't tell me—you picnicked like a good little girl."

Marie Fleur smiled sheepishly over her friend's exasperation, aware she had allowed a golden opportunity to slip by. "He said he could get me one."

"Never rely on what men say. Haven't you learned that by now?"

To Marie Fleur's growing consternation, Count Bezak did

not visit her during the following week. The shock of his abandonment made her realize how important that pass had become. Without it she was trapped forever in this dingy quarter sewing for fat merchants' wives with barely enough money to buy food.

She even contemplated going into the city in search of the count, rejecting the idea at the last minute as sheer idiocy. She had not the first idea where to begin her search, nor was she eager for another sample of the liberating troops' lust.

Chapter 13

SPRING SUNSHINE BATHED the ancient city in gold. In the parks budding trees burst into life, the grass turned green, and flowers unfurled their petals. Though she welcomed warmer days, Marie Fleur did not fully appreciate the beauty of Paris in the spring. The rapturous season immortalized by the poets left her strangely unmoved.

She was hurrying home one warm April afternoon, a parcel of sewing from Citizeness Martelot beneath her arm, when someone hailed her. Turning, she was surprised to see Hector in a guard's uniform sprinting after her.

"Marie Fleur, stop," he shouted as he raced toward her. Out of breath, he managed a smile of greeting, his sallow face unusually animated. "How's Corinne? I never see her lately."

"Oh, she's well." Marie Fleur had not the heart to tell him Corinne had taken a second lover besides the aging magistrate. "You're a guard now. Congratulations!"

Hector proudly straightened his shoulders. "Yes, last week. The foundry work was too hard. The Russians made many new guards, and Papa recommended me. And they won't be disappointed. Being a guard is much to my liking. Would Corinne like some violets? You, too, Marie Fleur. I got paid today."

They passed a flower seller on the corner, and Hector stopped to purchase two bunches of violets.

"Oh, they're lovely. Thank you. So fragrant."

Marie Fleur buried her nose in the velvety purple blossoms, breathing in their delicate scent. Suddenly the dingy street with its spindly poplars bursting into lime-green leaf seemed not so sordid, nor dirty. She smiled in surprise and took a deep breath. Today even the stench was not as pronounced. The usual perfume of old drains, cabbage water, and trickling sewage was overlaid by the age-old scent of rebirth.

"It's spring!"

Hector blinked solemnly and looked closely at her, wondering at her curious statement. "Yes, it's spring," he replied seriously. It was easy to see why Corinne had tired of Hector.

Such seriousness was not for a woman like Corinne.

"Will you come up to see Corinne?"

"Oh, no, no. Just tell her I miss her," Hector said, backing away. "There is something though."

Marie Fleur turned in the doorway. "What's that?"

"That man you were asking about."

Her heart lurched sickeningly. "Yes."

"Well"—Hector moved closer, glancing about to make sure they were not being overheard—"he's been sentenced."

"Sentenced! What was the sentence?" she demanded, gripping his bony wrist in agitation. "Do you know?"

Hector swallowed, surprised by her intensity. "Death," he said.

"Oh, God, no! Are you sure?"

"Quite sure. His time's set for next week. I have it on the best author—"

"Yes, yes, I'm sure you do. Thank you for telling me, Hector."

Marie Fleur left him standing in the street. She began the arduous trek up the steep stairs, stopping on the first landing, unable to see for tears. Brandon was going to die! It did not matter that he no longer loved her; she still loved him, no matter how hard she tried to deny the emotion. All those lies with which she had soothed herself, her anger over his apparent indifference, were swept away by stark reality. If she did not help him, Brandon would die. Whatever aid might be forthcoming from the British government or hopes for eventual leniency from the Russians were futile. Time had run out. His sentence was set.

Corinne answered her knock, not giving her time to speak as she dragged her over the threshold. "You stupid bitch, out again. That man's going to give up on you. You should've seen that filthy Monique all over him, clinging to his arms, whispering invitations in his ear. If he's not riding that one before the week's out... What's the matter? You look like you've seen a ghost."

"Brandon's been sentenced to death!"

"Brandon? Who's he?"

Catching her slip, Marie Fleur quickly added, "Nick—his last name's Brandon."

Corinne's eyes widened at the news. Biting back a sharp comment in the face of her friend's genuine grief, she enfolded the other girl in her arms, rocking her, kissing her tangled hair in an offering of comfort.

"He still matters that much to you, eh? Bah! I should've known you were lying when you said you didn't care. Maybe the Russian can help."

"Possibly, but Count Bezak doesn't come here anymore," Marie Fleur sniffled piteously, hugging Corinne's substantial body for comfort.

"Oh, yes, he does, stupid goose. That's what I've been trying to tell you. While you were out traipsing around town, he was here looking for you. You've missed him, and he didn't say he would be back."

Aghast, Marie Fleur digested the news. "What did he say?"

"That if you're interested in seeing him again return this to the soldier in the street." As Corinne delivered the message she produced a gold signet ring from her apron pocket.

"He's sure of himself. What if I'm not interested?"

Corinne grinned. "In that case he said you were to keep it and buy yourself a new gown."

Marie Fleur dried her eyes, and while Corinne made two cups of chocolate, she considered the situation. She alone had the power to free Brandon. Once she accepted the Russian count's terms, she knew she destroyed her own chance to leave Paris, yet she had been given little choice. The Russian had not actually spelled out his terms; there was no need.

"Where is this soldier?" Marie Fleur asked resignedly as she went to the window and scanned the usual ragged habitués of the grubby rue de Chat.

"So, you're not so uninterested in the Russian after all, or is this self-sacrifice just for that bastard's release? No, I believe there's another, less noble motive lurking behind it."

Marie Fleur found she could not truthfully answer Corinne because she did not herself completely understand her motives.

The dusty spring sunset had already suffused the room with pale gold before the steady clop of hooves announced a horseman riding by. Marie Fleur ran to the window, eager to see if this was to be her contact. The mounted soldier wore a dark cloak and a leather shako. He made no move to dismount, just waited below, not even glancing up at her window. At the corner waited another half-dozen men, ready to come to the aid of their comrade if needed. She wondered if she should go down to speak to him.

Corinne made the decision for her. Yanking open the window, she shouted to the man below, "Hey, are you from Count Bezak?" The soldier understood little French, recognizing only the name of his commander. It was enough. He nodded vigorously, the white plume on his shako waving up and down as if possessed of a life of its own. "Come closer." When he was directly below the window Corinne dropped the gold signet ring. Grabbing at it wildly, the soldier caught the ring; then, saluting to them, he clopped back to his comrades. A few minutes later they had ridden out of sight.

"Well, so much for that. What do I do now?"

"Have patience. Can't you wait another few hours for such a magnificent specimen?" chuckled Corinne.

At Corinne's urging Marie Fleur borrowed one of her new gowns, a gift from the magistrate. The high-waisted, long-sleeved dress was of pink-and-jade-striped watered silk; the neckline was trimmed with black satin ruching to match the triple bands around the skirt. Corinne pressed into her hands a fringed pink-and-green paisley-patterned silk shawl and a matching pink bonnet with a fluffy green plume, both gifts from her new admirer, Alain. Although Marie Fleur thanked Corinne for her generosity, she was not wholly appreciative of the gaudy finery. The loud dress made her feel highly conspicuous and something of a tart.

When Marie Fleur was ready Corinne clapped her hands in rapture over her magnificent appearance, tweaking her golden curls onto her brow to form a fluffy halo beneath the brim of the pink bonnet.

The minutes ticked by as Marie Fleur waited on a chair by the window. It was going dark now, and shadows moved furtively in the street below as the inhabitants of the dingy rue de Chat left their lodgings for a night's work, or pleasure, both frequently outside the law. Her mind seethed with a dozen half-formed plans to save Brandon, all of which she discarded as useless. One plan alone ensured his freedom. And she may have waited too long to take advantage of it. Marie Fleur was virtually resigned to this conclusion when there was a rap on the door.

A neighborhood urchin stood on the landing holding a paper.

"There's a carriage waiting at—the—the corner," he stammered, awestruck by Marie Fleur's brilliant finery. He had never seen a woman dressed so grand. "The driver gived this to me."

Marie Fleur accepted the folded parchment addressed in a bold hand.

Take the carriage. I await. Andreas.

Corinne peered over her shoulder, laughing in delight as she struggled to decipher the simple message. "How romantic! I wish I was coming into the city with you. Alain said he'd be 'round later, so I'd better wait. Though I fancy if I came with you I could find a very nice Russian of my own."

Though Marie Fleur would have welcomed some moral support, she did not think the Russian count would be expecting company. Besides, she was afraid Corinne's actions, when faced with so vast a selection of men, might prove embarrassing.

"I promise to tell you all about it. Thank you again for the dress." Marie Fleur hugged Corinne good-bye before she hurried downstairs after the boy.

A discreet dark carriage waited at the corner, the rue de Chat being too narrow to admit the equipage. The top-hatted driver bowed before handing Marie Fleur inside. In no time they were off, traveling through the shabby sector on their way to the city center. The illuminated banks of the Seine gleamed ahead as they wound through the narrow streets approaching Notre-Dame. The carriage finally drew up outside a café whose adjoining garden was strung with lighted lanterns.

"This is your destination, *mademoiselle*."

Marie Fleur alighted nervously and glanced about for the count. Couples were seated at the outdoor tables for the weather was mild. There were uniforms galore, so many different styles and colors she gave up trying to identify the troops' nationalities. She did not see Andreas nor any soldier in a similar uniform.

The carriage departed, and Marie Fleur went to an empty table to wait. Presently a party of horsemen rode up to the café and dismounted, all but one of whom quickly mingled with the crowd. Marie Fleur's heart lurched as she recognized the tall uniformed man who glanced about at the patrons as though searching for someone before he strode purposely toward her.

"*Mademoiselle*." The count bowed formally over her hand, his face solemn. "To what do I owe this honor?"

There was a hint of sarcasm in his voice. Marie Fleur swallowed uncomfortably, finding this not exactly the delighted greeting she was expecting. Should she lie and pretend she merely wanted to see him or should she be honest and tell him the truth? Truth won over deception.

While the count called to the proprietor to bring wine and something to eat, she mentally rehearsed what she would say.

"Are you hungry?"

"Not really."

He shrugged and pulled out a chair. "So. You've still not explained yourself."

"I thought you wanted to see me."

"I do."

"You don't seem overjoyed."

A waiter came to the table with their meal, which the count had ordered earlier in the day. He also carried a bottle of wine and two glasses.

The count's expression was sober as he directed the waiter to serve them steaming portions of *coquilles* in a cream sauce, tender young asparagus *hollandaise,* and crisp golden rolls fresh from the oven. He offered Marie Fleur a pat of golden butter stamped with the Russian imperial arms in tribute to the conquerors.

"Marcel's is a very popular place," he remarked as he saw her examining the elaborate design.

"I didn't know. Thank you for bringing me here. It's very nice."

At a nearby table laughing women shrieked hysterically, causing heads to turn in their direction. They were gaudily dressed in tall-crowned feathered bonnets awash with looped ribbons. Over their brightly colored gowns the women wore fringed silk shawls. Self-consciously Marie Fleur compared her borrowed finery with the near uniform of the demimondaines, finding her doubts concerning her costume well founded. Flushing in discomfort, she pulled the shawl tighter about her shoulders and hunched down in her chair.

"Are you to make the supreme sacrifice, *mademoiselle?*" the count said after a sullen silence. "I see you've dressed for the part."

She gasped in horror at his remark, longing to hide under the table in shame. "I had no decent gown to wear. This one's borrowed from Corinne," she hissed angrily, annoyed with him for embarrassing her by drawing attention to her appearance.

"Forgive me. I supposed the selection to be yours. Well, what can I say? I am right about the supreme sacrifice, however?"

"I wouldn't phrase it that way, but yes, I am considering that move."

"Ah, getting impatient for your travel permit?"

"Not only that."

"More?"

"Remember I told you about the man in prison." She hesitated, waiting for him to nod, before she continued. "He's been sentenced to death."

The count went on with his meal without remarking on her disclosure.

"Please. I'm begging you to release him. I promise not to see him, if only you'll release him."

"See him by all means. I've no wish to deprive you."

"Will you do it?"

He leaned back in his chair and placed his knife and fork carefully on his plate. "You do understand the price?"

"Yes."

The count resumed his meal while Marie Fleur waited in agonized suspense. When he was finished, he glanced up. "The *coquilles* are superb. You've barely touched yours."

"Please, don't taunt me. If you intend to do as I ask, say so. If the favor's too great, tell me now. Don't let me hope in vain."

He smiled slightly as he reached for her hand on the white tablecloth. "What's his name? And what's his crime?"

"He uses the name Black Nick. He's a highwayman and sometime smuggler. They've charged him with spying."

"The prison?" The count was writing the information in a small book he had taken from his pocket.

Quickly she supplied the name, her stomach churning. How unlike what she had been expecting: a romantic meeting, being swept into his arms, the tender smiles, the whispered love words—all were missing. Leaning on her hand, Marie Fleur gazed at the count solemnly writing in his notebook. Could it be that she did not really know him after all?

"I'll see what I can do."

And Marie Fleur had to be content with that. This inconclusive ending to her highly charged plea left her puzzled and distressed. "We haven't much time. He's sentenced to die next week. Is there hope?"

"It should take only a few words and a signature. Have no fear."

He refilled her wineglass and urged her to eat a little more of her meal. Marie Fleur obliged, finding the food tasteless as sawdust. Finally satisfied with her performance, the count paid his bill.

They left the café, threading their way between the crowded tables. The leafing trees along the riverbank were strung with twinkling lanterns, which spilled bright fingers across the Seine, winking as a light wind ruffled the water.

"How important is this man's release to you?"

"More than life itself."

"What assurance have I that you won't leave with him?"

"I've no travel documents."

"Nor will you have unless I provide them. You do understand?"

"Yes."

They walked a little way in silence. Marie Fleur's stomach knotted as she contemplated what that innocent exchange had obligated her to. For a piece of paper, she had promised herself. Hers was also a sacrifice for England, yet she doubted Brandon would view the situation in quite the same light. They paused beside the iron-spiked wall bounding the river where boats creaked on their moorings and banged against the small quay.

"This isn't the way I wanted it to be."

"The terms were yours, Count Bezak."

"Payment shall not be demanded until the goods are delivered," he said in a feeble attempt at humor. "I'm an honest trader."

They walked on, leaving the street of noisy outdoor cafés behind. Here beneath the trees it was more tranquil. Willows spilled low to the water where it lapped against ancient stonework. He slid his arm around her shoulders and hugged her against his side.

"Poor little Marie Fleur. No doubt this isn't quite what you wanted either. Will you tell your former lover you've set him free?"

"No."

"Meet me tomorrow afternoon at that last café we passed. I'll tell you then what can be done."

"Please don't let him die."

An unfathomable expression crossed the count's handsome face lit by the wavering glow of a lantern bobbing from the branches overhead.

"Good-night, Marie Fleur," he said, taking her small face between his hands. He gazed down at her lovely face bathed in gold. "This is the most joyful moment since my arrival in France," he whispered as he stooped to kiss her mouth.

Marie Fleur was surprised by her reaction to his kiss. While not the ecstatic surge of passion she had felt for Brandon, the count's kiss did not leave her unmoved. The pressure of his lips, his hands, of his body against hers imparted a pleasure she had not known for some time.

The sound of a horse clopping slowly along the boulevard alerted them, and Marie Fleur saw the carriage that had brought her to Marcel's Café. The count helped her inside the carriage, and they rode back to the café, where they parted most formally.

As the carriage slowly continued its journey, Marie Fleur watched the colorful sidewalk scene through the dusty window. Just before they reached the corner she saw the count join his fellow officers at a table overflowing with wine bottles. Then a pang of something she could identify only as jealousy gripped her as she watched one of those women in the frivolous bonnets slip her arms around his shoulders and, drawing his face down to hers, give him a resounding kiss on the mouth.

The following day dawned cloudy. Long before Marie Fleur reached Sacré-Coeur a light rain had begun to fall.

Street urchins scampered for cover. Flower sellers retreated under their tarpaulins, leaving the jewel-bright buckets of tulips, daffodils, hyacinths, and lilies of the valley exposed to the spring rain.

The count waited for her inside the café. Impatiently he motioned to her to enter. Today Marie Fleur wore her own blue wool gown and cashmere shawl, and he nodded approval of her changed appearance.

"Today you look more like the woman I know. You won't ever have to borrow dresses again. I'll buy you a multitude of gowns fit for a—" He stopped, checking the rapturous turn of his speech. "Sit down. Will you have chocolate or something a little stronger?"

"Chocolate."

The beverages ordered, he sat staring at her, drumming his

long elegant fingers on the glass-topped table. At last, after the waiter had brought them two blue-striped mugs foaming with whipped cream, the count withdrew a folded paper from inside his pelisse.

"Here. Your man's as good as free."

With trembling hands she accepted the paper, almost afraid to read it. Rain pattered gently against the café's wide windows, trickling as softly as tears over the gold-etched name of the establishment's owner. "Am I to take it to him?" she whispered in horror.

The count smiled. "That would have been poetic irony—but no, I'm not that unfeeling. I merely want you to see if everything's in order."

Marie Fleur scannèd the document authorizing the release of one English criminal known as Black Nick. "Thank you," she whispered, the words barely audible as tears choked her voice. "You'll not regret it."

"No, I'll certainly not regret it. I'll see to that," he remarked with a smile. The creamy chocolate had etched a mustache above his upper lip. "You have permission to visit him tomorrow, or this afternoon, whichever you wish. He's not to be released till morning, so at present he doesn't know. Perhaps you can make him squirm for his past mistreatment of you. No? Very well, that part's entirely up to you."

She accepted a folded paper giving her permission to visit the prisoner. "When . . . when am I to . . . come . . . to you?"

"Eager?" He smiled, amused by her woebegone expression. "I'm not a two-headed monster. I might be the first man who's truly known how to treat you."

"Perhaps." She allowed him to squeeze her ice-cold fingers, but her replying smile was wan.

Later that afternoon Marie Fleur reviewed their conversation as she walked through the rain-washed streets to the prison. The stark reality of Brandon's death sentence had aroused the love she had tried to smother. Despite his own lukewarm emotion, she still loved him intensely. For the past few hours a plan had been building in her mind, a plan so glorious she could hardly breathe for the excitement of it. Tomorrow, when Brandon was released, she would be waiting for him. He would have the necessary papers to leave the country as well as money and a prepaid passage to England. And she intended to travel with him. Now that Hector was a guard at the nearby customs post, she must gamble he would let her through without papers. Later on, nearer the coast, she knew money would effectively blind lesser officials to her lack of travel documents. With Brandon at her side, armed with a sheaf of official papers, she was convinced she would be able to get a passage aboard ship.

She hugged herself with delight, walking faster and faster, eager to reach the prison. Today, when she revealed her plans to him, Brandon would be excited. A cynical smile stole over her full mouth as she realized that, whether he actually loved her or not, a man like Brandon would welcome a female traveling companion.

The guards taunted Marie Fleur that her beloved would soon be kissing the angel of death. Ignoring their jeers, she smiled impassively, impatient to deliver the news to Brandon of his impending release. The new authorization from the Russians caused a great deal of comment.

"What's this? Pilou not good enough for you now?"

"His authorization is no longer valid," Marie Fleur retorted quickly, hardly expecting to be questioned about her credentials.

Toad glared at her, barely able to contain his rage. When she had walked through the door he had mentally arranged a sale to a prisoner in the west block always ready with money for a pretty woman. Now this. The official Russian paper made him uneasy. He had heard things about the Russians, rumors he had no wish to put to the test. The little bitch!

"Russians make better-paying customers, eh?" he snarled, kneading her shoulder with his beefy fist.

Ignoring him, Marie Fleur looked at the guard behind the desk. "I'm paying for a few minutes privacy today. It's fitting, considering he's to die tomorrow." And she handed the man a folded wad of money, pressing the crackling paper in his palm.

"That's up to English," Toad growled, snatching the money from the other man. "He might just be enjoying himself too much to leave. Anyway, you're just in time for the celebrations. He's having a farewell party. Got some cash for a watch—the last thing he had worth selling."

As she followed the guard Marie Fleur realized that Brandon had held out all this time without exchanging the watch for food or fuel because it was the gold watch that had belonged

to his grandfather, one of his most treasured possessions. On
the eve of his death such sentimentality must have seemed
misplaced.

Long before they reached the inner courtyard sounds from
the farewell party could be heard as shouts and drunken laughter
penetrated the tomblike passages of the prison. A long table
had been set up in the courtyard and on it were plates of chicken
legs, platters of sliced rye bread, and an array of green wine
bottles. The jailor indicated the gathering, making a mocking
bow before he turned aside to punish someone who was beating
against his cell door.

Marie Fleur paused in the archway, jolted out of her pleasant
thoughts by the unexpected spectacle before her. A bearded
Brandon, having sold his coat last month for food, stood in his
shirt-sleeves, a woman clasped in each arm. Too finely dressed
for inmates, for the female prisoners were generally ill-kempt,
these women wore feathered bonnets and striped gowns in
nauseating parody of the outfit Corinne had lent her. Marie
Fleur clutched the wall, fighting the cold sweat that crept over
her body. The women were laughing up at Brandon, expectant
smiles on their painted faces. Now they kissed him, running
their fingers through his black hair, taking his hands and burying them in the secret depth of their bodices. Cackling inmates
pressed cups of wine on them. Someone struck a chord on a
battered fiddle, the whining, discordant notes sounding macabre in the squalid, rain-spattered courtyard. The two painted
women pulled Brandon from the table, making him dance with
them, swaying in time to the music, and sidling against him
in sensual invitation.

One of his fellow prisoners noticed Marie Fleur standing in
the doorway, and heads snapped about. Men beckoned eagerly
to her, thinking she had come to help them celebrate the Englishman's farewell meal. Mutely she shook her head and retreated a pace.

Toad, having finished with the unruly prisoner, pushed his
way past, elbowing her out of the way. "Hey, English, do you
want to see little Marie? The bitch is asking to see you, wants
to speed you on your way."

Marie Fleur could not see Brandon's reaction to the news
because Toad's greasy bulk blocked the archway. Excitement
trembled through her body as she anticipated his answer, and

the time they would spend together while she revealed her cherished secret to him. Sincere or not, his joy would be expressed in passion. And she ached to feel his arms about her, to have his kiss and his whispered endearments. Then his chilling reply sliced keenly through her dreams.

"You know I've no money for any more women. Tell her to go home, Toad. You're wasting your time bringing her here—unless you intend to make me a gift of her. If you do, then bring her along. Any bitch from the Bellefleur is bound to make the party livelier."

With a guffaw, Toad stepped aside to reveal a white-faced Marie Fleur standing in the doorway. By now Brandon's face was buried against the neck of one of the painted women, his hand busy inside the other's full bodice. He glanced up, and for one horrifying moment their eyes locked. There was shock there, but no yielding warmth, no betraying emotion, only blankness slowly filling the void.

"Oh, Marie, so you're here already, sweetheart," he uttered, his voice thick, strangled.

She gaped at the stranger standing there, making no effort to thrust aside the women who glared challengingly at her, sensing competition. Brandon did not come forward to take her in his arms, nor did he leave his roisterous companions, even though to his knowledge this was his last night on earth. Stunned, they stared at each other, then Marie Fleur spun about, anger and pain surging like fire in her veins. Toad shouted after her, bellowing for her to stop, but she ignored him, her only thought to be free forever from the bond between herself and that bearded stranger. Her wonderful plan of accompanying Brandon seemed foolish now. She could never be content with crumbs of affection. If he did not want her, then she was far too proud to grovel.

She opened the street door of the deserted guardroom and stumbled outside, eager to be rid of the sight and smell of this place. Tomorrow Brandon would be free, and he would never know who had bought his freedom. Injury and anger mingled inside her veins until she considered telling the count she no longer wanted her lover's pardon, that she was withdrawing from their bargain. But she could not let Brandon die. A part of her still ached for the Brandon she had known: not the unshaven, shirt-sleeved convict with his cackling doxies, but that tender, considerate lover who had filled her soul with beauty. On the strength of those poignant memories she would keep her bargain with Count Bezak.

Marie Fleur began her homeward journey, wishing she had never come. This final pain of shattered plans need not have been. Had she stayed away she would have known only the pleasure of granting Brandon life without the bitter aftertaste of truth.

Hardly able to believe his miraculous good fortune, Brandon Nicholas hurried along the damp street, chilly in the early morning gloom. In his waistcoat pocket he carried a pardon and a passage aboard a vessel bound for England. For the hundredth time he wanted to pinch himself to make sure he was not dreaming. Someone in Liverpool's cabinet must have quietly pulled the right strings to get his release. If so, they had taken their own sweet time about it; he had been saved from the jaws of death at the eleventh hour. It seemed impossible that by tomorrow he would be breathing clean English air and seeing the green shores of the land he loved.

Love. The word evoked exquisitely painful memories of her. Brandon winced to recall what had taken place yesterday. He had not known she was standing there listening. If only he had seen her first, he would never have said those things. Intent on maintaining the lie he had manufactured to appease Toad, he nonchalantly wounded her when she had come to bid him good-bye.

He paused to lean against a building, fighting for composure. Pain and rage mounted within him until Brandon was ready to comb the city in search of her, to ask her forgiveness, to beg her to come home with him. Yet he had not the first idea where to look for her. Combing Paris for a woman named Marie Fleur would be a futile endeavor. Besides, he had little time for such a search. His generous liberator had granted him twenty-four hours of freedom to leave the country. After that, he would be arrested and the imposed sentence carried out. Even if he found her, she would still be in grave danger of arrest, for he would be unable to protect her. When he reached England he would send someone to bring her safely home. . . . That's if *they* could find her.

His mouth set in a bitter line, Brandon walked around the

corner into the rue de Guerre and hailed a passing vehicle. His guardian angel had given him money enough to journey to the coast in comfort.

Marie Fleur waited for the Russian count beneath the dancing golden lanterns on the banks of the Seine. The heady scent of lilac drifted in the breeze. The spring evening was mild, the air refreshed after the rain. Her heart still ached for what she had witnessed yesterday, the discovery one more nail in the coffin of idealistic love. Tonight she felt devastated and betrayed, totally vulnerable.

"Marie Fleur, how I've longed for this moment."

Setting her full lips, she turned, trying to feign happiness as she heard his deeply accented voice at her elbow. Now it was time to pay for her purchase.

She found the count overpowering in his red, heavily gold-braided uniform, his fur-lined pelisse slung across his shoulder. Tonight he was not wearing his fur-edged cloak. His black bearskin helmet adorned by gold tassels and a white plume and his tall, highly polished boots gave him the appearance of having stepped from a splendid military painting. He seemed unapproachable and remote.

"At last you're mine. I thought tonight would never come," he said huskily, his hands gentle on her shoulders. He stood gazing down at her lovely face. Absently he stroked her silky blond hair and twined his finger through the tendrils curling over her fair brow. "I could love you very much, if only you'll let me."

She smiled, feeling foolish for she could find no reply to his ardent confession. However, so involved was he in his own thoughts, the count seemed unaware of her discomfort.

Marie Fleur was again wearing her blue wool gown topped by a red cashmere shawl she had borrowed from Corinne. The count slipped his finger through a frayed black ribbon loop on her bodice as he said, "I've a new gown for you, a splendid creation. Not nearly as grand as you deserve, but the best I could manage." Laughing at her surprise, he swept her in his arms, raining kisses on her upturned face. "No more borrowed finery for you. Come, we go. Yes?"

Marie Fleur's emotions were in turmoil. Tonight Count Bezak was boyishly eager. His dignified formality was gone. Had his attitude changed because he considered her his own?

By now Brandon would be safely aboard ship, tossing on the Channel, probably already in sight of Dover's white cliffs. She clamped her teeth down hard. What utter foolishness to allow herself thoughts of *him!* She had cast her lot with the Russian. And not before it was time. This morning Corinne had confided to her that Alengon had invited her to share his pension. She intended to give notice on their lodgings unless, of course, Marie Fleur wished to continue paying the rent. When she said she did not earn enough to maintain the dilap- idated garret, Corinne assured her she could stay at Alengon's pension until the Russian issued her travel documents. Some- how Corinne had never grasped the fact that there would be no travel papers. Once France's monarchy was restored and order ruled again, Marie Fleur might not need papers to travel. Ironically, by then, neither would she have money for the boat, for she would need that jealously hoarded fare to survive.

The count was billeted with his fellow officers in a former palace. The magnificent white stone-columned building was larger than Langley Chase and surrounded by gardens almost as grand. Marie Fleur could hardly believe such splendor ex- isted so close to the crowded heart of the city.

"My room's fit for a prince," he confided, squeezing her hand in the dark carriage as they drew up before the entrance.

When they entered his apartment Marie Fleur marveled at the magnificent painted wall panels, gilded furniture, and white painted doors. The count fired a brace of candles in a silver candelabra and held it aloft to allow her to better admire her surroundings. The candlelight shed a soft welcoming glow over the high-ceilinged room. Rose silk brocade swagged draperies were drawn across the tall windows, their gold-fringed bottoms brushing a matching flowered carpet. Cornflower blue satin upholstery gleamed on the elegant gilded couch that stood be- fore a glowing hearth; blue satin curtains embroidered with nosegays of flowers hung from a circular diadem above the carved bed.

"Oh, Andreas, it's lovely!"

His mouth curved in pleasure. "Finally you've used my name. I think it must be the first time."

Marie Fleur swallowed uncomfortably at his reminder. Ever since she had obligated herself to this man, she had tried to visualize him as Andreas, an attractive Russian, rather than

Count Bezak of the Sumsky Hussars. Yet so long had she referred to him as "the Russian" or "the count," the transition was not easy.

"I'll try harder," she assured him with a smile.

The candlelight threw his shadow larger than life across the elaborately painted ceiling on which cherubs and nubile maidens frolicked on gilded clouds. He put down the candelabra, his expression solemn. Almost as an afterthought he removed his bearskin and pitched it to the sofa. Now his thick hair gleamed like gold in the light, curling crisply on his brow, which was damp with sweat.

"Marie Fleur, I don't want you to have to consciously *try* to be anything to please me."

She smiled guiltily, knowing he had read her mind. When he placed his hand on her shoulder she did not flinch, not even when he pulled her against him. The gold buttons on his uniform pressed into her breasts as she stood on tiptoe to receive his kiss. Their lips met, and he automatically tightened his arms about her, pressing her close. The unspoken message of passion fired a like response in her blood. This elaborate apartment seemed unreal as the heady feeling gripped her, making the room in all its gilded splendor rock slightly before she blinked and it righted itself once again.

"Oh, I feel faint," she gasped against the heat of his neck. "I've not eaten since breakfast."

"This feeling's not from lack of food. I felt it too," he replied huskily, as he gently kissed her closed eyelids. Joy leaped in his veins; the response he had longed for had been kindled at last. Inside her cool exterior burned a passion he must learn to unleash.

"First you shall have your magnificent new gown. Food will arrive shortly. I thought, since this is our first night together, we would dine here beside the fire."

There was a note of hesitation in his voice as if he awaited her approval. Marie Fleur steadied herself against the gilded frame of the sofa. "What a good idea," she said. "We can get to know each other much better in privacy."

"Soon we'll know each other better than anyone has ever known us," he vowed, his prominent blue eyes darkening as he gazed at her. "But first you must see your finery."

Andreas went to a white gilded armoire and flung open the doors to reveal a froth of brightly colored garments. Laughing boyishly, he pulled armloads of dresses from the armoire and threw them on the bed.

Marie Fleur gasped at the magnificent clothes, wondering whether he had purchased or plundered them. She felt it was not prudent to ask.

"When next we go out I want you to wear this." He withdrew a gown of ice-blue satin overlaid with white Brussels lace; posies of silk wildflowers caught up the overskirt and nestled in the froth of lace edging the neckline. A pale yellow high-crowned straw bonnet festooned with ice-blue satin ribbons and a band of wildflowers he placed beside the gown. Returning to the armoire he produced a pair of matching satin slippers and a posy-trimmed satin and lace reticule. Gasping with delight, Marie Fleur held the lovely gown against her body, going to the cheval glass to admire herself. Andreas came to stand behind her, his handsome face reflected over her shoulder.

"Try it on to please me. Since I first saw it I've longed to see you wearing that dress. The others aren't new; this is. There's a modiste tucked away on the rue de Valery who was making this exquisite creation for a member of the emperor's household. I'm afraid they left Paris in too much of a hurry to claim it."

Marie Fleur's eyes widened. "Oh, no wonder it's so beautiful! It must have cost a lot of money."

He smiled and kissed her hair. "Not a lot. Please, put it on."

He went back to the fireplace. At a sidetable he poured champagne into two crystal stemmed glasses.

Marie Fleur stepped behind a painted brocade screen, her fingers fumbling in excitement as she pulled off her threadbare dress. It seemed a lifetime since she had worn something pretty. Praying the gown would fit, she carefully slipped it over her head, straining to hook the back of the bodice. The snug satin cupped her breasts like a second skin, clearly revealing the protrusion of her nipples. Next came the bonnet. She carefully tied a bow beneath her chin. The satin shoes were tight across the instep yet wearable, for all that.

"See."

Andreas turned from the hearth to discover a vision in ice-blue satin.

"Even lovelier than I imagined," he breathed sincerely. "You look like a queen. Or maybe a Czarina. Come, you can be my little Czarina."

Andreas held out a glass of champagne, and Marie Fleur took the crystal flute, admiring the flowers etched on the stem. The champagne bubbled up the back of her nose, making her cough. It seemed an eternity since she had drunk champagne as well.

When their glasses were empty, he drew her against him, slipping his hands over her back. The warmth quickly penetrated the satin, causing a shiver of excitement to run down her spine. Andreas unfastened her bonnet and dropped it to the carpet. Slipping his hands into her silky hair, he drew her closer. This time Marie Fleur anticipated his kiss, holding back, trying not to respond. Her body ached to be loved, to be cherished. At moments like this it betrayed her. Anguished over the discovery, she opened her eyes and stared into his, seeing herself mirrored in the pale blue iris, the candles reflecting a halo behind her. He was not Brandon, and she did not love him as she had loved Brandon. Yet Brandon no longer wanted her. The stark pain of that statement made her gasp.

"What is it?" At once Andreas was all concern as he took his face from hers.

"Nothing. It's just that . . . that—"

"I'm not he."

Stricken that Andreas should have guessed her secret, Marie Fleur raised her eyes to his. She was surprised to see pain there.

A knock came at the door, and he left her to answer it. While he spoke to someone in the corridor, Marie Fleur examined the garments spread over the satin bedcover. There were two pale summer muslins with puffed sleeves and satin trimmings, a heavy watered silk day dress with long braid-adorned sleeves, a stylish frogged pelisse edged with chinchilla over a matching wine velvet gown. Her inventory was interrupted by the count's return.

"Here's our supper. I trust you'll enjoy it more than you did the last time."

She laughed in surprise to find the identical menu they had been served in Marcel's Café. "Ah! You're going to wear me down until I clean my plate."

"Exactly. Shall we eat beside the fire?"

They dined from a cabrioled side table that Andreas had

drawn to the sofa. It was pleasantly warm before the fire. While they ate he told her about his childhood on the Russian steppes before he had gone to join his father in St. Petersburg. Their estates were vast. The Bezak family's serfs bound for life in servitude to their master, numbered in the thousands. Andreas's mother, Louise, had been a famous Viennese court beauty before her marriage to Count Bezak. His own name was Germanic in origin, preferred by his mother to the Russian version, Andrei.

"My father was in the Czar's personal guard," Andreas was saying, gazing into the leaping flames where he pictured their tall town house on the banks of the Neva. It was there he had last seen his father, resplendent in the uniform of the Imperial Guard, riding his huge white charger into battle. "He was killed at Austerlitz with over twenty thousand of our countrymen. I'm count by default," he added bitterly, forcing a smile as he pushed aside the table.

Andreas drew Marie Fleur to her feet. "We are two piteous refugees, adrift in this vast sewer called Paris," he whispered, touching her face, her hair.

The champagne had made her lightheaded and unusually happy. No longer did he seem such a formidable stranger with whom she had struck an intimate bargain. She was lonely and she felt terribly unloved. When Andreas smiled at her gently and squeezed her fingers, she squeezed his bony hand in reply, glad of the contact.

"This evening's been marvelous. Such good food. These lovely clothes and these beautiful surroundings..." Her voice died away as he stared intently at her, an unfathomable expression on his handsome face. She swallowed, knowing before he spoke what it was he would say.

"The best is yet to come."

Andreas slowly turned her about and began to unfasten her gown. He was unusually skillful in unhooking a lady's garment, and Marie Fleur decided he had probably had much practice.

"Go to the bed and find the lavender negligée with the black lace. That, too, was purchased especially for you. There's a silly ribboned cap to match. Though I told the modiste it would be wasted, she insisted on me taking it."

The lavender negligée and its matching filmy gown lay beneath the heap of dresses. After carefully smoothing out the garments, Marie Fleur was taken aback by the transparency of the fabric. In this froth of lavender she would look most alluring. Such a wisp of a garment would have delighted Brandon—no! She tightened her mouth in anguish as she fought the hot prickle of tears. She must not keep thinking about *him*. Andreas, Count Bezak, was her lover now. It was he whom she would arouse with this seductive apparel.

She turned about with a stricken expression to find him leaning against the mantel, sipping champagne as he watched her. Without a word she picked up the outfit and the matching ribbon cap and walked behind the screen. When she had changed her clothes, Marie Fleur did not even look at her reflection in the mirror. It was a sight she could not have borne.

Andreas glanced up at her approach. He had been staring at the flames, not knowing how to erase the painful memories that haunted her. He tried to swallow the tightness in his throat as she floated toward him, barefoot on the plush carpet. With each movement the filmy material revealed further glimpses of rounded ivory flesh, tantalizing him almost beyond measure. The weight in the pit of his stomach increased, the hot surge roaring through his loins. She stopped several feet from him.

"Do you like it?"

He nodded, not trusting himself with words. Her dusky pink nipples peaked the soft fabric over those heavy white globes of perfection. His hands opened and closed, possessed of their own will, longing to capture that beauty.

Of her own accord, Marie Fleur came to him and slipped her arms about Andreas's neck, aroused by the knowledge of his desire. In the tight breeches of his uniform his was a poorly kept secret. When he kissed her this time, his mouth was on fire. She received his kisses with increasing pleasure as she clung about his neck. This man was her lover; she must keep repeating that fact until her wayward heart accepted it.

Andreas nuzzled her neck, his breath hot, his kisses passionate. His hands closed over her breasts, and she felt a surge of pride when he visibly shuddered at the longed-for contact.

"Come, torture me no more," he urged, his voice husky against her ear.

Arms about each other's waists, they went to the bed. Andreas pushed the glittering finery to the floor, clearing a place for them to lie. Almost lazily he drew her down beside him, pressing their bodies full-length. Now Marie Fleur could feel the matching fire in his loins, the thrust, the pressure. So controlled had been his actions, had she not known otherwise she would have thought him only slightly aroused.

"We'll love like no others before us," Andreas vowed as he untied the negligée's ribbon fastening. His fingers trembled as he slipped the neck of the nightgown down to expose her breasts. It took both hands to encompass the fullness of each perfect globe. He weighed their sweetness, marveling at the firm upthrust of such heavy flesh. Almost reverently he caressed her ivory flesh, tracing his forefinger over and around her pink nipples until they pouted invitingly.

Not finding her response entirely to his liking, for she did not return his caresses, Andreas unlooped the cord of his dolman. He opened his linen shirt, baring a hard chest furred with crinkly blond hair. Then he took her little hands and pressed them against his flesh, urging her touch.

Andreas kissed her neck and shoulders, tracing his tongue over her breasts. As Marie Fleur leaned over him to stroke his hot, smooth shoulders, he captured the weight of her breasts in his hands, drawing her closer until he could touch the pink buds of her nipples with his tongue. Marie Fleur shuddered deliciously at the hot, wet contact, at the heated insistence of his mouth, which shot fire between her legs. With an anguished sob, she finally relinquished that part of her that had remained loyal to Brandon, burying her ideals beneath a wave of passion. She fingered Andreas's own hardened nipples; she stroked his fevered cheek; she kissed and caressed him with an abandon she had never known before. In her subconscious she understood this arousing man was Count Bezak, and yet she did not understand it. His virile, pulsating body, his tender, knowledgeable hands merely spelled passion. And she found the pull of that primitive response far stronger than the beautiful ideal of faithfulness she had vowed to uphold though she would never again set eyes on her beloved.

"Andreas, oh, Andreas." Breathlessly she whispered his name, her violet eyes moist with emotion. His hot mouth welded to hers, igniting the torch of desire. His tongue probed her mouth, searching, possessing, as he pressed her deeper into the soft feather mattress.

Eagerly Marie Fleur slid her hands over his firm buttocks and muscular thighs, steel-tense beneath the formfitting breeches. Anticipating her next move, Andreas unbuttoned the flap of his breeches, then the inner band. Taking her hand, he molded her slender fingers about the fiery surge of his arousal.

At the searing touch Marie Fleur gasped anew with desire. How full and large he felt, how hot, how smooth. She admired the bursting strength of his pale, blue-veined flesh in the fire's glow. And as she fondled Andreas, tremoring with the promise of fulfillment, she no longer made a mental comparison to *him*. Her intimate caresses made Andreas respond with an even greater wave of desire, until he thought he would explode with need.

Hunger flooded between them as their breaths mingled in a ravaging kiss. His face grim, Andreas recaptured the smooth perfection of her breasts, his touch no longer gentle. The burning pressure of his mouth swept her throat, her shoulders, until Marie Fleur was consumed with fire. So enflamed was she that she rejoiced in the crushing possession of his hands on her flesh and the sudden demanding thrust of his manhood against her thighs.

"Love me. Oh, Andreas, please, make me forget," she murmured, barely aware of her throbbing plea.

Too involved was he in positioning her beneath him to heed her words. The liquid fire of her silken limbs drove him to the brink of insanity. He swept his hand over the quivering softness between her thighs, he placed a searing kiss on the soft mound before desire drove him relentlessly on. With a sob of frustration, Andreas invaded the final barrier to fulfillment.

Marie Fleur threshed beneath him, lost in a secret world of her own making. When he entered her the burning thrust of his flesh assuaged the craving of her body. She cried out as she clutched his back, straining to absorb all of him, desperate to reach that place where there were no conscious memories of time past, only the thrill of now.

Together they strove in the ancient battle of love, driving harder into the deep feather mattress beneath its blue satin diadem. No longer able to hold back, Andreas forced her onward, plunging her into that blackness from which there was no return. Marie Fleur cried out, lifting her hips from the confining softness to meet the strength of his vanquishing thrust. Then, in a throbbing wave of satisfaction, she allowed herself to slowly relax into the bed as she held him against her and kissed the hard bare shoulder she found beneath her mouth.

It was only when he whispered endearments and praise in his own tongue that the devastation of what had taken place

gripped her. The relieving flood of emotion-charged tears became a solemn obituary to her forsaken love. And she must
crush her lids tight to shut out the vision of his handsome face,
which mocked her from the gilded shadows of this palatial
suite.

❧ Chapter 14 ❧

MARIE FLEUR AND Andreas mingled with the afternoon strollers waiting to pay their toll of one sou apiece for admittance to the narrow Pont des Arts spanning the Seine. This privately owned iron bridge had been a sensation at its opening, being the first of its type and solely for pedestrians. The owner maintained two greenhouses, where a magnificent display of hothouse plants were kept. Against the rail, benches were placed between large orange trees planted in brightly painted tubs.

The gaily dressed crowd swept them to the center of the bridge before Andreas was able to draw Marie Fleur to an empty bench.

Today she was wearing a filmy muslin gown over a pink silk slip, the long mameluke sleeves gathered into puffs with pink satin ribbons. Her blond curls, which reached to her shoulders, peeped from under a yellow straw bonnet tied with pink satin ribbons. Andreas had purchased a nosegay of frilled pinks from a flower seller at the corner of the rue St-Honoré, and he had threaded the flowers under the ribbon hatband so that every time Marie Fleur moved their nostrils were filled with spicy fragrance.

"You look like an angel," Andreas breathed as he gazed at her silhouetted against the sun-sparkled water.

"Thank you, kind sir." Marie Fleur dimpled happily at his compliment.

"I've a wonderful surprise. All day I've been longing to tell you, but I wanted to wait for the right moment." Andreas rested his booted foot on the railing and leaned forward on his knee until his handsome face was very close to hers.

Marie Fleur had seen women watch them pass with stark envy on their faces, eager to attract a glance from the splendid Russian. Andreas strutted rather arrogantly, it was true, knowing how magnificent he appeared in his summer uniform of cream breeches and tailored dolman heavily adorned with gold Brandenburgs. His mirror-bright black boots were tasseled in red; his black bearskin cap tasseled in gold. Around his slender waist was a red sash from which hung his sabre in a gold sheath emblazoned with his family's arms. His pelisse was slung over his left shoulder in the customary style, attached by gold lacing. There was little uniformity about the dress of the Cossack regiments. Many of their officers had uniforms tailored to their own design. This lavish uniform had been styled purposely to emphasize Andreas's broad-shouldered, slender-waisted body. The skintight breeches displayed his muscular buttocks and thighs to perfection, allowing just enough bias for him to sit and ride.

Confidently she smiled up at him, waiting. She felt a surge of emotion as she met blue eyes in which she saw herself reflected in miniature.

"A surprise?" she prompted, "Surely not more clothes."

"No, not clothes," he dismissed, his face grave as he stared beyond her to the slender spires of Sainte-Chapelle. "We're soon to leave Paris."

Marie Fleur swallowed nervously, wondering if he was returning to St. Petersburg. Yet he had not said "I." "Where are *we* to go?"

"I've been chosen to accompany the Czar to an official victory celebration, and you're to come with me."

"Where?"

Unsmiling still, Andreas took her small hand encased in white lace gloves and placed a lingering kiss on her wrist.

"To London, my beautiful Czarina!"

For a moment Marie Fleur was speechless with shock. Tears of joy surged forth to dim her vision as his statement registered. Home to England at last! Eyes shining, Marie Fleur whispered, "Oh, Andreas, that's what I want most of all. When do we leave?"

"Do you think next week will give you time enough to pack?"

"Oh, yes, more than enough."

So excited was she, Marie Fleur embraced him, something she was not wont to do in public. Overjoyed by her spontaneity, Andreas kissed her passionately, his eyes glowing with pleasure at having pleased her.

Laughing, chatting, they continued their journey across the bridge. Marie Fleur was so elated she could hardly wait to get back to their apartment so she could begin packing.

It was only later, when she was alone, sorting through her

finery and deciding which garments were most suitable for the English climate, that she realized a truth that up to now had escaped her. Brandon would be in London! In all the swirling excitement of the moment, never once had she considered that he would probably attend all the fashionable gala events to which Andreas would be invited. The inevitable gossip and the raised eyebrows when she appeared in public on the arm of a handsome Russian officer she was prepared to take in stride. It was a heated confrontation with Brandon she dreaded. There would be no satisfactory way to explain Andreas to him. He would be convinced she had taken up with the Russian from choice.

Angrily she thumped her fist on the bed. What did it matter what Brandon thought? It was not she who had first forsaken their vows. Furthermore, he had told such humiliating lies after she had risked her life to save him. A man like that was not worthy of her affection; she was fortunate to be free of him.

Tears rolled slowly down her cheeks, flushed by the afternoon sun. If she was so glad to be free of him, why did her heart ache at the thought of his name? Why did it matter what he would think about her relationship with Andreas? Absently Marie Fleur fingered the mound of jewel-bright dresses, all gifts from her Russian lover who delighted in dressing her like a princess. Who could blame her for taking the passion of his magnificent body in an attempt to assuage the pain in her heart? Yet even while Andreas's kisses and his lovemaking soothed her, in the background there always lurked the specter of Brandon Nicholas, to whom she had vowed love eternal. Anger and pain surged through her body as she fought tears. Damn him for spoiling what could have been blissful happiness! His dark presence pervaded even this luxurious room, taunting her with memories of what might have been and was not.

Taking a deep breath, Marie Fleur got up and walked with determined step to the windows, where she lifted the rose brocade curtains to peer outside at the balmy darkness.

At the head of the shallow steps leading into the rose garden burned two wrought iron lanterns, casting lacy fretwork designs over the grass. A fountain tinkled unceasingly among the carefully laid-out beds. She had walked there in the moonlight with Andreas; he had kissed her and given her his love. She had even tried to love him in return, desperate to recapture the remembered intensity of that emotion. The silver moonlight, the scent of roses lingering in the warm air, the tinkling fountain had all played their romantic parts in her self-deception. It was only tonight while she stood here alone—for Andreas drank with his fellow officers in the mirrored banqueting hall below—that she finally faced the truth. Her experience of genuine love had not been of joy, nor of pleasure; rather, it was a painful reality that left her shaken and bereft. Though her body vowed devotion to Count Bezak, her heart had remained faithful to another.

During the month of June, 1814, London was *én fête*. Flags and streamers decked the streets. Doves of peace and banners conveying patriotic sentiments adorned the houses of the rich, while even the poor expressed joy over the allied victory by burning candles in their windows. The glorious month of June became a nonstop round of breakfasts, suppers, banquets, balls, and theatrical galas as the nation rejoiced over Napoleon's defeat and subsequent exile to the island of Elba.

Unfortunately, at the same time as they carried news of allied victory in Europe, the London papers seethed with reports of a classic royal row between the Regent and his wife, Princess Caroline. Though their public disagreements were nothing new, this current domestic squabble was ill-timed now that London was crowded with illustrious foreigners. The avid reporting in the press of his latest marital conflict proved to be a source of acute embarrassment to the Regent.

Furthermore, the Russian Czar had demanded a suite at Pultney's Hotel, Piccadilly, where his sister, the Grand Duchess Catherine, had been staying since March. This went totally against the Regent's plans, for he had intended to house the Czar at St. James's Palace. Obligingly he reserved the hotel for Alexander and his entourage, discouraged by the deterioration of his relationship with the Russian couple. A white banner proclaiming "Thanks Be to God" flapped across the hotel's facade to mark the auspicious occasion.

The warm June night throbbed with noise and laughter as the common people danced and drank in the streets, making the most of the official sanction on making merry.

Marie Fleur rested her head against the upholstery as her carriage sped toward the opera house. She was to attend a gala performance of *Aristodemo*. Czar Alexander, the king of Prussia, the Austrian Prince Metternich, and countless other foreign dignitaries were to be there as guests of the prince regent.

Andreas had gone on ahead to make arrangements for His Imperial Majesty. The blond, baby-faced czar had proved immensely popular with the Londoners, who hailed him as a savior. He had also endeared himself to the common man by walking in the park with his sister Catherine without attendant pomp or ceremony. Czar Alexander basked in such adulation, dividing his time between joyous public appearances and attempts to seduce every pretty woman he met. Both he and his sister had become increasingly hostile toward their royal host, going so far as to voice support for Caroline, the Princess of Wales, in the current marital squabble. Their open acceptance of his hated wife had further humiliated the already suffering Regent.

Marie Fleur smiled as she recalled the handsome young Czar's predictable romantic advances. Wherever he went, women swooned over him, desperate to be noticed, whereas she, who had been embarrassingly noticed on more than one occasion, wished the philandering Czar would turn his attentions elsewhere.

Tonight Marie Fleur wore a sumptuous new gown especially made for this grand opera gala. Of periwinkle-blue silk, it had a broad panel of crystal-beaded embroidery from the low-necked bodice to the padded satin hem. She wore an heirloom pendant of a huge sapphire surrounded by diamonds and a pair of matching earrings. The priceless jewelry was from the Bezak family's collection. Andreas had sent a special courier to bring back these pieces, and they had arrived in time for their departure for England. She wore a small jeweled tiara perched atop a mountain of curls that cascaded to her shoulders in a shower of golden ringlets, a style that had taken a maid over an hour to arrange. To complete her splendid outfit Marie Fleur wore a blue satin spencer edged with ermine. On her feet were dainty, low-heeled blue satin slippers spangled with brilliants.

Never in her life had she felt so grand, yet at the same time so miserable. She knew in her bones that Brandon would be at the theater tonight. He was a good friend of the Regent, and tonight Prinny would surely choose to be surrounded by his friends, if only for moral support. Though she kept trying to rehearse what she would say to Brandon when they met, each time she pictured his face, her mind went blank.

The theater was ablaze with lights. Marie Fleur shuddered

to recall the last time she had attended the opera. That hideous ordeal had begun an unhappy chapter of her life that she hoped was over.

The carriage stopped, and she alighted. She ascended the carpeted steps to the foyer. Everywhere she looked seemed to glitter with gold and diamonds. The men wore elaborate dress uniforms or impeccable evening dress; their ladies were visions in satin and silk, feathered and flowered, veritable hothouses of luscious perfumed blooms atop elaborately coiffed hair.

As soon as he saw Marie Fleur, Andreas came to her side, making her feel more at ease. As she had expected, from the instant she left her carriage vicious tongues began to wag: the pointed stares, the knowing smiles, the whispered asides behind gloved hands as heads snapped about to verify what the gossips had been saying.

Nodding regally to her acquaintances, Marie Fleur walked on, Andreas striding stiffly beside her, resplendent in his magnificent uniform, prouder than the Czar himself. In their box, which was three boxes away from the major dignitaries, he seated Marie Fleur amongst a handful of other ladies belonging to lesser foreign nobility before he excused himself to attend the Czar.

By now Marie Fleur's neck had begun to ache from the effort of holding her head high. Her face was flushed, her ears burning with the imagined comments from the *ton*. They probably already classed her as a Cyprian, which was, though she hated to admit, what her alliance with the Russian count had made her. Her attention was attracted by the Czar entering the royal box in military uniform, his chest ablaze with medals. The other allied dignitaries filed inside the royal box to thunderous applause. There was Prinny, fatter than ever, beaming with joy and pride over this lavish entertainment. The operatic stars of the evening, Madame Grassini and Signor Tramezzani, came to the footlights to bow in homage to the assembled crowned heads.

Just as the curtain parted, Andreas slipped into place beside her, his hand warmly comforting as he affectionately squeezed her arm. To Marie Fleur's surprise tears pricked her eyes as she pressed his steel-hard arm beneath the gold-decorated sleeve. Let them stare and gossip, she thought fiercely; she was not ashamed to be seen with Andreas. He was a man to be proud of.

Before the orchestra began the overture she noticed the Earl of Cranbrook gaping at her. He probably still did not know how she had escaped his clutches. The memory of those depraved theatricals hidden behind the gilt and plush facade of his sumptuous town house made her shudder with revulsion.

A Scotch divertissement and a ballet were scheduled to follow the opera. During the first interval the stars sang a hymn of welcome, which was followed by the national anthem. A flurry of movement opposite the royal box announced the unexpected arrival of Caroline, Princess of Wales, in the middle of "God Save the King."

Though from here she could not see his face, Marie Fleur knew Prinny would be furious. His wife was the last person he would have wished to attend his opera gala. A ripple of applause for Princess Caroline came from the pit, and redfaced, the Regent began to applaud the artists in an effort to cover the incident. The theater was aflutter, and laughter, some of it cruelly gleeful of the prince's discomfiture, rippled through the jeweled assembly.

After the second interval, an event occurred that affected Marie Fleur far more than the unexpected appearance of the Princess of Wales. To her horror, amid thunderous applause, a familiar dark-haired figure tripped onstage clad as a swan in ice-blue and white feathers. Gabriella Vasco's pure soprano voice soared free, reaching the topmost tier of gilded boxes. When the Italian song, which Marie Fleur assumed was in praise of a swan, was over, cheers and much applause resounded through the theater. Andreas was no less enthusiastic than the rest.

Gripping the railing of the box, Marie Fleur froze as a man moved out of the orchestra pit to the footlights bearing a beautiful bouquet of roses. She could see it was Brandon as he handed Gabriella the bouquet. The Italian singer curtsied and prettily blew him kisses.

At her side Andreas clapped, delighted by the gesture, completely won over by the vivacious brunette. He could not understand why Marie Fleur appeared so taut nor why she did not respond to his flattering comments about the woman's performance.

After the gala the area where one could walk from wing to wing behind the pit was crowded with chattering patrons. Acquaintances pressed themselves on Marie Fleur, eagerly de-

manding to be introduced to her handsome foreigner. She
smilingly obliged them with an introduction that included all
of Andreas's grand titles. At his most charming self, he bowed
solemnly to each gentleman and kissed the hand of every gush-
ing female. Highly aware of the mingled glances of envy and
spite from certain females, and ignoring the obvious cut she
received from Lady Marchope and her ilk, Marie Fleur valiantly
acted the part of glittering social butterfly. They had entered
the Green Room when the moment she had been dreading was
suddenly upon her.

"My dear Lady Dowling, how enchanting you look."

The sound of that lazy, affected voice sent a spear of pain
through her heart. Turning, she felt weak as she beheld Brandon, impeccably dressed in black swallowtail coat and body-
hugging breeches, a snow-white cravat tied beneath his firm,
determined chin. To his arm clung Gabriella, resplendent in
gold-embroidered satin with a long rope of fluffy swansdown
looped casually about her neck.

"The lady with the lovely voice! Introduce, please," commanded Andreas, his whisper loud enough to be heard by the
others who laughed in delight over his obvious impatience.

Stonily Marie Fleur complied, her voice brittle as she said,
"Signorina Gabriella Vasco—Andreas, Count Bezak." Andreas took Gabriella's hand and raised it to his lips.

"Charming. Such a lovely voice ... such a lovely lady."

"And her escort, the Honorable Mr. Brandon Nicholas."

"Sir, you are the envy of all men."

"Ah, surely tonight other men's envy is something we share
equally," drawled Brandon, giving Andreas a polite nod, his
eyes on Marie Fleur.

She tried not to meet his gaze but found herself irresistibly
drawn like a moth to the flame. When their eyes met she saw
anger and surprise reflected there before he cleverly masked
the emotion.

The others crowded around them. Marie Fleur swayed, refusing to move despite the crush of laughing humanity. It was
as if she stood rooted to the spot, staring at him, foolishly
awaiting his explanation. Abruptly Brandon turned away to
begin a spirited discussion with Lord Westerham about the
merits of tonight's performance. A rush of relief washed over
her, almost as if she had been released from bondage.

"A very pleasant Englishman," Andreas commented as he

handed Marie Fleur a glass of champagne he had taken from a passing waiter.

"His father is in the government."

"Oh, is that so?" Andreas watched Brandon's broad-shouldered figure a moment before turning his attention to Gabriella, who was smiling flirtatiously at all the men.

Nursing her champagne, Marie Fleur retreated against the wall to lean upon a brocade panel, fighting to regain her composure. Voices repeating snatches of gossip drifted to her. Most of it rolled over her and was gone. That terrible feeling of betrayal as yet again he had refused to acknowledge their attachment absorbed her attention. Surely she had not imagined that unguarded emotion in his face. Could it have been pain because he had lost her? A bitter smile tugged her full mouth. What a fool she was being all over again, forever presuming to put romantic thoughts into a head in which undoubtedly there was no room, the space already being filled with pictures of luscious Gabriella.

"The little nightingale ... charming villa ... Brandy's done this one proud, eh, what? Set her up with everything from carriages to silver ..."

Heat blazed in Marie Fleur's cheeks. She choked as her throat constricted, and she hastily gulped champagne to quench her torment. So they were openly living together! No wonder everyone accepted them as a permanent twosome. Pain and rage throbbed to her temples. If only she could will herself a thousand miles away from that attractive couple surrounded by chattering friends. Gabriella's high-pitched laughter, and her frequent squeaks of delight grated on Marie Fleur's nerves.

She sought Andreas, searching amongst the gaudy uniforms for his. He raised his head, saw her, smiled and nodded, then rapidly brought his conversation with a bewhiskered general to a halt.

"Are you ready to go home?" he asked huskily, his hand sliding possessively over her exposed back.

"Yes, please. All this noise gives me a headache."

"A headache! You're surely not going to disappoint me," he whispered, his lips against her hair as they were pressed closer by the milling patrons. "And I had such wonderful plans for tonight."

Over his shoulder Marie Fleur saw Brandon watching them, paying scant attention to the bosomy dowager who clung to

his arm. Pain stabbed afresh as she recalled all the torment he
had inflicted with his wayward love. Soon anger replaced the
hurt, the two emotions conflicting until she did not know whether
to rage or cry.

"Yes, let's go home. I'm tired of all this noise and especially
the company." Here she allowed her head to droop against
Andreas's shoulder, keeping her eye on Brandon to be sure he
still watched as she delivered her final thrust expressly for his
benefit. "I like it best when there's only the two of us." Marie
Fleur would not have known if Brandon heard her words over
the mounting noise had she not seen the characteristic tautening
of his stubborn jaw, the set of his mouth. Oh, how his mouth
evoked such exquisite feelings of longing, or desire.

"You'll never know how happy you've made me tonight,"
Andreas breathed, moved by her declaration. "I'll have the
carriage brought 'round at once."

Marie Fleur steeled herself not to look back. She could feel
Brandon's gaze boring through her back. Let him squirm a
little, let him know some of the pain she had experienced when
he appeared with Gabriella Vasco on his arm. Head high, she
tucked her hand beneath Andreas's arm and walked serenely
from the Green Room.

Brandon put down the glass he was holding, carefully controlling the rage throbbing through his body. So that was how
it was. Her Russian count meant far more than mere sustenance
as the gossips had suggested. She was in love with him! Damn
them both! he raged inwardly, clenching his fists. There was
no denying they made a glitteringly handsome pair: two tall
blond deities with flawless complexions, arrayed as brightly as
peacocks.

"What's the matter, *caro*, you aren't listening to me," pouted
Gabriella at his side, twining her hands about his arm.

"I'm sorry, darling, I've got a damnable headache. Haven't
you had enough of this? I certainly have."

"We'll go when you're ready. Surely you don't begrudge
me my hour of glory."

"You're more than welcome to your hour. Why don't I
leave and send the carriage back? Then you can come home
when you're ready."

"No." Gabriella's face hardened. She had not missed the
telltale change in his expression when he had looked at that
blond beauty, the action creating the same feeling she had

experienced before in Marie Fleur's presence. Gabriella had an animal's instinct for danger, and the Dowling woman was not mere danger—she was disaster. "I'm ready to leave now."

"Good. Here, I'll get your wrap."

Shouldering his way through the crowd, which was beginning to thin, Brandon grimly made his way to the theater entrance.

Gabriella waved a gay farewell to her admirers, shrugging and rolling her dark eyes expressively to explain their hasty departure. Her suggestive hints brought chuckles and knowing winks, for Brandon's healthy libido was a well-known fact. And who could blame him? The little Neopolitan nightingale was a splendid armful.

Though she could have allowed him to go home alone, thereby enjoying another hour of adulation for herself, Gabriella did not trust her magnificent Englishman for one minute, not while that woman was in the vicinity. Brandon moved in and out of her life as casually as a tomcat, never revealing when, or if, he would return. Lately, however, she had to admit he had been far more attentive. She had no intention of changing that welcome state of affairs.

On the return journey to Blackheath, clopping through the lighted London streets, Brandon had little to say. Gabriella was alarmed by his brooding silence. She stroked his face, she playfully nibbled his ears and fingertips, coquettish little ploys she used to great advantage to stimulate a man. Tonight his response was vastly disappointing. By the time they entered their darkened villa she was seething over the cause of his indifference. It was that icy blond who had bewitched him, damn her! Wasn't the good-looking Russian enough?

"*Caro*, unfasten my gown," Gabriella invited in a throaty voice to which she reverted when necessity dictated. They had retired to their bedroom where Brandon lounged before the hearth, a glass of brandy in his hand. Though it had been almost an hour since their return he was still in a morose mood. She was at her wits' end to cheer him. Sitting before the fire like old fogies was not quite what she had in mind as a finale to tonight's gala.

Obediently he put down his glass and came to her. Gabriella pouted at his frown, tracing the furrows on his brow.

"I don't think the opera agreed with you tonight."

"I'm all right. Just tired."

"Tired! What a terrible admission from my beautiful black stallion," she whispered wickedly. "We must wake you up. *Così!*" Taking his hands, she placed them over her ample breasts, which, as the gown slid lower, were tantalizingly revealed.

Against his will Brandon felt answering fire stab his loins. Gabriella kept at her arousing game by taking his index finger and rubbing it gently about her large brown nipple until it stood hard and full as an acorn. As always, Brandon was struck by the unusual appearance of her breasts. A huge areola surmounted by those strangely swollen protrusions covered half their golden surface. The accentuated development of her nipples must come from having suckled her two babies fathered by Murat, Napoleon's appointed king of Naples.

"You witch, you won't be satisfied till you're laid," he growled as he swung her about and covered her mouth with his own. There was no tenderness about him tonight, only rage and the desire to get even, to inflict pain for pain. He would have preferred his victim to have been Marie Fleur, the cause of his anguish, but Gabriella would have to do.

"Ah, so you aren't dead, after all. I was beginning to wonder." Gabriella's fingers were busy molding the strength of his mounting erection beneath his black knitted breeches. "You alarmed me, *caro*. I thought you no longer cared."

"I'll show you how much I care."

He took hold of her golden satin gown and peeled it like a skin to her waist. With a growl he captured her, his hands moving to her waist, her hips, as the gown slithered to the carpet. Bending his head, Brandon sucked on a protruding nipple until Gabriella gasped; when his teeth meshed she cried aloud in pain. Her nails raked his back, but his coat protected him from injury.

"Tonight you're a tiger. Let's not waste any more time."

Gabriella half fell amongst the rumpled bedclothes, her breathing labored as she watched him pull off his clothes. Brandon's aroused organ leaped from its confinement, and she gasped in delight at the towering strength of him. Wise in the ways of love, having serviced others besides the king of Naples, she had found few to satisfy her as well as this Englishman. Whether he visited her with the faithlessness of a tomcat or not, she would always be waiting for him, eager to claim whatever crumbs of passion he had to offer.

Her full lips pouted to receive his kiss. Gabriella was mildly surprised when he virtually threw himself upon her. *Assault* was the only word she could use to describe this lovemaking, for he dispensed with his customary kisses and caresses. Yet the novelty of his approach filled her with raging desire. Crying out in anguish, she desperately tried to hold on to her passion a little longer, drawing her long nails down the length of his back, biting his ear, pounding her fists against his buttocks. Now she kicked him in an effort to direct his movements to please her; Brandon remained oblivious, suiting his actions to his own speed and desire.

Flinging her on her back, he drove Gabriella into the mattress, moving her a foot up the bed with the force of his entry. She gasped, then squealed in mounting delight as she locked her arms and legs about his wonderfully virile body.

"You're the best lover in the world," she crooned, fighting for breath as he drove harder, until she finally succumbed in an animal cry of torment.

When she would have clung to him, keeping him beside her, Brandon wrenched free, disgusted by what he had done. He had sought to relieve his frustration on the closest object, which tonight had proved to be Gabriella. The fact she was more pleased than hurt by his action mattered not at all. This was the closest he had ever come to raping a woman.

Later, when Brandon had bathed and drunk another two glasses of brandy, he returned to the bedroom, hoping by now she would be asleep. She was. Brandon went to the desk in the corner, where he placed his lighted candle. He had decided to write a letter to Marie Fleur in an effort to explain his actions in Paris. After seeing her with the Russian he doubted she still cared, but it was something he must do to relieve his own conscience. Clear up loose ends, so to speak, he thought, his mouth bitter.

He wrote a few lines, the words drawn forth with much difficulty. There was no need, nor any prudence in trying, to explain his liaison with Gabriella. That he had been ordered to woo the Italian singer to learn the secrets of Joachim Murat would mean nothing to her. He doubted she would even believe him. Unwittingly Gabriella had provided much information about the father of her two children, the knowledge assisting the allies in winning Napoleon's puppet to their side. Brandon's

satisfaction in the matter, based somewhat on fulfilling his duty
but largely on bodily lust, had been rewarding—until he fell
in love with Marie Fleur.

After that fatal turning point, whenever he took the Italian
woman he knew a sickening stab of guilt, a painful sense of
disloyalty that robbed him of total abandon. For the smattering
of valuable information this liaison provided it hardly seemed
worth destroying his chances of a lasting relationship with
Marie Fleur.

Angrily Brandon dashed papers to the floor. What relationship? Quite clearly she had demonstrated her affection for the
Russian. And though he despised his very existence, Brandon
had to acknowledge that Bezak was a handsome devil. It was
whispered the jewelry she wore tonight came from the count's
estate. The stuff must be worth a king's ransom. There again
he could not compete. Undoubtedly she had experienced pain
over his treatment of her, yet she had wasted little time dwelling
on her misery. The Russian could have been waiting in the
wings even then!

Brandon poured another glass of brandy. Tonight this fine
imported French spirit failed to soothe his irritation. Nor woman,
nor drink, . . . he thought bitterly. Suddenly all the furtive
scheming he performed in the name of his country seemed
pointless. The act of depositing insignificant papers in an urn
in a derelict garden behind a dilapidated St.-Germain tavern
was almost ludicrous. Likewise, his galloping masked around
the countryside pretending to be a highwayman or masquer-
ading as a smuggler when he crossed the Channel for paltry
shipments of Holland gin and French brandy seemed more like
cheap theatricals—especially when he considered how much
it had cost him.

He ran his hand over his chin where black stubble rasped
beneath his fingers. That woman who slumbered peacefully in
the large rumpled bed, her black hair spread like a banner over
the pillows, was the leavings of Joachim Murat! He clenched
his fists at the distasteful thought. Usually the knowledge did
not bother him; tonight it did.

Murat, the flamboyant son of a Gascon innkeeper, with
barely the intelligence needed to keep his hat on, seemed a
poor target. What did it really matter that he had turned from
Napoleon to the allies? Murat was merely a purchased husband
for the little Corsican's sister, needed to help Bonaparte hold

onto the remainder of the Continent. Even so, Murat, as had the great Napoleon himself, had played his part in destroying the only love affair in his life that had ever meant anything to him.

Uncharacteristically Brandon sobbed deep in his throat as he laid his head on his hands, aware of the demeaning moisture in his eyes. God! Marie Fleur had brought him that low, toppling him from the pinnacle of unshakable masculinity, which denied such weakness. She haunted him like no other woman ever had, or ever would again.

It was a beautiful summer morning when Gabriella woke and stretched. Vaguely she recalled someone knocking on the door in the night. Brandon had exchanged a few words with whomever it was, then soon afterwards he had left. She had been aware of him bumping about in the dark, cursing as he tried to find his clothes, stumbling, crashing into the furniture. At the time she had sleepily wondered at his clumsiness. This morning she needed puzzle over it no longer. Brandon had been drunk! An empty brandy bottle lay beneath the desk; papers were scattered everywhere. He must have drunk himself to sleep.

She sighed and stretched again, wondering when he would be back. Last night he had displayed a whole new facet in his lovemaking. Would she never stop being amazed at the versatility of her Englishman?

Gabriella slipped her arms into a black lace negligée and padded to the window where the curtains fluttered in the sweet breeze. She went out on the balcony, careless of the titillating view she presented to two gentlemen riding below. The riders slowed their mounts and raised their top hats. Gabriella smiled sunnily in acknowledgment of their greeting as the breeze wafted her filmy negligée most enticingly about her body. Always aware of bodily sensations, Gabriella sighed, enjoying the soft caress that stirred her slumbering desire until she longed for Brandon's return.

She floated downstairs to the sunny hall, wondering if Tomkins knew when his master would return. The servant, who was preparing to take out his master's dispatch box of letters, said he did not know when to expect him. Tomkins generally annoyed her, but today he acted even more supercilious than usual.

"Tell cook I want my breakfast," Gabriella ordered imperiously.

"But, madam, I'm going to catch the mail."

"That's not vital. Am I not mistress of this house? Are you not bound to obey my commands?"

The long suffering Tomkins bowed slightly in deference to her shrill order, and he disappeared into the nether regions to summon the cook.

Gabriella glared stormily after him. How dare Tomkins refuse to obey her! What could be so important in the dispatch box anyway? Gabriella found the red Morocco leather box unlocked. She extracted a sheaf of letters, one to Brandon's lawyer, his uncle, a friend in Richmond . . . her face grew hot as she stared at a sealed envelope addressed to Lady Dowling at Pultney's Hotel. He was writing to *her*. Thin, so he had not written much, but he had written.

A soft tread on the floor made her spin about to find only Ottavio, her Italian servant, standing in the doorway.

"Take the master's letters," she commanded in Italian, holding open the front door as she thrust the dispatch box in his hands. "They are important, so hurry."

Obediently Ottavio disappeared, clutching the tooled leather dispatch box, bursting with pride to have been entrusted with so important a task.

As Tomkins appeared in the gloomy entrance to the servants' quarters, Gabriella held the letter behind her.

"Your breakfast is being prepared, madam. The usual."

"Thank you, Tomkins," said Gabriella with an ingratiating smile. "Now, to save you trouble, I've done a favor for you. Ottavio has taken the letters to the post."

"Thank you, madam, but it is my place to take care of the dispatches, as well you know," Tomkins replied in agitation. "The master will be most displeased."

"There's no need to tell the master. I assure you Ottavio will guard the precious dispatches with his life."

With that she swept past the haughty Tomkins and went back upstairs to dress more modestly for breakfast.

Angrily Gabriella ripped open the letter to read what Brandon had written to that woman. She seethed with rage as she read the pathetic sentiments. Well, his drunken ravings would go no farther. With shaking hand she lit a candle and held the white pages to the flame, watching the words blacken, then curl into ash.

"Darling . . . sorry . . . did not mean . . . love . . ."

She could make little sense of his ramblings. Vindictively she ground the ash into powder in the cold hearth. The action made her feel much better. That was that for Lady Dowling. She would never know what sentiments the weakness of drink had driven Brandon to pen.

Gabriella turned back to the sunny morning beckoning to her from the open window. As she listened to the gaily chirping birds she decided to ride on the heath. She had a lovely new white velvet habit she had not yet worn; in the morning cool, the costume would be perfect.

Bursting into song, which rivaled the birds' for purity, Gabriella slipped on a pink satin dressing gown and went downstairs to breakfast.

☙ Chapter 15 ☙

IN CELEBRATION OF Napoleon's defeat, White's threw a grand masquerade ball at Burlington House. Prinny, anxious to prevent his wife from attending, tried to make members of the exclusive gaming club give their tickets only to relatives.

The Russian Czar, Frederick William of Prussia, and a multitude of nobility, both English and foreign, were among the four thousand guests received at the grand affair by the young Duke of Devonshire and his cousin, the Duke of Leinster.

This splendid event was the most talked-about party of a splendid season. Men not disguised in masquerade costume were resplendent in full-dress uniforms. There were slave girls, several Madame Pompadours in panniers and high powdered wigs, magnificent turbanned sultans, kings, queens, devils, and buccaneers. Some men were dressed as women, some women as men. Colonel Armstrong appeared as a stout dowager of the time of Queen Anne, while Julia Johnstone aped a young boy in black satin breeches and blue silk jacket.

The refreshments were plentiful and extravagant. Iced champagne flowed like water. There were mounds of imported caviar, hot and cold soups, sliced roast goose, roast beef, roast lamb, pastries both sweet and savory, silver platters heaped with exotic fruits. As waltzing made thirsty work, liveried servants continually passed amongst the guests to offer refreshment.

Marie Fleur came dressed as Nell Gwynne, mistress of Charles II. The costume had been provided by Anabelle Reid, who had visited her at the Pultney, greeting her like a long-lost sister. Only when it was far too late to obtain an alternate disguise had she experienced second thoughts about the wisdom of portraying a king's mistress. Could this be a subtle joke at her expense? After all, the Reid family were notorious cutups.

It had been with some trepidation that Marie Fleur donned the full-skirted emerald-green satin gown. The low-cut, tight-fitting bodice was worn over a white lawn chemise whose lacy edging made a provocative frame for her breasts. This seventeenth-century style displayed to perfection Marie Fleur's perfect creamy shoulders and bosom. Knowing the Regent's passion for overheated rooms, an obsession growing out of his boyhood hatred of the icy palaces in which Farmer George had forced the royal children to live, Marie Fleur hoped the accompanying wig of red curls would not prove too uncomfortable. Like many of the other women she wore a black silk mask to conceal her identity. On her hip she carried a wicker basket of oranges into which laughing gentlemen dipped, placing kisses on the cheek of "Pretty, witty Nelly" in payment for the fruit.

Andreas smiled at her across the room, finding her disguise enchanting. He remained unmasked, as did all men in uniform. When Marie Fleur put down her wicker basket of oranges to waltz about the brightly lit ballroom with a multitude of different partners, jealousy flared uncomfortably in his stomach. He followed her movements with narrowed gaze. Since their arrival in England Andreas had been tormented by jealousy. These men had been part of Marie Fleur's life before they met, and he could not help suspecting each well-dressed stranger of being a former lover. Abruptly he turned aside, clicking his heels smartly as His Imperial Majesty impatiently addressed him for the second time.

The lilting music accompanying the dance introduced by Madame de Staël last season filled Marie Fleur with pleasure. She spun round and round like a beautiful animated doll, lost in the magic of the soaring violins. Her magical world was short-lived as curious partners, becoming aware of her identity, teased her to reveal where she had been hiding. Even Poggy Reid pressed her for details of her life during these past months. His cousin, Teddy Brooks, began his cross-examination where Poggy left off.

It was almost a relief when between waltzes Anabelle came over to show off her sumptuous pink and silver brocade gown. She was dressed as Madame de Montespan, mistress of the Sun King. A glittering, diamond-trimmed silver mask cleverly camouflaged her roving gaze as she boldly assessed the handsome uniformed officers, mentally evaluating their romantic potential.

"You naughty girl," Anabelle hissed behind her painted fan. "Everyone said you were entertaining a stuffy cabinet minister, and to think all the time you were with *him*. He's absolutely splendid. I wonder, can he bend in those breeches?" Here she went into peals of laughter. "I'd like to ask you far more intimate questions, but this is hardly the place. . . . Oh, look, the royal dukes are arriving."

Anabelle darted away, her wide skirts sweeping across the floor as she sought a better viewpoint from which to examine the corpulent royals in their elaborate costumes.

Marie Fleur wiped her brow. It was like a hothouse in here. To her disappointment she found Andreas still in attendance on His Imperial Majesty, who was having the time of his life kissing all the pretty masked women while laughingly pleading ignorance of their identities. Desperate for a breath of cool air, Marie Fleur stepped onto the balcony.

The black June sky was a breathtaking carpet of stars. The scent from tubs of potted roses wafted on the breeze. Out here the orchestra was muted, the melody more ethereal. She shut her eyes and listened to the lilting music. She should go indoors, but she was reluctant to return to the crowded ballroom. A few minutes ago she had seen the Earl of Cranbrook dressed as Nero in toga and laurel wreath. However effective she had thought her disguise, it clearly did not hide her identity from him, because he gave her a polite nod of greeting as he passed. Fortunately he had not attempted conversation. She was not sure she could keep her temper if he had the audacity to approach her.

The confrontation with Brandon and Gabriella, which she had been dreading, had not taken place. In this multitude of exotic costumes she might have overlooked them—after all, there were four thousand guests—yet Marie Fleur hoped Brandon and his Neopolitan nightingale had decided to stay at home.

The silver moonlit path tempted her down to the marble fishpond. Enjoying the landscaped gardens of others would be her lot from now on, for the buyer long sought for Langley Chase had finally been found. Silas Lawrence, the aged family solicitor, having suffered a recent stroke, had handed the business over to his nephew, Bartholomew. The younger man seemed less dependent on the good graces of the earl then his uncle had been. Still, she could not be sure Cranbrook was not Langley Chase's new owner because Bartholomew insisted on protecting his buyer's identity until the closure. It did not matter. She had no intention of returning to Langley Chase. The servants could pack her few possessions for shipping. The lease on the Mayfair property had lapsed some time ago, and though Andreas had generously offered to buy it back, she had declined the favor.

If her creditors continued to be generous, she had decided to settle at the Norfolk hunting lodge. Nowadays the memory of Yew Trees Lodge set against the wide expanse of Norfolk sky brought a deep sense of comfort. Over the months her initial attachment to the Gothic-turreted flint and brick lodge had grown, until she began to look upon it as a haven. There, amidst the solid squirearchy, she intended to begin anew. She would ride to her heart's content, enjoying the countryside, away from the tinsel glitter of society. Perhaps, at last, she might even find peace.

Marie Fleur walked down a shallow flight of steps to the pond where pink and white water lilies gleamed ghostly on the unruffled surface. It was so peaceful here. As she stood in the balmy, star-sprinkled darkness a sudden chill came over her. She felt as if someone watched her. Was it the earl intending to recapture her? Her heart raced as she glanced about the silent garden, which had rapidly lost its enchantment. Hastily retracing her steps, Marie Fleur was partway across the lawn when a rustling in the shrubbery convinced her the watcher was not in her imagination. Spinning about, she demanded, "Who's there?"

There was no answer. She quickened her pace to a run. She gasped in shock as a white shape loomed before her. Her assailant proved to be an armless Venus de Milo standing guard over the Italianate garden. Marie Fleur clutched her racing heart, knowing she was being foolish. Yet even as she managed to convince herself she was allowing her imagination to run riot, an unmistakable masculine step crunched behind her on the gravel walk. A tall, silver-doubleted figure rounded the corner of the maze.

Marie Fleur bolted forward, her high-heeled shoes turning over in the gravel. She was quickly seized from behind and pulled off balance so that she fell against her assailant.

"Let me go!"

"Be quiet! Do you want someone to come?" Marie Fleur stiffened, nausea gripping her as she recognized Brandon's voice.

"Yes!"

Laughing unpleasantly, he clapped his hand over her mouth

to stifle her screams. "Your tin soldier's far too busy dancing attendance on his Czar. He won't hear."

Eyes wide above his confining hand, she struggled to free herself, finding her movements only brought her in closer contact with his body. An overwhelming wave of faintness washed over her until she was unsure if it was generated by fright or desire.

"If you promise to keep quiet we'll go to that bench and talk like civilized human beings."

Calming somewhat, Marie Fleur nodded, agreeing to his suggestion. When Brandon warily released her, she jumped away from him. She quickly straightened her bodice, which revealed far too much white bosom; then, smoothing her skirts, she stalked haughtily to the bench inside the moonlit box arbor. The area was not too secluded; they would be visible to anyone strolling in the garden. Besides, she needed only a few minutes to tell him exactly what she thought of him.

Despite building anger, which made her legs tremble and her hands shake, Marie Fleur could not fail to notice how handsome Brandon appeared in his sixteenth-century costume. A white standing collar accentuated his curling dark hair and made his face appear swarthy in contrast. His doublet of raised silver stripes on silver tissue glittered in the moonlight. The placement of the stripes emphasized his already broad shoulders and drew attention to his compact waist. Silver knitted hose and knee-high dark kid boots showed off his strong muscular legs.

"I take it, after that scrutiny, you approve of my costume."

"It's well enough. Are you supposed to be Henry VIII?"

He grinned at her strained question. "Hardly. Much too thin for that, don't you think?"

She gave no reply, merely stared ahead, her mouth tight as she mentally rehearsed her speech. "Why did you do this?" she finally ground out.

"This! Anyone would think I'd attacked you."

"You did."

"Only because you tried to run from me. We'll have things out once and for all, Nelly Gwynne, and you won't get away till I've had my say. Why didn't you acknowledge my letter?"

"What letter? I've barely had a civil word from you since you abandoned me at that shabby inn."

"Last week a letter was dispatched to your hotel. Don't pretend you didn't receive it."

"It's no pretence."

They glared at each other. Though they sat several feet apart maintaining a safe distance, tension rippled between them. Brandon's fists were clenched as he stared at her, so palely beautiful in the moonlight. Surely those heart-rending sentiments, torn from him with the help of contraband French brandy, had not fallen into a stranger's hands. Tomkins assured him his letters had been posted.

"No matter," he said at last. "I'd as soon say what I have to say to your face."

"That's exactly what I've been waiting for: a face-to-face confrontation with you! I don't know how you even dare speak to me after the way you've treated me. You used me, and when I was no longer any use to you, you callously cast me off. No doubt, had you had the cash, you'd have welcomed me with open arms if only to help relieve the tedium of prison—oh, how dare you treat me so! After all I went through, all I believed. I trusted you, you, you—"

"Stop it!"

He seized her, his long fingers closing like a vise about her slender wrist. "Now, you listen to me. What I said and did in that French hellhole was to save you from imprisonment. Surely you're intelligent enough to realize that. My God, do you think I enjoyed saying what I did? My heart ached for the pain I caused you. I couldn't risk displaying deep attachment for you. Even so, you came very close to arrest. Have you any idea what they intended for you?"

"Certainly. Your loving greetings made them consider me a whore, and their offers were in keeping with that profession. Oh, don't act surprised," she retorted through clenched teeth. Thrusting at his arm, she found his muscles steel-tense beneath the elaborate silver fabric. "Release me at once! You've no right to lay your hands on me."

With a muttered oath, he obliged, flinging her wrist against her lap. "There! Satisfied? And what about my rights? I had the strangest feeling we swore vows of undying love—"

"You were the one who chose to cast them aside, not me!"

"It's not I who bed a lusty Cossack, madam."

"No," she hissed, her eyes narrowing, "you chose an Italian

streetwalker for your amusement."

Again they glared at each other, the balmy night air charged
with hostility. "So that's it—Gabriella. I should have known.
You never accepted my explanation. I knew her before I ever
set eyes on you—"

"Yet you never thought it important enough to tell me."

Marie Fleur began to rise, unable to continue in this vein.
Tears pricked her eyes, and her trembling lips made speech
difficult. Her pride would not allow her to weep openly before
him.

"I'm not finished," he snarled, thrusting her back on the
seat. The abrupt movement jarred loose her waiting tears, and
she swallowed, gulping for breath.

"Then finish," she ground through clenched teeth.

"You apparently didn't grieve long. Did the Cossack wait
outside while you visited me?" he sneered, his face dark with
anger. "Maybe you'll also tell me why you crossed the Channel?
You little fool, didn't you realize the Continent was at war?
Not parade games presided over by a red-faced prince who
merely imagines he fought in battles, but real warfare fought
by real soldiers who bleed and sweat and die."

"I knew that. I had no choice."

"What do you mean, no choice? I provided for your welfare."

"And much good it would have done me while you were
in a French prison. Do you think the landlord would have let
me stay without pay till your release?" Brandon was silent as
he considered her statement. There were tears in her voice, her
grief out of anger over his supposed betrayal.

"You actually believe I abandoned you in Paris. You still
haven't explained why you were witless enough to come to
France. Did you think to rescue me from prison?"

Blinking back tears, she stared at him, pain and rage knotting
up inside until it was hard to speak. "You must think I'm an
imbecile, but I suppose even that is preferable to being a whore.
All along I tried to excuse you by thinking you sought to protect
yourself, or perhaps me. Until that last time. Your farewell
party was the final indignity."

For a long time he did not speak. Strains of gay waltzes
and bursts of laughter echoed across the lawn, a constant reminder of the grand masquerade taking place inside palatial
Burlington House.

"I didn't know you were there. I was only reinforcing the lies I'd already told about you. I wanted them to think we had met in Paris," he croaked at last, his knuckles white. "Every time you left I hoped you'd have sense enough to leave before they arrested you for questioning. Toad never wholly accepted my story."

"The humiliation of watching you with those creatures," she shouted, wanting to strike him to vent her anger.

"Such farewell parties are commonplace in prison. How was I to know you'd be there? If it hadn't been for the government coming through in the nick of time, I'd be a corpse."

"You can't even say you're sorry after all I suffered to save your life. Jake, who may be dead by now—"

"He is."

"—brought news of your danger. I intended only to keep you from sailing. Then I found Cranbrook had followed us from London. I had to get away from him, so I ran aboard a loading ship. There I fell and hit my head, and when I came to, we were already under sail. I'd no choice but to go to France. Fortunately the captain's sister was very kind to me. During those hideous months in Paris I stayed with her and sewed to put bread in my mouth and in yours, too. I hope you enjoyed the gift."

"What about the Cossack? Surely he had money enough for bread?"

"Whether you choose to believe it or not, Count Bezak saved me from rape by a band of drunken soldiers. I owe him much."

"Fully repaid, I'm sure," Brandon sneered unpleasantly. "Let me see, how many nights have you been together?" He seized her wrists to deflect a blow. "You took up with the first likely soldier you found. I don't condemn you for it. Had I been female without means I'd likely have done the same."

"How dare you speak so scornfully when you owe us your life? It's he who released you, not your glorious, patriotic friends in the government."

"You're lying."

"Am I? Of course, the count has no idea who you really are. He thought he was releasing a petty criminal, a highwayman named Black Nick."

"Are you saying you...bought...my freedom?"

"That's right. Now, haven't we both said enough? Let me go indoors."

Brandon stared at her, wanting to believe her, yet at the memory of her head resting against the Russian's shoulder while she breathed soft sentiments, he hardened his heart.

"It's a pretty lie. What else can I expect? A woman must give some alibi to explain why she changes horses in midstream."

"I won't stay here and be insulted." Marie Fleur sprang to her feet and ran from him.

Swearing, Brandon followed her, anger making him clumsy. He stumbled to his knees, righting himself in time to see her gown fluttering around the entrance to the maze. He pounded after her, gaining on her though she ran as fast as she could in her high-heeled shoes. He easily captured her as she raced panting around the never-ending turns of the boxwood labyrinth.

Brandon pulled her hard against his chest. His fingers bit into her soft flesh until she sobbed unashamedly, her resistance faltering.

"Haven't you tormented me enough?"

"Tormented you? What of that romantic little performance the other evening? 'I like it best when we're alone,'" he mimicked, furiously shaking her in accompaniment to his words. "That precious statement almost made me puke!"

"The way I feel when I see you nuzzling Gabriella."

Her retort surprised him, but by now his anger was so great it blazed on, sweeping aside all caution. "Gabriella's part of my work, nothing more. At least now you know I live dangerously for a purpose, not merely seeking thrills as you supposed."

"I hardly think the government intended to support your love life," Marie Fleur snapped as she struggled to be free of his grasp.

"Love life! I don't *love* Gabriella Vasco and I never have. I've never loved any woman but you."

"You've got a strange way of showing it."

"How should I show it? Like this?"

Rigid with anger, he thrust her against the clipped shrubbery. Bending her backward, he pressed his burning mouth over hers. At first her lips were hard, then slowly yielding, salty with tears. To arouse her had not been his intention; in fact, he had no intent beyond the dictates of his flaring rage.

Tears trickled silver down her cheeks as she looked up at him towering masterfully before her. His anger was a tangible force, the emotion leaping from his limbs to hers. Overcome, Marie Fleur shuddered in his arms, grief raising a choking lump in her throat.

"Haven't you hurt me enough?" she whispered, trembling so she was hardly able to speak.

"Hurt you? And what of me? Don't you think watching you with that prancing popinjay causes me pain? I love you, dammit, I'll always love you. You swore to love me whatever happened. I should've known it was an easy lie."

This time when she shook herself free of him he did not stop her. "It was no lie. Your actions alone destroyed my love. Sometimes I don't even think you know what the word means." Then, mustering her utmost dignity, she picked up her skirts and fled.

At first Marie Fleur thought he would not pursue her, then she heard his relentless footfalls. When he seized her, she sobbed in frustration. Brandon swung her about, driving her painfully into the hedge, his body pressed hard against hers.

"Damn you for saying that, you cheating little wretch! I'll show you what the word means all right." He swung her back into the open, forcing her down; he kicked her legs from under her so that she fell beneath him.

Marie Fleur lay on the ground, the breath driven from her body by his weight and the shocking impact of her fall. Moonlight speared silver shafts between the tall box hedges, illuminating his glittering costume, his dark, angry face. Could this be the man she had loved? she thought in dismay as his face loomed above her, carved as if from granite. Angrily he snatched away her red wig, which had slipped awry, and flung it beneath the hedge.

"No," she cried out, suddenly interpreting the changing emotion in his face. "No!"

"Why not? You're mine. Didn't we make such vows?"

"No," she cried again, determined to free herself. Tears of rage choked in her throat when she could not budge his entangling legs. "I'll never love you again."

Rearing back, he momentarily considered her bitter words. His breathing had grown ragged, the sound magnified in this tunnel of clipped box. "Is that so?"

"Yes, damn you, it's so!"

"Then I'll take you against your will. It will be a novel experience for us both."

Marie Fleur shrieked in fright and indignation, pummeling his scratchy, glittering doublet as he pressed upon her. She tried to rake her fingernails down his face. With a curse he caught her wrists, thrusting her arms above her head, pinning her helpless beneath him. Now her legs were locked within the painful vise of his steel-hard muscles. He watched her struggling, allowing her to tire herself until, with a sob of resignation, she lay still.

"Now, pretty Nelly Gwynne, if you're quite finished."

She stared up at him in the moonlight, seeing ruthless determination on his handsome face. Relieving tears flowed effortlessly down her cheeks and dripped into her hair as she finally accepted defeat. Emotion screamed through her body— anger, pain, desire mingling into one. The temptation to taste again the pure pleasure of his passion tore her apart. Pride and rejection warred with the soft weakness of desire as she stared up at this handsome, arresting stranger who had successfully conquered her, who was even now contemplating violation. She knew she was powerless to stop him.

"You win."

Her rancorous utterance merely heightened his anger. With a growl of rage Brandon pressed hard upon her, driving her soft yielding form into the ground. His throbbing mouth, furnace-hot, devoured hers. Marie Fleur fought against response as she was engulfed by the distinctive scent of his body, that heated perfume that intoxicated her beyond measure. Despite the savagery of his kiss, the touch of his mouth proved her undoing. Mentally she yielded her body to him with an aquiescent murmur, softening unmistakably beneath the demanding pressure of muscle and bone, and pounding, throbbing blood.

"Say you love me still. Don't lie," he murmured against her hair. The unintentionally soft tone caught him unaware. Brandon cursed his unexpected weakness, knowing he was no longer in control, betrayed by his own vulnerability.

"Oh, Brandon, yes, always."

Again his mouth engulfed hers. He had released her hands, and she wound them about his broad shoulders, thrilling to hold him in her arms. His body burned against hers, his demanding flesh cutting painfully into her thighs until he shifted slightly to unite mutual fire. Marie Fleur strained up to meet him, grinding her hips against his, devouring his mouth, his face, her fingers twined in his thick black hair.

"I love you, sweetheart, no one else. God, I want you more than any man should ever want a woman. Love me, darling, love me."

The heat of his hands slid inside her green satin bodice, sending flashes of fire to pierce her skin. Now he untied the laces, and her beautiful breasts spilled free. Brandon could hardly bear the torment of touching her, so long had he ached to feel her firm flesh, to taste her fragrant nipples. They writhed in mounting rapture as he traced a path of fire with his mouth, engulfing her exposed shoulders, her breasts. He fumbled with her skirts, raising the green satin until he could sweep his hands over her deliciously smooth thighs, moving even higher until he possessed that blazing mound throbbing to receive him. There were so many erotic things he longed to do to her, so many artful caresses not yet bestowed, but there was not time. Someone could come at any moment. Yet tonight, even the danger of discovery heightened his passion until he shook so hard he could barely negotiate the unfamiliar fastenings of his clothing.

Eagerly, her breath issuing in a joyous gasp of pleasure, Marie Fleur seized the burning flesh he released. She shuddered ecstatically as she explored every marvelous inch of that pulsing brand, recalling each ridge, each vein. Longing to caress him at leisure, she, like he, was growing increasingly aware of their danger. This passionate coming together would be more furtive than any they had shared before.

Brandon ravaged her mouth, his hands and lips increasingly demanding. He murmured love words in two languages, and she reciprocated, the torment of their passion born out of months of betrayal and longing. Sobbing with desire, she placed the burning head of his swollen manhood between her thighs, desperate to receive the bounty of his lovemaking while there was still time. What anguish if they should be disturbed and her passion go unfulfilled.

Shuddering at the delicious contact, Brandon kissed her neck and traced the tip of his tongue across her face as instinctively their bodies joined. Needing no assistance, the velvet heat slid home, consuming her with fire. Marie Fleur struggled to take him deeper, eager to absorb every inch of that swollen flesh as Brandon plunged up to the hilt in the sweet furnace of her body. Slowly, rhythmically, he moved, heightening her ecstasy until Marie Fleur began to lose control. Desperate, she seized his hair, she smothered his burning face with kisses, whispering love words as she begged for the vanquishing thrust to end her torment. Tides of passion washed over her as he crushed her breasts, ravaging her mouth with his tongue, creating pleasure so intense she thought she would faint. Never before had she been so aware of his throbbing wholeness inside her, growing fuller, hotter, until he consumed her entire being. Tears mingled in their kisses, and her teeth snagged his lip as she strained, arching high as he drove harder, faster, forcing her to release her slender hold on reality. Brandon plunged with her into the abyss of passion so that she cried out; he covered her mouth with his own, swallowing her cries lest her wild abandon betray them. Deeper, deeper she swirled, writhing in the exquisite torment of fulfillment, neither knowing nor caring where she was, knowing only that this man was responsible for the most wonderful storm of passion she had ever known.

Brandon kissed away her tears while he held her soft, yielding form against his body, soothing her until she had returned to her surroundings. Awed by the terrible rapture generated between them, Marie Fleur gazed through tear-glazed eyes at his dark face.

"You're all I ever want."

"Darling." He kissed her again, his mouth softer, more vulnerable. The tension had left his face. She stroked his smooth cheeks, his sensual lips, tracing the arch of his heavy brows and the hard bridge of his nose.

"I never dreamed this was possible for us now."

"I won't let you go again. Promise to wait for me."

"Wait," she repeated, beginning to doze until he shook her awake, remembering where they were. "You know I'll wait."

"I'll arrange for you to go to Chalfont. When I can, I'll come to you there."

Chalfont! The name echoed through her head from a great distance. Shaking herself, Marie Fleur opened her eyes and stared at him. "Chalfont? Where's that?"

"It's a place I own in the country. There no one will know who you are."

"But I want people to know. Why must I be hidden? Why can't we love openly?"

"I'm not free at the moment to do as I please. There are things I must do, not of my choosing . . . official things."

The slow throb in her veins was not passion. A cold numbness began to settle in her limbs as he drew away to rearrange his clothing.

"What things? Surely now the war's over, you still aren't playing cloak and dagger."

"We hope the war's over. Napoleon may still have some tricks up his sleeve. Anyway, you're not to worry yourself about that."

Silently Marie Fleur accepted the strong hand he proffered to pull her to her feet. Though he kissed her mouth warmly, that old suspicion crept back to destroy her pleasure.

"Brandon, I want the truth. Is Gabriella still part of your job? Is it she I'm to be hidden from?"

He whipped his head about, startled by her blunt question. At least he had the decency to look away. Her pain erupted in a groan, and she clenched her fists in anger.

"You don't want *her* to find out, do you? Answer me!"

"Look, it's not my plan. She's vital to its completion. Perhaps next week things will be different, but not today, Please, sweetheart, believe me when I say she's only a job."

"You liar! After all you led me to believe, you're still going back to her."

"No. I'm using her—"

"You're quite good at using women. Not until now did I accept that fact."

Brandon stared at her stricken face, his expression stern. "Marie Fleur, I order you to go to Chalfont. Wait for me there."

"Order me? I'm not paid by the government; you have no control over me. I'll go wherever I please."

"Damn you, listen to me!"

He grasped her arm, and she shook herself free. "No, *you* listen to me. You've betrayed me once too often. No more! When you've put both Gabriella and your precious job behind you, perhaps then I'll listen. No more furtive coupling in secret hideaways, then barely acknowledging me by daylight."

"Christ, you stubborn woman! Why won't you listen?"

Marie Fleur began to run, instinct leading her around the correct turns until she finally saw the stretch of moonlit lawn spread before her. Shadows moved across the terrace, and she realized they were no longer alone.

Ashamed of being seen like this, she drew back into the shadows of the box hedge where she was immediately recaptured. Brandon pulled her into his arms and pressed his mouth fiercely over hers. Marie Fleur steeled herself not to react to his kiss. Her legs felt so weak she wondered if she could stand, calling on pride to reinforce her will. When he finally took his mouth from hers, his face was grim.

"Go back to your tin soldier then! I hope you enjoy him, you damned teasing bitch! I've had enough of you."

"The feeling's mutual."

She was free. As she careened over the grass, she remembered too late her red wig lying forsaken in the maze. When the wig was found everyone would guess what had taken place. Her gown was rumpled, and her bodice lacings not correctly tied. She shook with emotion, feeling terribly used and deserted. So intense was her reaction she felt the beginnings of nausea swirl in her stomach. To have succumbed to Brandon's passionate wooing yet again, only to part in bitter anger, had been the ultimate humiliation.

Marie Fleur entered Burlington House by a side door, anxious to stay out of sight. Feigning illness, she sent a servant for Andreas.

"What is it?" he asked in concern, going to his knees beside her when he saw her distress.

Andreas's arms were so comforting, Marie Fleur clung to him, sobbing out her pain and grief. "Please, take me home. I feel so ill."

"Yes, at once." His wide mouth quirked at secret, satisfying thoughts. This abrupt onset of illness might mean she had conceived. Soothingly he patted her shoulder. "Don't worry. It may be nothing. Perhaps you are *enceinte*."

Enceinte! She tried to smile, forcing her trembling lips to obey. "Perhaps," she whispered, hearing the ill-concealed excitement in his voice and not wishing to destroy his illusions. Were her illness from so simple a cause she might even be grateful. She could not tell Andreas the real reason she sat here sobbing and clutching her stomach. Let him enjoy his delusion.

It was only later, while they clopped the short distance to their hotel in the dark carriage, that Andreas noticed she was not wearing her wig. "You've left your basket and your wig. Tomorrow we must return them to your friend."

Marie Fleur's stomach lurched at his reminder. She hoped

no one would consider the discovery of an abandoned wig in the maze sufficient cause for comment.

Her hope was doomed. The next morning when Andreas brought her a breakfast tray of chocolate and croissants, his angry, scowl alerted her to the truth before he spoke. Marching to the window, Andreas drew back the moss green velvet draperies with a crash, flooding the room with sunlight.

"About your wig," he began gruffly, turning from the window.

Uneasily Marie Fleur regarded him, appearing so formidable in his full-dress uniform, impeccably groomed, his boots mirror-bright. "What about it?"

"Where did you say you left it?"

"I don't recall saying."

"Would it have been in the garden?"

She swallowed, wondering how much he knew. "Why do you ask?"

"Because a red wig was found abandoned in the garden. It's the talk of the hotel. And everyone knows who wore a red wig last night."

"Surely other women wore red wigs besides me."

Andreas strode to the bed and he gripped her wrist, his long fingers bruising her flesh. "Ah, true, but they didn't arrive home without them, did they, my love?"

Their eyes met, and she saw anger smoldering there. It was no use pretending to misunderstand. "I was hot. I walked outside, and someone attacked me in the maze. That was why I felt so ill. But then I couldn't bear to tell you."

"The gossips are whispering that you met your lover there and forgot your wig. Who is he? Tell me!"

Mutely she shook her head. "I can't. Have no fear; it won't happen again. I hate him for all the pain he's caused."

"That sounds similar to the speech you made about your highwayman."

Marie Fleur was immediately put on guard by his angry accusation. Miserably she wadded bread in her fingers until Andreas, furious at her silence, wrenched the breakfast tray from her.

"I'll be a laughingstock!"

"Is your pride all you care about? Besides, no one need know unless you tell them."

"What about your friend?"

"I'll get another wig. Anabelle will be none the wiser."

"How clever of you," he sneered, regarding her with distaste. "So my little Czarina is not faithful after all. How many other peccadilloes am I to be called on to overlook?"

Marie Fleur's angry retort was cut short by a knock on the door. Andreas marched to the door and brought back a letter.

"For you, my love. Perhaps in thanks for a delightful interlude."

Her heart pounded uncomfortably as she opened the hand-delivered letter. Marie Fleur read the bold copperplate handwriting, and her throat constricted with shock. The letter was from Bartholomew Lawrence to inform her that Mr. Brandon Nicholas had decided to press for payment of her debt. So far no definite agreement had been reached, but the gentleman indicated he would consider the Norfolk estate fair compensation.

Fair compensation! Viciously she crushed the letter, her mouth set in a grim line. Even Andreas, who watched from the sofa, declined to approach Marie Fleur when, with a torrent of curses, she pitched the crumpled ball of paper toward the hearth. Then, succumbing to a storm of angry tears, she dashed into the adjoining dressing room and slammed the door.

Andreas retrieved the letter. Smoothing out the paper, he took it to the window where he laboriously translated the precise, legal English. When he was finished he stared down at the trees forming a leafy canopy beneath the window. The Norfolk estate had been Marie Fleur's final possession. Now she was totally dependent on him. He had partially overcome the shock of discovering she had a lover. In fact, it was almost a relief to have his worst suspicions confirmed. Now that she was no longer independent, she must yield more readily to his will. That brief, exhilarating time of blind love was over. Philosophically, Andreas likened the past to adolescence, which he must leave behind. Maturity, when reality destroyed all dreams, lay before him.

When Marie Fleur finally emerged tearstained and disheveled from the dressing room, Andreas awaited her with a glass of vodka. "Here, this will revive you."

Marie Fleur accepted the fiery brew in which hot peppers had been steeped, for once not caring about the searing damage to her stomach. "Did you read it?" she asked, seeing the letter on the satinwood bureau. "And you understand? I'm penni-less."

"Not entirely. You didn't read it carefully. There's a small allowance to be made you from your late husband's estate. It might be enough to keep you in ribbons."

Marie Fleur glared at him as she gulped more of the fiery vodka. Gone was the caring, tender lover she had known, replaced by this arrogant nobleman. He was much the way she had assumed him to be when they first met in Paris. The welcome change their love affair had created had been only fleeting, after all.

"Damn you! The news pleases you immensely, doesn't it?"

"Far more than the news I learned about last night."

"And I suppose you've never been unfaithful to me."

"Not since we took up lodging together."

The obvious truth of his statement was no surprise; he had little time to spare for other female company. Remorse touched her, and she reached for his hand. Andreas hesitated, then he took her fingers in his.

"I can't say I'm sorry for last night, only that it wasn't my intention. I loved him once—no longer. As for that letter, Mr. Nicholas has broken his agreement. He promised not to..." Unable to continue, Marie Fleur turned away to stare at the canopy of summer-green swimming in a haze of tears.

"What of this earl? Who is he?"

"The earl? Does it mention him?"

Andreas took the letter and quickly scanned the page. "Here, it says he had purchased your home. 'The Earl of Cranbrook is deeply distressed by the news as he intended to bid on the Norfolk property also.'"

So Brandon had snatched the estate from under Cranbrook's nose! Deeply distressed would hardly be a description for dear Geoffrey's towering rage. Why had Brandon done this? He knew she had hoped to make Yew Trees her home; they had even discussed it. Clenching her fists, Marie Fleur stared un-seeing at the cloud-wisped sky. It must have been for revenge. She had chosen Andreas instead of him, and Brandon would never allow her to forget it. A sob choked deep in her throat, and she felt Andreas's arm slip lightly about her waist.

"That part of your life is over. It will make our move far easier," he assured gruffly, fighting to dispel a tormenting picture of Marie Fleur in another's arms. Mentally he had already reviewed her partners from last night's ball, wondering which of the many dandies had secured her favor.

"Our move," she whispered, hardly comprehending, still too angry over Brandon's vengeance. He had done something she never dreamed he would do; he had taken her sustenance from her. Anger throbbed through her veins and left cold hatred in its place. Finally in control, she turned to Andreas, surprised to see deepened age lines on his frowning face. "Are we to move?"

"We're to accompany the Czar to St. Petersburg."

Whereas once she would have welcomed the adventure, now Marie Fleur recoiled from it. "To Russia! Oh, no, I can't."

"You have nowhere else to go." Andreas stepped away from her, his mouth tight. "I must leave now. Perhaps, when I return, you'll be more agreeable." Stiffly he marched to the door, opened it, and left without glancing back.

Marie Fleur swayed slightly, clutching the bureau for support. In a few short hours her world had crumbled to dust. Brandon she had found and lost, and because of it, now Andreas, too, had become hostile and withdrawn. If that were not misfortune enough, this hateful letter confirmed her worst fears that Cranbrook was the new master of Langley Chase. It also shattered the last vestige of hope she had clung to, that desperate lie that in his heart Brandon still cared for her. He had no need of her Norfolk estate. The act had been deliberately to hurt her, to punish her for daring to choose Andreas. And now her brief infidelity with Brandon had destroyed Andreas's fickle affection. It was a vicious circle she could never break. Weeping, she flung herself across the bed. She was penniless. There was nothing to do but travel to Russia with Andreas.

Once he became used to the idea, Cranbrook would probably welcome the Norfolk sale. With his twisted logic, he would consider only one possible alternative: She must come to him for charity. Doubtless his original offer still stood—board, clothes, attention—in exchange for what? The answer made her shudder.

For some time she lay there reading and rereading the letter. A dim possibility emerged. The allowance Lawrence referred to might be sufficient to support her in modest circumstances. Though it was not to her liking, she could probably take lodgings in the better part of the Soho émigré district. There neither

Brandon nor the earl would be able to find her. And Andreas? Tears slid from her eyes as she reviewed the unpleasant change of character he had exhibited this morning. Whatever affection she had felt for him was not sufficient to permanently bind them together. If she could support herself by supplementing the small allowance she need be dependent on no man.

Marie Fleur got up and washed her face and straightened her hair. She selected a plain muslin gown with pale green satin bands and a matching spencer trimmed in black soutache braid. Grimly she set her leghorn straw bonnet on her fluffy curls, recently shorn to a more fashionable length. She would go to see her solicitor and determine exactly what she could afford.

Chapter 16

MARIE FLEUR HURRIED toward her Soho lodgings feeling breathless and weak. She had barely avoided a confrontation with the Honorable Fulke Greville, a friend of the Regent and known both to Brandon and the Earl of Cranbrook. That he would have failed to recognize her so plainly dressed and living in this rather dingy quarter never entered her mind. The constant dread of discovery that could bring a visit from one or both of the aforementioned gentlemen was with her always.

Uttering a sigh of relief, Marie Fleur reached the sanctuary of the dim vestibule of the four-storied house where she lodged. Mrs. Day, the landlady, poked her head out of her door and called to her as she passed.

"Letter, Madame du Lac."

Marie Fleur accepted the folded paper and went upstairs. In hope of avoiding detection she had resumed her maiden name. Besides, no one with a title would lodge here; she could hardly have presented herself as Lady Dowling.

The September days were drawing in, the early sunset bringing premature darkness. It was so dark on the second-floor landing she had to fumble for her key. Safely inside her small, tidy room, Marie Fleur lit a candle and took off her straw bonnet.

It had been almost three months since that day of liberation when she had packed a traveling bag and walked away from the Pultney. By now she supposed Andreas was happily reunited in St. Petersburg with the woman he had kept before his arrival in France. To say she had not missed him would not be strictly true, yet she did not ache for the sight of him; she reserved that deep emotion for another.

This room at Mrs. Day's boarding house was plain but clean. Heavy rep curtains hung at the windows. The rush matting on the floor and the rubbed velvet cushions on the threadbare armchair were attempts by Mrs. Day at providing luxury for her refined tenant. Marie Fleur's bedding was laundered once a week, also an unheard of luxury, but a necessity for a lady

of her quality. Marie Fleur smiled as she considered the landlady's kindness. Mrs. Day was eager to be accepted by her
"betters." And though she was definitely down on her luck,
when compared to that of the landlady's other tenants Marie
Fleur's obvious breeding marked her as very special indeed.

While the water boiled for tea, Marie Fleur opened the
grubby letter. She was not unduly concerned over its contents,
knowing this cheap paper could not have come from any of
her noble acquaintances. It was probably from someone re-
quiring her sewing skill. To her surprise, when she finally
deciphered the signature on the poorly written missive, Marie
Fleur discovered the letter to be from Nancy. A smile brightened her face as she set to with a will to read what her friend
had written.

Yewr Ladyship
   I seen yew coming from ere last week. Please forgive
me askin, but food's what I need's most. Can yew come.
No one els cares now. We needs yewr elp. God bless
yew.

                              Yewr affictonate
                              Nancy.

Shock over Nancy's desperate plea took Marie Fleur back
downstairs to ask Mrs. Day in what part of London the address
could be found.

"Coo, you don't want going there this time o' night, madam,
friend or no friend. This be in St. Giles, not far from the
rookeries. Most decent folks don't go there by daylight neither."

The following morning, wrapped in her plain wool cloak,
for the September morning was gloomy and chill, Marie Fleur
set off with a basket of food for the address in St. Giles. The
district neighbored Soho, but it was a long walk through depressing streets. As she entered St. Giles proper the buildings
grew even more ramshackle, leaning drunkenly against each
other, paintless and dilapidated. People of all ages thronged
the streets, mostly standing in doorways and leaning against
walls, listlessly watching passersby. Filthy urchins groveled in
the foul gutters or clambered atop great refuse heaps choking
the entrance to even fouler courts.

Now that she had seen the squalor of St. Giles, Marie Fleur was glad she had not come here after dark. Even in the cold light of this September morning the district sent a chill through her bones. The farther she went into the warren of mean streets, the worse grew the smell. So strong was its foulness, the revolting miasma permeated even the folds of her cloak, which she had pulled over her mouth and nose. Though it was daylight, huge rats squeaked about the gutters and over the refuse heaps, boldly running close to her feet. Barefoot ragged urchins ran behind her; loitering men holding bottles leaned against windowsills and watched her pass. Fortunately her dark dress and serviceable cloak did not attract too much attention.

Finally, after repeatedly asking directions, Marie Fleur was guided to a court behind a tumbledown tenement from which poured dozens of creatures like vermin vacating their holes. The narrow entry through which she had to go to reach Nancy's lodgings was foul with the stench of years trapped in its slimed, narrow-sided confines. Holding her breath, Marie Fleur plunged forward, virtually running out of air before she reached the other end.

The entry gave onto a court around which three-storied dwellings leaned, windows missing, doors hanging on broken hinges. This slum was even worse than the area where she had made her desperate bid for freedom during her kidnapping. Though not well-to-do by any means during her childhood, Marie Fleur thanked heaven she had never been forced to endure such squalor.

Here there were no numbers on the doors. She asked directions to Nancy's room from several old women gossiping in the court. They barely answered, then turned to stare after her, muttering amongst themselves. Up the broken treads of the rickety wooden stairs she went, jumping aside as rats scampered past. The stairway reeked of filth; the crumbling plaster walls were caked with it. Over all hung the stifling odor of dirt, urine, and cabbage water.

Marie Fleur knocked on Nancy's door. There was a feeble call, and she waited while someone shuffled to the door.

The two women stared at each other, both shocked at the sight of the other. Not waiting to be invited inside the squalid room, Marie Fleur stepped over the threshold and closed the door behind her. Quickly she put down her basket and took

Nancy in her arms, appalled by her changed appearance. All this time she had carried a mental picture of rosy-cheeked, dark-haired Nancy, sturdy of limb and spirited in disposition. This poor creature wearing a soiled pink wrapper bore little resemblance to the Nancy of her memories.

"Oh, Your Ladyship! You did come after all."

Nancy's haggard face crumpled in tears as she clung to Marie Fleur, sobbing against her shoulder. Finally pulling herself together, she drew away self-consciously, sniffling and thrusting back her lank hair.

Marie Fleur swallowed, dismayed by Nancy's fevered appearance. The pallor of her face was relieved by twin spots of color high on her cheekbones; her eyes burned unnaturally bright in her haggard face. When they embraced she had been terribly aware of Nancy's harsh breathing rasping and rattling through her chest. Her skin was on fire.

"Nancy. You're ill! Here, I've brought you food."

"Oh, I'm not so bad today. I've bin worse."

Eagerly Nancy delved inside the basket and grabbed a couple of rolls, which she crammed into her mouth. A faint mewing cry came from a heap of rags in the corner, and Marie Fleur gasped in surprise when she saw small white legs kicking feebly in the air.

"You have a baby!"

Nancy glanced toward the rags, no smile on her cracked mouth. "Yes, he's mine, poor mite. That's not much recommendation. Don't suppose ye brought any milk?"

Marie Fleur shook her head. "Why didn't you tell me about him? Why didn't you answer my letters? I wrote frequently."

Nancy hung her head. "You knows I don't read and write none too good."

"I wouldn't have cared. I wanted to know how you were. If we'd kept in touch you'd never have sunk to such straits."

Nancy pointed to a rickety chair where Marie Fleur gingerly seated herself.

"Looks like you're in straits yourself, from the place you're staying, Your Ladyship."

"William left me virtually penniless. I must sew to supplement the meager allowance I receive from his solicitor. Yet even at that there would have been enough for you. Why didn't you go home?"

"Mum died last winter, Dad was at sea, and I was too ashamed to tell our Betty, 'er being Chapel and all. She thinks I've a good place at a fine house."

"Why are you living in this terrible place?"

Nancy's head came up, displaying a remnant of pride. "It's none so terrible when it's all you've got!" she declared hotly.

"I'm sorry, Nancy. It's just that I never expected—where's your husband? Has he left you?"

A bitter smile twisted Nancy's face. "There's no 'usband, Your Ladyship. Folks like me don't get married jest 'cause they's breeding."

"Then the baby's father. Did he desert you?"

"I don't even know who he was or where he is," said Nancy, hanging her head in shame. Her dull, sweat-stranded hair fell over her face, and she made no effort to brush it back, finding it a convenient curtain to hide her discomfort. "When they threw me out, I took to the streets."

"Who threw you out?"

"Where I worked at 'is Lordship's. That old harridan, Mrs. Medley, threw me out when she found I was in the family way."

Horror crept through Marie Fleur's veins. Surely not! There had to be more than one Mrs. Medley. "Not the Earl of Cranbrook's housekeeper," she whispered in horror.

"That be her. Oh, 'is Lordship's a fancy piece and no mistake, generous to a fault—until he loses interest."

"Oh, Nancy, why did you go with him?"

Defiantly Nancy's head came up. "He said I was pretty. He treated me like a woman instead of a stick of furniture in someone's parlor. Besides, there was nothing shameful about it, not then."

"Why did you believe his lies?"

"He met me in Rye one day and told me they needed a parlormaid at Cranbrook House. Called me Miss Cross, jus' like he allus does. I fair jumped at the chance to see London."

Sickness gripped Marie Fleur as she imagined poor, simple Nancy's delight at having this distinguished nobleman single her out for attention. All the better to lure her to take part in his infamous pleasures. "He became your lover?"

"Love wasn't what I'd've called it. After he went to the country, I found out I was expecting. Anyways, old bitch Medley found me puking one morning and twigged it righ away. On the street before dark, I was, and 'is Lordship away not able to 'elp me."

Marie Fleur wanted to reveal it would have made no difference had she told him, but she kindly spared Nancy this final disillusionment. "What did you do?"

"Got another job, but when they finds out, it's the same story. I wasn't showing much, so I was able to work on the street for a while."

Nancy went to the baby and picked up the feeble wisp of a creature. While she watched her, Marie Fleur recalled Nancy had told her she did not know the father of her child when it was clearly the earl. When Nancy had settled the baby and was trying to nurse him at her meager breast, Marie Fleur said, "There's no use protecting him. Cranbrook's obviously the father of your child."

Nancy colored slightly and she glanced away, fixing her gaze on the rag-stuffed window. "Well, it's not that easy, Your Ladyship. You see, one night he gived me champagne and some funny stuff to smoke at one of them parties. He says if I did like I was told, I'd be paid well"—Nancy stopped, too ashamed to continue. "I don't know which one done it to me."

"There's no need to remind him of that. We'll go to the earl and demand he support your child," Marie Fleur announced with determination.

Aghast, Nancy stared at her. "Oh, no, I can't—" Her protest was cut short by a bout of coughing, which left her sweating and weak.

Marie Fleur took the baby and laid him down where he squalled and kicked in rage while she helped Nancy to the bed of rags on the bare floor. Tears pricked her eyes as she took in the terrible poverty of this room. Telltale noises in the corner betrayed the presence of rats, and huge black insects crept out of the cracked plaster.

Nancy continued to cough, her body contorted as she fought for breath. Finally able to speak, she whispered, "A bottle . . . over there."

Searching through a jumble of soiled rags, Marie Fleur unearthed a medicine bottle with a drain of dark liquid in the bottom. Eagerly Nancy grasped it, but there was not enough to quiet her cough. Gasping, she said, "There's a shop on the corner. . . . Get it there. I've money."

A handful of coins were hidden inside a holey shoe. Marie

Fleur put the coins inside her glove and agreed to purchase more cough medicine.

When she reached the littered court it was spitting rain. These streets looked even more impoverished beneath the lowering sky. At the corner shop she asked for a refill in the bottle. While she waited for the shuffling old man to return with the medicine, she went to the doorway to escape the sour smell coming from the unwashed secondhand garments hanging around the shop.

The money was just enough. Out of her own small funds, Marie Fleur bought milk for the baby. The shopkeeper grumbled because she had not brought her own pitcher, so she had to give him an extra two-pence deposit on a chipped enamel jug.

When she reached Nancy's room, the baby was no longer crying. Nancy was asleep. Marie Fleur searched for the cleanest dirty rag and rolled it into a cylinder, which she soaked in milk. The baby wouldn't open his mouth; even the smell of milk seemed unable to rouse him from his listlessness. Presently Nancy woke and took over the task of feeding the baby, touchingly grateful for Marie Fleur's kindness.

Using half the cheese from her basket Marie Fleur made Nancy a sandwich. There was no safe place to put the rest of the food, and she supposed before morning the rats would have eaten it. Nancy grasped the bottle of cough medicine and took several gulps, more interested in the elixir than the cheese sandwich.

"Makes the pain go away," she revealed with a gap-toothed smile.

Laudanum probably formed the basis of the medicine. Marie Fleur had heard the Regent himself consumed the opiate in vast quantities.

When she had eaten the sandwich, Nancy reached for the bottle again and took another long swallow. Finally feeling at ease, she propped herself against the wall, prepared to hear Marie Fleur's adventures since they had been apart.

Halfway through Marie Fleur's account, Nancy began to nod. Marie Fleur did not want to leave her alone, so she busied herself trying to feed the scrawny baby. This time she had more success. Nancy had not said how old her baby was, but he seemed so tiny he could not be more than a month. When the baby was settled she tried to tidy the room, which contained little of value beyond the rags that served for bedding and clothing. A used chamber pot stood in the corner. The inhabitants of the tenements emptied their slops into the street, for in this district there were few sewers. The foulness of the reeking dirt privy in the courtyard penetrated the lower floors of the building, and Marie Fleur could not enter it. Instead she emptied the chamber pot on the closest rubbish heap.

As soon as she reentered the room, Marie Fleur knew something had changed. A chill swept over her as she saw Nancy sprawled in a strange position on the rags, her chest strained forward, her hands stretched back, as if she fought for breath. The medicine bottle lay empty beside her. Marie Fleur ran to Nancy's side, her heart thumping with dread. Beneath her hand Nancy's shoulder felt bony and terribly fragile.

"Oh, Nancy, love, speak to me," she urged tearfully, trying in vain to rouse her. Marie Fleur's plea became a stifled sob as the girl in her arms stayed inert. It could not be! Only a few minutes ago she had been talking to her. After the food, Nancy had seemed a little better.

Marie Fleur pressed her hand against Nancy's emaciated chest, but she could find no discernible heartbeat. Nancy was dead! It was too much to accept that plump, jolly Nancy, her friend and confidante, had expired alone in this terrible hovel. If only she had known she was ill. If only she had contacted her earlier, she could have taken her away from here. With proper housing and adequate nourishment perhaps Nancy's ailment would not have proved fatal. Tears welled in Marie Fleur's eyes, spilling down her pale cheeks as she held the lifeless body in her arms until gradually she could accept the truth: She had arrived too late.

It took Marie Fleur some time to gather her wits sufficiently to go for help. There must be someone in the building who could help her make the necessary arrangements. It was customary to send for a doctor, yet under the circumstances she doubted any doctor would venture into St. Giles. Besides, she had no money to pay him. Last week, last month, was when she should have sent for a doctor to examine Nancy.

After knocking on several neighboring doors, she finally roused someone. The news about Nancy's death spread rapidly, and soon a small crowd of ragged tenants congregated in the open doorway staring at the dead woman, muttering and whispering amongst themselves before they slunk away. No one appeared unduly concerned about Nancy's death.

The friendly woman across the landing sent her grandson for the undertaker, assuring Marie Fleur she would take charge of matters. The woman had been Nancy's friend for they shared the same profession until Nancy grew too ill to ply her trade. The woman insisted Marie Fleur sit on a stool by the open window. Her grand visitor seemed so distraught, she was afraid she would collapse. However, the shock of this vermin-infested room and of the abominable stench rising from the overflowing privy below was a great incentive to recovery. Marie Fleur was soon able to return to Nancy's squalid room to care for her crying baby.

The rough voices, the distressing sights all swirled together through her brain while she waited for the undertaker's men to arrive. The skeletal figure in its gaudy wrapper on a bed of rags was not the Nancy she knew. It was hard to accept this nightmare, and she longed to wake to discover it had never really happened.

Presently the burly undertaker's men arrived to take away the dead stranger; they wanted money and Marie Fleur had not enough, so after a great deal of swearing they took what little of value they could find in the room.

Within the hour a bedraggled family of six were already climbing the rickety stair to occupy the vacant room. Nancy's sleeping infant, wrapped in his soiled blanket, was thrust in Marie Fleur's arms; the family had enough children of their own.

At the undertaker's Marie Fleur pledged the price of a simple coffin and headstone for Nancy. She had not the money now, but perhaps she could get an advance on next month's allowance from Bartholomew Lawrence. As for the writhing bundle in her arms, she supposed she was now the guardian of Nancy's orphan son.

Clutching the mewling baby, and without her basket, which the undertaker took as partial payment for services, Marie Fleur headed toward her lodgings. She had no idea what she would do with this child. His noble father probably dined off Sèvres porcelain, unaware a son of his body survived in the most abject poverty. She walked away from this ramshackle district, wracking her brain for a solution to the infant's future. Marie Fleur decided to risk rejection and write to Nancy's sister Betty asking her to take the baby to raise with her own. On a Dorset farm the boy's life would be decidedly more rosy than in this poverty-stricken neighborhood. Yet marvelous though that solution was, it did not answer the baby's immediate needs. Dorset was a long way off. A stab of guilt accompanied her sensible decision not to try to care for the child herself until she heard from Betty. She knew of a woman in a neighboring street who fostered babies. Mrs. Lumm appeared to be a decent country woman whose charges were reasonably well fed and decently clothed, unlike the majority of foster children. Unscrupulous baby tenders often starved the children in their care, interested only in the money they brought in. Mrs. Lumm could care for the baby until Betty arrived to claim him. And the Earl of Cranbrook would be made to pay for his support!

An hour later, in the gloomy, rain-splashed dusk, Marie Fleur handed the baby over to Mrs. Lumm, who agreed to take him on condition she had not to wait long for the money. Times were hard, and she definitely could not take another mouth to feed without pay. Marie Fleur assured her she would make arrangements as soon as possible for the baby's support.

A concerned smile creased the woman's fat face as she looked inside the threadbare blanket at this forsaken waif.

"Oo 'e looks like a drowned rat! 'E's all skin and bone." Mrs. Lumm cradled the small bundle in the crook of her fleshy arm, assuring Marie Fleur if anyone could make him thrive, it would be she.

The following morning, during a light shower, Marie Fleur set off for Cranbrook House. Though she could ill afford it, she hired a hackney with the last of her weekly budget, deciding it would not be prudent to arrive at the earl's residence soaked and bedraggled. The servants would probably turn her away.

Her high-waisted dress and matching pelisse were of fine wine wool trimmed with black braid; her bonnet was black velvet. She would never cut a swath as a leader of fashion in this outfit, but the garments marked her as quality.

The haughty butler himself opened the door, peering down his long nose at this uninvited female.

"I'm here to see the earl," she announced, cleverly putting the toe of her black kid slipper in the door before he could slam it shut. "Lady Dowling."

"The master isn't receiving company this morning."

"He'll see me. Kindly tell him I'm here."

Reluctantly the butler allowed her to enter. Marie Fleur waited on a mahogany claw-footed sofa in the dim hallway listening to rain pattering against the stained glass windows that framed the door. Her stomach was in turmoil. There was a curious choking sensation in her throat, and her hands were sweating. It was difficult not to wrench open the door and flee from this place with its hideous memories. But she could not do that. Nancy would rely on her to provide for the child, and that is exactly what she intended to do.

After a long wait, she heard a click as the double doors to the morning room opened an inch. Sitting stiffly erect, she pretended not to hear. A moment later, the door was flung wide and the earl himself appeared, impeccably dressed in a morning coat and starched cravat, his light hair arranged in casual curls on his high brow. His dark, superbly tailored coat was of Bath superfine, and beneath it he wore a white marcella waistcoat. Under his arm he carried a folded copy of the *Morning Post*.

"My dear! I thought Reeves had lost his mind, but it's really you at long last. Welcome to my home."

Steeling herself not to be taken off guard by his apparent friendliness, Marie Fleur nodded in acknowledgment. To the casual listener it would seem that she had never been here before, had never participated in those vile entertainments in which he delighted.

"I didn't come for a social visit."

"Indeed. Why have you come?"

"I'll tell you in a more private place," she replied stiffly as she glanced toward Reeves, who waited in the open doorway, disapproval plain on his thin face.

"By all means. Bring us refreshment, Reeves. We'll take it in the blue drawing room. Come, my dear, there's a good fire in there. Have you been in London long?"

"Some time," she replied as they walked toward the door he indicated.

The small room was paneled in blue brocade painted with birds of paradise. Exotic ceiling moldings combined pineapples and palm trees, the fireplace surmounted by columns of the same. The sofa and wing chairs were upholstered in navy and white silk. The remainder of the furniture was imitation bamboo in the Chinese style.

From a cabinet japanned in black and gold, the earl selected two glasses, and he poured a couple of inches of claret. He offered a glass to her.

"Have you finally decided to relinquish your pride?" Marie Fleur smiled and continued to sip her claret. "No? Too bad. Will you at least consent to call me Geoffrey?"

"I've much cause to hate you, Geoffrey, after your abominable treatment of me," she began evenly. "However, that hideous episode is behind us."

"Quite. Quite." The earl leaned against the mantel, surveying her above the gold-edged rim of his claret glass. "Tell me one thing. How did you give me the slip on the quay that night?"

"I ran aboard a waiting ship."

"So that explains it. You're far more clever than I gave you credit for—that fact evidenced by your appearance here today. The hunting will be good this season at Langley Chase. Will you do me the honor of spending a couple of weekends there?"

"As I told you before, I'm not here on a social visit."

He smiled sardonically. "No, I suppose one would not call begging for charity a social call. However, I am a gentleman: I shan't hold it against you."

"It's not my intention to beg for charity."

"Oh, you surprise me. By what means are you surviving in your genteel poverty? I hear the handsome Russian is no longer at your side. In fact, you appear to have dropped out of society."

Marie Fleur remained deaf to his questions.

"Some time ago you seduced my former maid, Nancy Cross." Cranbrook's face tightened, and he put down his glass.

"What possible concern is that of yours?"

"Of great concern. Nancy died yesterday." His lids fluttered slightly in acknowledgment of her statement. "You haven't even the decency to offer your condolences."

"Servant girls die every day in London."

"Yes. And many of them have been forced to Nancy's intolerable circumstance by noblemen like you."

"What circumstance?"

"She had to turn to the streets to live. There's a son . . . your son."

"That's a lie!"

"No. You know I speak the truth."

They glared hostilely at each other, all pretense of social conversation gone.

"Any number of men could have fathered her bastard."

"You are the father. Nancy was turned out of here *after* you impregnated her. Your housekeeper will vouch for that. I'm not the only one who knows about it," Marie Fleur added recklessly, searching her mind for the names of guests at his exclusive parties. "Need I name the others privy to the matter? Must I show you the parish record where you are named as father? Nancy was a decent girl from a loving home, not a prostitute nor one of your poor urchins from St. Giles who're glad to perform any abomination for a few pennies." The earl blanched at her scathing reminder.

"You said the girl's dead. What do you expect me to do about it now?"

"Provide for the child whom I've placed with a Mrs. Lumm in Soho. Here's her address and what she charges. You'll find it very reasonable." Disdainfully he accepted the folded paper and glanced at the carefully written address.

"And if I refuse?"

"There are many secrets you would not wish to be made public."

"I'm not the only one with secrets, my love. There's a certain card game, the stakes of which I need not remind you. . . ."

Marie Fleur was on her feet, seething with anger. "Don't threaten me with that now! After all you forced me to endure in this vile house. You even took my home, though you've little use for it. Now you're threatening to take my honor. Take it then, if you will, spread your stories. It matters little to me now. All I want is your word that you'll support Nancy's son. That's little enough recompense for what I've suffered. There's also the small matter of a coffin and a headstone for her grave. On the reverse side of the paper you'll find the address of the undertaker's where your poor victim lies. Such paltry sums of money being meaningless to one of your vast wealth, it should be small sacrifice."

Their eyes met, and before she looked away she saw shock in his pale gaze—shock that she dared defy him, that she dared challenge him to do his worst. She doubted there was any shock for the outcome of his actions, for Nancy, like the others, had been an expendable commodity.

"So, now you've had your say. Have you any idea the irreparable damage I could do were I to reveal what I know about you? No one would ever admit you to polite society again."

As Marie Fleur stood, putting down her empty glass, the door opened and Reeves entered the room.

"Thank you, Reeves. On the side table, if you please."

Twisting her gloves together in agitation, Marie Fleur waited for the butler to take his leave before she continued. When the door closed, she took a deep breath, then turned to face the earl. Cranbrook had made no move to touch her, yet she was uncomfortably aware of his pale eyes flicking searchingly over her body. The thought that he knew how she appeared without her clothes made her flesh crawl. At this moment he was probably reliving that horrible charade of lovemaking in his gaudy Oriental pleasure palace.

"Say what you wish about me; I no longer care. Yet, if it prove too damaging, be warned of the secrets I know. Those debts are pressing, and though small, they are important to the parties concerned. Pay them, and I'll say nothing of the vile practices I witnessed in this house."

The earl laughed sarcastically. "Oh, my dear, you set me quaking in my boots. There's one other mystery I've pondered these months past. How did you escape my despicable clutches? I believed my plans to be foolproof."

"A gentleman of your acquaintance, a guest at dinner that night, rescued me." Marie Fleur was gratified by his sharp intake of breath, by the tension betrayed in his arrogant face.

"Who?"

"I shall not tell you."

"Who is he, dammit? Tell me. I have a right to know."

"He prefers to remain silent, awaiting the right moment to make his story public."

"Westerham? Is it he?"

"I cannot say."

"Nicholas then? The devil take him! It is Nicholas!"

"You could guess all night. Your dinner parties are usually quite large."

Forcing composure she did not feel, Marie Fleur leisurely walked to the door. "Now, will you please summon a hackney for me?"

He glared at her, his fists clenched as he searched his mind for the probable identity of the traitor. Several guests had left early that night. She had been alone when he had spotted her flying along the highway as if her life depended on it. Westerham had always had his eye on her, and he took no part in their private parties, expressing his disapproval in no uncertain terms. Yet again, Nicholas, too, declined his invitations, and he had far more reason than Westerham to champion her cause, being the one who had won Marie Fleur's body for that stolen night. Nicholas, however, had demanded settlement from her, not something a man smitten with a woman would do. Dammit, if only he had been more alert, he could have had Martin invite her to the back, slip something in her drink—but it was too late for that.

Marie Fleur was at the door, her hand shaking on the cold brass knob. "Good afternoon, Geoffrey. I do hope we never meet again."

Coldly polite, he followed her into the hallway, where he summoned a footman to hail a hackney.

Bidding him good-bye at the door, Marie Fleur hurried into the steady rain. She gave the hackney driver an address outside Holborn, just in case the earl had paid him to reveal where he dropped his passenger. Belatedly she remembered she had no money, but she need not have been concerned for the earl had already paid the driver.

While she walked the rest of the way home through the rain, the tension of the past hours relieved itself in tears, which mingled with the raindrops splashing down her cheeks. The ordeal of reentering that hideous mansion revived memories she had tried to forget. Were she not so ashamed of what had taken place at Cranbrook House, she would have made public the earl's crimes. She did not know whether her threats to do so had concerned him sufficiently to provide support for Nancy's son. She could only hope he would not insist on seeing the parish record, which she was sure did not exist. Even if it did, no one would have dared charge the Earl of Cranbrook with fathering a prostitute's child. The father would be listed as unknown. Hopefully the earl's guilt would force him into believing her blackmail.

The depressing memory of Nancy's squalid lodgings invaded her mind, the smells unpleasantly fresh in her nose, the sounds loud in her ears. If it were not for the modest allowance received from William's solicitor, she, too, could be forced to live in greatly reduced circumstances. The money she earned from sewing was not enough to pay the rent on her room. The growing fear of sharing Nancy's fate haunted her, her distraught state of mind magnifying the emotion.

When she finally reached her lodgings Marie Fleur was soaked to the skin, her hair plastered over her brow. While she walked she had come to the decision to seek work as a governess. That way she would always be assured of respectable housing if and when William's exchequer ran dry. She spoke fluent French, she sang, she sewed, she embroidered, even her academic education had not been neglected, for her mother had prepared her to marry a gentleman. Surely, with those qualifications, she would soon find a suitable post.

ᘯ Chapter 17 ᘯ

MIST WREATHED THE treetops, hiding the browning leaves, and the unmistakable smell of autumn was in the air. It was the last week of September, and Marie Fleur had still not found a post.

Every day she set out hopefully to apply for vacancies. Prospective employers often supplied names of friends who were also seeking a governess, yet her efforts had been to no avail. As the disappointing search dragged on, Marie Fleur gradually came to the conclusion that Mrs. Day had been right. When she first told her landlady she intended to seek employment as a governess, Mrs. Day had flung back her frizzy gray head and laughed.

"You?" she had cackled in great humor. "A pretty piece like you! There's not a wife in this city'd have you under the same roof as their menfolks. Not on your life! Plain's what they want, no competition. A man's eye roves soon enough without making it any easier."

At least one of her immediate problems had been solved, though. To her surprise the Earl of Cranbrook had not only settled the bills at the undertaker's and the mortuary, but he had paid Mrs. Lumm for one year's board in advance for Nancy's son. His responsible action relieved Marie Fleur of the unpleasant necessity of a return visit to Cranbrook House. As she had hoped, Nancy's sister had replied to her letter expressing a desire to do right by Nancy's son. When the money for harvest had been paid, Betty promised to come to London for the boy, now named Sam after his maternal grandfather.

The dark chill of the dying season cut through Marie Fleur's wine wool gown as she wearily trudged home after another fruitless day. She had no more addresses of people desirous of employing a governess.

Yesterday when she had tried to pin him down, Bartholomew Lawrence revealed he could not guarantee her allowance forever, that the sum hinged on continuing availability of assets, or some such double-talk.

Tears of frustration stung her eyes as she let herself inside her room. She set her jaw, determined not to give up. Teeth gritted, she spooned out the last of the tea. There was an uncompleted sewing job on the table. Perhaps if she sewed into the night, she could earn enough to buy food. She was too proud to ask for a further advance on her allowance, especially after she had airily informed the solicitor she was managing quite well.

The tea brewed, she sat down to enjoy this final cup when there was a knock on the door. She did not take her candle as the draft up the stairwell inevitably blew it out.

"Who is it?" she called, surprised when there was no cheery hello from the landlady, who often came upstairs to chat, valuing her friendship with a woman of quality, as she referred to Marie Fleur.

She opened her door a crack and peered out. It was very gloomy in the hallway. Two thin slivers of candlelight slid beneath the doorways across the landing. She could tell her visitor was a man by the bulk of his shoulders, by the tall solid shape blocking the feeble light.

"Yes?"

"Have you forgotten me so soon, little Czarina?"

"Andreas!"

Marie Fleur swayed in the doorway, as shocked as if she had seen a ghost. "How can it be? I thought you were in St. Petersburg."

"'I couldn't leave London without you. I stayed on at the embassy on General Lieven's staff."

"Everything all right, Madame du Lac?" Mrs. Day came to the foot of the stairs. "He did say he was a friend of yours." The landlady had allowed the handsome young foreigner upstairs only because he was obviously a nobleman. She scented romance, and she prided herself on being a matchmaker.

"Yes, thank you, Mrs. Day. It's an old friend."

Andreas smiled tenderly at her, and Marie Fleur's heart pitched. She was not sure what brought the unexpected surge of emotion racing through her body as she grasped his coat sleeve to draw him inside and found it stiff with braid. Tears filled her eyes at the reminder of his glorious, extravagant uniforms.

"Come in, Andreas. I'm so very pleased to see you," she whispered brokenly.

The click of the closing door sounded so final, trapping her in this small room with him. Andreas appeared overwhelmingly virile, seeming to take all the available space, the air.

Mutely he held out his arms. For an instant she hesitated, fighting the pounding fury in her chest. Then Marie Fleur yielded to his invitation. Andreas crushed her so hard against his body, she gasped for breath. Slowly the resistance left her body as she dissolved in his arms, giving herself up to his supporting strength.

"You're so lovely," he breathed against her hair. His legs and arms trembled with emotion, for he had longed to hold her in his arms night and day since they had been apart. It no longer mattered that she had sported with an unnamed lover at Burlington House. She had said it would not happen again, and for his own peace of mind he had to believe her.

"Hold me. Oh, I feel so alone, so unwanted."

Her tears soaked the shoulder of his wool cloak before Marie Fleur finally regained command of her emotions. Gently wiping away her tears, he smiled down at her, his heart lurching with joy at her tremulous, inviting smile.

"You've never been unwanted. I've thought of you constantly. Tonight I gambled that you still thought of me."

"How did you know where to find me?"

"Your attempt to find work gave you away. The Austrian ambassador heard of a striking Frenchwoman seeking a governess's post. I knew immediately it was you."

"I didn't find one. No one would hire me."

He smiled affectionately as he detected the woebegone note in her voice. "You've no need of one now," he whispered.

They kissed deeply, and joy shot through her veins. Last month she would not have viewed his arrival with pleasure; tonight it seemed the most wonderful event she could have imagined.

Andreas was most reluctant to let her go. Marie Fleur took his heavy gray cloak and laid it on the bed. Beneath the cloak he wore a dark red uniform encrusted with gold braid; a fur-trimmed pelisse was slung over his shoulder. Though he was still the same Andreas, now he did not appear so tall or so overpowering.

"Are you hungry? I haven't much to offer. Some cold tongue and a few slices of bread. And broth—I've some good lamb broth."

"Whatever you wish. I could eat dirt and enjoy it tonight."

While Marie Fleur sliced bread and cut the tongue, she made him stay in his chair so she could concentrate on her task. They each related their adventures of the past months, carefully leaving out any reference to their quarrel after the ill-fated party at Burlington House.

Andreas enjoyed the simple meal, barely taking his eyes off her face while he ate. The candlelight burnished his dark blond hair like gold, warming his skin, making him appear so handsome, Marie Fleur marveled she ever had the courage to leave him. Andreas slid his hand across the small table and grasped her fingers, his expression intense and full of tenderness.

"Please come back to me."

"I don't know if I can. We quarreled once; we could do so again. Perhaps it won't work for us now."

"I'll make it work," he vowed intently, his face grim. "Did you tell me the truth about that man? You don't intend to see him again? Haven't seen him since?" He stopped, gritting his teeth, afraid of the truth.

"No. I've no intention of seeing him again. Andreas, much as I'm pleased to have you here, I—"

"Don't you care for me anymore?"

She was moved by the deep concern betrayed by the furrows on his brow, by the sudden intensity of his blue eyes. Impulsively she touched his face, finding it hot and smooth beneath her fingertips.

"I care."

"Two days from now I'll be gone. I beg you not to hesitate. It will be too late."

"Gone? Back to Russia?"

"No. I'm to attend the Congress of Vienna. I'm already late, but when I heard about this lovely Frenchwoman, I had to investigate the story. God be praised it was no lie."

Marie Fleur turned away. Andreas intended to begin where they had left off, as if nothing had gone wrong between them, but she could not. She was not the same person she had been then.

"I can't accompany you to Vienna."

"Why?"

"I don't know if I can be comfortable as your mistress. I've changed. When you purchased me—"

"Don't say that. Oh, sweetheart, the price I pay now is out of love."

The sincerity of his words touched her. She came to him

and slipped her arm about his broad shoulders and rested her head against his. Andreas pulled her to his lap.

"I love you. Will you come to Vienna and marry me?"

"Marry?"

"Yes. That should set your mind at rest. There'll be no stigma of purchase then."

Marry! Marie Fleur closed her eyes, burying her face in the heated hollow of his neck. The standing braid-trimmed collar of his dolman gouged her cheek, but she barely noticed. To marry Andreas would mean renouncing her adopted land. Worst of all, it meant relinquishing that slender hold she kept on her dreams of Brandon. By marrying another she would permanently sever the tie. Though Brandon had humiliated her, discarded her, and taken away her last refuge, fool that she was she still could not close the door on their love. Marriage was too final a step.

"Well?" Andreas demanded impatiently, nuzzling her throat. He took her face in his hands, holding her there, eye to eye, determined to have her decision. "Will you come to Vienna?"

Horrid visions of Nancy and her starving baby condemned to the horror of St. Giles passed through Marie Fleur's mind. The solicitor had been unable to guarantee a continuing allowance. What if next month, next year, it stopped? Her hopes of securing a post as governess were becoming increasingly dim. It was easy to say she would never be driven to the streets to support herself; doubtless Nancy had believed that too, once.

Marie Fleur gazed down at Andreas, remembering the brief flowering of their love before jealousy and pride drove them apart. Their passion had been sweet. Andreas loved her; she could see it in his face. What did it matter if their attachment was not deep enough to survive the years? Now was all that mattered. His warm arms, his tenderness would soothe away this terrible feeling of abandonment. The lonely days and nights would be over. He loved her. What more could she ask? Feeling as bleak as she did tonight, God knows she needed Andreas's love desperately. He was an oasis in a vast desert of hopelessness. This wonderful, handsome Russian was the answer to her most heartfelt prayers.

"Andreas, I'll come to Vienna with you—"

He cut short her answer with a passionate kiss, his eyes alight with pleasure. "Oh, sweetheart, you'll never regret it. I promise."

"But I can't marry you." She swallowed uneasily as temper flared in his face. Placing her fingers on his lips, she soothed, "Please, no anger. Just give me more time to think about it. Perhaps when I get used to the idea of living in Russia I'll want it as much as you."

His anger gradually dissolved, and he hugged her. "We need not live there. We can go anywhere you wish."

Marie Fleur smiled, not wholly believing his extravagant promise. Andreas was Russian, and that is where he belonged; his title, his rank, his livelihood came from the Czar. There was simply no other choice to be made.

"What about that woman you told me about? Tanya?" she whispered after a few moments, remembering the confession he had made to her one rainy night in Paris. "She'll be waiting for you."

"Let her wait. I'll palm her off on Mikhail; he'll be eternally grateful. Now, no more about her. I swear you're the only woman I want. And, oh, how much I want you!"

The deep throb of passion in his voice excited her. She had been a fool to cling to visions of a man who no longer wanted her. Love with Andreas, though not as earth-shattering as she had known with Brandon, was nevertheless supremely satisfying. And now that she knew there was genuine love behind his desire, he became even more appealing. Tingling excitement swept through her body as she looked down into his handsome face, finding his eyes dark with longing, his nostrils flaring. Wild abandon gripped her. She slipped her arms about his neck and kissed him passionately. He was hers, offered up to her this night, an assuaging balm for all the loneliness of the past.

"Andreas, darling, I want you too."

The leaping fire against her thigh revealed how much her words excited him. His mouth answered hers hungrily. While they kissed, his hands slid to her breasts, feeling the rounded contours inside her wool bodice, fingering her nipples, hard beneath his caress.

Marie Fleur unfastened Andreas's dolman. Sliding her hands over the fiery smoothness of his shoulders, she tangled her fingers in the wiry golden hair on his chest. She pressed her breasts against his bare chest until he shuddered with delight. Unable to withstand the torment, he seized her mouth and ravaged it with his tongue. As his passion mounted, Andreas plunged deeper, simulating the act he trembled to consummate.

"Shall I take you here?" he whispered, his hands sliding along the silken heat of her thighs and over her firm buttocks. When she agreed "here" would be acceptable, he braced the chair against the wall, his booted feet against the bureau.

"If I were to die this moment I'd be supremely happy," he whispered, his eyes tightly closed, moisture seeping beneath his abundant lashes.

She studied his tense face, seeing the awesome change such ecstasy had wrought. His mouth was hot and hard, his tongue quicksilver as she grasped his shoulders. She locked her legs about his slender waist and buried her face in his neck. Then suddenly she surrendered. Their passion burst like a rocket, soaring to mutual climax. Breaths rasping, they shuddered repeatedly, clinging together, backed against the wall.

Belatedly Marie Fleur wondered if the occupants of the adjoining room had heard their cries or the rhythmic banging of the chair against the plaster. Opening her eyes, she looked down at Andreas. His lids were closed. A thin patina of sweat bathed his face, which seemed cleaner, softer, more youthful than she had seen before.

"I love you. Oh, God, how I love you," he groaned without opening his eyes. "I've never felt quite like that before."

"I love you too, Andreas," she forced herself to say. Forced, because Marie Fleur was still not sure a woman could love two men at the same time. And whomever else she might pretend affection for, she had to confess that, in her heart, she still loved Brandon.

Napoleon's Grande Armée defeated all who opposed it. Of France's enemies, only Britain on her island stronghold remained inviolate. That is, until Napoleon's ill-fated invasion of Russia in 1812. There, amid the interminable miles of ice and snow, battling blizzards and bone-numbing cold, the ambitious emperor's exploits were finally checked. France's sons froze to death beside the roads, dropping by the thousands in a disastrous retreat through winterbound Russia.

After this Russian defeat, Prussia, Napoleon's former ally, remembering she was German and not French, turned against him. Austria, Britain, Prussia, and Russia allied against France. Yet not until the last, when the remnants of his army struggled against overwhelming odds, did Napoleon finally concede defeat. His troops reduced to a rabble before the allied onslaught, Napoleon agreed to abdicate.

After the emperor's fall and subsequent exile on Elba, the victors, mutually suspicious, met to redefine the boundaries of Europe. Each faction suspected the other of treachery, each nation its neighbor of secretly planning to go over to the enemy. In a grand gesture designed to demonstrate their collective goodwill, the allies agreed to convene the Congress of Vienna to formally discuss the peaceful redistribution of European territory to the satisfaction of all concerned.

Austria's foreign minister, Klemens von Metternich, organizer of the conference, was determined to stop Prussia's dangerous emergence by hampering her power with a German confederation consisting of Austria and the combined lesser German states. Russia alone did not conspire to crush Prussian ambition. Thwarted by this united front in his attempt to seize Saxony, Frederick William of Prussia had to be satisfied with the coal-rich Saar Valley and considerable territories in the Rhineland.

The Congress of Vienna opened in September, 1814. It was the grandest diplomatic extravaganza ever organized. Prince Metternich took credit for arranging both the marriage of the Austrian emperor's daughter, Marie Louise, to Napoleon and, now that the tide of war had changed, for arranging this historical congress to divide the spoils of war.

The Austrian capital played host to the Russian Czar, the kings of Prussia, Bavaria, and Denmark, crown princes, grand dukes, and a multitude of lesser members of the blood royal from all the nations of Europe. England was ably represented by its second-ranking politician, Lord Castlereagh, France by the great Talleyrand. Accompanying these worthies were vast retinues of relatives and servants. As the congress stretched through winter with no sign of settlement, the Austrian emperor was at his wits' end to provide entertainment for the glittering multitude.

While delegates squabbled about the redistribution of Europe after the allied victory over Napoleon, the baroque city of music blossomed. Operas, balls, and banquets took place in glittering, never-ending succession. On days the diplomats were not verbally tearing the territories to bits, there were picnics in the nearby Vienna Woods and hunting parties that terminated in invitations to the Augarten, the imperial hunting lodge.

At first Marie Fleur had plunged wholeheartedly into this exciting round of entertainment, feeling for the first time that her love for Andreas was deep and lasting. And he, proud to have such a beautiful woman at his side, showered her with gifts and attention. They attended operas in the gilded magnificence of the opera house; they worshipped in the Augustinerkirche, the parish church of the imperial court. They strolled under the bare winter trees in the Kaisergarten in the company of archdukes and their ladies. And only occasionally did she hear whispers of the impropriety of Count Bezak's lady. Under the bare chestnuts and lindens, in the sparkling frost of winter days, she existed in a glittering, artificial dream.

It was well into *Fasching*, that traditional Austrian season of balls and gaiety stretching from New Year's Eve until Ash Wednesday, when Marie Fleur finally came down to earth. There had been a snowfall in the night, and Andreas had taken her for a sleigh ride. Tomorrow they were to journey to a nearby town where he intended to introduce her as his intended bride to his mother's Austrian relatives.

Laughing as she crunched over the pristine snow, Marie Fleur allowed Andreas to capture her. When he kissed her his mouth was icy, but their warm breaths soon mingled to dispel the chill, ready passion flaring as their tongues touched. Marie Fleur was smothered in furs, leaving only her face exposed. The tip of her nose was red with cold, and Andreas kissed warmth back into her flesh as he held her against him, transferring throbbing life from his body to hers. The unspoken message that these days passed so readily between them was relayed, his face tightening, his breath becoming shallow.

They slid their arms about each other's waists and walked indoors, abandoning the gaily decorated sleigh in the snowy courtyard of their rented home within sight of the Hofburg, the emperor's domed palace.

Marie Fleur's dreams of passion were cut short by a man-servant who bowed respectfully. "There is a visitor, Count Bezak. For the lady."

They paused in surprise at the doorway of the drawing room where a heavily cloaked figure stood warming himself before the hearth. Marie Fleur recognized him as Sir Michael Soames, one of Castlereagh's secretaries.

"Sir Michael."

"Lady Dowling. How well you're looking. Count Bezak." Andreas bowed stiffly, clicking his heels.

Marie Fleur's breath choked a moment with shock. How unused she was to hearing that title pronounced in precise English accents. Here she always used the name Marie Fleur du Lac.

"I have a letter and a package for you. Our mutual acquaintance, Brandon Nicholas, thought you'd like to have this. He found it in a drawer at Yew Trees with some letters. You must have left it there some time ago. Now, I must be off; it's back to England for me. Good afternoon, Lady Dowling, Count Bezak."

Again Andreas clicked his heels, bowing stiffly as the visitor walked into the hallway.

Marie Fleur had gone white. The writing on the envelope was his. She could scarcely draw breath as she considered that she held the paper where Brandon's hands had rested. What foolish, romantic notions! Angry with herself for her weakness, she tore open the envelope.

> My Dear Lady Dowling:
> I trust you mislaid the enclosed on a previous visit to Yew Trees. The locket appears old and is probably a keepsake, therefore I am sending it to you by courier. May you continue to enjoy good health.
> Yours faithfully,
> The Honorable Brandon Nicholas.

Her breath was ragged when she finally allowed herself to draw it. Andreas had been reading over her shoulder, and though at first she was devastated to find Brandon's message so formal, now she was thankful he had the good sense to betray nothing of their former intimacy. Inside the small packet was an old silver locket engraved with roses.

"How pretty. Yours?"

"My mother's. I never knew where I'd lost it." Marie Fleur gripped the cold silver in the palm of her hand and went to the fire.

"It's good of him to send it. Now, come, forget lockets and messages, except for the one that lies closest to my heart," Andreas breathed as he drew her into his arms and pressed his mouth on her brow. He slipped back her fur-lined hood, his hands gentle. "Or maybe the message comes from another, less controllable force," he suggested huskily as his passion flared against her.

Marie Fleur tried to respond to him. She smiled, she touched his face, she kissed his lips, but behind it all burned memories of Brandon. Damn him! Could he never leave her alone? Must he forever intrude in the new life she had carved for herself? Andreas was where her future lay, not with the Honorable Brandon Nicholas. He was welcome to Yew Trees. May he never spend a happy moment there!

They made love beside the blazing hearth, slowly, tenderly, while Marie Fleur tried her utmost to dispel that invading presence. When her passion was spent, she wept, not out of deepest passion as Andreas believed, but out of pain for all that had been and was lost.

The next morning, Marie Fleur dressed for her journey to Leopoldsfeld in a red, sable-trimmed pelisse over a matching gown. She carried a sable muff and wore a tall Russian hat pulled well down over her ears.

Andreas tucked a fur lap robe around her legs. He whistled cheerfully as he took his place behind the horses. The air was crisply invigorating. If it were not for the bright sunshine he might have thought himself back in Russia. A pang of nostalgia made him momentarily silent, his thoughts straying to the tall house beside the Neva that was his family's St. Petersburg home. Marie Fleur would love it there, he told himself stubbornly. There would be many carefree days like this, rushing through the snow in his gilded troika, dancing at the imperial palace. But later, when he must return to the steppes to direct his serfs—what then? The lonely, hard life would seem alien to her. He glanced down at Marie Fleur, beautiful in her soft nest of fur, and his heart twisted with love. Impatiently he tugged on the reins, urging the horses forward.

They soon left Vienna with its snow-frosted eaves and trampled, snowy streets to emerge in a world of pristine white. Sleigh bells jingling merrily, they sped through the gleaming diamond-bright countryside. The horses' breath floated in great icy clouds as they sped along the glittering road. Towering black pines overshadowed the sleigh, forming ice blue lakes on the snow and making windblown ripples of darkest blue fading to black beneath the trees.

Used to traveling long distances in the snow, Andreas expertly guided their horses over the tree-dark mystery of the plain stretching to the foot of the Alps. This sleigh, with its brightly painted garlands of roses on every exposed inch of wood, proved to be a fast conveyance.

The icy air stung Marie Fleur's cheeks, and she turned up her sable collar to keep out the cold. This lovely white world was new and exciting, so exciting, in fact, she had managed to thrust her pain over Brandon's message to the back of her mind. From time to time disturbing memories successfully invaded her self-imposed barrier, and she had to fight to regain her peace of mind. It would never be easy, but she was determined to overcome her deplorable weakness where that man was concerned.

Andreas laughed down at her, appearing strikingly handsome in the dazzling sunshine, his eyes bluer than the clearest sky beneath his tall beaver hat. Today he was not in uniform. Instead he chose to travel in his regional dress of full white breeches, tall black boots, and fitted embroidered white tunic, which fastened on the left shoulder and was belted about his slender waist. Over that he wore a fur-lined hide coat decorated with red braid and reaching below his knees. In this exotic dress he was a totally new Andreas. Marie Fleur had seen him only two ways before, uniformed or naked. To his utmost delight she had laughingly confided to him this morning that it was hard to choose between the two for magnificence.

"How much farther?" she asked, when they had been on the road for several hours. They were speeding down a slope, the long runners sending up showers of snow in their wake.

"Not long. We're going to stop for refreshment in that village."

In the sheltered valley below stood a green onion-domed church towering over a huddle of dark wooden buildings. When they entered the village street, Marie Fleur found the wooden buildings were as gaily painted as this sleigh. Some houses had life-size scenes covering their walls while other householders preferred scalloped window boxes and ornamental gilded carvings.

The outside walls of the snow-covered inn where they stopped were decorated with twining red roses and buxom, golden-haired maidens. The building's interior was low-ceilinged and dark. The inn had several private rooms, and Andreas ordered their meal brought to the best room. Uneven board floors and rough-paneled walls in the best room indicated the simplicity of the establishment. A quarter of the room was taken up by a massive green tiled stove, its huge bulk reaching to the ceiling. Though ugly, the stove filled the room with heat, and they were forced to remove their furs, being much too warm for comfort.

"Oh, you're wearing your locket," remarked Andreas, seeing the gleam of silver against her red gown. He reached for the silver heart, purposely allowing his firearm to rest upon the swelling of her breasts.

"I thought my other jewelry too elaborate for travel. We don't want to be robbed."

He smiled at her as he casually flipped open the catch to look inside. "Ah, a lock of your mother's hair. Strange, I'd have thought her to be blond like you—Ah, here's our food, at last."

While Andreas raved about the steaming liver dumplings and bubbling veal stew, Marie Fleur took off the locket. She had not remembered there being anything inside it. And her mother's hair had been blonder than her own. Numbly she stared at the gleaming black curl filling its blue-enameled interior. A shudder passed over her. Brandon had placed a lock of his own hair inside her locket. Must his memory always reach out to spoil her every happiness? Tears pricked her eyes, and she snapped the locket shut.

Unseeing, she stirred the dumplings about in the liquid with a brightly decorated wooden spoon, trying to overcome a wave of melancholy that threatened to engulf her. In this alien snow-bound land, England seemed so far away. She pictured wind-swept Norfolk with its vast expanses of winter sky. Though she had spent little time at William's hunting lodge, the fact it stood in familiar country had endeared it to her. Did Brandon gallop over the salt marsh or hunt in the sparse thickets on the high ground? Which of the rooms had he taken for his own? And did *she* share Yew Trees with him?

"What is it?" asked Andreas in concern as tears trickled down her flushed cheeks.

Marie Fleur reached up to brush them away. She gave him a wan smile. "I was feeling homesick."

"Homesick? Within the month we're to travel to Russia. I might delay until late spring, but by then the going will be hard. Once it starts to thaw the mud comes up to the horses' bellies. Far better to travel in the snow. I thought you'd overcome your longing for England."

"So did I."

She swallowed and forced herself to eat some veal stew. Until the arrival of this confounded locket, her plans had been secure, her love for Andreas strong enough that she had decided to marry him in St. Sophia's in a Russian Orthodox ceremony. Now she knew she could never do that. To pretend enduring love she did not feel would be too unkind. Unlike many others, they were not being forced to wed for money or possessions; their marriage was to be from choice. Therefore, she realized, she could not hurt Andreas like that. She could not deceive him by marrying him so long as she was haunted by the memory of another man.

"Do you still love me?"

"Yes, I love you, Andreas. But to spend the rest of my life in Russia—I am not certain I could do that. Isn't it better to discover that now than to doom ourselves to unhappiness?"

Sullenly he ate, his mind seething. Perhaps she was right. Sense told him he would be a fool to take her to Russia while she still felt this way. What had happened? Their love had seemed so sure. Bonded, it was true, by bodily desire, but they loved nonetheless. He looked at her with narrowed eyes, pondering the alarming change. The locket had been the turning point. Had he known such an innocent bauble would shatter his dream, he would have done anything to stop that fellow from delivering it. England drew her with a force he could not combat; he had always known it was so. And the men she had known—the reckless highwayman whose life he had spared, the Burlington House dandy—did they, too, exert a force too overwhelming to be denied? Was it England or her forsaken lover that caused her the most heartache?

"What do you want to do?"

"I've got to be sure. Let me go home with the ladies from the English delegation."

"No. You'll never return."

"England's the only home I've known."

Andreas slammed down his spoon, splattering gravy across the wooden table. "I forbid it!" His hard face appeared so formidable she quailed inwardly. Fear fluttered in her chest over his sudden intractability.

"Please, Andreas, if you love me, let me go. You always promised if I wasn't sure, you'd give me the freedom to return one last time."

"Such promises are easy to make and hard to keep. Besides, how will you live over there? You've severed all ties."

"There's still my small allowance. And I've relatives in Norfolk," she declared, desperate to be free. As the time of departure for St. Petersburg had drawn near, her unease had manifested itself in countless ways: Dancing till dawn, exhausting moonlit skating parties, barely stopping to sleep and, even then, being unable to relax without the quieting release of passion. All were symptoms of her malaise. Such reckless gaiety had been a desperate race to evade an unsettling fact she had thrust to the back of her mind. It was true she pined for England, but there was far more involved. England meant Brandon and the painful pleasure of their stormy love. In the soft green land, in the gentle rain, lay the promise of delight unfulfilled. Until she had finally laid to rest the haunting specter of her old love, she could pledge herself to no man.

They continued their journey to Leopoldsfeld in strained silence. Marie Fleur longed to comfort Andreas, to tell him there was nothing he could have done differently. No man could have erased those precious memories forged during that long summer night. Yet the remoteness of his expression, the faraway lifelessness of his eyes, hooded against the glare, warned her to keep silent. Andreas must come to terms with pain in his own fashion.

The great *schloss* at Leopoldsfeld perched on high ground beyond the Vienna Woods. From its battlements could be seen a spectacular view of the surrounding countryside. To the left the land swept majestically to the Alps glittering silver in the sunshine, while before them, beyond the dense Vienna Woods, the brown Danube girded Austria's capital. The interior of the forbidding gray stone *schloss* proved to be a pleasant surprise. In recent centuries the stronghold had received several renovations, bringing it from the Middle Ages to the nineteenth century in grand style.

Liveried servants admitted them, welcoming Andreas as enthusiastically as if he had been their master. Three huge dogs bounded forward to greet him. They were a breed Marie Fleur had not seen before. Almost three feet tall, the silky lemon-and-white hounds had a majestic appearance. Their long narrow skulls atop beautiful wavy coats gave them unusual grace and beauty, while their powerful, muscular legs betrayed their speed.

"Bistri, Zorka, Lada," cried Andreas in delight. He temporarily forsook Marie Fleur to greet the large dogs who hurled themselves at him, overcome with joy.

When at last Andreas managed to extricate himself from the wagging, yapping circle of canine devotion, he turned to Marie Fleur. "Aren't they beautiful? These are Borzois from the Czar's kennel. His Imperial Majesty presented me with a litter in payment for faithful service. These fine hounds are the grandchildren of the original animals. You should see them run; they're like lightning. When you come home with me you'll see what I mean. And I promise to breed a pair especially for you."

There again was the ever-present reminder of Russia. Marie Fleur swallowed and turned her attention to the dogs, who came to her shyly to be petted.

"Andreas, my boy, welcome, welcome. And who is this beauteous creature?" boomed a genial voice.

Andreas's Uncle Leopold appeared, resplendent in his red military uniform, which strained uncomfortably across an expanding paunch. One sleeve was empty and pinned across his chest; over his right eye he wore a black patch. His white hair settled like snow about his rosy, cherubic face.

"Marie Fleur du Lac, meet my brave Uncle Leopold. He was the hero of Austerlitz," Andreas said, laughing as he thrust her forward.

"Heroes sometimes don't come back in one piece, as you've probably noticed." Leopold enfolded Marie Fleur in his embrace, chuckling as he kissed her cheek.

"I hope to make Marie Fleur my wife."

"An admirable choice."

They walked deeper into the gloomy stone *schloss*. Ancient armorial banners fluttered from the rafters of the vast hall. The dark paneling was softened with shimmering silken draperies. The flickering orange light of a roaring fire warmed the somewhat forbidding grandeur of their surroundings. A huge pine log was burning in the gigantic hearth and giving off a pungent scent, the resin hissing and popping in the blaze. Several large dogs toasted themselves before the fire. At the stranger's approach the animals rose, growling menacingly. Their master quieted them good-naturedly, ushering his guests to a fringed settle.

"Those Russian wolfhounds of yours are amazing," Uncle Leopold commented in awe. "I only wish you could stay to watch me put them though their paces—Ah, here's Mitzi. Come here, dumpling. Greet your favorite nephew. He's come a long way to pay us a visit."

Aunt Mitzi tripped forward, a rosy-cheeked woman almost as broad as she was tall. Her gown of maroon watered silk decorated with gold fringe was so tight and vast it suggested she had been upholstered rather than dressed. About her thick throat glittered a triple collar of diamonds. For the most part, Austrian women wore no jewelry, having patriotically contributed gold and silver to the government to finance the war.

Marie Fleur felt increasingly uncomfortable and out of place as the family lapsed into German. Sometimes, for her benefit, they reverted to stilted French, but more often they used their native tongue, which Andreas spoke fluently.

Eager for news of their nephew's daring exploits in the war, Leopold and Mitzi pressed him to recount his adventures. Frequent gasps from his aunt and bluff interjections of his own similar experiences from the old soldier stretched the story into several hours. While she listened to them, understanding little, Marie Fleur sipped spiced wine and nibbled small flaky pastries topped with sweetened whipped cream.

Later, when Aunt Mitzi suggested they would soon be retiring to the dining room for dinner, Marie Fleur felt too full to eat more than a few bites. She knew, however, she must stuff down a little of the meal so as not to appear impolite. From her scant knowledge of German Marie Fleur gathered they were awaiting guests who were traveling from a distance to welcome Andreas to Vienna.

Andreas smiled at her, viewing her speculatively. While they waited for the guests' arrival he took Marie Fleur on a tour of the ancient *schloss*, showing her portraits of his father and mother.

Marie Fleur listened to his pleasant voice recounting the family history in his strangely accented French, knowing this tour, which included thumbnail sketches of Austrian history in general, was Andreas's way of marking time. They had already been invited to spend the night, and he had privately expressed his disappointment that, for propriety's sake, they must take separate bedrooms. Yet whenever Marie Fleur attempted to reopen the subject of her return to England, he ignored her. All her pleas for understanding fell on deaf ears. Anger and frustration mingled in tears, which she had to blink back, too embarrassed to cry before his relatives.

It was not until after the other guests had retired for the night and they stood in the baronial splendor of the massive stone hall bidding Uncle Leopold and Aunt Mitzi good-night that Marie Fleur knew Andreas had finally reached a decision.

"What a charming young lady," gushed fat Aunt Mitzi, turning Marie Fleur about for what seemed like the hundredth time to admire her. "When's the wedding to be, you darling boy?"

Andreas smiled down at Marie Fleur, his hand possessive on her back. "We've set no date, Tante Mitzi. Marie Fleur has to return to England with their delegation. But soon, I can assure you of that."

Marie Fleur turned to him, her eyes moist with grateful tears. Andreas had given her his answer.

Chapter 18

SPRING PAINTED THE English countryside green. Clouds of pear and apple blossom softened bare roadside orchards whilst early flowering blackthorn capped the hedgerows with snow. The pussy willows hung heavy with silver catkins dusted with pollen and small crimson blooms brightened the stark wych elms. Stars of stitchwort, blue speedwell, and golden celandine threaded the roadside grass with color, and the woodlands were sweet with purple violets and yellow primroses.

This rebirth of life glimpsed from the coach window filled Marie Fleur with poignant longing for something she could not name. Instead of experiencing overwhelming happiness as she traveled north through the land she had yearned to see, she felt increasingly melancholy.

At Norwich the coach stopped overnight at the Bell, a local cockfighting haven. Marie Fleur was glad she had written ahead requesting a night's lodging from Mrs. Graham at the top of Elm Hill. That was where she had spent a pleasant night on her ill-fated bridal journey to Kent.

The narrow twisting cobbled street leading up Elm Hill was poorly lit and crowded with roisterous patrons leaving the Briton's Arms. Outside the thatched inn stood the huge elm from which the hill took its name. Marie Fleur was vastly relieved when kindly Mrs. Graham opened the door and ushered her inside the sanctuary of her cozy parlor where the only distractions were the ticking of the grandfather clock and the purring of the cat.

After a good night's rest, Marie Fleur felt much restored. Mrs. Graham provided her with an appetizing breakfast of poached eggs, rashers of fried ham, buttered home-baked bread, and strong tea.

London had buzzed with news of Napoleon's escape from Elba. Brandon's well-remembered warning that Napoleon was not finished yet had unfortunately proved correct. The would-be conqueror of the world had not given up his ambition that easily. Many soldiers were immediately recalled to their regiments. The general assumption that the war was over had been premature. Peace had been merely a lull between battles. Marie Fleur knew Andreas must have heard the news in Vienna, and she hoped the resumption of hostilities did not put him in immediate danger.

Though it was late when she arrived, Marie Fleur wrote a letter assuring him of her own safety and inquiring about his plans in view of the startling world developments. At Andreas's insistence before she left Vienna she had accepted a hundred pounds for traveling expenses, much of which she had left in trust with her London solicitor before boarding the Norwich coach. She had, however, held back enough money to purchase an inside seat for the journey. Before long the gusting east wind had brought rain, and she was even more thankful she had not tried to economize by riding outside.

The Edgerton Heath mail coach did not leave until later that day. As she took her leave in the cloudy afternoon, Mrs. Graham assured Marie Fleur she would post her letter to Vienna.

At her solicitor's suggestion Marie Fleur had written to her uncle from London to tell him of her impending visit. As they pulled out of the cobbled innyard to the waves and shouts of the ostlers, she was filled with impending gloom. Though Lawrence had appeared unduly eager to have her throw herself on her uncle's charity, Marie Fleur doubted the solicitor understood James Fox's precarious financial state. In fact, if Uncle James's finances had plunged as close to disaster as he had glumly predicted, there might be little welcome for her at Toppings. It had been difficult to swallow her pride and go begging, hand outstretched, for the second time in her life. Ever since she left Norfolk she had been vaguely concerned that her untimely return would somehow let the family down. They had entertained such high hopes for her future, she hated to shatter their dreams. She had no intention of living off her relatives' charity. She would try to obtain a post as governess. In Norfolk, people would be unfamiliar with her past.

A flush suffused her cheeks as she recalled the stares and pointed snubs she had received from the wives of the returning English delegation. In fact, the return journey to England had been so unpleasant, she tried not to think about it. Most respectable matrons would never dream of employing as governess a woman who had been mistress to a Russian count. Anxious to dispel all vestiges of that frivolous time, Marie

Fleur had dressed demurely and kept her eyes modestly downcast as befitted a governess. No one would recognize her in
her serviceable blue merino gown and dark gray cloak.

If news of her lapse from social grace had reached the
provinces, she knew her chances of finding respectable employment were dim. She could give in to Andreas's demands
for marriage; then she would need distress herself no further
about the matter. It was foolish to refuse him, still clinging to
a forlorn hope of love long dead. Foolish—but the course she
had chosen. Resolutely she raised her stubborn chin, not allowing herself the luxury of such painful thoughts. From now
on she would manage on her own, beholden to no man.

Black clouds were already gathering above the spire of Norwich Cathedral as they rattled over the narrow medieval bishop's bridge spanning the Wensum. Picking up speed on the
open ground, the coach rattled across furze-dotted Mousehold
Heath. Yellow gorse flowers shut tightly against the approaching night, while silver birch and greening alder saplings bent
before the rising wind. From the top of St. James's hill was a
splendid view of the city, but the coach turned sharply west,
taking the low road over the heath.

They recrossed the Wensum and clattered over the Yare as
Marie Fleur dozed to dream of Andreas inviting her to waltz
in the blazing chandelier-bright ballroom of Vienna's magnificent Hofburg. She had taken his hand, smiling up at him, her
white gown aswirl with pink and gold ribbons, when a resounding clap of thunder jerked her awake.

The other occupants of the coach—a farmwife, her harelipped daughter and corpulent brother—shrieked in fright. Marie
Fleur attempted words of consolation, but they stared uncom-
prehending at her as if she spoke a foreign tongue. Soon driving
rain lashed the sides of the coach. On the box the coachman
turned up his collar, loudly cursing the elements. For ten minutes the spring storm raged, the sky rent apart by jagged lightening flashes. Then, almost as suddenly as it had come, the
storm died; the wind dropped to a breeze and only dripping
trees and bushes betrayed its passage.

After the rain the air was sweet with the scent of growing
things. The spring freshness seeped inside the coach, a distinct
change from the aroma of ale and strong cheese wafting from
the other travelers, who carried their supper with them.

A narrow sunken lane forced the coach to slow to a crawl,

and in the ensuing quiet, broken only by the clopping hooves, Marie Fleur heard the eerie cry of a wood owl searching for prey. She had begun to feel like a stranger in her own land. All her questions directed to her fellow passengers were met with blank stares. Surely her short stay abroad had not destroyed her ability to speak English.

Marie Fleur closed her eyes, trying to sleep. Her dream of Vienna had made her even more melancholy. Andreas loved her enough to want to make her his wife. In searching for an elusive goal, she had cast him off to return to Norfolk, knowing as long as she was haunted by another man's memory they could find no permanent happiness together. The untroubled years she had spent at Edgerton Heath before she had ever heard of Brandon Nicholas were the closest to peace she had known. Perhaps, in the loneliness of heath and salt marsh, she could find peace again and finally lay his disturbing memory to rest.

The moon had risen, and its silver beams shone inside the coach. When they changed direction, heading onto the open heath, passing stands of trees cut off the light, then it reappeared, creating a distracting flicker across her face. Marie Fleur pulled down her bonnet brim and pretended to doze.

Galloping hoofbeats, followed by the barked command, "Stand and deliver!" snapped her awake.

Marie Fleur's breath strangled in her throat, and she went rigid. Stark memories of another time when the same challenge came out of the night set her nerves jangling. The three other passengers were wide-eyed with fright. The harelipped girl began to babble hysterically, and her mother cuffed her across the face to silence her.

Amid the curses of the coachman and the two outside passengers and the neighs of the startled horses, the coach came to a skidding halt. A black shadow cut off the moonlight as the highwayman tapped on the window with his pistol.

"Ladies and gentlemen, out!"

The masked rider was having trouble with his mount. The storm had made the beast skittish, and it shied, threshing the air with its forelegs.

The highwayman did not appear to have any accomplices, but the coachman was taking no chances. He threw his blunderbuss to the ground and quickly raised his hands to demonstrate his good faith. Two cocked silver pistols gleamed in the highwayman's gloved hands, and he wanted to live to see his grandchildren. Not being a hero, the coachman had no intention of dying to save King George's mail.

In the lull following the highwayman's unexpected appearance, the coach's passengers clambered from their seats. The others thrust Marie Fleur into the corner, eager to be first out in case the highwayman thought them disobedient.

She finally climbed down the step in the sharp breeze, shivering with fright and cold. Though her possessions were modest, tonight she carried far more of value than the time Black Nick had stopped them on the Tenterden road. Her shabby valises held everything she owned.

The highwayman clattered back from the group of shivering topsiders, thrusting a modest collection of watches and signet rings into his pocket. He turned his attention to the coach's passengers.

"Please, good sir, we be simple folk. Nothing of value 'ere," whined the fat man. "A watch, me grandsire's, but ye're welcome to it if ye'll leave the womenfolk unharmed."

The highwayman pointed to Marie Fleur with the muzzle of his pistol.

"Oh, no, good sir, she's not with us. A foreigner she be. We be good Englishfolk."

The highwayman walked his horse closer. The moon, surrounded by fitful clouds, tossed like a ship at sea, suddenly plunging the road in darkness. The masked man slid from his horse, and leading the animal, he came toward her.

Marie Fleur glared at him defiantly. As he stopped before her her heart began a frightening tattoo. She must be mistaken, she thought in shock. It could not be he! The highwayman was the right build, the right height, his horse was black, as were his voluminous cloak and tall black hat.

"From what country do you come, Duchess?"

Her breath stifled in her throat. No other man's voice had quite that same husky quality mingled with a caressingly intimate tone.

"Black Nick!"

"You remember me. I'm flattered. Now, you others, hand over your valuables. I haven't all night."

Marie Fleur's legs trembled until she wondered if she could stand. The March wind was chill as it whipped against her burning cheeks. Of all the coaches heading out of Norwich why had he chosen this one? What was Black Nick even doing in Norfolk? Brandon had no smuggling contacts here, so he could not pretend he played highwayman to aid his country. She had the uneasy feeling Brandon had been privy to her movements from the minute she had landed and that his selection of this particular coach had been no accident.

Paying scant attention to his haul, Black Nick thrust the assortment of cash and jewelry into his saddlebag. Shouting a warning to the coachman, he threw him the mailbag.

"Here, you can keep the mail. I've no fancy for reading tonight."

The coachman uttered a tentative chuckle, watching the highwayman warily. When the firm mouth beneath the concealing black mask turned upward, the other men joined the coachman in nervous laughter.

"For my pains I require something worthwhile, this hardly being worth my time. The pretty foreign piece will be a nice bonus."

To Marie Fleur's horror she was seized and dragged toward his waiting horse. None of the men raised a finger to help her, even though she cried out to them to save her. They watched impassively, thankful it was she the highwayman had demanded in payment for his trouble and not their own lives.

Tiring of her struggles, Black Nick twisted Marie Fleur's arm behind her, hurting her until she cried out in pain. "You're cowards, all of you!" she shrilled, furious that the men docilely watched her abduction.

"Shut up, woman. They know what's good for them, that's all. Good-night, gentlemen. Have a pleasant journey."

Wheeling about, Black Nick waved his pistol in farewell. Then discharging a shot harmlessly in the air, he headed for open country. The coach horses whinnied in fright, threatening to bolt. It took the men's combined strength to stop them as they pawed the air, wide-eyed, nostrils flaring. When the men finally turned to see which direction the highwayman had taken, he was out of sight.

At first Marie Fleur fought Brandon. As they pounded over the spongy turf her will gradually ebbed until she had no further strength to pit against him. Sullen, she sat there, her heart pounding.

When he had put what he considered a safe distance between them and the coach, Brandon slowed his pace and drew rein.

"That was a damned poor reception you gave me."

"What did you expect? A red carpet?"

He chuckled throatily. "Well, that would have been a change."

"I demand that you let me go!"

"Out here on the heath?"

"The heath will be fine."

"Don't be an idiot," he growled, clicking to the horse, urging him forward with his knee. "There's nothing for miles."

"I've little to fear from rabbits and foxes."

"And a hell of a lot to fear from me, is that it?"

"Yes."

"You haven't changed a bit, you featherbrained wench."

Marie Fleur exploded in rage, raising her fist to strike him. Adeptly Brandon pinned her arms against her body. In the brief struggle his corded forearms brushed the soft prominence of her breasts and she shuddered, trying to deny the sparks of fire his touch had kindled.

"How did you know I was on that coach?" she demanded, her temper rising when he chuckled but did not answer. "Where are you taking me?" she persisted in her questioning, daring him to maintain his silence.

"A secret hideaway."

She bristled at the ill-concealed humor in his voice. "Another?"

"Of course. I have them all over the country."

"I don't doubt that! And do you keep a mistress there also?"

"I'll have one when you arrive."

His growled retort silenced her, and they continued their journey through the rain-drenched countryside without exchanging more verbal thrusts. In the dark the land was unfamiliar, yet when they passed through a sleeping village, the horses' hooves thudding loudly along the road, Marie Fleur thought she recognized the parish church.

"Where are we going?"

"To my estate."

Her back ached with tension. She tried to relax without touching him, being forced at last to lean against the hard heat of his chest. The contact was nerve-wracking as she fought the sudden urge to sink into the warmth of his arms, relinquishing her will to his. Tears of anger for her hopeless weakness stung her eyes and she let them spill to her cheeks, confident he would not see them in the dark. They were approaching tall wrought iron gates set in a dark stone wall. She recognized this gatehouse, but when she had seen it before, she had not known it belonged to him.

"Yew Trees lies five miles to the south," she blurted, filled with new hope.

"More or less. I now own much property in this region. In ancient days it would have been large enough to be called a kingdom. My mother's family comes from Santon Downham beyond Emily's Wood. The adjoining village of Brandon supplied many of the gun flints used by the army during the war. Mother took my name from there. She had a whimsy for such things."

Marie Fleur refrained from comment. She recalled passing through the village of Brandon, the houses built of flint from whence the local industry came. She had never dreamed then the innocent name would become the abiding passion of her life. She would never again read that name on a milestone without experiencing a sickening lurch in her stomach.

The broad driveway bordered with rhododendrons led to a shallow flight of steps at the entrance of the house. In the darkness the square, Gothic-turreted dwelling was not unlike Yew Trees, being constructed of flint and brick. Disdaining the front entrance, Brandon rode around the back to the stables. He had removed his mask and appeared no more sinister than countless other soberly dressed travelers.

He swung from the saddle, his stern expression cautioning Marie Fleur to silence as a groom came forward carrying a lantern.

Brandon held his hands out to her. She did not want to accept his aid, but knowing no other way to dismount, Marie Fleur steeled herself for the feel of his hands on her waist.

He swung her lightly to the flagstones. Pausing to exchange a few words with the groom, Brandon followed Marie Fleur as she headed toward the archway over the side door. Lights gleamed brightly in the windows, and she was anxious to be indoors. She could have run from him, she could have told the groom she had been brought here against her will, but she did not. And her own puzzling inaction merely added to her building rage.

Brandon led her inside a warm parlor decorated in paneled oak, the walls hung with portraits in gilt frames. A blazing fire was in the hearth. On a side table a cold supper was laid.

"Come to the fire. You must be chilled."

She disdained his hand when he would have helped her shed her cloak. The heat from the fire was welcome, and Marie Fleur turned around to warm her back. Her limbs were stiff from the long ride and her increasing tension. Brandon handed her a warming glass of spirits, and she accepted it, being careful that their hands did not touch.

"Your silence surprises me. You've usually far more to say," he remarked casually, his mouth full of sliced ham and pickled onions. "Here, you must be hungry."

She wanted to decline the offering, but her stomach growled in protest. Silently she took a slice of bread piled with pink ham and chopped pickle. The wine had imparted needed courage, and when she finished her sandwich, she picked up her cloak and marched toward the door.

"Going somewhere?"

"Home. Or at least to my intended destination, seeing that, thanks to you, I now have no home. We must be less than ten miles from Edgerton Heath."

"And you intend to walk, I suppose?"

"Yes. Unless you'll kindly provide me with a mount."

"Christ! Anyone would think we were paying a polite morning call. You shall go nowhere with, or without, a horse!"

"You can't stop me!"

He turned, his face grim. She did not flee from him as he half expected, merely stood there glaring at him defiantly, her face set. "I'll do anything I must to keep you here, Marie Fleur du Lac. Anything."

Her lips quivered. "Why are you doing this? We're no longer of any consequence to each other."

"I see you took me at my suggestion and returned to your wild Cossack. Soames tells me you were the toast of Vienna."

She swallowed, fighting tears. Shame filled her at the unkind reminder. Those were things she had wanted to put behind her, not because she was actually ashamed of her life with Andreas, more because of the way polite society now viewed their liaison.

"What do you want?"

"Apart from the obvious. . . ." His mouth quirked slightly at his thoughts. He indicated a chair beside the hearth. "Please, spare me a few minutes. If, when you've heard me out, you still wish to leave, you may."

His assurances were too good to be true. Eyeing him warily, Marie Fleur retraced her steps to the fireside. Brandon unbuttoned his greatcoat and threw it across a nearby chair.

She tried to ignore the betraying emotion that forced her to acknowledge how attractive he appeared in a dark wine coat and fawn breeches, a plain cravat at his throat. Without his hat his black hair curled close to his head, the way it had been that other time when Black Nick had unmasked for her benefit.

"I'm listening."

"Some time back I took Yew Trees Lodge in payment of the massive debts owed me by your late husband. Whatever construction you put on my actions, it was doubtless in error."

"Oh, come to the point!" she cried, clenching her fists.

"The point being, I'll return your home to you. That way you can be free of obligation to anyone."

"Except you!"

"I said I'll *give* it back, no strings attached."

"And you expect me to believe that? When did you do anything without strings attached?"

"If it will set your mind at ease, I'll give you the deeds now."

"My mind would be more at ease if you'd order a horse saddled for me."

He spun about, his jaw set. "Very well, madam, I shall do that."

He stalked to the door and called a servant. During the minutes it took for Brandon to convey the orders, Marie Fleur tried to calm her nerves. Her legs were shaking and she felt sick. If she made a dash for the outside door, would he allow her to go or would she have to fight her way out? The opportunity to escape passed when he returned and slammed the door.

"Satisfied?" he snarled, his face hard.

She gave no reply, nor could she meet his gaze. The shimmering softness she had always admired in his large gray eyes was gone. The man who stood before her had changed from lover to adversary.

"I took Yew Trees to keep it out of Cranbrook's hands, and that's the only reason. You must be mad if you think I took the place out of vengeance for your unfaithfulness."

"My unfaithfulness?"

"The Cossack was your lover, my sweet."

"While you dwelled pure as the driven snow." Her violet eyes flashed and she jumped to her feet. "I'll accept that horse now. He'll be returned at my earliest convenience."

Brandon swallowed, trying to calm his rage. "Keep it as a gift. There are plenty more in the stable."

"No. I want none of your gifts."

"You haven't always felt that way."

"What do you mean?"

He seized her arm and spun her about. "Perhaps you recall a modest allowance paid to you by Bartholomew Lawrence, Esq."

A dull thud began in her veins. "How did you know about that? I'd thought my affairs confidential."

"I not only knew about it, I paid it, my love."

"You what!"

"The money came out of my pocket."

"You liar! That money was what was left of William's estate."

"No. Lawrence only told you that to salve your precious pride. Will's coffers were drained long before you returned from France."

"I don't believe you."

He smiled, his expression without humor. "All you have to do is ask your esteemed solicitor. He'll confirm my story."

Aghast, Marie Fleur stared at him, her face blanched. All these months she had prided herself on managing on the modest sum—or not managing, as the case may be—but at least she had considered the allowance her own, the final trickle of William's vast estate. To think all that time she had been living off Brandon's charity!

Unreasonably she lashed out at him. "My God, so it was you who arranged for me to live in near-poverty. Thank you, sir, for your generosity."

"All you had to do was ask for more."

"No one told me that. Oh, how dare you interfere in my affairs?"

"I dare because you belong to me. A man doesn't risk his life galloping about the countryside disguised as a highwayman for fun. I was desperate. Had I approached you in the normal bones. "Well, my dear Brandon, ride post haste to London and comfort her. You have no more need to waste your time in Norfolk. I can manage quite well alone. Keep your charity. I wouldn't knowingly touch another penny of yours!"

These final words were flung over her shoulder as Marie Fleur raced for the door. He shouted after her in rage, but she ignored him, her feet flying down the tiled hallway and into the night. Virtually blinded by tears, she raced over the flagged yard, finding the groom standing there holding a saddled horse. Wrenching the reins from his hand, she scrambled clumsily in the saddle, sobbing in angry frustration as she yanked the animal's head about and set him toward the open ground.

The horse was swift and excitable. She had a hard time controlling his speed when he shot across the turf, careening about the rhododendron hedge as she forced him to take the driveway. They had nearly reached the wrought iron gates when shouts told her Brandon was coming after her. Fortunately the gates stood open. Urging the animal to greater speed, she crouched lower, setting her teeth as she rode into the March wind.

Out on the highway she was more familiar with the terrain. Searching her mind for details of this part of Norfolk, having ridden past here less than a half-dozen times, she recalled a crossroads about a mile north. There she would be able to find the signpost to Edgerton Heath.

Rage made her clench her teeth till her jaw ached. Tears trickled down her cheeks and splashed on her cloak. How dare Brandon cheat her, pretending the money came from William? She felt an utter fool for counting out the shillings, wondering how much longer the small allowance would be forthcoming. To think she had been living off him all this time, the obligation she had shunned binding her unwittingly.

seemed to have receded. Surely Brandon had not given up easily! A sob was torn from her. She did not know if she cried out of relief or disappointment.

Across the fields she went, disdaining the highway as she grew more familiar with her surroundings. She would reach three-mile corner around the next bend. Recognizable farmhouses, barns, stock ponds, and a small mere flashed past, restoring her confidence. She had traveled this way dozens of times. Brandon had little chance of overtaking her now.

To her annoyance Marie Fleur found she was holding back, listening for his hoofbeats. There was no sound. Disappointment that he should have given up his pursuit so easily washed over her before she angrily thrust the emotion aside. Hadn't she been anxious to outride him? Why else was she careening over the countryside in the moonlight, hell-bent for Edgerton Heath?

Perversely, the fact that his chase was over, that he had decided to let her go her own way filled Marie Fleur with pain. She had not really wanted Brandon to give up. Though his very presence infuriated her almost beyond endurance, it thrilled her with the same intensity.

Bleating sheep guided her to Brow Farm as she took a shortcut down a narrow lane. A few minutes more and she would be able to see the chimneys of Toppings through the trees.

The drive leading to Toppings wound up an incline through dense shrubbery. Gravel had once covered the drive but it had been largely washed away, leaving in its stead potholes and clumps of grass. Coming around the final bend, she reined in, sobbing deep in her throat at the welcome sight of her childhood home. Though she had spent more years in London than in Norfolk, Marie Fleur remembered Toppings with affection.

Life as a companion to selfish Lavinia Fox had not been overly pleasant, yet it had been the happiest time she had known.

All reason for speed behind her, Marie Fleur slowed the horse to a walk up the drive. Lights shone through two uncurtained windows revealing that someone was still awake. Uncle James would be surprised to see her. Perhaps, given the slowness of the mails, she could even have preceded her letter. It was possible that Lavinia might be married now, for though she had written to the Foxes several times during the past year, she had received only one letter, which announced Lavinia's impending betrothal.

At the sound of approaching hoofbeats, the side door opened and a woman in a mobcap poked her head around the doorjamb.

"What be you wanting at this hour?" she cried suspiciously. "I've got dogs, so you'd best be warned."

Marie Fleur reined in, not recognizing the woman. Uncle James must have replaced Mrs. Rose with a new housekeeper.

"Are you the housekeeper?" she called, not dismounting, for low growls warned her of the validity of the woman's threat.

"Housekeeper!" came the indignant snort. "What cheek!"

"I'm here to see Mr. James Fox."

"Oh, indeed," replied the woman mockingly. "And shall I tell 'im the Countess of Muck is 'ere?"

"I'm his niece!"

Marie Fleur was becoming annoyed by the woman's rudeness. Braving the growling dogs, who as yet had not put in an appearance, she walked her horse closer to the light.

"Niece, is it? Well, you can just take yourself off again."

"How dare you!"

"Fancy talking ain't yer. Well, some of us don't recognize our betters, do we?"

Mentally agreeing with the observation, Marie Fleur smarted beneath the woman's insolent attitude. "I am Lady Dowling," she announced sharply. "Please be kind enough to inform your master of my arrival."

The woman was temporarily silenced. "Lady Dowling...hm...well, I never," she remarked at last in surprise.

Another voice came from inside the house, a rumbling, masculine protest. A bent man dressed in a voluminous nightshirt, a tasseled cap on his bald head, appeared in the circle of lamplight behind the woman.

"What is it? Waking a body up at this hour! You should be ashamed. A man needs 'is sleep, 'e does. What do you want, you good-for-nothing?"

Marie Fleur swallowed uncomfortably. It was not Uncle James. In fact, she had never seen the man before.

"Says she's Lady Dowling," muttered the mobcapped woman.

"Dowling? Dowling? Never 'eard of 'er."

Clanking chains followed by deeper growls warned Marie Fleur to stay astride her horse. "Where's Mr. Fox? Is he away from home?"

Her innocent question brought a burst of bronchial laughter, which temporarily incapacitated the old man. Rallying at last, he leaned against the doorjamb for strength as he peered into the darkness.

"Don't know who ye is, woman, but I'll tell ye this: Ye've come the wrong way to see James Fox, that you 'ave."

"James Fox owns this farm. Tell me where he is."

"Debtors' prison, last I 'eard."

"What? Oh, no! It can't be true! I wrote to him from London telling him I was coming—"

"Oh, aye, we got the letter. Couldn't make 'ead nor tail of it. So you's the one."

"Are you sure he's in debtors' prison?"

"Sure as I'm standing 'ere. I bought this place at auction. Reckon 'e got in too far ower 'is 'ead, did James Fox. Allus had fancy ideas. Thought he was gentry. Well, he's gone, and I can't say I'm sorry."

"What of Lavinia, his daughter?"

"She married some upstart young ensign. Gone orf to foreign parts, so I 'eard tell. And good riddance if ye asks me. A surly piece of goods she was, and no mistake. Now, woman, you've 'eard all I know. I'll thank ye to be off and let honest folks get some sleep."

"Is my uncle in Norwich jail?"

"Most likely. Could be took to Lunnon, though. 'Eard some folks was. Maybe they'll send 'im to the colonies to work off 'is debt. That would be a right comeuppance, that would. Now go on, get going afore we turn the dogs on ye."

For a few minutes Marie Fleur did not move, merely sat there aware of the throb of emotion in her veins, the sheer feeling of hopelessness washing over her. Her very last sal-

vation had been stripped from her. The comforting thought that
if all else failed she could beg charity off Uncle James had
blown away in the March wind.

Disconsolately she turned, blinded by tears. The night seemed
so dark, so empty. The couple shouted at her, urging her to
hurry, repeating their threats of turning the dogs loose. She
ignored them. Back down the drive she plodded. The young
horse seemed to sense her dejection, for he plodded too. Back
into the country lane they went. She did not know what to do
now. She was alone in the night.

The faint sound of hoofbeats echoed in the distance, but
she paid little attention. At Brow Farm a dog ran out yapping
at the horse's hooves, startling the animal and making him shy.
Dawn would be lightening the sky soon, she knew because she
heard a farmer's milking pails clanking in the nearby shippen.
Dawn, and she still had nowhere to go.

The hoofbeats were louder now as Marie Fleur reached the
crossroads. She knew she must ride to Norwich and try to see
Uncle James, to help him if possible. To be cast into debtors'
prison was a terrible fate. Though her experience of prisons
was limited to that hideous time in France, she supposed most
prisons to be alike whether on this side of the Channel or the
other.

Marie Fleur heard the thud of hooves drawing closer. The
Norwich signpost lay ahead. The few minutes it took her to
read the words in the fading moonlight allowed the approaching
rider to catch up with her.

Glancing up, she cried out in distress as she saw Brandon.
She charged forward, setting the animal toward the narrow lane
to the right, following the signpost to Norwich. She could see
Brandon astride a black stallion, bearing down on her. His
cloak billowed behind him in the wind. The huge black horse
appeared devil-sent as it swallowed the ground at an alarming
rate. She had little hope of outpacing him, but stubbornly she
tried, diving through a break in the hedge in the hope of giving
him the slip. In time he discovered her ruse and followed her
across open country, narrowing the space between them.

Sobbing in frustration, Marie Fleur tried to go faster, but
the skittish young horse was winded; after having his fun, he
wanted to rest. She had no crop to whip him on, so she kicked
his flanks sharply with her heels.

"Stop, damn you! Am I to chase you to Norwich?"

"If you've a mind," she spat through clenched teeth, plunging back into the lane. As the gap between them lessened Marie Fleur tasted defeat, yet not until the last would she give up.

Brandon galloped ahead, cutting her off, placing his great plunging stallion across the narrow lane. She wheeled around, trying to go back the way she had come, but he leaned over to seize her reins and wrenched her about, almost unseating her in his anger.

"No, damn you! You won't get away from me again."

Great heaving breaths robbed her of speech. Marie Fleur glared at him, unyielding in the white moonlight. His face was in shadow, but she could see the determination in his jaw, the set of his mouth.

"Do you intend to hold me prisoner like Cranbrook?"

Brandon swung from the saddle and, reaching up, he dragged her to the ground. "If that's what I must do. Is that what you want?"

"I want you to leave me alone! Go back to Gabriella. I won't share you."

He gripped her shoulders, shaking her, hearing the tears in her voice. "You fool woman, you no longer have to."

She stared up at him, her vision blurred by tears. "What?" she mumbled incoherently. "What?"

"Sweetheart, let me love you. Let me look after you. Put all the rest behind us."

At first she resisted his embrace; not until he rammed her against the hot pulsing life of him did she give in. The rigidity left her legs, and she felt weak and lightheaded. For so long had she fought against this moment, this time of yielding, somehow she could not release her control. All pleasure was suppressed, her feelings numb. Not until he seized her stubborn chin in his hand and turned her face up to his, not until he possessed her mouth in a blazing kiss of passion did she unlock those floodgates. Moaning deep in her throat, she clung to his hard shoulders, allowing that feeling to wash like the tide over her vulnerable body.

"I love you, Marie Fleur, like no other woman's ever been loved before. Say you love me too."

The terrible pleasure of Brandon's embrace left her unable to speak. The well-remembered scent of his skin overpowered her senses while the unspoken message of his muscular body pressed to her own touched that primitive inner self, unbound by pride or rage or wounded ego.

"Oh, Brandon, darling, I love you too. I'm sorry for all the pain, the anger..."

He kissed away her tears, his hands trembling against her back. "So am I. We'll never let pride and temper get in our way again. Promise me that. No more foolish masquerades pretending to be something we're not."

"I promise. Oh, I love you so."

She swayed against him, driving hard, longing to blend her limbs with his, to shelter behind his strength and never again go forth to battle the world. At last she had found her haven, her peace, her love.

"Why did you run from me? You're such a perverse, absurd little creature," he muttered in repressed rage.

"I was going to Uncle James's. Oh, Brandon, he's gone."

"Gone. What do you mean, gone?"

"They've taken him to debtors' prison!"

"My God! How do you know?"

"Those awful people at Toppings bought the farm at auction. They think he's in Norwich jail."

"And that's where you were going?"

"Yes."

"What for? Did you think to storm the prison and rescue him?"

"I didn't think. I just knew he needed me."

"That's your problem: You usually don't think. You just follow your emotions—damn you, woman, you've led me a hell of a chase. I lamed one horse coming after you."

"I thought you'd given up," she sobbed, burying her face against his coat, feeling overwhelmingly weary and vulnerable.

"Thought what? Do you suppose after all this time I'd give up? That I'd allow some hotheaded woman to outride me?"

She no longer bridled at his insults, too tired to take issue with his choice of words. "You didn't come after me, that's all I know."

Brandon held her at arm's length, his expression incredulous. "You wanted me to come after you? Christ! You mean this was a game?"

"Not a game. I hated you, I was angry with you. I never wanted to set eyes on you again—but, oh, how much I still loved you."

His mouth softened, his stern expression dissolved in a grin.

"Never, if I live to be a hundred, will I understand you, Marie Fleur. You are a total mystery."

The warmth in his voice told her he had forgiven her, that the overwhelming love they shared had wiped out all anger.

"Isn't that why you love me?" she whispered against his warm neck. "Because I'm so confounded puzzling."

Brandon chuckled, pulling her tightly against him. "Aye, maybe that's exactly why I love you."

"Shall I tell you why I love you, Brandon Nicholas?"

"Please do, but preferably in a warm room on a soft bed."

He brought her up hard, holding her under the arms. They stared at each other in the fitful moonlight, aware of the awakening dawn chorus in the woods. Birds chirped in the leafing trees and woodland creatures stirred in the grass.

"Tell me you won't ever see Gabriella again," she whispered, needing to resolve that dispute between them. "I couldn't bear it."

"Am I to get a similar promise that you won't see the Cossack?"

The tension in his face tore at her heart. The pain she had known because of Gabriella she had made him feel over Andreas. It was a just exchange.

"He wants to marry me, to make me a countess," she could not resist adding, a stubborn streak in her nature not allowing her to relinquish all without a fight.

Brandon snorted in anger. "Indeed. Countess over a flock of stinking peasants and a couple of pigs."

His scathing words struck her as funny, and she giggled. "He's very wealthy. How dare you ridicule—"

"Enough games. Forget the Russian. You're mine now. Gabriella's already returned to Naples, eager to rejoin her king. All our scheming was for nothing: Murat's gone back to Napoleon, that's if he'll have him."

His mention of Gabriella set her nerves on edge. "You still haven't convinced me you didn't care for her."

"Sweetheart, I told you Gabriella was part of my job. I'll not lie and say in the beginning it wasn't a pleasant part—but it was a job nonetheless. She was mistress to Joachim Murat, Napoleon's puppet king of Naples, and they kept in contact. When Murat became disenchanted with his emperor, he was considered a valuable asset to our cause. Through Gabriella, who unintentionally revealed valuable information about him, we learned how best to approach Murat for maximum advantage. Secrets were ultimately disclosed, including the fact there was more than one general ready to throw in his lot with the allies. Unfortunately, before everything fell into place, Napoleon escaped from Elba, and Murat, afraid of losing his kingdom, switched affections again. Now, I can't tell you anymore. In fact, if my uncle knew I'd told you this much, he'd have an apoplectic fit. Can you accept my faithful promise never to have to see her again?"

"Or *want* to see her?"

"Or want to see her," he repeated softly, pulling Marie Fleur close. "Tell me how much you love me one more time."

"I love you more than life itself," she vowed sincerely, tears filling her eyes for the depth of her emotion. "Is that not enough for the Honorable Brandon Nicholas?"

"More than enough," he whispered huskily, crushing her body against his. His mouth was like fire, awakening the sweetness and the heat of her passion, bringing forth her long-buried trust.

"Shall we go home?"

"I thought you'd never ask."

Brandon raised her face to his, overcome by her beauty as the faltering glimmer of breaking day tinged the eastern sky with silver.

"I've waited a lifetime for you, sweetheart. You're all the world to me."

And he gently kissed away her tears of joy before he lifted her to the saddle and turned the horses' heads toward Yew Trees Lodge.

Turn back the pages of history... and discover

Romance

as it once was!

_____	05470-4	**CRYSTAL HEART** Lisa Gregory	$2.95
_____	07100-5	**THE WAYWARD HEART** Jill Gregory	$3.50
_____	07071-8	**A GLORIOUS PASSION** Stephanie Blake	$3.50
_____	04628-0	**THE FIFTH JADE OF HEAVEN** Marilyn Granbeck	$2.95
_____	867-21205-5	**CAPTIVE DESIRE** Kathleen Victor	$2.95
_____	04729-5	**PRAIRIE FLAME** Jessica Howard	$2.95
_____	06045-3	**RENEGADE LADY** Kathryn Atwood	$3.25
_____	04756-2	**A SHARE OF EARTH AND GLORY** Katherine Giles	$3.50
_____	05908-0	**TOUCH ME WITH FIRE** Patricia Phillips	$3.50
_____	07251-6	**MARIE FLEUR** Patricia Phillips	$3.50